Matt Hilton worked for twenty-two years in private security and the police force in Cumbria. He is a 4th Dan blackbelt and coach in Ju-Jitsu. He lives in Cumbria with his wife and son.

Praise for Matt Hilton and Dead Men's Dust:

'Joe Hunter takes you in at the deep end . . . and never lets up. It has an unflagging pace and you'll love Joe's no-nonsense approach to sorting out the baddies. Breathtaking.'   Adrian Magson

'Hilton writes well . . . A promising start'

Observer

'Breathless, page-ripping stuff'
Peterborough Evening Telegraph

'Hilton is more adept at humour than Lee Child . . . the series should be electrifying.'   *Daily Mail*

'Hot, blood-spatterd and unrepentantly hard-hitting . . . This is an old-fashioned, dark, dangerous and gripping page-turner, full of anxiety and brutal tension. Thriller fans who like gun-toting and fast-fisted, flawed heroes will undoubtedly enjoy Joe Hunter's first outing in *Dead Men's Dust*.'

Australian Independent

THE FIRST JOE HUNTER THRILLER

MATT HILTON

DEAD MEN'S DUST

HODDER

First published in Great Britain in 2009 by Hodder & Stoughton
An Hachette Livre UK company

First published in paperback in 2009

5

A CIP catalogue record for this title is available from the British Library

ISBN 978 0 340 97823 8

Typeset in Plantin Light by Hewer Text UK Ltd, Edinburgh
Printed and bound by Clays Ltd, St Ives plc

Hodder & Stoughton policy is to use papers that are natural, renewable
and recyclable products and made from wood grown in sustainable
forests. The logging and manufacturing processes are expected to
conform to the environmental regulations of the country of origin.

Hodder & Stoughton Ltd
338 Euston Road
London NW1 3BH

www.hodder.co.uk

This book is dedicated in sad memory to my beautiful girl, Megan Rose Hilton (1989–2006). My first and foremost fan and critic. I miss you dearly, Megs. Your energy, I know, goes on. When the time is right, I will see you again.

Meet Joe Hunter and play the game at
WWW.JOEHUNTERVIGILANTE.COM

I

Pain and fear transcend everything, and know no boundaries. It doesn't matter where you are. You could be in any metropolis in the world – New York, London, Paris, Moscow – and the parallels would remain consistent. There are differences in culture, in law, in language, but at its most basic level, civilization shares one undeniable truth: the scream of a victim sounds the same the world over.

Stepping off an airplane into the sticky heat following a Floridian thunderstorm, the screams of my past were ringing in my ears. Somehow, I knew that the hunt for John Telfer would add further memories of pain and anguish to my already overfull heart.

It's difficult to pinpoint where this tale starts.

Was it while I was a Special Forces soldier on seek-and-destroy missions to bring down the tyrants and terrorists of the world? Was it after I retired and turned my hand to beating down the thugs, criminals and mobsters that preyed on those weaker than themselves? I couldn't really say.

Maybe my story doesn't start until I stepped off the Boeing 737 at Miami International airport. I would find John Telfer in the States, but I would also find something that would test me to the very extremes of my skills. And, yes, there would be screams.

Even though my quest would begin in the tropical heat, I began it all two days previously and an ocean away. There were screams then, too.

It was just like the old days. I was back doing what I was good at. Where I crouched, broken glass and rubbish littered the floor. Nearby, a train rattled towards Manchester Piccadilly. Last week's front-page news fluttered in the alley. It wasn't all that stirred; the stench was terrible, a mix of urine and shit.

It chilled me.

Jennifer Telfer's curtains twitched.

She was scared. But that was to be expected, I suppose. She knew I was there. And why.

It wasn't me she was afraid of.

Some people call me a vigilante. That's their prerogative. I prefer to think of myself as a problem-fixer. When you're a single mother whose children have been threatened by violent men, you send for Joe Hunter.

A black BMW slowed at the end of the street.

'Here we go.'

It halted in front of the apartment building. Gangsta rap blared. The music was harsh and aggressive, just like the men inside. There were three of them, indistinct behind cannabis smoke. Just as I'd expected.

A large bald-headed man stepped out, pulling on leather gloves. From the back came a man equally tall. Unlike the first, his frame was lanky and sparse. Together, they moved towards Jennifer's home.

The rap music covered my approach. The driver was too busy rolling a joint to notice. The first he knew of my presence was when I tugged open the door.

'What the fuck?' was all he got out before I hit him.

I aimed for the carotid sinus and struck bull's-eye. Such a blow could prove fatal. Call me compassionate if you want; I chopped him just hard enough that he approached unconsciousness.

The BMW should've carried a government health warning. Used hypodermic syringes were the least of it. Leaning over him, I grabbed at the seat belt. It made a good noose. The remainder of the belt looped round the headrest and jammed into the door frame made it even better.

I caught up with the other two before they'd reached the apartments.

With a bent back, a cap pulled down over my hair, I moved towards them. I might as well have been invisible.

I straightened up and thrust the 'V' of my thumb and index finger into the bald man's windpipe. As his hands went to his damaged throat, I slammed my clenched fist into his solar plexus and he folded over my arm. Breath exploded from his lungs as he performed a slow dive, meeting my lifted knee midway. He hit the floor hard, but it didn't matter: he was already oblivious.

There was no time for taking satisfaction from my work: Skinny was already going for something inside his jacket. Could be a gun.

Grasping his wrist and tugging his hand out of his jacket, I saw that he held a knife.

'Now isn't that just typical of you, Shank?' I flexed his wrist, hearing bone grating on bone. Made it easy to pluck the knife from his fingers.

His name was Peter Ramsey, an idiot who began his criminal career stealing pushbikes over at Oakwood Park in Salford. But – like all third-rate gangsters – he loved his nickname. He favoured a knife when threatening desperate mothers. Shank should be a scary handle for someone wielding a blade. Me, I just thought it was pathetic.

I bunched a fist in Shank's hair and pressed my knuckles against his skull.

'Listen closely,' I growled. 'One thing, and one thing only.' I snatched his head towards me, meeting him eye-to-eye. 'Jennifer Telfer is off your books. *Permanently.* You hear that?'

'Jennifer Telfer? Who the fuck—'

I slapped him hard.

'You know who I mean.'

Wiggling the knife, I asked, 'Tell me you weren't thinking of cutting her.' I lifted the blade. Sharp edge beneath his nose. His breath misted the steel. 'You know something, Shank? Just thinking of that makes my blood cold.'

'I wasn't gonna cut nobody,' Shank said.

'Good. You won't be wanting this back then.' I dropped the knife into my coat pocket. 'If I see you around here again, I will hurt you bad.'

'What have I ever done to you?'

'Fucked with the wrong person,' I told him. 'That's what.'

To punctuate the point I backhanded him across the face. 'When you walk out of here, you keep on going. If you as much as look back, I'll be all over you like a bad case of hives. You got that?'

'Yeah, man, I get you.'

'See you, then.'

'Not if I see ya first,' he said, turning quickly away, 'you psycho!'

'Believe me,' I said, 'if there is a next time, you won't see me coming.'

2

'Come in, Joe. Quick.'

Jack and Beatrice huddled in front of a television. A cartoon vied for their attention and they barely spared me a second. Empty bowls were at their feet, remnants of food drying in the forced heat of a gas fire. Next to an easy chair, there was an empty wine bottle and the remains of a takeaway Chinese meal. They weren't the leftovers of a celebration.

In a hurry, Jennifer shut the door. Behind me came the clink of a security chain, the ratchet of a dead bolt.

'You won't need as many locks in future, Jenny.' I pulled off the hat and jacket. 'Shank won't be paying you any more visits.'

Jennifer hugged herself. Barely above a whisper, she said, 'There's worse out there than Shank to worry about.'

Fourteen years working as a counterterrorism agent had already convinced me of that. If I required reminding, all I had to do was look at the kids. Only six and four years old, they already had the look of the infinitely wise about them. 'Hi, kids, what're you watching? Cartoons?'

'SpongeBob,' Jack said matter-of-factly.

'He's got square pants,' Beatrice added.

'Interesting,' I said. I gave her a lifted eyebrow. She was too young to know who the Rock was, but she appreciated the effort. Her giggle was like soft music. A baby again. The resilience of children never fails to amaze the cynic in me.

Her mother wasn't so easily calmed. My hand on her shoulder was waved off with a desultory gesture. Jenny took the coat and hat from me; she abandoned them on the arm of a settee, then crossed the room. Perched on a chair next to a battle-scarred table, she had the look of a condemned prisoner.

'You can quit worrying. I guarantee you: Shank'll look somewhere else for his cash.'

She plucked at a pack of cigarettes next to an ashtray overflowing with half-smoked stubs. The ashtray was testament to prolonged worry.

'For now,' she said. 'But what about when you leave? What's to stop them coming back?'

'I'm only a phone call away.'

Jennifer hacked out a cough. She stabbed the cigarette into her mouth.

'What about when I can't pay you, Joe? Are you still gonna come runnin' then?'

'You think I did this for money?'

With her skewed sense of the world and of men in particular maybe I should've thought my reply through first. She tilted her face to stare up at me. Her fingers plucked my shirt. 'You want me to pay you another way, Joe?' Her gaze flickered to the children, as though they were an obstacle. 'If that's what you want. But not here . . . not in front of the kids.'

I gently extricated myself from her.

'Jenny, you know that's not what I meant.'

Turning away, her arms went beneath her breasts.

'What's wrong? Am I not good enough for you? You think I'm ugly.' Her reflection swam in a mirror over the fireplace. Patina twisted the image, compounded her self-revulsion. 'Well, I can hardly blame you, can I?'

'You're not ugly, Jenny. I helped you because I wanted to.' I swept my arm in an all-encompassing gesture. 'You needed help. All of you.'

'But *you* don't work for free, Joe. Didn't you tell your brother that? Why didn't you help John? If you had, then maybe he'd still be here . . .' Fresh tears trembled on her lashes. 'Why didn't you help us then, huh? I'll tell you why, shall I? It was about the *money*.'

I didn't answer.

She struck a light to her cigarette and went at it as if it were a lifeline. She glared at me. 'You wouldn't help John when he needed it. I can't pay any more than he could.'

I had to say something. First, I settled in opposite her. 'Jenny, you don't really understand what happened between me and John. It had nothing to do with whether he could pay me.' She snorted, sucked on the cigarette. I said, 'I don't know what he told you, but I guess it wasn't the truth.'

Her eyes pierced me.

'What're you saying, Joe?'

I sighed. 'It's water under the bridge, Jenny. Forget it, OK.'

She shrugged, flicked ash that missed the ashtray. 'Suit yourself.'

Silence hung in the air between us, mingling with her blue-smoke exhalations.

Once I watched a heron spearing trout from a stream. Jennifer's hand made similar stabbing motions to douse her cigarette. Then, like the greedy heron, she reached for another. I gently laid a hand on top of hers. She met my eyes. Hope flickered beyond the dullness but only for a second. She prised loose her hand, drew the pack to her. She lit up and took a long gasp. Through a haze of smoke, she said, 'I want you to find John.' She reached out and twined her fingers in mine. 'I want you to find your brother and bring him home.'

'That might not be as easy as it sounds. He's not in the country any more.'

'No, he isn't. He's in America,' Jenny said.

'You've heard from him?'

Jenny withdrew her hand. Searching in her pocket, she pulled out an envelope and held it to her breast. After a moment, she placed the envelope before me. I looked up at her. However, she was looking over at the kids. 'You two, go into your room while me and Uncle Joe are talking. You can watch telly in there.' Before they could argue, she hurried over, took them by their elbows and ushered them into their bedroom. Closing the door, she said, 'I don't want them listening. After all's said and done, John's still their dad.'

I concentrated on the envelope. It was a standard white manila dated more than a fortnight ago. It was stamped *Little Rock, Ark.*

'Arkansas?' I asked.

I received a pinched expression. 'Where else?'

The tattered edge of the envelope produced two sheets of paper. On first inspection, it was like the hurried note you scrawl and display in a prominent position when you have to leave in a hurry. Only longer. A Dear John letter. Or in this case a Dear Jenny? But it wasn't my brother's handwriting.

I sought Jenny's face. 'Go ahead. Read it,' she said. I did.

Jenny, it read, *I probably have no right contacting you like this. No doubt you hate me, but I hope you'll listen to what I have to say.*

John has gone, and I don't know what to do. Don't get me wrong, he hasn't just left me as he did with you. When I say he's gone, I mean vanished.

Maybe you don't care, maybe you think I deserve everything I get, that John definitely deserves it, but I don't think you're that kind of person. John has got himself in some kind of trouble. He was jumpy for two or three days before he disappeared. He was frightened. I think something terrible has happened. And that's why I'm writing to you now.

I placed down the first sheet of paper, looked across at Jenny. She'd retreated to the opposite end of the room, staring vacantly into space. The letter was my problem now.

John said that he's got a half-brother over in England. Someone he called Hunter. I know they didn't get along

that well, but John once said that if ever anything
happened to him I had to send for Hunter because he
would know what to do. So I'm asking, no, I'm begging,
please do this for me. And if you won't do it for me, do
it for John. Send for his brother.

    Please. L.

The note struck me as odd.

'This woman,' I asked, 'who is she?'

Jenny returned to stub out her cigarette. Her words held more vehemence up close. 'John's bitch.'

I raised an eyebrow. 'American?'

'No. She's English.'

'What's her name?'

'Louise Blake.'

'How did John meet her?'

'She worked for the same company as him.' She gave me a pointed stare. I just watched her, and Jennifer added, 'By all accounts they were seeing each other for six months before he left me.' She gave me the pointed look again. 'Everyone knew but me.'

'I didn't.'

She wiped at her mouth with the back of a hand. 'Well, you're about the only one.' Her words became softer as she recalled the betrayal. 'Louise stole my husband from me, Joe. Now she wants help to find him. What does she want me to do, just hand him right back to her?'

'Have you ever met her?'

'Not formally. I saw her a couple times at John's workplace.' Jenny laughed. 'When I think about it, I suppose you'd say she's a younger version of me. Without the baggage round the belly from carrying two kids that is. John traded me in for a younger model.'

'But you still want me to find him?'

She sighed. Her gaze flickered towards the bedroom. The kids were very quiet and I wondered if they had their ears to the door.

'He's still their dad, Joe. He should be doing more to support them.'

Yes. A sad fact. But not something I was about to put into words.

Jenny said, 'Probably Louise is right: John does deserve everything he gets. But my kids shouldn't be made to suffer, should they?' She could look all she wanted but she wouldn't see any sign of reproof from me. After a few seconds, she asked, 'So . . . what do you think? Is there anything you can do?'

'There is,' I promised her.

I meant it.

3

When working, I don't use a vehicle that I care about. I use an old junker picked up at auction for a couple of hundred pounds. That way, when the disgruntled dig a key into it the length of the paintwork, I don't get too upset. It carries many scars. The only concession to roadworthiness I demand is that the engine is regularly overhauled and the tyres are of the new puncture-proof variety. Both things have proved invaluable in the past.

Before setting up the takedown on Shank and his goons, I had parked the old Vauxhall Corsa a couple of streets away. OK, I wasn't that protective of it, but neither was I going to make my wheels a sitting duck. I was approaching it when the BMW swung into the street behind me. To be fair, I'd thought I'd seen the last of Peter Ramsey, yet here he was, back for more.

Maybe I should've done a better number on him the first time. My fault, but, as I said, I am sometimes a compassionate guy.

'This time . . . no fucking about,' I promised.

In an effort at stealth, the music volume had been turned down. Still, the thud-thud rhythm sounded like the heartbeat of a predator coiling for the death lunge.

Thick tyres whistled on tarmac. The engine growled. Even without looking, I'd have known they were coming.

It was like patrolling bandit country all over again. Only then, I was an inexperienced rookie, immortal in my battle fatigues and holding a sub-machine gun. Unprepared for what happened, I hadn't even realized I'd been shot until I surfaced through a morphine haze the following day and blinked up at my nurse.

You don't hear the bullet that kills you. Which meant the two bullets Shank fired at me missed their mark. Good job I'd leapt forwards at the right time. The pavement was a little unforgiving, but a scraped elbow and knee were the least of my worries.

The BMW was a sleek black shark, as dangerous as the .38 Shank aimed at me. It made sense that the driver swung the BMW on to the pavement. A half-ton of metal on my head would finish me as quickly as a slug in the heart.

'Get that muthafucka!'

Even as I rolled away from the car, I had to smile at Shank's pseudo-gangsta lingo: it was more Salford, Greater Manchester than it was South Central LA.

The BMW bumped down from the kerb, knocking value off the alloys. I rose up behind them. From beneath my shirt-tails, I drew my own gun. SIG-Sauer P226. Unlike these cretins, I had a full load. In addition, I knew how to shoot. One round into the rear nearside tyre, two in the boot and one through the back windscreen for good measure. More than the deflated tyre, panic spun the car across the road and drove it into my parked Vauxhall.

In this part of town, gunfire would ensure witnesses kept their heads down. On the other hand, a good old-fashioned car wreck would bring the ghouls running.

'Out of the car,' I shouted. 'Now!'

The driver was slumped over the steering wheel, blood frothing from both nostrils. Sound asleep for the second time that evening. Shank wasn't in much better shape. Half out of the window when the car collided with my Vauxhall, he was now on the road, crying like a baby and cradling a busted elbow. His gun had slid harmlessly beneath my car. Only the big baldy posed any threat.

'I said *out of the fucking car.*'

Staring down the barrel of a SIG is enough to motivate most men. He was surprisingly sprightly when offered the correct form of stimulation. His hands went up. 'OK! Easy, man, easy.'

His gloves were gone. Heavy gold rings made a rich man's knuckleduster on his right hand. Fancied himself as a pugilist.

'Pick Shank up,' I told him.

Conditioned to taking commands, he didn't object. He quickly stooped down and lifted Shank to his feet.

'Up the alley.'

Opposite us a narrow alleyway ran between a vacant lot and a video rental store that was closed for the night. Maybe the store had closed for many nights, judging by the faded posters.

I knew what was going through the big guy's mind. He thought that the ignominious alley was where he was going to end his days. Give him his due; I think he was braver than he was stupid.

'You aren't taking us up there to shoot us.'

'I'm not?'

'If you're gonna do it, do it now. Out here in the open.'

'OK,' I said.

Not so keen, Shank whimpered.

Baldy gave his boss a look that suggested that there were going to be changes in their arrangement. That was if they managed to get out of here alive. Shank was left swaying as the big man stepped away from him.

'Go on,' he challenged. 'I don't think you've got what it takes.'

I gave him my saddest smile.

The big man took that as a sign of weakness. He snatched at a gun tucked into his waistband.

I caressed the trigger and his right kneecap disintegrated.

He collapsed to the floor, and despite his bravado he screamed.

'What about you, Shank? Do you think I haven't got the balls to do you?' I aimed the SIG at a point directly between his eyes. 'After you tried to shoot me?'

Think of an air-raid siren and you'll imagine the sound that Shank made.

'You know something, Shank? You should have listened to me.'

I pulled the trigger again.

Shank fell next to his friend, clutching at his own shattered knee.

'Next time I will kill you,' I promised.

4

He had the desire and the passion. He certainly had the ability. But that wasn't everything: Tubal Cain also had an agenda.

Right now he was short on materials.

There wasn't much hope of acquiring what he needed here, but for these assholes, he'd make the effort.

'You know something? You should all be damned straight to hell!'

There weren't too many things that got him riled, but these pigs on wheels were the exception. Motor-homes! These monstrosities of engineering were a blight on the landscape. Colossal steel bullets fired from the devil's cannon to cause woe and destruction wherever they landed.

Without their intrusion, this oasis turnoff beside route I-10 in Southern California held its own beauty. A semi-circular drive ran up to an artesian well, and trees had been artfully arranged to block the view of the interstate. Laurel trees made a pretty silhouette against the star-filled sky, but not when a goddamn Winnebago hunkered beneath them, square, unnatural, and spewing light from a cabin the size of the flight deck of the *USS Enterprise*.

'It's enough to make you sick,' Tubal Cain said.

Neither Mabel nor George or whatever the hell they were called argued the point. George was equivocal on the entire subject. However, that was to be expected. Speaking could be difficult with a gash the width of your thumb parting your trachea.

For her part, Mabel was pretty verbal, but nothing she'd said up until now would change his opinion. She was more intent on screaming for her unheeding husband. Another thing: she wasn't giving any clues to George's actual name. She'd only refer to him as Daddy. It was obscene, like a wrinkly Lolita.

'Aw, for crying out loud!' Cain said. 'Put a lid on it, willya? How do you expect me to work with all that racket you're making?'

Mabel hunkered in the kitchen compartment. She was a hunched package stuffed beneath a fold-down counter, looking like the garbage sack George had been about to drop in the bushes when Cain surprised him.

'Daddy, Daddy! Help me, Daddy!' she screamed for about the hundredth time.

'Daddy's not interested,' Cain pointed out. 'So you may as well shut up.'

Daddy sat in the driving seat, surrounded by the luxury of leather and walnut. But he was of no mind to point out the lushness of his surroundings. The elderly man was currently preoccupied with trying to stem the tide of blood flowing down the front of his pullover. Chalk-white, his features showed he was losing the battle.

'Daddeeee . . .'

Cain took the man's hands away from the wound, guiding them to the steering wheel. His final earthly experience was gripping the wheel as though with the intention of taking the Winnebago through the Pearly Gates with him.

The knife snicked through tendons and gristle, the old man's death grip loosened and his hands flopped on to his thighs. Sans thumbs, his hands looked like dead squid.

Moving towards the woman's hiding place, Cain slipped the thumbs into a sandwich bag and dropped them in a pocket.

'People have to learn to take their trash home with them, Mabel.' If there was something that got his goat even more than motorhomes it was the irresponsible and harmful littering George had been engaged in. Bad enough that he destroyed the picturesque beauty of the desert with this huge beast – then he deposited its shit before he left. 'Maybe if George wasn't so indiscriminate with his garbage I wouldn't have had to call on you and teach you such a valuable lesson.'

'You killed Daddy because there were no trash cans?'

'Yes. And for his ridiculous taste in vehicles.'

'You're insane!' Mabel shrieked.

'No, Mabel. I'm angry.'

'You killed Daddy!'

'Yes.'

He stooped down, pulled her from beneath the counter. She slid out as boneless as an oyster from the shell. Cain didn't like oysters. Didn't like anything boneless.

He rapped a knuckle on her head. Just to be sure. The clunk was only partway reassuring.

'How old are you, Mabel? Seventy? Eighty?'

Her turquoise-framed spectacles lent an extra dimension to her incredulous blink. Confusion reigned, terror tamped down by befuddlement. Her mouth drooped. At least she'd stopped screaming.

'I wouldn't ask, but it is pertinent,' Cain said.

'Eighty-three.' Saliva cracked at the back of her throat.

'Hmmm. Quite elderly.' Cain gripped her shoulder. He kneaded with a masseur's skill. 'Frail under all that padding. I bet you suffer from arthritis, eh?'

She showed him her misshapen knuckles.

'Thought that might be the case.' His sigh sounded genuinely remorseful. 'What about osteoporosis?'

He was offering hope, and she wasn't so distraught that she didn't recognize it. Even after such a long life, when faced with dismemberment an octogenarian can still desire further years. 'I'm riddled with it. I only have to sneeze and I can break a rib.'

'Doesn't bode well.'

'What do you want from us?'

'Nothing.'

'You cut off Daddy's thumbs . . .'

'I did, Mabel. I have a purpose for them. But you needn't fear. You have nothing that I want.'

'Thank the good Lord!' Mabel sobbed.

'But only for small mercies,' Cain concluded as he slipped the knife back in his pocket. He didn't require a knife when dealing with an invertebrate. The heel of his shoe would be all he'd need.

Ten minutes later he was back on the road.

The Mercedes SUV he drove made a fine chariot. Interstate-10 stretched out before him, an umbilical cord drawing him ever westward, towards the fertile stalking-grounds of Los Angeles.

Billy Joel was cranked high on the SUV's CD player. A window open so that the warm breeze ruffled his fair hair. He was a happy man. Beside him on the passenger seat were the tools of his trade, flagrantly displayed in total disregard of law or common sense. If someone saw them, well, so what? A cop died as easy as any man did.

With that thought in mind, he reached over and lifted the flap of the pouch. Inside was an array of knives, scalpels and other cutting utensils. *Tap, tap, tap.* He ran a finger over the dozen or so hilts. *Tap.* Rested momentarily on the sturdy hilt of a bowie knife.

'Ah, sweet baby,' he said. Such fond memories.

A would-be knife fighter back east in Jacksonville had bestowed the knife upon him. What unashamed Southern generosity. Such a polite man, too.

'You're going to have to take it from me first, sir,' he'd offered.

'Gladly,' Tubal Cain had agreed.

The blade was broad and easily a foot long. Whenever it was thrust into flesh, it made a satisfying *thunk!*

A firm favourite for instilling fear in the hearts of his victims. Sadly, it lacked finesse. If carnage was your only desire, then fine. Ever the artist, he preferred a little more delicacy to his cutting.

Now, this was more to his liking. Black plastic hilt, slim and unadorned. Grasping it lightly, he teased out the cutting edge. Muted moonbeams played on a curved, very utilitarian blade backed by saw-toothed serrations. Beautiful in its simplicity. It was a fish-scaling knife acquired during a northern foray to Nova Scotia. The blade had seen employment on a number of occasions since, but never on anything so mundane as trout or salmon.

Happy with his choice, he pulled the scaling knife free and held it up for closer inspection. With a thumb, he tested its keenness. 'As keen as I am, eh?'

The knife went into an inside pocket of his sports jacket.

Billy Joel was winding down, Christie Brinkley demanding his full attention. The CDs spread over the passenger seat beckoned. He selected a Robbie Williams collection: Stoke-on-Trent's best-known export doing his best to capture the cool of Sinatra and not doing a half-bad job. He changed the CD, then bobbed his head along with the tempo swinging from the speakers.

'My kind of music,' he whispered. An aptly named track – a cover of 'Mack the Knife'. He cut lazy figures of eight into the air with his right hand. Like conducting a big band, but instead of a bandleader's baton he imagined a blade in his hand. With each swing of the music, he cut another strip of meat from a faceless victim.

'Swing while you're sinning,' he said with a grin. A nod towards the title of the album.

5

That evening, after the episode with Shank, I returned home to a house in darkness. Nothing new there. It's been like that since Diane and I divorced.

The Vauxhall wasn't registered to me, so I was happy to leave it *in situ*. A taxi took me to the lock-up garage I used, so it was my other car, an Audi A6, I parked in the tree-lined street. My two dogs, Hector and Paris, were inside the house, and I could just make out their forms as they pressed their noses to the glass doors leading to the patio area. I must've made an indistinct shadow against the deeper night. Hector, largest of my German Shepherds, huffed once, then I watched as the two dogs became animated.

I was conscious of disturbing my neighbours, but it was pointless trying to be quiet; Hector and Paris were making enough racket to wake the neighbourhood. I pushed open the patio door. Instantly I was assaulted by twin black-and-tan whirlwinds. We went through a round of play fighting before the dogs would obey my command to sit.

As always, the TV cabinet became a receptacle for my car keys and wallet, a habit my ex-wife used to frown upon. It was only one of the many things that annoyed her before our split. Probably the very least of them.

Sometimes I wished Diane was still there to keep me right. As soon as I tendered my resignation from the army, the death toll for our marriage was rung. Probably she understood me in a way that I never could. Physically I'd resigned, but mentally?

'Married men can't just rush off, placing themselves in life-threatening situations all the time,' Diane told me the night she left.

'So you just want me to sit at home and die of boredom?' I demanded.

'No, Joe.' She'd shaken her head sadly. 'I just don't want to be the one who has to bury you.'

Diane wanted someone she could grow old with. Understandable, but it wasn't something I could promise her. I'm way too impulsive for that. My promise to Jenny was nagging at me to get going, and I wanted to make a start with some phone calls.

The clock on the wall had to be telling lies. Not too late, though, I decided. Hector and Paris scuttled out into the back garden. I followed them, pulling out my mobile phone. Four years on, I still had Diane's number on speed dial.

'Hello?'

'Hi, Simon,' I said, concealing any trace of jealousy. 'Can I speak to Diane?'

Diane's very safe office-bound husband grunted, muttered something unintelligible, but handed over the phone.

'What do you want, Joe?'

'I'm going away,' I told her.

There was a momentary hitch in her voice. 'So why are you telling me?'

'Thought you might want to wave me off at the airport.'

I heard her sigh. 'I already did that. Too many times.'

It was my turn to sigh.

'Can you take the dogs for me for a few days?'

'Simon has allergies,' she said.

'Fuck,' I said. 'Isn't it a good job we never had kids?'

Her silence said everything.

'I'm sorry, Diane. I shouldn't have said that.'

'No, Joe. You shouldn't have.' In the background, Simon was whispering something. 'Simon said we can take them, but they'll have to stay in the garden shed.'

My dogs were gambolling around the garden, play-fighting amongst the rhododendrons. Full of life.

'So long as they're exercised they'll be fine,' I said.

'OK, then.'

'I'll drop them off in the morning,' I said.

'No,' Diane said, way too quickly for my liking. 'I'll come there with Simon.'

Then she hung up.

With the dogs sorted, I returned indoors, settled into an armchair. Then I dialled a number in Tampa, Florida.

'Hey, Hunter, what's up?'

Jared 'Rink' Rington's voice is a rich Southern drawl that always reminds me of that guitar-playing wedding suitor in the John Wayne movie, *The Searchers*. He has the honky-tonk twang of a country and western singer that always surprises people; it's a strange anomaly coming from a mixed parentage of Japanese mother and Scottish father.

'You busy with anything?'

'Got my heel planted on a weasel as we speak,' Rink said.

'I take it you're talking metaphorically?'

'Uh-huh,' Rink said. 'I just gotta finish up a little one-on-one business with my client, then I'm all yours.'

'So what's the deal? Anything exciting?'

'Nothing startling. Guy paid me to do a little eyeball on his wife. He grew suspicious when she started doing too much overtime at work. Thought she could be playin' away from home.'

'Maybe she was just after more money,' I offered.

'Yeah, you might say she was after a raise.' Rink chuckled. 'I got the goods on her last night. Filmed her giving head to her boss in the back of his limousine.'

'So you just have to hand over the evidence and that's you finished?' I asked.

'More or less, yeah. Anyway, what's up?' Rink asked. 'You haven't rung for the sake of idle chit-chat. That's not the Joe Hunter I know and love.'

'I've got a job for you . . . if you're interested?'

'Uh-huh.' It could've been agreement but more likely he was waiting for more.

'Could be a long story,' I told him.

'Fire away, it's your dime.'

It was so still I could have been in a mausoleum. But habit caused a quick over-the-shoulder glance to make sure I was alone.

'I'm going to be coming out there,' I told him.

'Out here? As in Florida?'

'Well, yeah, I was thinking of stopping over a day or so, but then I have to get myself to Little Rock, Arkansas.'

White noise reigned. Then a faint exhalation tinged with humour. 'My old stomping ground?'

'It's why you're the man for the job.'

'You think I'm a tour guide all of a sudden? Get yourself a map.' Good-natured sarcasm was rich in his drawl. Why anyone could dislike Rink is a supreme irony. What's not to like about a sarcastic curmudgeon?

'Local knowledge is half the battle,' I told him.

'I ain't been home in eight years, Hunter. Don't know how up to date my local knowledge'll be.'

'How much can Arkansas have changed in eight years?' I asked. 'It's not like it's the centre of American culture or anything.'

'Yeah, but it's not like it's simply rednecks in pick-up trucks either,' Rink said, sounding exactly like a redneck in a pick-up truck. 'They're as cultured as any place else, Hunter. They know the difference between Paris, France and Paris Hilton.'

'It'll do you good to get yourself back there, then.'

Rink chuckled. 'So what's the deal?'

'Missing person,' I said.

'That all? I thought it was going to be something exciting.'

'There's more. The missing person is my brother.'

'You mean John?'

'Yeah. He's finally surfaced, only to drop off the face of the earth again.' I gripped the phone tight. 'I'm worried, Rink.'

'You know what guys are like. He's probably gotten himself drunk, picked up a coupla hookers an' holed up in a motel someplace,' Rink said. 'Give him a day or two an' he'll be home with his tail between his legs.'

'Maybe,' I agreed. 'And with John it wouldn't be the first time.'

'You guys had a big falling-out. Why you lookin' for him now?'

'He's in trouble,' I said.

'Always was.'

'I'm not doing this for him,' I lied. 'My sister-in-law asked me to find him. I promised her I would.'

'Figures.' Seems like Diane wasn't the only one who could read me from a thousand paces. Rink asked, 'So is he skipping out on the alimony?'

'Has done for years,' I said. 'But that's not what this is about. Yeah, there're kids involved, but it all goes a lot deeper than that.'

'Pray tell,' Rink said. It sounded like a car engine burst into life, the sound only slightly muffled by the intervening thousands of miles.

'You driving, Rink?'

'Just setting off. But you can keep on talking; I got a twenty-minute drive. Just ignore me if my language gets foul, but the I-75's a bitch even at this hour.'

Rink manoeuvred his Porsche through the Florida traffic. My run-in with Shank and his goons was just another war story to us. The creative use of a seat belt as a noose won me kudos. So did the fact two major arseholes would be walking with crutches for a while.

I got round to the note from John's current girlfriend and the plea made by Jennifer. My promise to help.

'You always were a soft touch, Hunter,' Rink said. 'Never could turn down a damsel in distress.'

'She's also my sister-in-law,' I reminded him.

'Sister nothing. If you'd never met her before, you'd still be coming out here.'

'Now you're starting to sound like Diane,' I said.

'Your lady was right in a lot of respects,' he pointed out.

'Even Diane would understand this time. It is my brother we're talking about.'

'No argument from me, Hunter.'

Even if I didn't crave the kind of action that keeps me alive, I couldn't turn my back on my brother. For all that the last time we spoke I threatened to punch his face.

'You've missed him, huh?'

'Like a hole in the head.'

It was a good place to lighten the conversation. 'So how's the Sunshine State?'

'A contradiction in terms, my man. Rain's coming down in torrents. Third day in a row. They sure don't show that on no "Come to Sunny Florida" TV ads, do they?'

'I'll pack for the weather, Rink. But can you set me up with the necessaries?' Mentioning a key word – particularly gun – over the telephone is never a good idea. Especially since 9/11. Conspiracy theories aside, all kinds of enigmatic government establishments known for their acronyms are tapping phones for just such words. I know. I've been there. Last thing I wanted was to land in Florida then get a one-way ticket to Guantanamo Bay.

Rink said, 'Leave it to me. You want I get you a coupla day passes to Universal Studios?'

'Best you do. Hopefully I'll have a little time for sightseeing; I don't want to be wasting time queuing.' More code. *Universal* was a cipher. It meant the entire package: passport, Social Security number, driving documents, credit cards, the business.

'Sounds like we could be in for some fun, Hunter.'

'Fun isn't even the half of it,' I said.

6

Tubal Cain was in his element. Driving a flashy car and dreaming about further slaughter.

Interstate-10 was one of his all-time favourite places, stretching all the way from Jacksonville, Florida in the east to Santa Monica in the west. A transcontinental artery with no fewer than three of the largest cities in the US straddling its route. Houston, Phoenix and Los Angeles were all territory he knew. But what appealed to him more than the cities was the transcontinental highway itself. It was a popular backpacking avenue across the states. Throughout its length no great change in elevation occurred, and even in winter the daytime temperatures were generally warm. He could almost guarantee a year-long stock of wandering lambs.

George and Mabel – or whatever they were really called – were good examples of what could be achieved by one as enterprising as himself. OK, he'd only gained a couple of thumbs for his collection, but consolation was his in the form of the scorched motorhome he'd left behind.

He'd spent some time in all the major tourist centres along the way, sampling the atmosphere of each before moving on. He'd thoroughly enjoyed the vibrancy of New Orleans, the Cajun flamboyancy of Lafayette, the history of San Antonio, where he'd used his Bowie knife in tribute to Colonel James Bowie who'd met his death there. He'd sampled the culture, the music and the southwest flavour of Tucson while hunting students in its universities. Forging westward to Santa Monica, he'd found easy pickings amidst the crowds jiggling for elbow space on the world-famous pier.

Then there was Los Angeles itself, his current destination. A city he found best suited his way of life, where he could ply his trade and fear little consequence. What with all the gangs shooting and hacking each other up, his two previous victims gleaned from South Central LA had barely raised more than an eyebrow.

His return was overdue. He intended executing a series of atrocities that would force even the jaundiced eyes of the LAPD to take note. If he could achieve that, then he would be cementing the foundations of his notoriety.

But that didn't mean a little fun along the way wasn't allowed.

Arriving in LA a few hours later than originally planned was no time at all to quibble over. Not for one whose name was destined to last an eternity.

He flicked on the turn signal, politely showing his intention to pull on to the wide shoulder, even though there was no traffic behind him. Politeness was a virtue Tubal Cain believed he possessed in abundance. The man waving for assistance by the side of the road would never guess that such a gracious driver could be so dangerous.

'Boy, is this your lucky day,' Cain said. The wing mirror made a fine TV screen for the man jogging up to his SUV: Road Runner kicking up a plume of trail dust as he charged into Wile E. Coyote's trap.

Cain noted the possibility of trouble. Though harassed and worn down with attempting to resurrect a dead engine, the man appeared moderately young and fit. Might put up a bit of a fight if not taken carefully, he concluded. Best not give the game away. Quickly, he concealed his knives under the passenger seat. He stepped out, tasting the silicon tang of the desert.

Cain wasn't the only one acting here. Conscious that few people would even stop to pick up hitchhikers, the man was careful to show that he was harmless. His gait was amiable, boyish, friendly. As fake as Tubal Cain's smile.

'You in trouble there, mister?' Cain asked.

'Yeah, bloody car's broken down and I can't get it going again.' Pushing an oil-smeared palm down a trouser leg gave him the look of a bumbler, but to Cain the act had been premeditated. His offer of a hand was no more believable.

'Hey, you're not from round here, are you?' asked Cain. 'Are you here on vacation?'

The stranded driver shook his head. 'It's been no vacation, believe me.'

Cain studied the man's eyes. Beyond deliberate innocence, a certain amount of deceit shone through.

He was hiding something, but that was all right. Everyone had something to hide.

'Not the best of places to break down,' Cain noted. The Mojave nightscape demanded their attention. 'Pretty barren.'

Nothing much other than sand and gravel, with sparse vegetation to offer neither shade nor protection from the extremes of the weather, surrounded them.

Concealment of a crime could be difficult here.

'No place is a good place to break down, mister,' the man said, 'but you're right about this desert. I'm only happy that it's night-time and I'm not stranded in a hundred degrees plus.'

'Yeah, things do get warm around here when the sun's up. It's a bitch having to walk any distance, believe me.'

'Oh, I believe you,' the driver said. He nodded toward the SUV. 'I bet that beauty's reliable.'

'Has been for as long as I've had it,' Cain agreed. That he'd only had it for eighteen hours was academic. 'You want me to take a look at your car for you? I know a thing or two about engines.'

A shake of the head towards his abandoned vehicle. With its hood raised to the star-filled heavens, it looked like a lizard attempting to swallow the distant moon. 'It's done. Blown a cylinder, I think.'

'Let's take a look.' Cain brushed past. Shoulders touched briefly. There was strength hidden beneath the man's denim shirt. Reasonably young, fit and *apparently* strong. Could be trouble. Cain slipped his hand inside his sports jacket, caressing the hilt of the scaling knife.

'There's really no need,' the man said. 'A lift out of here'll be fine.'

Cain turned round slowly. Was that a demand? Am I supposed to be obliged? 'Let me take a look at the car first. If I can't get it going, then, fine, I'll give you a ride.'

'You're wasting your time.' The man shifted his hands to his hips, inclined his chin at the broken-down vehicle. 'Piece of crap won't be going anywhere.'

'Let me take a look,' Cain said again.

'Suit yourself . . . but it won't go,' the driver said. Subtle words concealing an equally subtle action. His scratch at an itch on his side wasn't as mechanical as it seemed.

'I insist,' said Cain.

Practice makes perfect. Cain had practised this manoeuvre a thousand times. He pulled the blade free of his pocket, held it braced along his wrist, took a quick step forwards . . .

And met the barrel of a semi-automatic pistol aimed directly at his face.

A short laugh broke unbidden from his throat. It was neither shock nor fear. His laughter was self-deprecating. Looked like a little more practice could be in order. Not least, the re-sheathing of his knife. Hidden from the man's view, he slipped the blade into an outer pocket of his jacket.

'No,' the man said. 'I insist.'

Cain shook his head in mock reproof. 'You know, I can't believe you've gone and pulled a gun on me, when all I want to do is help.'

'I appreciate your concern, mister, but I don't need your help. All I need is your car.' A jerk of the gun was an invitation for a walk in the desert.

Casting his eye over the terrain, Cain saw a deep arroyo. It was steep-sided, the bottom choked with rocks and stunted sagebrush. A good place to hide a crime after all.

'So . . . you're going to shoot me?'

The driver sucked air through his teeth.

'You're going to put me down in that hole for the coyotes to find?' Cain shrugged his shoulders. It wasn't as if he hadn't done the very same thing to many others.

'I'll only shoot you if I have to,' said the driver.

Was that so? BIG MISTAKE. Rule one: never show weakness to your enemy.

'You're no killer.'

'I will be a killer if I have to,' the man said. The new edge to his voice held a tremor. Fear or anticipation – either could cause a nervous man to pull the trigger. 'Climb down in that ditch and kneel down. I'm warning you, mister, if you don't do as I say, I will use this gun.'

Cain lifted his hands in supplication.

'Come on, man. You can't do this to a Good Samaritan.'

'I can and I will.' The man jerked the gun again. 'Get moving. Down in the ditch.'

'I'm not dressed for climbing.'

'Well, jump.'

Cain started towards the arroyo. 'You think you could let me get something from my car? You're going to leave me out here in the middle of nowhere; at least let me get a bottle of water.'

'In the ditch.'

'It's called an arroyo.'

'Well, get in the fucking *arroyo*. If you don't, I'll put a bullet in your head and then throw you the hell in.'

Cain shook his head again. No urgency to his tread. 'Easy now, I'm going.'

The man watched him clamber down the embankment. Cain turned and peered up at him. His face was a spectral grey in the starlight. A blob of silver that'd prove an easy target for a gunman. 'Turn round, kneel down and put your hands on your head.'

'Why the amateur dramatics?' Cain asked. 'You're going to take my car. There's no way I can climb out and stop you, so why do you want me to kneel down?'

'Because I said so,' the man answered.

'It's going to ruin a perfectly good pair of slacks,' Cain said in a singsong voice, choirboy sweet. He turned and kneeled in the gravel as though at a pew.

'OK, stay right there,' the man said.

The scuff of shoes through sand marked the man's progress. Fetching something from his own abandoned vehicle, Cain surmised. He heard the unmistakable thud of a hood being slammed, then the sound of footsteps returning to the brim of the arroyo. Glancing over his shoulder, he saw the man outlined against the stars. In his hand he carried a backpack. He delved in the bag, pulled something out and cast it down.

Cain's assumption was justified. Definitely not a killer. A plastic bottle three-quarters full of water settled against a boulder ten feet in front of him.

'Don't say I'm not grateful for your help,' the man called down. Then he turned to go.

'Wait,' Cain shouted.

'What?'

'I'll do you a trade.'

'There's nothing you have that I want.'

'You sure?'

'Positive.'

'How's about the keys to my car?'

That got his attention.

'Throw them up here.'

'No.'

'Throw them up here or I'll shoot you.'

'No. Like I said, I'll do you a trade.'

'Just throw the fucking things here or I'll put a bullet in you.'

'You do that and you won't find the keys. While you were off gallivanting, I hid them. Fair enough, they're not too far away, but it'll take you a while to find them. Are you sure you want to waste all that precious time looking for them for the sake of one little request? You know, you could kill me, but what if someone was to come along while you were still searching for the keys? Are you prepared to kill them as well? Could even be a cop.'

The Englishman swore impolitely.

Cain grunted in amusement. 'One little request,' he repeated.

'All right, but you give me the keys first.'

'No. You get something from my car first.'

More profanity, then, 'So what the hell's so important?'

'Look under the front passenger seat. You'll find a utility belt. Bring it to me please.'

'OK, but then you give me the keys. And no messing about.'

'Deal.' Cain lifted one hand off his head and gave the driver a thumbs-up.

What could the man do but acquiesce?

'Don't move. I'll go and get your fucking utility belt. But if I come back and you've moved as much as an inch I'm going to do you.'

'Deal.' This time he put up two thumbs.

He knelt in the gravel, ignoring the sharp edges of rocks against his knees like a monk in penance. Zen tranquillity was attained through the mantra of 'Mack the Knife' hummed to himself.

'You liar.' The man's voice broke the trance. 'The keys were in the car all along.'

Without looking round Cain shrugged.

'I've got a good mind not to give you your bloody bag for that.'

'It's no good to you,' Cain pointed out. 'You may as well leave it.'

'I took a look in your bag, mister. Hope you don't mind, but I wanted to check there wasn't a gun inside. Didn't want you chasing me up the road taking pot shots at me.'

'Well, you know there's no gun now. Just leave it there for me, please.'

'What's with all the knives?'

'Just a passion of mine.'

'They don't look expensive. Not the kind of thing anyone would collect.'

'I use them in my work, that's all. And you're right, they're not expensive. So it'd be pointless stealing them.'

'What the hell's so important about them if they aren't expensive? You were prepared to risk a bullet for the sake of a few old knives?'

'Just call it sentimental value. I've had them a long time. They hold a lot of memories.' Cain turned and peered over his shoulder. He held the gaze of the driver. 'Indulge me, will you?'

The man dropped the utility belt on the floor, kicked it down into the arroyo. 'Don't climb up from there until you hear me driving away. I'll be watching.'

A wink. 'Understood.'

'Good.'

As he was commanded, Cain waited until he heard the SUV grumble to life, then recede into the distance. What would be the good of rushing? A footrace with a 4 × 4 wouldn't offer good odds.

First, he retrieved the bottle of water. It felt tepid against his palm. Then he grabbed his belt. He didn't need to make an inventory of its contents; he could tell merely by its weight that something was missing.

'You thieving asshole!' He tore open the pouch. His Bowie knife was gone.

This changed everything. He practically hurled himself up the arroyo wall. Reaching the top on his elbows and knees, he lurched up, took half-a-dozen running steps towards the road. The tail lights of the SUV were mere pinpricks in the distance.

'I'll see you again, *thief*.' His promise was as righteous as his fury. 'I'll see you again. And when I do there's gonna be hell to pay.'

7

So, there you have it. Why I hotfooted it to Florida.

I took an evening flight to Miami. On the first leg out of Manchester, I slept for hours. I dreamt of people screaming. After transferring planes in New York, the nightmare was with me still. I couldn't sleep, so sat staring out the window. Surreal cloud formations were a mild distraction. They piled all the way down the east coast. Rink hadn't been exaggerating; storms were raging across Florida.

The air-conditioned terminal tricked me. I stepped out into rain. That I was used to, but the cloying humidity slapped my face like a hot rag.

Damp with the rain and wringing wet with sweat beneath my clothes I walked towards Jared Rington's Porsche Boxster with a grimace of greeting for the big guy. Christ, I hadn't seen the brute in two years. Rink pressed a button and dropped the passenger window.

'What's with all the bags, Hunter?' he asked, nodding at my two holdalls. 'Figuring on staying a month?'

'As long as it takes.'

'Fine by me.'

I nodded at him. 'Are you gonna invite me in or must I stand out here all night getting even wetter?'

' 'S long as you don't get any stains on the upholstery,' Rink said.

I checked out the Porsche, then down at my sodden
clothing. 'Maybe I'd best take a taxi,' I said.

'The hell you will. Jump in. Toss your bags on the
back shelf . . . if they'll fit. Otherwise you're gonna
have to keep them on your knee. That's the problem
with these beauties – no trunk space.'

'Not much room for anything.'

'I didn't buy a Porsche for its capacious luggage-
handling qualities,' Rink said.

'You got it to impress the young ladies, huh?' I
clambered in, clutching my other bag to my chest.

'Yup. But to be honest, I don't score as often as I
used to in my old pick-up truck,' laughed Rink.

Previously clean-shaven, he now sported what
looked like a hairy caterpillar on his top lip. He
caught me staring at it. He checked himself out in
the rear-view mirror. 'What's wrong with my
moustache?'

'Makes you look like a porn star,' I said.

Rink grinned unabashedly. 'Yeah, so I've been told.
But then again,' he puffed out his chest, 'I've also got
the *goods* of a porn star.'

'Dream on, Casanova,' I said. 'Don't forget, I've
seen you in the showers.'

'Yeah,' Rink agreed. 'But you're forgettin' what
battle-stress does to a man. Sometimes adrenalin
makes you shrink up like that.'

'Never seemed to affect me,' I told him as he was
pulling away from the kerb.

'Trouble is,' Rink said, his tone losing its bantering edge, '*nothing* ever seemed to affect you the way it did us mere mortals. I sometimes used to wonder if you know what fear is.'

'Oh, don't you worry,' I said. 'There were plenty of times I was scared to death.'

'It didn't show.'

'It was there, Rink. I just didn't let on.'

We joined a freeway headed west. 'I made a coupla calls,' Rink said as our journey took us towards Tampa. 'Spoke to an old friend out in Little Rock. You don't know him. Harvey Lucas. Ex-military. A good man. I worked alongside him during Desert Storm. Met him again by chance a few years back an' kept in touch since. He's done some digging around for me.'

'So what's he come up with?'

'Not much. First day on the job.'

'Anything's a help.'

'He went round to see this Louise woman.'

'And?'

'She wasn't exactly friendly. Said she'd speak to nobody but you.'

I nodded. Her reluctance made sense. 'In her letter, she said that John had been acting strange, afraid of something. She could also be scared. I suppose she's not going to say too much to a stranger asking about John.'

'Even after he mentioned your name, she wouldn't give Harvey diddly-squat,' Rink said. 'But he was able to set up a meeting with her. Tomorrow afternoon, three o'clock, after she gets off work. Another thing he found out: seems your brother liked to gamble.'

Yeah? That was quite an understatement. 'You think it's because of the gambling that he's done a runner?'

'Could be. By all accounts, he's left a large IOU with a local shark called Sigmund Petoskey. Petoskey's not the most forgiving of people. Could be a good starting-off point to go round and see what he's got to say for himself.'

'As good a point as any,' I agreed.

'I remember Petoskey from years ago,' Rink said. 'A no-good punk with delusions of grandeur. Siggy likes to think of himself as some kinda new world Godfather type. He's gathered a gang of scum around him to do his head-bashing when the punters are a little slow to pay up. Maybe John's simply had the good sense to get out with all his limbs intact.'

'What's Petoskey into?'

'He's into all sorts. Got hisself a good cover as a businessperson. Real estate. Used-car dealerships. Those kinda things. But he makes most of his money from the gambling and corruption.'

'Corruption?' I asked.

'Yup. Has a few names in local government by the balls. Certain cops won't touch him either.'

'What's he like?'

'An asshole of the highest order,' Rink said. 'But I suppose with a gang behind him he's dangerous enough. To someone who's easily frightened, that is.'

'Yeah, just like every other arsehole we ever went up against,' I noted.

Rink often seems to know what I'm thinking. 'I've got the guns and stuff back at the condo,' he said.

I nodded at his foresight. We both knew that when you went up against someone like Petoskey or Shank you had to show them that you weren't about to take any shit from them. Shank could be intimidated by a nasty promise, but in a land where every other blue-rinsed grandma toted a sidearm, you had to bring something even nastier to the negotiating table.

'Does Harvey know where Petoskey is?'

'I've got him on it. By the time we arrive in Arkansas, he'll be able to tell you where Petoskey squats down to take a dump . . . and at what time.'

I said, 'All I need to know is where he'll be this time tomorrow.'

'Leave it with me. I'll call Harvey again soon as we get back to my place.'

'Sure,' I said.

Business sorted, Rink turned to me. A smile lit up his features. 'It's good you're here, Hunter.'

'Good to be here.'

8

Duty and soldiering go hand in hand. The same could be said for family. I may have been a little remiss in supporting my loved ones since retiring from the forces.

Diane and I were history. She had made a new life with Simon. Nevertheless, there were others I could still help if they needed it. I was ashamed that my niece and nephew were living in such squalor, that Jennifer had fallen so low that my skills for pressuring people were all I could offer them.

John is my brother. If you want specifics, he's actually my half-brother. My father died and my mother remarried. Then John came along. Maybe it's because we have different fathers that we've turned out like chalk and cheese. I was the war hero, John the stay-at-home layabout. Of course, in some eyes that doesn't mean much. Funny how our parents always took his side.

Over his fifth beer, my stepfather had once said to me, 'While you've been off gallivanting all over the world, John's been here. John's the one who we've had to call for if we needed help. You've never been around. It's all right for you, Joe. You've had everything you ever wanted. What's that boy ever had?'

I hadn't had it in me to argue. I just walked away.

John I found at a bar just off Deansgate, swilling down his wages alongside a couple of friends. I cornered him by the pool table. Grabbing him by the collar of his shirt, I pushed him against a wall. His friends knew better than to step in.

'Where the fuck's all the money I gave you, John?'

His eyes wouldn't meet mine. 'I've got it back home.'

'Don't fuckin' lie to me, John. I've just seen Dad. He told me you've been round begging him for a loan.' My jaw was aching from clenching my teeth. 'He just gave me a load of grief about how I should help you out. Again.'

John shook his head.

'Don't tell me you've gone and blown it?'

Shame made his cheeks burn. 'I got an inside tip,' he said. 'Five to one odds, what could I do?'

'Oh, for God's sake –'

I turned away from him.

John's fist thumped into my shoulder. Turning slowly, I saw my little brother setting himself up.

'Don't fuckin' dare,' I warned him. 'I don't care who you are, I'll punch your fucking face in.'

'Come on, then,' he said. 'Why don't you do it, huh? Every other fucker round here wants to.'

I almost did. But right then he was just too pathetic to waste my time on. Staring him down, I backed away. Lifting a finger, I aimed it at his face. 'You're not worth it, John. I'm done with you. You got that?'

Pushing my way through the crowd of onlookers, I heard him call out. 'I don't need you, Joe. You're done with me, are you? Well, fuck you! You mean nothin' to me either. You're not even my real brother. Just some sad *bastard* that I've been stuck with all my life.'

Our eyes met over the shoulders of the drinkers making a wall between us.

'I'm not your real brother?' I asked. 'Fair enough. If that's what you want, John?'

The light of anger went out of his eyes and he turned away. I turned away, too. Didn't look back.

They were angry words on both sides.

Despite them, John would always be my little brother.

We didn't get a chance to make amends.

The time had come to put things right again.

As a soldier, I hunted and killed men. That's what soldiers do. But with me the killing was up close and personal. It does something to you when you have to look into the eyes of those you kill. Violence breeds a sickness of the human spirit. Hatred consumes and gives birth to self-loathing. It doesn't matter that the deaths were sanctioned, just or righteous. It's still death. Fourteen years tracking terrorists left me changed forever.

Maybe that's why I turned my back on my brother. If I'd stepped up to the mark then, maybe John wouldn't have run.

I took my leave of the forces, determined that I'd settle down with Diane, lead a life of normality and peace.

I should've known I was pissing into the wind.

In some respects, John made me what I am. I dealt with his debts in the only way I knew how. I backed down his debtors. On the streets that gave me a certain reputation. It wasn't long before my natural ability pushed my other, gentler attributes aside. Subtly, what began as a foray into private security consultancy metamorphosed into clients who demanded more. Occasionally I had to crack skulls and bloody noses. For fourteen years I'd met violence head-on with even more violence, and it seemed for all my good intentions that nothing had changed.

In another world I could've ended up a hitman like those I'd waged war against, or as muscle for some lowlife gangster. Only because I had morals and – yes – compassion could I find any peace at all. Without my sense of decency, I'd be nothing more than a bigger thug amid all the little thugs.

I promised Jennifer I'd find my brother.

Nothing was going to stand in my way.

9

Yesterday morning Tubal Cain's rage was epic. Little wonder. First, he'd lost his SUV, stranding him out on the highway like road kill left to dry in the increasing heat. Then he'd realized that the unscrupulous bastard who'd abandoned him had also stolen his second-favourite knife. Next, he'd discovered that his penny loafers were no good for walking any distance. But, as the saying goes, that was then and this is now. Almost twenty-four hours later Cain was feeling rather pleased with himself.

For one, he was lying on a soft bed, wiggling his hot feet in the draught from a wall-mounted AC unit. Freshly showered and wearing clothes that weren't sticky with perspiration, he was a new man. Beside him on the bed was the quiet, still form of the Good Samaritan who'd brought him to this place.

She was dead, of course, not sleeping peacefully as her pose would suggest. Her hair was spread across the pillows like a sheaf of spilled corn, hiding her slack features. Deliberate posing so that her unnatural pallor wouldn't give the game away

'Now, I'd appreciate it if you'd just lie there like a good girl,' he said. 'Like you're sleeping off the effects of a heavy party. It was a good party, believe me, and you certainly deserve a nap.'

Cain prided himself on his expertise at covering his tracks. This was why he remained the USA's most prolific *undetected* serial murderer. Take George and Mabel, for instance: he'd rigged the explosion so that both of them would be so charred, it would take a determined investigator to guess that they'd been murdered. Essentially, Mabel hadn't been too careful with the gas cooker when preparing their supper. Either the explosion or the subsequent fire would cover the fact that George was missing a couple of digits while his wife had suffered numerous broken limbs.

Here, though, it wasn't as dramatic as flames and carcass-ripping devastation. Subtlety was the order of the day. He'd cranked up the AC so that the growing stink wouldn't alert anyone too soon. And he'd tucked the comforter up to the woman's chin. That'd help dissuade the blowflies as they searched out decaying matter as nurseries for their brood. By the time the proliferation of insect life made the room unbearable, he'd be many miles away.

The comforter served a threefold purpose. It absorbed the blood leaking from her body and would take a lot more before it showed. It also concealed the missing digits from her right hand. Ideally, Cain would've preferred to deliver her entire corpse to his repository in Jubal's Hollow; there were some nicely shaped bones under that alabaster skin of hers. For now, he had neither the time nor the inclination for further diversion. The fingers stripped from her hand would have to do. They were easily concealed in the pocket of his jacket, easily transported, and could be dropped off next time he visited his secret place.

It was like preparing for a school picnic. He'd wrapped the fingers in cellophane, packed like snack-sized hot dogs, and secreted them alongside the baggie holding George's thumbs. When he had time, he'd strip the flesh away and keep only the bones. He preferred them that way. Without the associated baggage of rotting meat. For now, he could content himself with fingering his souvenirs through their plastic casing without fear of getting her filth on his hands.

In his other pocket was a similar package. Fingers taken from the woman's boyfriend, who had kindly given Cain the fresh set of clothes and the keys to his VW Beetle. The boyfriend himself was in the shower, no more alive than the girlfriend was. Locked in the cubicle from prying eyes, he'd stay undiscovered for as long as the girl did.

Finally, Cain raised himself up. Bedsprings squealed in protest at the redistribution of weight. A creaking eulogy for the woman as she settled deeper into the mattress.

'I'd love to stay and chat a little longer,' he said. 'The woman remained unresponsive beneath the bedsheets. 'I'm not normally the type who just has his way with a girl then makes off with hardly a thanks. It's just that I've got something that needs doing and time's a-wasting.'

He sat on the edge of the bed amid further creaks and groans and pulled on a pair of thick hiking socks.

He had some intense blisters on the balls of both feet but the socks alleviated some of the discomfort. Socks in place, he tucked the hems of his jeans into them, before tugging on sturdy lace-up boots. Then he retrieved the lightweight anorak containing his souvenirs and pulled it over his checked shirt. A black baseball cap emblazoned with an American eagle completed the ensemble.

He paused to admire himself in the full-length mirror on the bathroom door. His fair hair and pale green eyes gave him a boyish air that he knew endeared him to the ladies. 'Well, hello there.' He smiled at his reflection. 'Who is that ruggedly handsome guy?'

He'd entered this room the epitome of Joe College. But he now bore the aspect of a seasoned hiker, exactly like thousands of others who passed along this highway day in and day out.

Before leaving the room, he wiped down all the surfaces he'd touched, as well as all those he couldn't remember touching. He used the cloth to wipe the door handle, then slipped out of the room, taking the cloth with him. 'Pays to be extra careful,' he told the woman.

Best that he didn't leave any incriminating friction ridges for a CSI person to find. That would really stir things up. He scanned the room for the minutiae he might have missed, but decided he'd been as thorough as ever. He wasn't concerned about hair or saliva, or even semen. His DNA wasn't on any *police* record. Of course, his fingerprints were another story entirely. Twice in towns out east, he had been caught with prostitutes in his car. Luckily, the cops had dirty minds; otherwise, they might have guessed his true motive for hunting the red-light districts. He wouldn't have gotten off so lightly with a fine and his prints taken – the old-fashioned way, thankfully, ink on cards.

A return to the bed allowed a straightening and tucking-in of the comforter. A soft pat of his hand on the woman's head. 'Now don't you worry. So long as I don't leave behind any prints, I'll remain anonymous. By the time the police get round to checking out a sample of DNA taken under warrant I'll already be one of two things: famous or dead. Probably both. And by then it won't matter, will it?'

His old set of clothing was packed into the dead man's backpack, along with other articles that could come in handy. His utility belt for one. He slung the backpack over his shoulder, took one last look at the woman on the bed, winked at her, then slipped out of the room.

The early-morning cool washed over him. Within hours this same place would be oven-hot, the air shimmering before his very eyes. But now everything was calm and he could see way off across the star-blasted wastelands to an orange haze on the horizon. Not the dawning sun – it was on the wrong horizon. The light he could detect was artificial, half a billion streetlights tainting the skyline with their putrid glow. Towards those lights he must travel. For it was there he'd find fame and notoriety.

Not to mention the thief who stole his knife.

The motel was your typical low-slung timber structure. A series of cabins set out in two parallel rows behind the booking-in office. The office was in darkness, as were the other cabins. Not too many patrons had stayed the night. Drawn up in the parking lot were only four vehicles, one of which was his recently acquired VW Beetle. True to his sense of destiny, the VW was an orange/yellow colour; just like the one driven by the man born Theodore Robert Cowell on 24 November, 1946. Cowell would later adopt his stepfather's surname and be known as Theodore Bundy. Ted Bundy, the talented serial killer who was soon to be eclipsed by the exploits of one Tubal Cain.

A quick reconnoitre of the area satisfied him that no other guest was out of bed. He walked towards the VW, jangling the keys in his hand. The aged car was more stubborn wreck than it was vintage model. A little temperamental to start, if memory served. Hopefully the chugging of the engine wouldn't alert anyone nosy enough to see him depart. But then again, why should that matter? By the time the bodies were discovered, he'd have arrived in one of the cities and acquired alternative transport. The Beetle would be a burnt-out shell in some vacant lot.

Opening the door of the car, he slung the backpack on to a back seat. Surprisingly the car started at the first attempt, and he disengaged the emergency brake and drove off without a look back. He drove without hurry, but with purpose. From his shirt pocket, he teased out a slip of paper, on it a handwritten telephone number. Beneath it, he'd written the address of the hotel it corresponded to.

'Stupid, stupid thief.' His laughter was as bitter as sucking on unripe lemons. 'If you want to get into my kind of game you have to learn the basic rules. First rule: cover your tracks.'

The amateur who'd hijacked him, taking his SUV and beloved Bowie knife, obviously hadn't thought of the consequences of wadding up the slip of paper and dropping it on the floor of his car – or at least trying to. It'd been a simple matter for Cain to ring the number and listen as a nasal girl had announced the name of the hotel in Santa Monica. The call didn't give him the thief's name, but that was academic. Cain knew where the thief planned to stay. A quick visit to the hotel itself would establish everything else he needed to know.

'Santa Monica, here I come,' he said, laughing again. This time his laughter wasn't so bitter, the lemon rind sweetened with sugar. As he drove he shredded the slip of paper, depositing a tiny portion of it out the window every so often along the way.

A couple of hours would see him on the west coast. Maybe he'd grab a little breakfast, see to the disposal of the VW, then go scout out the location of the hotel. He'd locate the thief, then by tonight he'd be ready to move. He didn't care about regaining the SUV. It had served its purpose and would likely have gone the way he was planning for the VW. But he did want his knife back.

Not to be sentimental about it, but the Bowie held a great number of satisfying memories. Some he liked to play back in his mind while holding the knife in his hand. He could soon buy or appropriate a replacement, but it wouldn't be the same. False memories just weren't gratifying. And besides, when he finally allowed the world to know his name, he wanted his arsenal right there beside him. The police should have the capacity to match the blade with each corresponding corpse it had been used on. He wanted the *genuine* knife to be kept as a museum piece to record his infamy, not some second-rate, virgin chunk of metal.

Westward he drove. And despite appearances, the VW was a steady if plodding workhorse. He only had two complaints. First, the air-conditioning system was archaic, achieved by winding down the windows to promote a cross-draft. Second, the facility for music was as outmoded as the AC unit.

He raked through the glove compartment, searching out a couple of music cassettes. One of them, some inane hip-hop crap, he tossed over his shoulder into the back seat. The second was more to his taste. Cain didn't recognize the band, but the bluesy guitar was to his liking. It wasn't as good as the swing music he preferred: playing air guitar wasn't as satisfying as imagining cutting away strips of flesh with a bandleader's baton.

The miles passed easily.

So did the gas in the tank.

Thirty miles short of his destination, he was forced to pull into a gas station. Ten dollars' worth of gasoline would more than suffice. He would have paid his bill with the credit cards stolen from the dead couple back at the motel, but a credit trail would easily set the law on his path. It didn't irk him to have to use his own cash, not when it was so readily available to one who knew how to acquire it. The teller thanked him California-style and Cain smiled unashamedly. The girl – sun-bronzed and blond with a smattering of freckles on a cute nose – smiled back at him. Hey, it was good to be back on the west coast.

Hungry, he purchased a pack of pre-packed sandwiches and a couple of Snicker bars, plus a pint of chocolate milk. Skimmed milk, less than ninety-nine calories, he had a waistline to consider. He finished it before he was even out of the door.

Outside the store, he stood for a while, watching traffic passing on the highway. Here the traffic flow was heavier than out in the desert. He watched vehicles sailing by like mirages through the shimmering heat, wondering what stories their occupants could tell. Where they were going, what they were doing. One thing he was certain of. None had a story to tell to match his.

Beyond the gas station was a rest area. Picnic tables were set out on a patch of lawn so verdant it had to be fake. Bordering the grassy area, the land remained parched and gritty, the home of dust devils and wind-blown detritus. A family had set themselves up at one of the tables. Bottles of soda and food wrapped in tinfoil were laid out in front of them. Father was pointing out what the children should eat, while they ignored him and went straight for the potato chips. Mother sat on one of the benches, trying her hardest to coax some enjoyment out of a cigarette while squinting against blown dust and the high-pitched squalling of the kids.

Cain shook his head.

'Family bliss,' he said to himself. God, but he was happy he'd left those trappings behind.

He surveyed the remainder of the rest area. There was a public convenience building abutting the gas station. A pint of chilled milk forging towards his bladder, he decided a visit was in order before setting off.

Someone else had the same idea. A heavy-built guy with uncontrollable hair raced towards the door. His moon face was contorting as though he'd been caught short many miles distant. He was the epitome of desperation.

When Cain entered the public restroom, the man had already disappeared behind a cubicle door. Cain could hear him struggling with his belt, issuing soft, urgent noises. Then there was a clunk of the seat followed by the indescribable sound of the man's very essence dropping into a porcelain bowl.

'Now that's either extremely gross or mildly amusing,' Cain said to himself. The man's disembodied sigh decided the issue for him. 'Extremely amusing.'

Smiling, he unzipped at a urinal and relieved his own body of a growing urgency. That done, he could concentrate on another more pressing ache that required assuaging.

The sink hadn't seen a cleaner's administrations in many an hour. He used a hot-air blower to dry himself.

Water flushed and the fat guy came out of the cubicle and bustled directly for the exit door. Cain caught his eye and the guy looked momentarily abashed, turned fluidly towards the sink to wash his own hands. Cain nodded at him. 'Things a little desperate there, buddy?'

Embarrassed, the man shrugged.

'Better out than in, eh?' Cain quipped.

'You betcha,' the man grimaced. 'Must have eaten some green meat. Didn't think I was gonna make it to the can.'

'Lucky for you that you did. By the sound of things you'd have made quite a mess of yourself,' Cain said. 'Best to stay clean, though, don't you think?'

'Cleanliness is next to godliness,' the man quoted, humiliated at having been caught out, 'even when you're in a hurry.'

The man made a brief run of his hands under the water, then turned towards the filthy-looking towel hanging on the wall. He paused. Looked to Cain for guidance.

'Seems a little pointless, doesn't it?' Cain said.

'You're telling me,' said the fat guy. His bulk formed a queue of its own behind Cain at the automated hand-dryer. Energized by his need to get about his journey, he hopped from foot to foot in anticipation of his turn at the hot air.

Cain took his time dry-washing his hands to a point where his skin began to stick together. A *tsk* of frustration from the man. Cain was pleased. Finally he stood aside.

'It's all yours.'

'Gee, thanks,' said the fat guy, not really meaning it.

'My pleasure,' Cain said. Not meaning it, either.

It would be nice to kill the fat guy. But in the end, he decided not to. Too dangerous. What if someone walked in before he was finished concealing the gross body in one of the stalls? He could obviously kill them too, but then he'd be right back to square one. Last thing he wanted was to end up in a loop where the only guarantee was that he'd finally run out of places to conceal the dead. He would allow the man to live but there was something he could do that'd bring him a modicum of fulfilment.

It was more than a friendly gesture as he patted the fat guy's shoulder. Two solid slaps of his hand. The man flinched at the contact, blinked at him.

'See you, friend,' Cain said. He moved towards the exit. Happy.

'Yeah, see you,' the fat guy intoned. Then, stupidly, he muttered something under his breath.

Cain turned and stared back at him. His look was that of a prowling leopard eyeing up a wounded buffalo.

'You say something, buddy?'

The fat guy blinked rapid fire. His jowls hung slack, framed by long, wiry curls. 'No, I didn't say a thing.'

Cain stepped towards him, and a piece of grit crunched beneath his boot. The sound was more invasive than loud, an expression of Cain's aversion to the man before him. The fat guy reacted as though it was gunshot. He reared back, lifting his chin in anticipation of avoiding a blow. Cain shook his head at the overreaction. He said, 'That's funny. I'm sure I heard you call me an asshole.'

Now the fat guy shook his head.

'Look, mister. I don't want any trouble, OK. I just want to dry my hands and get outa here. Wife and kids are waiting for me in the car. We're going down to see my wife's mother for a day or two is all. So I don't want any trouble with you. Gonna get enough of it off the mother-in-law if I'm more than a minute late.'

Funny how people babbled when they were afraid.

'I was being polite to you,' Cain said. His smile was mock whimsy. 'Even looked after your health and well-being for you. Not many people would've bothered. Quite happily could've let you go and get back in your car with your wife and kids. Could've allowed you to spread all those nasty little germs to them. Take them on down to Grandma's house too, no doubt. But I didn't. I thought I'd be nice and remind you to wash your hands. No big deal?'

'No,' the fat guy said. 'No big deal.'

'So why'd you have to call me an asshole?'

'I didn't . . .'

'Don't lie to me. Please?'

'I'm not lying. I didn't say a goddamn thing.'

'Ingratitude. Lies. Now profanity?'

Sometimes even scared fat people got to a point when enough was enough. 'Look fella, I don't know what your problem is with me, but I'm outa here.' He shoved by Cain, heading for the door. His exit was as desperate as his entrance.

From the open door, Cain watched him go. A hot breeze lifted whorls of dust in his wake. The man kept glancing back, his hair waving Medusa-like. Cain waved at him. The man jumped in his station wagon, babbling loudly in distress, hands stabbing for the ignition. His prodigious wife and two equally fat children looked over at Cain. Red-haired with pie-dish faces, they looked like orang-utans in a zoo. He waved at them too. Then the station wagon was headed for the highway with a little more haste than was sensible.

Too quickly, the show was over. While it lasted, the slight distraction had proven enjoyable. Would've been more satisfying if he'd sliced up the fat guy. But at least the look on the guy's face was a bonus.

'And I got another trophy.'

In his palm was a strip of plaid cloth. A patch taken from the man's shirt when he'd patted him on the shoulder. Not just a friendly farewell, it was a well-rehearsed move. It was all part of a game he played. If he could get a sliver of clothing and remain undetected he let the target live. Those who felt the tug at their clothes or the slice of the knife against their flesh he had to kill immediately.

'Fatty, you just don't realize it yet. Today is the luckiest day of your life.'

10

Rink's condominium was set in a small community in woodland near Temple Terrace, north-east of Tampa. Set on a limestone outcrop, it was elevated above the flat country all around. Across the way, I could see families in their backyards, reclining on deckchairs with a cool drink at hand, some splashing in private swimming pools. A different world from the one I knew back home. Rink had obviously been pulling in decent work to afford this kind of accommodation.

From the front of the house, I heard an engine growl, Rink announcing his return. Rising up from the chair, I wandered into the lounge area and met him coming in with his arms full of takeaway food.

'Let's eat,' he announced.

'You bet.'

The food wasn't too fancy, but it was more satisfying than the artificial slop the cabin crew offered on the flight over. I chewed without really tasting anything other than the liberal quantity of Corona I washed it down with. After we ate, we collapsed in front of Rink's widescreen TV and he put on a fight DVD. Rink passed me another beer.

Then we got round to business.

'Harvey called,' Rink said. 'He's gonna come to the meeting with Louise Blake. Then he wants a private meet with us after we're finished with her.'

I took a sup from my beer, said, 'Makes sense.'

'He's got the location Petoskey does his night shift business from. Says he'll take us there if we need him.'

Something was coming that I might not like. I nodded encouragement; might as well get it over with.

'Says he'll take us, but that's his involvement over with. Doesn't want a backlash from Petoskey if things turn sour.'

'Fine by me,' I said. 'Things are bound to turn sour.'

It was Rink's turn to nod.

'Thought they might,' he said. 'This nonsense about John leaving town because he owes money sounds like a cover story. I want the truth from Petoskey. If that means hitting him hard and fast, so be it.'

'I'm with you, man.'

'Never doubted you.'

'Good.'

'Shut up and drink your beer,' I said.

And that was that. The planning would come later. When we arrived at Petoskey's front door. When we had a better idea of what we were up against. I hadn't been a secret agent; it wasn't for me to use guile and trickery to root out the bad guys. I was – along with Rink and a select few others – the weapon sent in when all the planning was done with and all that was left was the arse-kicking. Arse-kicking I was good at. It got results.

Ergo, there'd be nothing fancy set up for when we paid Petoskey a visit. Either he'd be cooperative, or we'd make him wish he had been. End of story.

Rink indicated the TV with his beer can.

'I was figurin' on havin' a go at this extreme fighting stuff.' On the screen, two buffed athletes were pounding the snot out of each other in an octagonal cage. Unlike pro-wrestling, this fighting was for real. The blows were aimed with intent, the strangles to a point people passed out, the arm and leg locks occasionally ending in fractures.

'I'm sure you'd do OK, so long as you didn't forget it was only a sport,' I said.

'Man, it's all in the control,' Rink said. 'I know when to kill and when not to.'

I shook my head. 'What about when the shit hits the fan? When one of those monsters has you up against the cage and is pounding the life out of you? You telling me you won't gouge out an eye or rip off an ear with your teeth?'

Rink shrugged. 'Biting's for the likes of Tyson, man. It was just an idea. Something to keep me fit.'

'Go for it then,' I said. 'If you're not too old.'

'Too old?' Rink looked scandalized.

'Well, you are almost forty.'

'I ain't too old. For God's sake, the damn heavyweight champ's in his mid-forties and he's still showing these young lions what a real fighter is all about.'

I had to agree. The champion was giving a man a foot taller and almost twenty years his junior some serious grief.

I'm a realist. I couldn't compete with the likes of those athletes. Not in their arena. But put them in mine, and I was positive that the man left standing wouldn't be the sportsman. My expertise lay in the battlefield and they wouldn't stand a chance. You couldn't go to war, then tap out when an opponent was getting the better of you. Fail in my arena and you were dead.

The same was true for Rink. He'd had the same training as me and was equally dangerous in a fight. What Rink possessed that I didn't were black belts to prove his expertise. Even before he'd signed up as a Ranger, he'd been an interstate karate champion three years running.

The first time Rink and I worked together, it wasn't during a covert operation. We were off duty, but Rink had taught me a valuable lesson.

I had been aware of the big American, but only as the silent new recruit who only seemed animated when in action. We hadn't bonded yet, and I was as confused as anyone why the strange-sounding Yank had been drafted into our team.

Near to our base at Arrowsake was a small fishing town. The bar next to the harbour was a favourite of squaddies when it came to downtime. Rink was standing by the bar. He was cradling a pint of brown ale but didn't seem to be enjoying it. I glanced across the barroom and saw why.

There were three of them, Special Air Service guys who'd been brought in on a joint training operation. There'd been friction from the start. Even over the murmur of the crowd I heard one of them call Rink a 'reject Nip'.

I saw Rink set his glass down on the bar and turn to leave.

The three SAS guys got up.

I didn't owe Rink anything, but for some reason I got up, too. There was a hush in the bar. The silence that preceded violence. Rink veered towards the side exit and the three SAS guys moved to follow him. No one tried to intervene. No one wanted to be pulled in as a witness.

The three men followed Rink into the backyard. Barrels were stacked against one wall, metal bins the other. At the far end, a metal gate stood open and Rink walked towards it.

'Hey, slant eyes,' one of the SAS guys shouted at Rink's back. 'Where the fuck d'you think you're running off to?'

Rink didn't answer.

The three of them laughed, started after him. Rink closed the gate. He turned round.

I saw the three SAS guys falter in their stride.

Behind them, I closed the door of the pub, placed my hip against it.

One of them turned and looked at me.

'Got nothin' to do with you, mate,' he said.

'Three against one,' I pointed out. 'I think it does.'

I noticed Rink looking my way.

'I can handle it,' he said.

'I'm just watching your back, buddy.'

Rink nodded his thanks. Then he turned back to the SAS guys. 'So who's first?'

'Fuck that!' one of them snapped.

The SAS guys weren't slouches. No Special Forces soldiers are. The one who'd spoken to me hung back while the other two moved in on Rink.

The first one to reach him caught Rink's front kick on his chin. He fell in a heap at the feet of his friend. The second one wouldn't be taken so easily. He feinted a punch but then turned and shot a sidekick at Rink's knee. Rink wobbled and I saw pain on his face. The man stepped in and drilled a punch into Rink's stomach. Rink folded at the waist as his hands sought the source of his pain. The SAS man stepped in, ready to finish it.

But Rink wasn't finished. He was play-acting. Even as the man threw his punch, Rink rammed his elbow upwards and drove the point into the man's throat.

At the same time the third one stooped and grabbed at an empty bottle lying on top of one of the bins.

I didn't stop to think.

I leapt after him.

The man spun, swiped at my head with the bottle. I was expecting that so I was already ducking. My shoulder caught him in his chest and I continued to drive him backwards, rushing him at speed across the yard. As we collided with the barrels, the bottle was knocked out of his hand. It shattered on the floor. The SAS man struck at me, catching me on my left cheek. I gave him one right back and he staggered away from me.

He ended up in front of Rink. Rink grabbed him, spun him round, then headbutted him in the face. The man dropped to his knees, but he wasn't as unconscious as I'd have liked. I stepped in to put the boot in his ribs.

Rink lifted a hand.

'He's done,' he said. 'It's over with, OK?'

Looking down at the SAS man, I saw him blinking up at me with dazed eyes.

Rink was right then.

And he was now.

'Sorry, Rink. All those years of competition; of course you could restrain your killer instinct. It's me who couldn't do it. I haven't had the etiquette ingrained in me the way you have.'

'You know your problem, Hunter? You're too cool about it all. You get off on the violence.'

'I thought you knew me better than that, Rink.'

'Aw, lighten up, will ya? Here, drink some more beer.' He underhanded me a bottle.

Despite what had just been said, my aptitude for hurting others has always been channelled, a skill forged for a strict purpose and with strict delivery in mind. The alcohol – or perhaps it was the jet lag – made me maudlin. 'You remember our training, Rink? I don't know about you, but it was about the hardest thing I ever did.'

'Sure was. An' that's counting the fifty-man challenge I had to complete to get my Kyokushin black belt.'

Unlike that of regular soldiers, our training hadn't simply been geared towards weaponry and technology, but the use of the body to achieve the desired results. Back in 1940, Captain William Ewart Fairbairn had revolutionized the unarmed tactics of the British military. He was alleged to have had 666 brutal encounters that he survived by using his knowledge of hand-to-hand combat. Basically, he was no slouch when it came to a fistfight, the ideal inspiration for headstrong squaddies like us.

Over the intervening years, other warriors had added to the roster of Fairbairn's skills and through intense training, their legacies were passed down to us. In effect, you could say we were the direct descendants of those masters of empty-handed combat. I can't claim 666 encounters, but I'm well into triple figures. My generally unmarked face was testament to my skills as much as Rink's black belts were to his.

'See, it's not just about finishing your man,' Rink said with a nod towards the screen. 'It's about doing it in style. Has to have entertainment value or the promoters won't be able to put spectators' asses on seats. What you do, Hunter, well, it just ain't pretty to watch.'

'Aren't you afraid you'll lose your edge?' I asked. I was being serious.

Rink looked pensive for a moment. Then he hit me with his enigmatic look, all hooded eyes and down-turned mouth.

'Hunter,' he said slowly, 'we ain't in the military no more. We don't have a licence to kill. Hasn't that sunk in yet?'

It didn't take much deliberation.

'Yeah,' I finally said.

But it was a sore point.

11

Only eight miles from Los Angeles International Airport and thirteen miles from downtown LA, Santa Monica was pretty much Tubal Cain's favourite place on the West Coast. He'd visited here many times before but never grew tired of it. How could you be bored with its striking contemporary style and architecture or its shameless attempt at snaring a buck from the tourist market?

Santa Monica was originally a chic Victorian playground. Then in the early 1900s it blossomed again with movie-star glamour. As early as the 1920s stars such as Will Rogers, Greta Garbo and Marion Davies built mansions here. During the 1980s it boomed again after a multi-million-dollar restoration transformed the city.

Many people thronged to take up residence here, but also many of those coming were transients with no roots to speak of. It was the perfect hunting ground for one who preyed primarily on strangers who wouldn't be missed.

Cain was hunting one of those transients now.

A certain thief of a certain knife dear to him.

Traversing Lincoln Boulevard in his Bundyesque VW, he grinned at the characters he witnessed thronging the sidewalks. Here were wannabe actors, wannabe directors, wannabe rock stars. You name it, they were here. Then there were the *others*. They were there to gawk in wonder at all the other wannabes, to rub shoulders with the wannabe rich and famous. To be sure, no one truly rich and famous would wander along those sidewalks for fear of being torn to pieces by star-struck souvenir hunters. Yet Cain could see a half-dozen Michael Jackson lookalikes, a handful of Marilyn Monroes. Who would know if the star was real or not?

The world was twisted full tilt in this wondrous place. But that was what Cain loved so much. It was an escape from the humdrum existence of reality, a dimension to which one of his kind belonged. He knew he didn't exist in the everyday world that most others inhabited. As a sociopath, he understood that what he was doing wasn't acceptable in ordinary society. But as a psychopath, he didn't care. Here in this modern-day Babel he could thrive and grow, easy in the knowledge that he was surrounded by myriad like minds.

Cain liked to speak to his dead victims. They tended not to butt in. For the same reason, he was equally happy conversing with himself. He could be as verbose as he wished. 'Rule two, thief: the easiest way to hide is to do so in full sight. Here I'm a sardine in a massive shoal of sardines. I'm indiscernible from the thousands of others, and unlikely to be picked out when there are so many to choose from.' Not that he particularly liked the sardine metaphor, but he had to admit that it served his purpose. He tended to think of himself more as a shark or a swordfish, lurking within the shoal, ready to spring forth from concealment to show his ripping teeth or flashing blade.

No doubt about it. The thief was likely holed up in his motel room.

'You're making it too easy for me, thief. You should be out here in the sunshine. Mingling with everyone else in this crazy, topsy-turvy place. What chance would I have of finding you then?'

He parked the car in a massive lot filled almost to capacity. Nearby was the promenade that led to the pier, an easy stroll he relished after driving so far. Day and night, it made no difference; people would be on the pier fishing, watching the waves, entertaining themselves in the arcades or shopping for souvenirs, riding the carousels or rollercoasters, laughing, yelling, screaming in delight.

Why bother locking the car or removing the keys from the ignition? If some thief should happen to steal his vehicle while he was gone, then all the better. It'd save him the job of disposing of it later. Wiping the steering wheel, console and doors was both sensible and necessary. Wouldn't like to think that a cop discovered the car before the joyriders did.

He strolled on the promenade below the bluffs, the windows of the Victorian houses reflecting the glare. Where the afternoon sun caressed his face beneath the peak of his cap, it was molten honey. A couple of girls roller-bladed by, thong bikinis barely concealing their cute little assets. It was all for show, but so was his reaction. He smiled and nodded, adjusted his cap as if in amazement. Just like any other first-time visitor who was male and red-blooded would do. 'Rule three, thief: it's an easy one to remember, this.' To avoid funny looks, he kept his words to himself now. 'When in Rome do as the Romans do.'

Good advice.

To Cain's delight, a woman rode by on a bike, towing a Jack Russell terrier on a skateboard. Screwball madness, insanity, and he loved it all.

He paused at a vendor to buy some food, then continued strolling to the pier, eating directly from the carton with his fingers. Man, but this really was the life!

The day and the sights were glorious. The sun was beginning its roll towards the Pacific Ocean, the sky and sea a holiday brochure cerulean blue. The beach was packed with beautiful people glistening under the sheen of tanning oil. All that was missing was Pamela Anderson in a red swim suit.

Cain felt good. Only one thing could make the day better. But that would blow his cover as a tourist. He dumped his greasy food tray in an overflowing trash-can, felt for the scaling knife in his jacket pocket. A little bone harvesting was out of the question, but he decided he had ample opportunity for a little game. With most people skimpily attired it might be a challenge, but that only made things more interesting. And, as always, with a challenge conquered came more satisfaction.

His first target was apparent immediately, a statuesque woman in khaki shorts and a vest top. She was standing at the rear of a line waiting to purchase ice cream. Cain didn't pause. He moved directly in, pretended to accidentally jostle the woman.

'Sorry, ma'am,' he said. 'I do apologize.'

The woman, forty-something but looking every bit of ten years older under her make-up, gave him a frown. Not used to the concept of strangers copping a feel from the likes of her, she wasn't concerned by the unsolicited contact. She flung back her hair and returned to the more pressing engagement of securing her place in the ice-cream line. Cain walked away, clutching a belt loop from her shorts in his left hand.

'One nil,' he whispered.

He secreted the trophy in the pocket of his windbreaker, pushing it alongside the film-wrapped fingers and thumbs of his collection. Light of spirit, he climbed a series of board-planks to a ramp leading on to the pier. From this high vantage, he spied the woman at the kiosk. She'd already forgotten him in her desire for raspberry whip delight. Behind her in line was a man in taupe shirt and chinos. He seemed to glance Cain's way. Only a brief glance, but their eyes met. Then the man looked away. Hmmm, interesting.

'Rule four, thief: *semper vigilo*. Remain vigilant at all times.'

On the pier, the pickings were even sweeter. The crowds were hemmed closer. Accidental collisions were the order of the day. Within a minute, he had a button from an elderly gent's blazer and the tassel from a woman's parasol. Neither were what he considered too great a challenge, but they joined his collection just the same.

Cain wasn't finished yet.

'The catch of the day!'

She was stunning in pale lilac swimsuit and matching sarong. Looked Hawaiian. A dark-eyed beauty with dusky skin and full red lips. Cutting her out of her bikini would make anyone a happy man.

She moved through the crowd with the fluid confidence that the masses would open before her. Sure, she was beautiful, but she had that innate disdain for the lesser mortals around her. Cain wouldn't hold that against her, she was a person after his own heart. He would have loved to teach her that there was at least one among the crowd who would not give way so easily. Trouble was, she was too high-profile. More than one man gave her a lingering glance. Some women looked too. But their stares were of the green-eyed variety.

The attention she commanded meant it wasn't a good idea to approach her. Someone would notice and remember. Guaranteed. An older woman sitting on a deckchair was much more viable. He took two steps towards her and stopped. Something registered. A flash of taupe walking by. He blinked slowly. The colour taupe wasn't something that would generally cause concern. Not unless you were as cautious as Tubal Cain.

He entered an arcade. Families fed coins into machines as though they were going out of fashion. A grandiose show of holiday overexuberance. Sweaty faces and the smell of popcorn. Cain absorbed and then discarded it all. He was in the Zone. He took five paces, then rounded on his heel and walked back the way he'd come.

The man entering the arcade had no option but to continue inside. The flicker in his eyes, the almost imperceptible pause in his step, was the give-away. Cain was more adept at this game. No one would guess that he was suspicious of the man.

Immediately outside, Cain turned towards the deck-chair woman. Spun on his heel again, just in time to see the man in taupe shirt and chinos come out of the arcade. Pushing his hand through his dark hair, he scanned the crowd for someone else. It was good cover. Not convincing to Cain, though. Should have stuck to buying ice cream, Cain concluded.

No doubt about it, now: the man was following him. Only thing was, he couldn't quite guess his motive. Slowly, Cain turned and began the walk along the pier.

He affected the look of one thrilled to be there, ogling the attractions like a country boy in the big city for the first time. But the storefronts and carousels held no real interest for him. They were cover for his own surveillance. In the reflective surfaces he checked behind him. Taupe shirt was still there. Plus another in a flamboyant yellow and blue striped number. He was being hunted down by at least two men.

'What have we got here then? Muggers or cops?' Neither assumption boded well. 'Time to go, I think.'

Escape beckoned via the steps leading back to the promenade. But a huge man blocked the way. He glowered like a bull mastiff as he whispered into his fist. Not muggers then. Definitely police.

Feign indifference. Just walk on past him. Good plan, but the man stepped in front of him, held up a hand and pushed it against Cain's chest. He was a stuccoed wall, wide, pale as whitewash, and a little rough up close. Not too polite, either. Didn't even have the good grace to introduce himself. All he was capable of was a nod over Cain's shoulder. Ergo, his intention was to distract rather than contain. Taupe shirt or the other in candy stripe must be moving in on him.

Cain blinked up at the man. The innocent look. 'Can I help you?' he asked.

'You can wait there a moment, sir.' He did the over-the-shoulder nod thing again. The slight urgency told Cain that the man's friends weren't as close as they should have been.

'What's this about?' Cain asked as he pushed his hands into his pockets.

'Security,' said the man. 'We'd like a word with you.'

'Security?' Cain's nervous laugh was real. But for a wholly different reason than he'd admit. 'That's a relief, friend. For a moment there I thought you were about to rob me or something.'

'We just want to ask you a couple of questions,' said the man. 'If you wouldn't mind waiting a minute or two?'

'Wait for what? What am I supposed to have done?'

'We've been having problems with pickpockets. Been watching you, and we'd just like to ask you to turn out your pockets.' The man, large and impressive-looking, had a nervous cast to his eyes. Not been on the job long, Cain decided.

'I don't think you're at liberty to do that,' Cain told him.

'If you'd just wait for my supervisor, he'll explain everything to you,' said the security man. His hand was as big and hot as a Sunday roast on Cain's shoulder.

'Hey!' Cain shrugged him off. Amiable enough. A lack of aggression ensured he didn't encourage a tighter hold.

Yes, the big guy was new to the job, obviously unsure of his level of authority here. His hand wavered in the air as though plucking at floating threads of lint.

Cain exhaled. 'Rule five, thief: if you're accosted, keep them thinking. While engaged in thought, the fools aren't acting. Gives you the opportunity to act first. Rule six: if you are going to act, do so immediately and without prejudice.'

'So where is your supervisor?' he demanded.

'Coming.'

Cain glanced round, saw that the man in candy stripe was about twenty feet away, attempting to skirt a group of kids on an outing. He couldn't see the one in taupe. Good, that gave him a few seconds to spare.

'I can't wait here all day.' Cain engaged the man's senses by locking eyes with him. Simple but effective. It was all Cain required. His hand moved below their plane of vision. Motion that was barely a flicker. A quick jabbing action between the man's legs. Very little contact. Hardly noticeable. Then he was past the man and taking his first couple of steps down the stairs. The security man was motionless, looking down between his thighs at the lake of blood pooling between his feet.

Cain counted the steps, one, two, three, four; then the caterwauling began. A horror-movie scream as the truth became apparent. Cain's feet gave a backbeat to the howl, clattering down the remaining steps to the promenade. On the pier, heads were swivelling towards the commotion, but Cain simply ran. He needn't look back to witness the result of that one simple knife-jab. A punctured femoral artery came with a guarantee: without immediate medical help, the security man would bleed to death in minutes. Confusion would erupt and allow him to escape. Also, attempting to staunch the flowing blood of their downed fellow meant the man's companions couldn't possibly pursue him, too.

Of course, Cain was also a firm believer that you didn't trust people to react the way you expected them to. A shout broke through the murmur of consternation rising behind him. The slap of determined footsteps down the stairs. He did glance back, a natural instinct that would not be denied. The man in taupe rushed after him. Cain swore and increased his speed.

As they had for the Hawaiian beauty, the crowds parted before him. Only the looks he received were anything but admiring. They were fearful. It was apparent to all that Cain was a fugitive. A dangerous fugitive, judging by the screaming overhead. There were no gung-ho heroes amongst the tourists, no one trying to snag his clothing or bring him down. But neither did they impede the man in taupe. Younger than Cain, and in reasonable shape, he was gaining fast, all this while shouting into a radio and – more worryingly – clenching a revolver in his other hand.

Cain cut to the right, charged up some more steps out on to the ramp arching over the highway, then raced head down for the anonymity offered by the stores a couple of blocks over. The man in taupe didn't stop, matching him step for step all the way.

Cain ducked down a service alley, away from the beach and into the twilit underbelly of Santa Monica that was immeasurably different from the glitz. The sights, the sounds, the smells, everything was tainted with neglect. He grabbed at a wheeled dumpster crammed with the ghosts of pizzas past, tugged it out to block his pursuer's path. Didn't stop running. He heard the man heaving the dumpster aside and realized that barely ten paces separated them. Sprightly son of a bitch, that one, not your usual run of the mill rent-a-cop.

Fortunately Cain gained the corner of the buildings first. He spun to his left into deeper shadows, rushed headlong through a narrow alley, trusting to luck that he didn't smash headlong into an obstruction. Thankfully, he saw a turn and ducked left again.

Cain hoped that the security man would act with caution. He'd witnessed what Cain was capable of with his knife. Only a fool would relish the possibility of bleeding out in a deserted alleyway with only the smell of garbage in his nostrils for the final journey to the afterlife. Fearing ambush, he would slow at the corner.

Cain sprinted on, gaining precious distance on his pursuer.

On a main shopping street parallel to the beach, Cain slowed down. It was surprising how much anonymity a single block's dash had given him. All around him the beachfront lunacy continued unabated. Not as much as a glance or a 'How you doing?' came his way.

A mini-mall enticed passers-by with the promise of major discounts on all purchases. From within the entrance Cain watched the man in taupe rush by. Problem solved, almost.

Ducking through a service door, Cain took off his cap and jacket and dumped them in a waste bin. He freed his jeans from his socks. His shirt hung loose over his waistband, concealing the scaling knife tucked in the small of his back, as well as the large bulges his trophies now made in his jeans' pockets.

Back out in the mall, he ambled in shopper mode. Shoplifting wasn't a skill he'd engaged in since his school days, but the appropriation of a pair of sunglasses was as dexterous as any swish he'd ever made with a blade.

Out on the promenade by the beach again, he looked towards the pier. A swarm of buzzing hornets, the paramedics and police had arrived. The bled-out security man was the sheeted-up load going into an ambulance. The man in candy stripes hung his head by the open doors. Two accounted for, one to go. Behind his newly acquired sunglasses, Cain squinted left and right. No more than ten yards away the taupe security man walked towards him. Cain wasn't concerned; he stood looking out to sea, hands bunched in his pockets around his trophies. The man made the slow walk of dejection back towards the pier, totally oblivious that he was in stabbing range of the person he sought.

Cain turned away. He'd lost interest in this pointless game. Better he return to the VW to see if he still faced the chore of getting rid of it.

Then the more pressing matter of finding the thief.

12

'So this is your home town, Rink? I have to take back what I said about pick-up trucks, huh?'

'Damn right!'

I don't mind admitting when I'm wrong. I thought that I'd be flying into a sleepy town full of wooden shacks and fond memories of Southern belles. Instead, I found a vibrant city to equal any in the mid-western US. I was knocked back by the sprawl of beautiful high-rise buildings, the fine museums and scenic parks along the banks of the Arkansas River.

Not that Rink was gloating. His smile was all pleasure while pointing out the major landmarks, reminding me that Little Rock was the capital of the Natural State, and not some piss-pot backwater as I'd thought.

'Pity we couldn't take the roundabout route so I could see *even more* of your fine town.'

We were in a rental car we'd picked up at Adams Field, otherwise known as Little Rock International Airport, following a four-hour flight from Tampa. The car was a regular sedan, nowhere near as flashy as Rink's Porsche, but clean and comfortable none-theless. More trunk space, too. Rink drove. It was easier that way. This was his old stomping ground and could get us to our destination much quicker.

That had been the plan. Yet it seemed to me that Rink must've been a cab driver in a past life, judging by the winding route we took through town.

'Yeah, Le Petite Roche sure has come on a ways,' Rink said as he pushed the sedan through a downtown convention and entertainment district. Rink himself was impressed. 'I think you're forgettin' that this was Bill Clinton's first capital city, Hunter.'

'I'm not forgetting, Rink. I didn't know. Full stop.'

'Man, you're just too ignorant for your own good. Admit it, you weren't expecting anything like this, were you? We've even got the brand new one-of-a-kind William J. Clinton Presidential Center and Park right here in Little Rock,' Rink said, indicating off to his right with a wave of his hand. 'It's sure a sight to behold.'

'Like Disneyworld?' I asked.

Rink frowned at me. I smiled unabashedly.

'We far off Louise's place?' I asked.

'Not too far. Another five minutes or so.'

'You said that five minutes ago.'

'I did. Now ain't that strange?'

'Harvey going to be there?'

'Said he'd meet us at a diner where we can speak to Louise on neutral ground. Doesn't want to be seen around her house in case anything comes back on him.' Rink gave a shrug. 'I don't know what he's gettin' all bowed up about, not as if Petoskey's the goddamn Godfather or nothin'.'

'Like you said, though, he's got connections,' I said. 'To be honest Rink, I'm starting to worry that we're underestimating his outfit. City this big and important, he must be a key player if he's controlling the politicians.'

Rink shook his head.

'Petoskey's a two-bit asshole playing at the big time, just like I told y'all. It's not as if he's got the Governor in his pocket, just some minor politicians and low-ranking cops who're taking bribes for favours.'

I grimaced, but nodded nonetheless.

Rink's eyes flickered over me. 'I'm telling you, man. There ain't nothin' to get riled up about. I know his type. Thirty years ago, he was frog-giggin' for meat to put in his momma's stew, now he's eatin' the best cuisine and drivin' around in flashy cars. He's poor white trash acting as if he's the big important businessperson. On the grand scale of things, he's nobody. An' he knows it.'

'Maybe, but he seems to have put the frighteners on John. He must have some sort of weight behind him.'

'From what you told me, John ain't too hard to frighten. Ran off from this weaselly Shank character. I take it your brother's not the bravest dude on the planet?'

My headshake was as much from memory as it was disagreement.

'He wasn't running from Shank. Shank was Jennifer's problem, not John's. There were others involved.'

'I know, he'd shacked up with this Blake woman, too,' Rink said. 'He was running from his marriage.'

'Amongst other things,' I said.

Rink pulled the rental over to the side of the road. He sat looking at me.

'What haven't you told me, Hunter?'

I shrugged.

'I didn't think this had anything to do with what happened before, but now I'm not so sure.' I was pensive for a moment. Rink continued to give me the eye. 'I told you me and John had a fall-out, yeah?'

'Uh-huh. But you never told me why.'

My face felt like putty, cold and clammy as I scrubbed my hands over my features. I was already tired, but more than that, thinking about John's predicament made me bone weary.

'Not long after I resigned from the job he came to me with a problem,' I said.

'Go on,' Rink prompted.

'He'd got himself involved with some real heavy duty shit. Stupid son of a bitch had been playing cards and writing IOUs he couldn't hope to cover. First went his car, then the house. But it wasn't enough. He had nothing left and had no one to turn to.'

'So you did the honourable thing?'

'Yeah, I bailed them out. Jenny doesn't know it to this day. I gave John the cash to pay off his debtors. But, an addiction being what it is, John went and blew it on another *sure bet*. I pulled him up about the money and that's when we had the falling-out. It was just a stupid argument.'

'You didn't speak to him afterwards?'

'No, Rink. I didn't even see him again.'

Rink nodded. 'That's when he ran out?'

'He must have been planning it.'

'Punk.'

I shrugged. 'After that, the only way I could think to help him and Jenny was to face down his debtors and make them back off. Wasn't easy. They weren't as easily intimidated as Shank was.'

'They didn't back off?'

'No.'

'You're slipping, Hunter.'

'Seriously,' I said. 'Short of going to war with them there wasn't much I could do. So, instead, I arranged for John and Jenny to disappear for a while. It was all set, they would go off together, assume new identities, everything. Then John went and fucked it all up. Unbeknown to all of us, he'd been seeing this Louise Blake on the side. Before we knew it, they just flitted. Gone.'

'Leaving poor Jenny and his kids behind to take the flak,' Rink concluded for me.

'Yeah,' I agreed. 'I did everything I could for her. Helped her get back on her feet. I had space in my house, but she refused. Said she needed a place of her own. John didn't even get in touch and let her know where he was.'

'And you want to help this pecker-head?'

'He's still my brother, Rink.'

Rink raised an eyebrow, but then gave a soft nod.

'Plus, I'm doing this for his wife and kids.'

'OK. But I'm surprised she wants him back.'

'Jenny doesn't want him back,' I explained. 'She's looking for some kind of closure. I think she wants me to find John so she can spit in his eyes.'

'I'm with her on that one.'

'Me too. Took a lot of sorting, the problems he left behind. As I said, they were a major outfit with major connections. They put out a contract on John.'

'Shit,' Rink said.

'In the end they saw reason. I explained that John had double-crossed us all, that we were all equally aggrieved. So, I made an agreement with them that they didn't go near Jenny or the kids. The alternative was that I'd call in back-up and wipe them out.'

'They believed you were capable?'

'I think it was more fear of the unknown,' I said. 'They didn't know who I was or what I was prepared to do. But some of them had heard whispers. I believe, in the end, they decided it was just a little more trouble than it was worth. You could say that going to war with me wasn't profitable.'

'Did they call in the contract on John?'

I shrugged. 'Who knows what they'd do if he ever showed up again?'

'Which is why you think he's still on the run?'

'Nah.' I shook my head. 'There's more to it than that. John has other reasons. I guess the point I'm trying to make is this: he's a selfish son of a bitch. Doesn't give a shit for anyone but himself. But I don't think he'd be running from the likes of Petoskey if it was only about a couple of hundred dollars' gambling debt.' I paused, summing up *exactly* what it was that I was trying to say. 'Something big has happened. Something he's so frightened of that he's done a runner again and he doesn't intend looking back. Louise Blake has been left high and dry, the same as he left Jenny. That means he's attempting to cut all ties, so he can disappear without a trace. You don't do that for any piddling gambling debt.'

Rink agreed.

'Petoskey's an asshole,' he reiterated. 'But I see where you're coming from. What's he gonna do? Maybe order an ass-whuppin', maybe a broken arm or something? He's not going to order John's death, is he?'

'Unless Petoskey's more dangerous than we're giving him credit for,' I pointed out.

'No, I stand on my first opinion. He's a small potato playing at the big time. He's too chicken shit to take someone out for real.'

'You've been gone a long time. People change.'

'Okay, I'll concede that. But it still leaves another option, doesn't it?'

'John's pissed off someone else. Someone who is prepared to kill him.'

Rink leant forward, turned on the engine and pulled out into the traffic. He turned to me, said, 'But you're still fixin' to start with Petoskey?'

'Yeah. We're going to do it loud and hard. We need to shake him up, Rink. Make him fear us, tell us where John is. Hopefully it'll end there,' I said. 'But I don't think so.'

'No,' Rink said. 'Now that you've got me thinking, I don't figure so either.'

The city was behind us now and we were entering a grimmer section of town.

'What are we doing here?' I asked.

'Just thought we'd take a detour and scope out the land. Harvey said Petoskey does business from an office downtown, also mentioned this place he visits when the dealings are a little more underhand. Thought we'd just drive by and take a look. It would be better to hit him there than downtown. Less chance of the cops arriving and saving his ass before we're through.'

Up ahead was a building right out of Gotham City. Rink raised his chin to indicate it.

'What do you think?'

'Is it haunted?' I joked.

'Only by hobos, I guess,' Rink said.

The building was a huge redbrick affair, but little of the original colour showed through the accumulated grime and soot. It stood five storeys high with a flat roof, rows of windows on each level. Not too many of the windows retained their original glass. Some were boarded over with mouldering chipboard, others bore remnants of glass like the shards of teeth in a crone's mouth. The uppermost windows had fared better; perhaps they'd been replaced more recently. Beyond the dull glass there appeared to be sheets of semi-opaque plastic.

'What do you think the plastic's for?'

'Not the obvious,' Rink said. 'It's not there to catch blood. More than likely it's to dampen down any sounds from inside.'

'Looks to me like there could be squatters on the lower floors.'

'Uh-huh. Good cover. Who in their right mind's going to want to run a gauntlet of crackheads and thieves?'

'Only those who really have to,' I said.

Rink spun the car in an abandoned lot so we could take a second drive by Petoskey's hideout. Second time around it looked no better.

'Time to meet Harvey?' Rink asked.

'Yeah,' I said. In the rear-view mirror the building took on the colour of old blood. It seemed to exude the promise of ill-restrained violence.

13

'Mr Hunter?' Louise Blake looked me up and down. 'You're John's brother?'

'Yes.'

'You look like him.'

We shook hands.

'Please. Sit down. I've already taken the liberty of ordering coffee,' I said.

She sat down and immediately reached for her mug. Quick gulp. Not so much a need for the caffeine as it occupied her trembling hands. She pushed the cup from her, almost empty. Fiddled with the handle, a faint knocking coming from the table as if the spirits were making contact at a séance.

You might say that she was a little nervous.

I'd never met her before, but I recalled John talking about the beauty he was working with. I'd suspected he was glorifying her through the bottom of his beer goggles. Seeing her now, I had to admit she was a good-looking woman. Even pinched with worry and nervously adjusting her clothing, she had the fine bones and full lips of a model. Not *Vogue* standard, but perhaps your mail-order catalogue girl on the way to the big time.

Something else struck me. Louise Blake *was* a younger version of Jenny. One undamaged by childbirth, and the ultimate betrayal of trust.

'I hope you don't mind meeting me here?' Louise said. She crossed her arms beneath her breasts to hug herself. More likely, it was another attempt at concealing the shakes. 'The thing is, I don't think it would be a good idea for you to show up at my house.'

'This place is as good as any,' I told her. I was nursing my cup of strong coffee, while Louise had drained hers and by the look of things wanted more. She required reassurance that she was amongst friends. I made the introductions.

Harvey Lucas had arranged the meeting with seclusion in mind. Neutral turf, he called it. More like minimal space. We were squashed into a booth in a greasy-spoon-type café at the end of a strip mall. There weren't too many customers at this hour of the afternoon, and those few apparently understood the concept of privacy. The booths either side of ours remained empty, which added to the ludicrous scene of the four of us packed together at a table designed for two. Rink and I sat at one side, Louise and Harvey facing us. Pressed into the corner by the window by Harvey's imposing bulk, Louise looked like a cornered rodent menaced by a panther.

When you think of a private eye, you might picture a middle-aged white man in dog-tooth sports jacket and mustard slacks. Possibly wearing a fedora hat to cover his thinning hair. Harvey was anything but. He was six feet five, 220 pounds of sleek muscle with a bullet head. And his skin was blue-black to the point that it reflected the overhead lights.

Harvey Lucas looked like a professional boxer, and dressed with the panache and flair of a movie star. I'd learnt that he was an ex-army Ranger, the connection to Rink now obvious.

Harvey cut in to the conversation in a rich baritone. 'Been some strange-looking people hanging around Miss Blake's place these past coupla days. Thought it best we did our business out of sight.'

'Petoskey's people?' I asked.

'Could be,' Harvey said. 'But if you ask me they look to be too slick to be involved with Siggy. Got a few good photographs of them if you want to take a look.'

'Yeah, we'll have a look when we're finished here,' I said. Then I turned to regard Louise Blake. 'Do you know anything about who's watching your place?'

She shook her head and her reddish hair momentarily covered her features.

Harvey stepped in again. 'Miss Blake was unaware of the surveillance of her home until I pointed it out to her.'

'I knew something was going on,' she offered in an attempt to keep face. Apparently, there was a tough side to Louise Blake. 'I could feel it. As if there were eyes on me everywhere I went. But, no. I didn't see anyone. Not that I'd know them anyway. I've never seen this Petoskey bloke.'

'What're your feelings, Harve?' Rink asked.

Harvey rolled his head on his broad shoulders, turned down the corners of his mouth. 'Don't like it one bit, Rink.'

Harvey had my complete agreement. To Louise, I said, 'In your letter to Jennifer Telfer you said that you thought John was in some kind of trouble. Was it because of something specific he said?'

Louise shook her head. 'He didn't say anything. That was the problem. What bothered me more was the way he was acting.'

'What do you mean? You said he was frightened.'

'Yeah, he was kind of jumpy. A car would pull up and he'd sneak to the window, peek out of a corner of the blinds, that kind of thing. He couldn't sleep too well, either. Tossed and turned all the time, jumped at any noises from outside.'

'Did you ask him what was wrong?'

'Of course I did. But he wouldn't tell me. Just said he had something on his mind.'

'But you didn't push him about what it was?' I asked.

'No. I just thought it was to do with him starting a new job. Maybe it was too much for him to handle or something. You know, like the pressure was getting to him?'

'John started a new job?'

'So he said. Told me he was doing a bit of driving for a local firm, delivering to customers, that sort of thing. I didn't press him about who it was for. He looked a little embarrassed at first.'

'Why'd he be embarrassed about a driving job?' I asked.

'Wouldn't you be embarrassed? To end up as a delivery boy's a bit of a comedown, don't you think?'

'Is that the way you saw it, Louise?'

Her gaze snapped on to me with power-drill intensity. 'That's not at all the way I saw it! What do you think I am?'

'Sorry, I didn't mean it like that. I was just wondering if he'd got the notion in his mind that he'd let you down, and that was why he was acting so jumpy around you.'

She exhaled noisily.

'Maybe he did have it in his mind, but he never mentioned it to me. Anyway, he wasn't jumpy around me; he was jumpy around everything else *but me.*'

'You said he was acting like he was watching for someone?' I prompted.

Louise shook out her hair again.

'Not just like he was watching for someone,' she said with a wave of a finger. 'More like he was waiting for something to happen.'

'Or something to arrive?' Rink asked.

'Yes.' The momentary anger had gone from her eyes. 'John said that if anything ever happened to him you would know what to do, Mr Hunter. So . . . I mean, do you?'

I swirled the coffee in my cup, pondering the patterns of froth, as if it was a psychic's divining tool. I saw less in the coffee swirls than I already knew. Which wasn't much. Finally, I switched my gaze to her face. My exhalation told her everything. 'I haven't seen or heard from John since he left England; I was hoping you'd be able to bring me up to speed on what he'd been doing since coming here.'

Louise's shrug was non-committal.

'We just got by. I took a job at a beauty salon. John went from job to job. Nothing startling really. Parking valet. Stacking paint at a warehouse. Fast-food cook.' She ticked off the jobs on the fingers of one hand. 'Then, most recently, this driving job.'

'But you don't know who for?'

'No.'

'Was he delivering locally?'

She shrugged again. 'Sometimes he'd be away for a few days, so I guess he got a few long-haul jobs. Don't know where he went though. He'd phone from a motel or something, but he'd never say where he was. I didn't think to ask. I wasn't really that bothered.'

'You weren't that bothered? Were you having problems with your relationship?'

Louise looked at me sharply. The hammer drill on overdrive. 'Are you asking if he was seeing someone else?'

'Was he?'

'No.'

'How could you tell?'

'Believe me: a woman knows these kinds of things.'

I thought of Jenny; how she hadn't had a clue about her husband's infidelity. But then again, with the constant money worries, the fear that bad men would turn up and take it from their hides, Jenny probably wasn't capable of detecting the subtle signs that Louise was now hinting at. 'If there wasn't another woman, was there anything else between you?'

Louise's lips trembled. I don't know if it was emotion or scorn. Then, to change the subject, she lifted a hand and waved over a waitress.

'Can I have another coffee?' she asked.

The waitress refilled her cup, offered more to the rest of us but we all declined. Louise waited, a manicured fingernail tapping her cup, until the waitress returned to the serving counter. 'As you know, John left his wife for me. Not exactly the ideal situation.' She glanced around the three of us checking for any sign of disapproval. We were like the three wise monkeys. See, hear and – definitely – speak no evil. 'Because of that, it wasn't really a good idea to keep in touch with anyone back home. We severed all ties. My family doesn't know where I am. John didn't tell his. There have been so many times that I wanted to pick up the telephone and speak to my mum, but I didn't.'

'Was that your choice?' I asked.

'No. John always argued against it. Said it was best we remained anonymous for a little longer. Just another six months or so. He said it was to give everyone time to reconcile themselves with what we'd done. So that they'd forgive us.' She laughed sadly at herself.

'Did you believe that?' I asked softly. 'That John was concerned about what people back home thought about you?'

'I'm not a complete idiot,' she said, and again a spark of anger leapt across her features. 'We argued about it a lot. But that's not why he left. Believe it or not, we do love each other. It's not important what anyone thinks.'

Her challenge was as direct as a laser-guided warhead. Aimed directly at me. After all, I was the only other constant here. I had come to America at Jennifer's request as much as because of the letter that Louise had sent. She wanted to know whose side I was on.

'You're right. It doesn't matter,' I told her.

She nodded, pacified for now. 'When we left England I knew that he was hiding something. That he was running from more than his wife and children. He was in some sort of trouble and he *had to run*. That's the bottom line.'

I sat back from the table, had to manipulate my shoulders so that I could lean against the booth wall without nudging Rink into the gangway. I said, 'It's not likely that the men who were after him have followed him here. The cost would exceed what he owed them.'

Louise looked more than a little stunned at my words.

'I . . . I didn't know.' Her eyes glazed over. 'Are they . . . uh . . . bad men?'

'Yes. Loan sharks. The type who take payment with body parts.'

She could've been slapped in the face and looked less surprised. 'I had no idea. I thought the debt he'd got himself into was just the usual type that everyone ends up with.' She shook her head, then slowly drifted up to meet my eyes again. 'Was it Jennifer's debt? He said he couldn't control her spending. He even cut up her credit cards, but it made no difference. In the end, they lost everything . . . and that's why he had to leave her.'

I chose not to comment. But Rink, who had only just heard the truth from me earlier, snorted in derision. Louise snapped her gaze between us. Challenging us to disagree with John's version of events.

'The men that were after him,' I said, to steer the conversation away from John's lies, 'are dangerous in their own right. But you needn't worry; they're not exactly an international outfit. They don't work outside the UK.'

'You know that for a fact?' Louise asked.

'Yes.' To allay any fears about unlikely possibilities I decided to elaborate on the truth. 'I've already had a . . . well, call it "a talk" with them. They've backed off. They know the consequences of doing anything to John or any of his family.'

'His family.' Louise snorted.

'Present company included,' I reassured her.

She looked at me again and I gave her my most open-faced promise in return. Her nose crinkled above a twisted mouth. She wasn't so pretty now. 'You didn't even know who I was. How could you make the same agreement for me?'

'My demands weren't open to negotiation. They harm John or anyone close to him and they'd pay the consequences.'

I saw fear creeping into Louise's face now. Not the worry that was evident before. Something new. Something scary that had just dawned on her regarding the man who'd traversed an ocean to help her.

'Who exactly are you, Mr Hunter?' she asked.

'I'm John's brother,' I told her.

'But, who . . . or what . . .?'

I held up a hand to ward her off.

'Just leave it at that,' I said. 'Best you don't know. All you need to understand is that I'm John's brother. And by association, you are family. I'm here to help you, OK?'

Louise picked up her coffee, drained it in one gulp.

'After you leave,' she asked, as she set down the empty mug, 'will it be safe for me to stay here?'

I gave a quick glance towards Rink, who shrugged. Harvey bowed his large neck, stared at the table. I shook my head slowly.

'Maybe it's time you phoned your mum,' I said. 'Ask her if it'd be OK to come home.'

Tears welled in her eyes. Fear, it seemed, has many expressions.

'You think John is dead.'

I didn't answer. It wasn't a question anyway.

'Don't you?' she asked.

The air I sucked through my teeth wasn't the ideal reply. In hindsight, I wouldn't have done it. I'd have considered the action, and spared Louise my concern. Trouble was, I did fear the worst and Louise was intuitive enough to know it. She leant forwards into her hands and wept. Around her, three big tough guys squirmed. I reached across and took her hands from her face.

'Sorry, Louise,' I said. 'I know that's not what you wanted to hear.'

Louise sniffed. Shook her head. Sat up a little straighter, teasing her hair; her way of attempting to regain composure. A smile forced into place didn't work; it was too redolent with misery.

'I don't know why I'm crying,' she said. 'It's not as if I haven't already considered it myself. He's been gone for ages now. I mean, surely he'd have called me if he was still alive, right?'

In reality, she was asking why John would bother to pick up a phone when he'd never done the same with his wife. He'd cautioned her from phoning her own mother, for Christ's sake! So just because he hadn't been in touch didn't mean he was dead.

'We can only hope that he's hiding some place. Maybe he is. Perhaps he won't call for fear of jeopardizing your safety.' I gripped her hands with a little more pressure. 'But you may have to accept the worst, Louise.'

'I know,' she said quietly. I gave her an extra squeeze.

'But,' I said, expecting the sideways glance from Rink, 'if it's possible, I'll find him. I will bring him back, one way or the other.'

After that there wasn't much left to cover. Louise was done speaking, and prepared herself to leave. Being the consummate gentleman, Harvey offered to give her a lift home but she declined.

'I feel like shit,' he announced after Louise was gone.

'No need to,' Rink said.

'The more I look at this, I think I should be helping you guys more than I am,' he said.

'We don't know what we're up against,' I told him. 'Don't know how it's going to turn out. So maybe it's best you leave things as they are.'

He shook his head. 'I've heard another whisper. I can't substantiate it, but some people are saying John disappeared owing Petoskey more than a bad debt.'

'Like what?' I asked.

'No one is saying. But Petoskey is screaming murder. Making him speak to you might not be as easy as it sounds. He might very well resist. Big time.'

'He's a punk,' Rink put in.

'A dangerous punk,' Harvey told him. 'You might go in there and not walk out again. All I'm saying is it'd be better if you had an extra pair of eyes watching your backs.'

'You live here, Harvey,' I reminded him. 'It's OK for me and Rink. We can shake up the local bad guys, but we don't have to hang around afterwards. We don't have to live with the consequences of making any enemies here. You do.'

'Appreciate that,' he said. 'But I still feel like a goddamn shit-heel. It's like I'm running out on you guys.'

'No need to,' Rink said. 'We ain't expecting you to put your head on the block for us.'

'Anyway, you've done a lot for us already,' I pointed out. 'All we need from you now is the stuff we asked for. If Petoskey's as dangerous as you say we'd better take it with us.'

'It's in the car with the photographs I mentioned,' Harvey said.

The stuff we were referring to was a twelve-gauge shotgun for Rink and a steel bodied, nine-mm parabellum, blowback semi-automatic SIG Sauer for yours truly. Added to that were a couple of military issue Kabar knives and an untraceable mobile phone. To corner Siggy Petoskey, we'd be like ninja warriors assaulting the shogun's castle. A shogun, self-made or not, would have his private army of loyal retainers. However we looked at it, it was going to be a dangerous mission.

Then we got back to Louise Blake. Since she'd arrived, something had been bugging me. 'There's something she isn't telling us,' I said.

'Yeah,' Rink agreed. 'I was getting the same vibe.'

Harvey simply raised his eyebrows, shrugged his wide shoulders.

'I'm not suggesting that she's involved in John's disappearance. But there's something that isn't gelling with me,' I said. 'She says that John was acting all jumpy and nervous, but she didn't press him for what he was concerned about. That strike either of you as normal behaviour?'

'No way. We're talking about a woman, here,' Rink joked.

'She also said that she didn't know who he was working for. I find that a little hard to believe,' I said. 'Even though my work was top secret, my wife still knew who the hell it was I was working for.'

'I suppose he could've been doing sub-contract work,' Harvey offered.

'Or a little private enterprise,' Rink said.

'Private *criminal* enterprise,' Harvey added.

'If not Petoskey who else?' I asked.

Harvey blew out in a harsh exclamation. 'Take your pick, Hunter. Could be anyone.'

'Yeah,' I agreed. If John was involved in crime he could be working for any one of half a million employers from anywhere in the States. 'Louise said that she didn't press him about his work, but twice she's mentioned that John told her to contact me if anything happened to him. People don't give you those kind of instructions unless they're pretty sure something *is* going to happen.'

'And,' Rink added, 'he has obviously been expecting something *real bad* . . . considering the business you're in, Hunter.'

'Yeah,' I said. 'That's what worries me the most.'

14

'Different plates, same SUV.'

Tubal Cain was in no doubt. The vehicle parked in the lot of the Pacific View Hotel was the one stolen from him yesterday. Even if it had been sprayed a different colour, furry dice hung in the window and white-wall tyres added he'd have known the vehicle for his own. It had a vibe that he could feel even from across the width of the parking lot. That vehicle had witnessed death and the pall of violence hung over it like a bleak miasma of poisonous fumes.

As nonchalant as a man with the right – which he certainly had, in his estimation – he ambled over to the 4×4. The locks were engaged. Not that they'd stop him taking back what was rightfully his if he was of a mind to do so.

Nothing on the front seat but an empty water bottle and the remnants of a KFC meal, but on the dash was a CD. 'Swing When You're Winning'; the very one he'd been playing prior to stopping for the stranded motorist. If ever he required confirmation, there was his proof.

He wandered to the rear of the vehicle. A cursory inspection of the registration plate spoke volumes. The area around the locking nuts was clean, unlike the rest of the plate that had a fine coating of trail dust. The clean areas proved someone had turned the locking nuts very recently. It was obvious to his expert eye that the plates from another vehicle had been removed then screwed in place on this one.

'Guy's a freaking amateur,' he reminded himself. But – and this was a caution he would heed – not to be underestimated.

Credit where it's due, then. Changing the number plates was on the way to being a good idea. The thief didn't know that Cain wouldn't be reporting the theft of the vehicle, so it was sensible to install a new identity.

Some constructive criticism was in order, though. It was good that the thief had tried to cover his tracks. It was just a pity that he hadn't taken the time to do so properly. Any cop worth his salt would notice the clean area around the locking nuts and know immediately that the plates had been switched. His headshake was pure reproof. 'I don't know if it's your lack of experience or whether you're just too lazy for your own good.'

A slow walk took him round to the driver's side. Peering inside he saw no sign of his stolen Bowie knife. It meant one of two things: either the knife was concealed or the thief had it with him in his hotel room. Considering the third possibility wasn't pleasant: the thief might have dumped the knife somewhere along the way.

Finished with the car, he made his way towards the front of the hotel. It was three storeys high, built on land barely a stone's throw from Route 405. Prime location, except that larger hotels blocked the view of the Pacific Ocean. The name of the hotel was a marketing lie; probably wishful thinking. Either that or the name was thirty years out of date.

Inside, overhead fans spun indolent circles in lemon-scented air, the lobby as cool and clean as a spring morning. Cain's rubber-soled shoes made a soft squishing sound on the faux-marble tiles, barely disturbing the tranquillity. On his right was a long reception desk, behind it a small office area. A young woman, a Californian cutie with straw-coloured hair and rosy cheeks, was bent over a computer. Cain smiled at her but she didn't as much as raise her head. Spreadsheets held more interest for her than a handsome man. Cain walked on past her towards the communal dining area.

The steward wasn't at his station. In fact, no one challenged him. The room was devoid of staff or any of the hotel's clientele. A glance at his wristwatch told Cain that it was too late for lunch and too early for dinner.

He stepped back into the lobby, deciding on his best move. There were alternatives but the sensible course of action would be to wait for the thief to show up at the SUV. From there he could take him out and regain what was rightfully his.

'Can I help you, sir?'

The blond woman had exited the office and now stood at the reception desk. She had a sheaf of papers in her hands and a smile on her face. Apparently, a handsome man did override the attraction of a spread-sheet.

To miss an opportunity would be tantamount to a crime. Without pause Cain swung towards her, affecting his best 'humble and caring guy' face. 'Yeah, ehm, I was wondering if someone could help me out. I didn't realize anyone was around when I first walked in.'

Like many before her who'd come into contact with Tubal Cain the receptionist was oblivious of his lies. The power of a smile and twinkling green eyes are never to be undervalued in a lunatic's arsenal. She waved the sheaf of papers in the general direction of her office. 'Sorry about that, I had my nose buried in some work.'

Cain waved off her apology. 'It's nothing really,' he said. 'I just pulled in and noticed that a car outside has its lights on. Thought I'd come in and let you know. Wouldn't like anyone to find a dead battery. Bit of an inconvenience for them.'

The woman swung sideways, pulling a large ledger towards her. 'What kind of vehicle is it?'

'Mercedes SUV. Black and silver. Has Nevada plates.'

The woman checked the register. Opportunities presented must be grasped with both hands. As calmly as possible, Cain leant over the counter, watching as she traced down a list of names with a well-manicured fingernail. In the split second before she looked up, Cain turned his head aside and scanned a poster on a wall at the rear of the reception area as if it had held his interest throughout.

'I'll give the owner a call and let him know. I'm sure he'll be grateful for your help,' she said.

'It's nothing,' Cain reassured her. 'There's nothing worse than a dead battery. And it's so easily avoided, too. I'd only hope that if I was ever so careless, someone would do the same for me.'

'Me too,' said the woman. 'I remember one time, I was at the mall and I left my lights on. Had to call a tow truck and everything. It was so embarrassing.'

'And costly, I bet?'

'Oh, not too bad. It was more the inconvenience,' the woman said. She covered the memory of her discomfiture with a hand over her mouth. To some the act would be coy, but to Cain it was reminiscent of a self-conscious halitosis sufferer.

'Pity I wasn't around that time,' Cain said. 'Could've saved you some trouble.'

The woman's amused laughter was the tinkling of Christmas bells. Humble and caring guy strikes again. When she looked at him this time, it was with more interest. 'Are you a guest here, sir?'

'No,' Cain said. 'I was just driving by and my phone went. I don't have a hands-free kit, so I pulled over. Hope you don't mind me using one of your parking spots for a few minutes? I'd have been gone by now if I hadn't noticed the lights on the car I told you about.'

'It's not a problem, sir. In fact, it's good of you to take the time to come in and tell me. Thousands of people wouldn't have even bothered.'

'That's true,' Cain said in agreement. But then again, he always did suspect that he was unique. 'Isn't it sad though that people have got to a point where they'll just walk on by without offering a hand?'

'It is.' The woman nodded. 'Not many people I meet are as nice as you.'

Ooh, the nice word. Cain thought she was nice, too. Unfortunately, he had wholly different reasons for his opinion. His estimation was based purely upon the judgement of the ossuary-building artist within him. Clark Kent's X-ray vision was no less penetrating than his scrutiny. She had a pleasing bone structure behind the rosy cheeks. A little plump perhaps, so that he couldn't easily define the fine skeletal lines he adored. He glanced from her face to her hands. They were slim and long-fingered, the nails polished to a sheen. Now there was a bunch of treasures he would cherish. Slowly he visually traced each digit in turn.

She was aware of this examination. She stirred, ever so slightly uncomfortable under his gaze. Cain acted startled, offering her an abashed grin.

'Sorry. You caught me staring,' he said. 'It's just that . . . well, uh, you have such beautiful hands.'

'My hands?' The woman didn't know how to answer, but she was flattered. Unconsciously, she gripped the sheaf of papers tightly in one hand while she held out the other and studied it. Cain leant towards her.

'I hope you don't think I'm hitting you with some sort of cheesy come-on line,' he said. 'I'm simply speaking the truth. Your hands are lovely.'

'Thanks,' she said. 'That's really sweet of you to say so.'

The catch in her throat gave her an appealing huskiness. She coughed. Eyes darting towards the office as though checking for a disapproving supervisor. The unashamed impression she was portraying was frowned upon by the hotel management, either that or she genuinely was as naive as she appeared. She discreetly slipped her hands below the counter. Her rosy cheeks had become twin candy apples.

'Sorry if I'm embarrassing you,' Cain said. 'I don't mean to.'

'No, it's OK. I'm not embarrassed.' Despite her words, her cheeks were growing even redder. She dropped her chin towards her chest, swayed in indecision, then laughed.

Cain laughed with her.

'Look,' he said. 'I have embarrassed you. I'm sorry. Please accept my apologies.'

He put out a hand and the woman reached for it reflexively.

They shook hands.

'Apology accepted,' said the woman, still laughing.

Cain was slow to release her hand. He allowed his fingers to trail along her palm, prolonging the sensation for as long as possible. One of his human frailties was a total lack of empathy, but what he lacked in compassion he more than made up for in sensory ability. He did not have the capacity to love a woman, but he did love to touch a woman.

He would lodge the sensation at some far recess of his mind, a memory to summon for later. If he couldn't have her hands, he could have the sensory recall of their touch whenever he desired. And that thought was enough to sustain him for now. Primary need on his agenda was his reckoning with the thief. Afterwards, if everything went well – as it most definitely would – he could come back at his leisure and take her hands as genuine trophies.

Finally, he stepped back, gave a slight wave.

'Well, I'd best get going,' he said. 'I've taken up too much of your time as it is.'

'Honestly, sir. It was no problem.'

'See you,' he said. 'And once again, I'm sorry if I embarrassed you.'

'Yeah, see you,' the woman replied. She lifted her hand in reflex. Caught it mid-wave. Then laughed and continued the gesture.

Cain gave her his most self-effacing grin. His wink was full of promise.

He walked back through the lobby. In the old Hollywood musicals, Gene Kelly or Fred Astaire would have made the walk a grand swagger, hands in pockets, whistling merrily before swooping round to catch her looking. Cain wasn't so flamboyant; at the exit he merely twisted at the shoulder. It was enough to confirm that, yes, she was still watching him. There was more than a little interest in her gaze. He waved again and she waved back, her face breaking into a wide smile. In true Astaire form he made a show of opening the door and pushing outside.

But as he walked away, his smile turned to a frown, then a scowl. Achieving his objective of flushing out the thief was one thing, but there was no way he could act on it now. The receptionist was a bit of a dim light bulb, but she still had enough about her that she'd remember the man who lured the client outside before he was brutally butchered.

Self-recrimination wasn't something he often indulged in, but even he could see he'd made a mistake. I shouldn't have flirted with her, he thought. I should've simply gone in, given her the story, then got the hell back out again. By flirting with the bitch, I've forced her to take a good look at my face. Stupid, Cain, stupid. If I take the thief now, she could give a good description of me to the police. *And that just will not do.*

He'd put his identity at risk for the sake of a minute or so of banter with a pretty girl. Not good when you are the USA's most current prolific and undetected serial murderer.

Making matters worse, it wasn't even as if he needed to lure the thief outside any more. While the receptionist had checked the ledger, Cain had watched her fingers pointing out the room number of the owner of the SUV. Why bother ambushing him in the exposed car park when he could go on up, knock on his door and call him by name.

Time for plan B.

Cain spun round, but all trace of Astaire was gone from his light tread. Once more, he headed directly for the entrance door. Quick inhalation for effect, then he bustled into the hotel with feigned urgency. The woman was midway between closing the ledger and reaching for a telephone. Thankfully, she never reached the receiver. Her startled expression was a mixture of delight and regret as Cain jogged to the counter and slapped down the palms of his hands.

'Hi,' he said. 'It's just me again.'

The woman still wore the startled look. She visibly fought to regain her composure, achieving the fixed stare and open mouth of an inflatable sex toy. Not that Cain had any experience of *those* kinds of things.

'You didn't call the SUV owner yet, did you?' Cain asked in breathless fashion. As the woman shook her head, he went on, 'Seems I might have been a little premature coming in about the lights. While I was inside the owner must've come back out and turned them off.'

'They're off now?' the woman echoed.

'Yeah, I guess there must be another exit. I didn't see anyone leave when I was in here.'

'There are a number of exits. I suppose he could've used one of them.' The ledger was still beside her and she flipped it open with professional dexterity. She nodded confirmation. 'Yeah, he's got a room at the back, so he could've used the rear stairwell. I guess from his room he could see his car and noticed that his lights were still on.'

'That's probably it,' Cain agreed.

'OK,' the woman said. Her face had regained its natural elasticity and a smile was beginning to bloom.

'OK,' Cain replied, giving her his version of a sheepish smile. 'I feel a complete idiot now.'

The woman crinkled her nose at him. 'What for?'

'I must look like the dead battery vigilante or something,' Cain laughed. 'I just thought I'd come back in and let you know everything's fine now. Save you the trouble of calling.'

'It's not a problem,' she said.

'Yeah, but the owner would've been wondering what the heck was going on.'

'I'm sure he wouldn't have minded,' she said. 'In fact, I dare say he'd have told me he'd already been out and turned them off. That would've been that, I guess.'

'Yeah, I suppose so.'

'Anyway, thanks again for going to so much trouble.'

'No problem. Just doing my bit.'

'Dead battery vigilante,' the woman smiled at him, crooking a finger in his direction. 'Sounds like a superhero.'

'You got it,' Cain said. A flippant gesture of his head and hands fisted on his hips was more Boy Wonder than Man of Steel.

They both laughed as he walked away the second time. Before he reached the door, she called to him.

'Are you sticking around town for a while?'

Cain looked back at her, feigning disappointment. 'No. Just passing through, I'm afraid. On my way to the east coast. Have to be in Mississippi early next week for a sales convention.'

Now it was the woman's turn to look dejected. 'That's a shame.'

'It is,' Cain agreed. 'But, hey, who knows what's around the corner? I might be back this way in a month or so.'

She gave him a lopsided smile.

'Well, if you're passing and you notice any lights on, give me a call will you?'

Cain lifted his fingers as if they were a gun and feigned shooting her. 'You got it, lady. If your battery is running down you can count on me.'

Quickly he left the lobby to the sound of laughter.

'Dimwit could do with a couple of thousand volts up her ass,' he assured himself.

Directly across the entry drive ran a walkway that led into the car park. From there he followed the side of the building, past bougainvillea shrubs arranged to add a little privacy to those rooms on the ground floor. At the rear of the hotel the grounds were laid out like an exclusive garden, verdant with golf-course-perfect lawns and bursting with colour from the proliferation of flowering plants. The grounds contained a private swimming pool.

There were a couple of female guests sitting out in bathing suits, drinking from glasses smeared with lipstick. Cain sneaked a peek at them. Ordinarily he might have lingered and enjoyed the show. Sadly, neither of them was pretty enough to hold his interest. He gave them no attention, searching instead for the stairway the receptionist had mentioned. He saw it within seconds, a tiled staircase spiralling up to a balcony on the two upper floors. Chancing a stiff neck, he craned upwards, seeking door numbers. Then, happy with what he saw, he rapidly moved away, skirting the building and returning to the parking lot.

Time for plan C.

He took the scaling knife from his jacket pocket as he approached the SUV. Bobbing down by the rear nearside tyre, he thrust the blade into the rubber seal next to the wheel hub. Pulling the knife out again, he noted that the narrow slash was barely detectable but the almost inaudible hiss of escaping air was encouraging.

'That'll hold you for a while,' he whispered. A flat tyre would royally piss off someone who couldn't even be bothered to rub a little dust on the licence plate.

He dropped the knife back in his pocket, straightened out his clothes as he returned to his own vehicle. The vintage VW Beetle had gone the way of the dinosaurs. Not that he required the intervention of a planet-destroying meteor; he'd merely dumped it in a dry canal bed then set it ablaze. It was quick work to replace it with an anonymous, light-blue Oldsmobile.

On the rear bumper was a sticker some might think pathetic: I BRAKE FOR WILDLIFE. Though tempting discovery by leaving such a distinct identifier on the car he'd allowed it to stay in place. For one thing, it added to the disguise he'd adopted of a meek-mannered sales person, plus it was a statement that actually resonated with him. He had no qualms whatsoever about butchering those of his own species, but he had no such desire to harm any other living creature. Torn between running down a rabbit and swerving into a line of children on a Sunday school outing, there was only one way to go. Sunday school would be missing a number of snot-nosed brats next meeting.

The temperature inside the Oldsmobile was a lot cooler than anticipated. When he'd driven the car here, the sun was thrusting wicked talons through the windows and the heat had grown almost intolerable. That was the drawback when appropriating an older model car: no climate control. Plus the driver's window had a fault and he'd been unable to open it with the rotating arm. Oh, how he suffered for his art!

When he'd driven into the parking lot, he'd parked the car beneath a stand of date palms to conceal it from the view of traffic on the interstate. Serendipity meant his fortuitous parking had also brought him some welcome shade.

Settling in the driver's seat, he prepared for a long wait. To pass the time, he took one of the film-wrapped packages from his pocket and teased the contents within. Kind of gnarly now, but they'd polish up nice. He imagined that the fingers were those of the rosy-cheeked receptionist. Yes, he could be in for a long wait, but he was happy to do so with his mind thus engaged.

15

Harvey had performed a decent job in monitoring the movements of Sigmund Petoskey. True to Harvey's word, as soon as the third-generation immigrant finished his daytime business he headed out to the derelict building Rink had shown me earlier. He left in a procession of three vehicles that snaked their way from the opulent business centre to the run-down building, driving in a fashion that said he wasn't concerned about police patrols pulling him over. In our rental car, Rink and I followed at a discreet distance.

When Petoskey ignored a red light, we pulled up; it wasn't necessary to keep a close tail when we knew where he was headed.

The lights were reflected in Rink's gaze.

'You up for this, Rink?'

He sniffed. 'Things could get messy,' I said. 'But I can't think of a better way to shake Petoskey than raiding him in the place he feels safest.'

'You take guns into a man's house, things always get messy.' He gave a melancholy shake of the head.

'Been a while since you done any wet work?'

'Been a while, yeah. But, it never leaves you, Hunter.' Rink looked across at me and, for a moment, we

made a connection. Only those who have taken another man's life would recognize the haunted imagery
flickering in our vision. He was right: doesn't matter
how hard you try to bury the memories, they never
leave you.

The green light saved us further agony.

When we arrived at the old redbrick, Petoskey and
his entourage had lined up in the lot to the right of the
building. As well as the original three they'd been
joined by a further two cars and a van.

A couple of bored guards stood to one side, nonchalant as they sucked at cigarettes. They weren't
expecting trouble. They were there for appearances'
sake.

These guards were of no immediate concern. We'd
be going in via a different route and would not be seen
by them. I was more apprehensive about the profusion
of street people who wandered around the area. We
were strangers and they'd be suspicious of us. It wasn't
known by any of us – Harvey included – if the bums
were belligerent to Petoskey or not. It'd ruin our
chances of bearding King Siggy in his castle if any
of them went running to him. I doubted anyone would
rush to warn Petoskey out of loyalty, but the promise of
a reward would be too much of a temptation for some.

Discretion *is* the better part of valour, and don't let
anyone tell you otherwise. Rather than chance early
discovery, we parked our vehicle the best part of half a
mile from the redbrick, donned shabby clothes we'd
purchased from a thrift store, and then wandered in on
foot. My SIG Sauer was tucked down the waistband of

my trousers, my Ka-bar down my boot. Rink however had a shotgun to conceal. Without the luxury of a violin case, he carried his over-under twelve-gauge in a large holdall. To further disguise the gun, he raided a nearby dumpster and pushed in a few old tin cans and a bundle of newspapers and magazines. On cursory inspection, his holdall would pass for the sum of a bum's possessions.

The walk in took about ten minutes but it was just what we needed to shake off the cobwebs of inactivity. Feeling keyed up we took up a position opposite Petoskey's building. Behind a chain-link fence was a small building. It had suffered over the years. The roof was gone. No windows remained and the interior was the domain of rats and wind-blown detritus. Even the graffiti was age-faded. No discerning street person would take up residence there.

We entered through a hole in the fence, negotiated a weed-choked courtyard and entered the building through a doorless void. We had then to push our way through heaped rubbish to one of the abandoned office rooms from where we could watch and wait. The sunset was a raw wound on the horizon.

Without spoiling the decor, Rink emptied the junk from his bag. He checked the shotgun and seemed satisfied. He fed cartridges into it while peering from the window. Following his gaze, I saw that lights had come on behind the semi-opaque plastic sheeting on the upper floor. Though muted, shadows wove sinuous patterns on the sheeting as people moved through the rooms.

'I'd like to know what the hell's going on up there,' I said over his shoulder.

'Don't hear nothing,' Rink replied. 'My guess is he's got a cook shop going.'

It was a likelihood that Petoskey had some kind of laboratory up there, producing crack cocaine or methamphetamine. On two counts, we would need to take care going in. If indeed it was a crack laboratory, inside there could be innocents who had been forced into this unwholesome line of work. Plus, the scum guarding the production line would be packing weapons. Scum with weapons plus innocent bystanders are never good mathematics.

'I don't know, Rink. Could be something else.'

The location wasn't sitting right with me. OK, we were in a run-down area of town, but normally crack laboratories weren't as public as this. People didn't turn up in limousines to conduct a quality control inspection, even if a few of the local cops had been paid backhanders to turn a blind eye.

Something I didn't doubt: whatever was going on, it was illegal. We'd be walking dangerous territory. 'Looks like your standard one-two assault,' I said to Rink.

He nodded slowly.

Where only two soldiers are involved in infiltrating an enemy stronghold, we always used a strategy termed a one-two manoeuvre. Like the name, there's nothing fancy about it. Advancing single-file the first – or point – man would engage and take out the enemy while the second would move on to the next position.

Roles would then reverse, and so on, until the head ground was gained and no enemy was left behind to cause further trouble.

Of course, there are inherent problems with such tactics. It leaves way too much to chance and the ability of the individual soldier to neutralize the opposition. If things go wrong, the mission has to be aborted in rapid fashion. In the past, I've had worse experiences gaining exit than I have during the initial assault. Because of this, I prefer the less formal sobriquet of 'smash and dash'.

It remained our choice of approach on this occasion simply because it was all we had the numbers for. Maybe I should've allowed Harvey Lucas to join us. With three men, it lessens the chance that the enemy can outflank you. But not by much.

'Where do you suggest we start?' Rink asked. His face was flat, but this was a front. Ghost-lights burned behind his eyes and I knew that he was anxious.

I pointed out the opposite end of the building from where the guards patrolled. 'See the fire escape? I'm guessing that there are doors at each floor level. We'll go in through one of them, huh?'

Rink inclined his chin in agreement.

On the lowest level the doors were likely shored up as tight as a miser's wallet. But the myriad broken windows would give us easy access.

It was a waiting game. The sun went down, and shadows moved in like furtive burglars in the night. The lights behind the plastic appeared to grow brighter. Like zombies from some B-movie, the street people drifted from their daytime hidey-holes, moving off in search of the necessaries to feed their vices. More vehicles arrived. From our position, we couldn't make out how many people arrived, but from the excited yapping, someone had brought a couple of dogs with them.

'You hear what I'm hearing?' Rink asked.

'Yup. But you didn't expect this to be easy did you?'

'Easy ain't a word in our vocabulary, Hunter.'

Maybe the dogs were extra security Siggy employed after dark. I severely doubted that he was conducting doggy obedience classes. Rink and I shared a glance. Dogs, large or small, always made extreme stealth an issue.

We waited another half-hour before leaving the derelict building. Rink went first, shambling across the waste ground and out through the gap in the fence. His pace was that of a man addled with drink with no firm destination in mind. When he was out of sight round the side of the redbrick, it was my turn to follow.

I followed the same route, joining Rink in the deep well of murk at the side of the building. There was an overpowering stench of vomit and urine. Welcome home, Hunter! It doesn't matter where my work takes me, it's always the same. I was only pleased that I couldn't see what I was standing in.

'You ready, Hunter?' Rink whispered. He had the shotgun out of its bag, ready for action. I pulled out my SIG, held it at my side.

'Ready,' I said.

Mounting the first set of stairs on a rusted fire escape, my mission to discover the whereabouts of my brother was finally underway. Whether or not John was inside the building wasn't the issue. Petoskey was, and he knew something about John's disappearance. Taking Petoskey was the order of the day.

Gaining the first landing, I laid a hand on the door. The locking bar, like much of the remainder of the building, was an item lost to the past desecration of this place. The door swung open to the slightest tug. Rink immediately stepped past me, sweeping the darkness with his shotgun.

'Clear,' he whispered, and I entered.

We stood still, acclimatizing ourselves to the ambient light leaking in from outside and listening to the natural sounds of the building. Far above, voices formed a discordant chorus. Someone was laughing. Then there were the dogs. No longer were they yapping, but snarling and barking maniacally.

'Dog fights,' I whispered.

'Son of a bitch,' Rink snarled. In the half-light, I saw his face grow hard. 'I'm going to feed the bastard his own balls.'

'Yeah,' I agreed. For one instant my mind clicked half a world away and I saw my own dogs, Hector and Paris. The prospect of them forced to fight to the death for the sick pleasure of the likes of Petoskey was enough to sicken even the stone-cold assassin in me.

Shake the anger loose, Hunter, I cautioned myself. It's bad enough that we were going in outnumbered. Never mind doing so with the wrong frame of mind.

Go in in a rage and we'd be dead before we reached the next level. I reached out in the dark to grab Rink's forearm.

'Go easy,' I cautioned him.

'I'm cool,' Rink replied. And I knew that he was.

'OK. You take point.'

'You want I go up or across?' Rink asked.

'Across,' I said. Judging Petoskey by the putrid essence of his soul, he'd have been right at home amidst the drifts of refuse on this stairwell. But, considering his penchant for fine suits and luxurious automobiles, it wasn't likely that he'd be found dead here. In all probability, the stairwell was exclusively used by the dropouts who squatted here during the daylight hours.

We had to go up by the route Petoskey would take, to ensure we took out any possible reinforcements.

The corridor could have been a set from a horror movie. Cobwebs brushed our faces. Dust sifted from above and clung to the lips. From behind closed doors, the spectres of this place tittered at our bravado. They beckoned to us: *Come and join us in hell, there's plenty of room for two more.*

The far end of the corridor didn't come too soon for me.

Rink was waiting in a vestibule area. A door that once held wire-reinforced glass, but was now blocked with a sheet of tarpaulin hung on bent nails, barred our progress. The faint buzz of conversation filtered from beyond.

'What do you think?' Rink whispered.

Ever the smart one, I made a quick calculation. Held up three fingers to Rink. Not that he didn't trust me; Rink placed his face to the edge of the tarpaulin to confirm the estimation. We moved back down the corridor a safe distance.

'Two guys on the stairs. Looks like another one sitting down in a chair to the left of the door, but I could only see his feet.'

'Armed?' I asked Rink.

'Nothing I could see.' Rink shrugged. 'Doesn't mean anything. They could still be packing.'

Armed or not, it didn't mean a thing. I could chew my lips all day, but it wouldn't change our options. 'We treat them like they're armed. OK?'

'Yup,' Rink said, hefting the shotgun so the barrel pointed skyward.

It's not what you want – and to be fair, it didn't lie straight with either of us – because it meant that we were going in with what's commonly known in our trade as extreme prejudice. In layman's terms: shoot to kill. These weren't international terrorists or even enemy soldiers, just half-assed gangland hoods. Killing them was extreme, maybe too extreme under the circumstances. As Rink had reminded me last night, we didn't have the prerogative to kill any more.

'No, Rink, we can't. You happy with defence only?' I suggested.

Talk about weight coming off shoulders, I'd swear we both grew a head taller.

'OK,' I said. 'We only shoot when necessary. Otherwise it's bone-on-bone.'

'I'm happy with that,' Rink said.

Rink again laid an eye to the edge of the tarpaulin. His raised thumb showed no change to the tableau.

OK, we're rolling. Action!

Rink ripped aside the tarpaulin and stepped into the hallway beyond. I was a fraction of a beat behind him.

Confusion is the result of prolonged inactivity dramatically kick-started into life. The three men in the stairwell were caught catching flies, with their hands in the cookie jar, with their trousers down, whatever your choice of image. Whatever, the sudden intrusion of two armed men in their midst caused shocked silence. But then, that was only a snatch frame of the action. Time jumped to fast-forward.

To my left a man erupted out of a wicker chair. He had a sawn-off across his lap and was grabbing for it. Rink swung both his barrels on the other two. It was an easy decision for me. I snapped my left hand sideways. Back fist strike to the bridge of his nose. The man went back into his seat like the world champion of competitive musical chairs. The fact that his hands didn't reach in reflex for his broken nose meant he was unconscious. The shotgun slipped out of his lap on to the floor and I swiped it away with the edge of my boot.

Giving them their due, the other two had more sense than to challenge Rink's shotgun. They stood like mute statues until he ordered them to come forwards. The one-two was on; I immediately mounted the stairs, heading upwards. From below me, Rink said something. Knowing him, it would be funny, but no one was laughing. The silence was followed by the thump and scuffle of feet and I guessed my suggestion of bone-on-bone was taking place.

The second landing was devoid of movement. Stepping into dim light that leached from the floor above, bringing up my SIG to sweep the space before me, I crept ahead. My darkness-adapted eyes sought the next flight of stairs. Below me, Rink mounted the stairs and you'd assume that it was safe for me to go on. Bad move. You know what they say about assuming anything; it certainly made an ass of me.

Maybe I'd grown a little ring rusty. I should have checked the corridor to my left before proceeding. As I committed myself to the stairs, a door opened behind me and a voice challenged me.

'The fuck are you?'

Then a second voice shouted. 'Five-O in the house.'

I've undergone extensive hand-to-hand training in the Fairbairn method of combat. What I neglected to mention is that I've also trained in Fairbairn's armed method known as point shooting. Like the hand-to-hand, it's based upon the principle of immediate and reflexive action. Point. Shoot. Simple as that.

While the two men were stunned at my appearance, I could have spun and put a couple of rounds into their bodies. They'd have been on their backs and I'd have been up on the next landing.

As I'd so recently agreed with Rink, unless necessary, this mission was to be carried out without lethal force. Shooting was out of the question. With that in mind, I'd no alternative but to turn round slowly, giving them ample opportunity to take stock of me on the stairwell. Not that I was about to give up an advantage. I kept my gun by my side, hidden from view by the angle of my body. If it came to it, I could shoot from the hip and take out both of them in a fraction of a second.

What is it with criminals? Both men were dressed in windbreakers and denims, both with the obligatory shaved heads that went with hired muscle. They could have been the American cousins of Shank's right-hand man. Perplexed at my appearance, they were caught in a limbo that stayed their hands as effectively as it did their brains. One of them had called out, shouting Five-O. Street slang for police. That gave me a second advantage over them. Where they probably wouldn't hesitate to take out a rival, it wasn't the done thing to kill a police officer. Do that and any agreement Petoskey had with the local police force goes right out the window. When it came to avenging one of their own, the police would come down on them like a blue avalanche.

The disguise didn't fool them, but that was fine. They saw through the shabby clothes, but saw something that wasn't true. So let them think I was a cop. It's what would save their lives.

'Police,' I said. 'You're both under arrest.'

A totally lame statement, I know, but something they expected nonetheless. They gawped at me, then at each other, before breaking into stupid grins.

'You gotta be fuckin' jokin', man,' said one of them.

'No,' I answered. 'I'm deadly serious.'

Tweedledum and Tweedledee, they again exchanged grins.

'What the fuck you on, man?' Tweedledum asked. 'You know that you don't come here.'

'Oh? You mean an officer of the law isn't welcome in your fine establishment?' I said. Any old nonsense was enough to keep their attention on me another second or so.

'No, you're not fuckin' welcome,' said Tweedledee.

'Ah, now that is a shame,' I told him.

'Yeah, a goddamn cryin' shame,' Rink echoed as he whacked the stock of his shotgun into the nearest man's kidneys. The man buckled to his knees, crying out as his hands went to the source of his pain.

The second Tweedle twin spun to face Rink, backing up against the far wall as he reached to his pocket for a concealed weapon. Rink wasn't a black belt for nothing. He lifted a boot and kicked the man in the pit of his stomach. He held the man with his foot, pressing him up against the rotting plaster of the wall.

'Go on up,' he said. 'Leave these punk assholes to me.'

'They're all yours,' I told him.

I was about midway to the next landing when the shooting started. Not from below, as you might expect, but from above. It's natural to throw yourself down when fired upon; what is equally natural is the way I brought up my hand and fired off a return shot.

Boom! There goes the neighbourhood, you might've said. And you'd have been right. All hope of engaging the enemy without shooting was gone now. Any remorse about killing had to be put behind me too. When fired upon there was only one recourse.

The stairwell echoed to the thump of feet. It could only be Petoskey's men looking for cover. There were four distinct voices as they called out to others in the building. Confusion was the reigning order. Someone was shouting that the police were here while another shouted that *Hendrickson's men* were in the building. It didn't really matter who the hell they thought they were up against; panic had turned their response deadly.

To buy a little respite I unloaded a clip towards the head of the stairs, following my bullets with a headlong charge as I pushed another magazine in place.

Rink was still below me, snorting like a bull as he finished off the two who'd tried to take me from behind. Undoubtedly eager to finish the fight and come to my assistance. Time to wait for him wasn't a luxury I possessed. I sprinted upwards to a point where there was a kink in the stairs. Suicidal I'm not, but suicide's what I'd have been committing if I'd poked my head round the corner for a look. Unfortunately, I had to get some kind of bead on the men waiting to ambush me. Choice made, I thrust my gun round the bend, firing three rapid shots. Just enough to force my ambushers to dive for cover. I spun into the cordite cloud searching for movement.

No one in sight. I sprang up the remaining stairs and into a recess on the left. I run regularly, occasionally go to the gym, yet I was still blowing hard. I blame it on the result of adrenalin dump rather than lack of condition.

The wall next to my shoulder was holed by one of my own bullets. I quickly pushed myself deeper into the recess, firing off two more rounds into a corridor devoid of movement. There were doors lining the corridor on both sides and any one of them could be concealing an enemy shooter.

'Rink! Are you about done down there or what? I could do with that scattergun up here.'

Rink appeared on the stairs below me. Blood was seeping from a shallow nick below his left eye. Other than that, he appeared unhurt.

'One of the bastards thought he'd do me with a set of brass knuckles,' Rink said. He dabbed away blood with the back of his wrist. 'I soon knocked that silly notion out of his skull.'

'Get yourself up here and give me some cover,' I whispered to him. 'Sounds like they're holed up in a room on my right.'

Rink came up the stairs, feeding cartridges into his shotgun. There was blood on the stock. Thug with brass knuckles versus Rink wielding a shotgun like a club: no contest.

'I'm going to try and get by that door there. If it looks like it's about to open, give them hell.'

'Leave it to me,' Rink said. He moved to the head of the stairs so that he could get a line on the door I'd indicated.

Cat-footed, I moved forwards, my gun extended before me. The defenders behind the door had to know I was moving into the corridor, but there was nothing for it. We had to stop them and stop them fast. I feared the arrival of reinforcements who'd be able to pen us in from below. Then there was the other consideration, that Petoskey was making a quick exit by another route. If he got away from us now, it'd probably be impossible to get a second chance at him.

Passing the door on the right, I nodded for Rink to follow, and he thumped up the corridor like Frankenstein's monster. True to form, the door exploded into splinters. Even the wall opposite was shredded, the bullets continuing into the rooms beyond.

As the first barrage curtailed, I swung in front of the shattered door, emptying my clip through the wood. Men yelled within the room, one of them making a series of guttural gasps. I'd hit one of them, at least. That left – what? – three more?

Rink lifted a boot and smashed open the door. Immediately he blasted the interior of the room before swinging back out of sight. Two seconds of carnage were all I required to insert a full clip of ammo. Exchanging positions with choreographed precision I opened up, firing off bullets as quickly as I could squeeze the trigger. Then I was in the room and had moved left as Rink let off another full load of pellets.

Armed confrontations do not resemble John Woo's battles of balletic gunplay; any somersaulting or leaping through space discharging bullets is reserved for the movies. Reality is not so pretty . . . I slammed my back to a wall, my gun out before me, and I emptied it at every target that moved. I was shouting something that was unintelligible even to me. An animal shout of loathing, fear and unrestrained rage.

It took all of a few seconds to deplete my gun of bullets, yet I felt as spent as the bullet casings littering the floor at my feet.

Rink hustled into the room, the stock of his shotgun to his shoulder as he sought targets. Smoke hung in the air. So did the unmistakable tang of blood. One man was huddled in a corner of the room, hands over his head as he sobbed in terror. Another was sprawled over a coffee table, a hole the size of a baby's fist in his shoulder. The man murmured, delirious with agony.

That accounted for two of them, but I couldn't see where the other two were. As Rink covered the cowering man I ejected my newly emptied clip, inserted a fresh one. Rink moved over to the open window. Sounds of flight ricocheted from the fire escape beyond.

'Careful,' I said. Both to Rink and as a warning to the man who cringed away from the business end of my SIG. Rink gave me a wry grin as he approached the window.

'Like rats down a drainpipe,' he observed. 'Two of them are running for it, Hunter.'

'Let them run,' I said. The cowering man peeked up at me through tears and smeared snot. I nudged him with a boot. 'Where's John Telfer?'

In those old Poe books, victims of terror often gave out a keening wail. I'd never heard one for real and couldn't imagine what one sounded like. Until now.

I nudged him harder. 'I said, "Where's Telfer?" I won't ask again.'

He must have read something in my face. Maybe my hesitancy to kill in cold blood. Whatever it was, his demeanour suddenly changed. 'Go fuck yourself, asshole.'

'So now you're the brave guy?' I put the muzzle of my gun to the centre of his forehead. 'You don't think I'll do it? Try me.'

As suddenly, he was keening and wailing again.

'Where's Telfer?' I asked.

'I don't know who you mean. Speak to Petoskey, man. Not us. For God's sake . . . don't kill me.'

I took the gun from his skull. There was a scarlet ring where the hot metal had pressed into his flesh. 'Second question, and the rules haven't changed. Where's Petoskey?'

He wanted to resist. Perhaps it was bravado, but more likely it was fear of his boss that held his tongue. Back went the gun.

'Where's Petoskey?'

Fear of a bullet in the skull now or *perhaps* one later from Petoskey if he survived; I could see the calculation going round in his head. It was a simple equation.

He nodded upwards, eyes on the ceiling above.

'He's upstairs?' I asked.

The man nodded again.

'How many with him?'

'How the hell should I know?' the man spluttered.

'Guess,' I said.

'Three, four . . . Could be as many as a dozen for all I know!'

'Armed?'

'What do you think?'

It was a stupid question.

'Yes. It's the end of the line, buddy,' I said. Then I slammed the butt of my gun against his temple, sending him sprawling sideways across a floor littered with debris.

'Maybe you should plug him and have done,' Rink said from behind me.

Was that really my friend speaking?

'Can't do it, Rink.'

'I know it's not right, but it makes more sense. We don't want to be going up there, leaving one of them behind us. Not when he's armed.'

'You're right. But I'm not a murderer.'

Rink's gaze sought the man with the new open-vent shoulder.

'He'll survive. Anyway, that was different,' I said. 'He was trying to kill me. But I won't kill a man in cold blood.'

Rink winked at me, his stern face softening. 'Just checking, my old friend,' he said. 'Like I said last night, we don't have a licence to kill no more.'

'I hear you,' I told him. And I meant it. But we still had a job to do, and it was my firm guess that others could die this night. My only hope was that it wouldn't be either of us.

16

There he is.

The thief.

Purloiner of second-favourite knives and sports utility vehicles. He was just as Tubal Cain remembered him, though subtly altered he had to admit. A handsome enough bloke as far as thieves go. Aged in his early thirties. He was dressed the way a million other guys do, in nondescript casual clothing with a ball cap pulled down to his ears. The sum of his possessions were packed in a knapsack and slung from one shoulder. It was the same knapsack he carried when he'd carjacked Cain yesterday. Mirror-lensed sunglasses concealed his eyes.

In essence, the thief was very similar to Cain, Mr Normal blending with his surroundings. The thought had occurred already, but now, watching the man who'd signed his name in the hotel's register book as David Ambrose, Cain came to a conclusion: you're hiding your true identity as carefully as I am. Why is that?

One thing was for certain, Ambrose wasn't hiding from Cain. He had no way of knowing that Cain would hunt him down. In his mind, Cain had been nothing but a hopeless freak he'd carjacked out in the middle of nowhere.

I'll tell you why. It means that you are afraid of someone else.

Cain leaned back in the driver's seat of the Oldsmobile, chewing his lower lip. Now, this was an unexpected turn of events.

'Who are you running from, Mr So-Called-Ambrose?' he whispered as he watched Ambrose approach the SUV. 'Who is it that frightens you more than Tubal Cain?'

Ambrose gave off a vibe, an electrostatic buzz of anticipation, almost as if he was steeling himself for a sniper's bullet between the shoulder blades. It was the unnatural way in which he moved, trying his damnedest to appear nonchalant, yet at the same time holding a posture as taut as piano wire. He could pretend not to, but Cain knew that behind the mirrors of his shades, Ambrose glanced around, alert as a mouse in a rattlesnake's den. Turning, the sunlight and dappled shadows of palm fronds played across his glasses. Cain thought of a beetle's eyes.

The insectile gaze skimmed over the Oldsmobile, pausing for less than a heartbeat before passing on. There was a momentary pinching of the thief's lips as he'd scanned the car, but the strained expression was gone in the next instant. No, it was merely an unconscious reaction, not recognition. Deep in the shadows of his parking spot, Cain felt protected from an amateur who'd made too many mistakes.

As he approached the SUV Ambrose dug for keys in a trouser pocket. Unhitching the knapsack from his shoulder, he unlocked the driver's door and slung the bag on to the passenger seat. Another glance around gave him the air of one of those hopeless spies that Napoleon Solo – and that guy with the Russian-sounding name Cain could never recall, let alone pronounce – used to thwart every week in *The Man From U.N.C.L.E.* television show.

Cain saw the headlights flick on. The engine coughed to life like a grizzly stirring from hibernation. The SUV barely rolled forwards a couple of yards before the parking brake was violently engaged. Ambrose had forgotten all about subtlety and blending in if the way he stomped to the back of the vehicle was anything to go by.

'Gotcha,' Cain said.

Ambrose crouched down at the flat tyre, running his hands over it as though he could magically restore it by touch alone. Unfortunately, he was no sorcerer. Defeated, he stood up with his hands on his hips, and even from across the breadth of the parking lot his language was choice.

It would be so simple to come up behind Ambrose while he was distracted. Push the point of his scaling knife into the juncture of his neck and clavicle. Dig down for the vital organs in one rapturous moment. End him right there and then. At his leisure, Cain could search the dead man's possessions and regain that which belonged to him.

Yes, that's as it could be.

That *was* exactly as his plan had gone. By now it was hours later, his discussion with the dippy receptionist wouldn't be connected to an apparent mugging gone wrong. Cain could go merrily on his way, his sense of justice appeased.

'But, thief, that isn't how it's going to be.'

The enigma of Ambrose's true identity, and what – or who – he was hiding from, was enough to give pause for anyone with an enquiring mind. And never let it be said that Tubal Cain was not a deep thinker. His needs might be basic, but he thought long on ways of satisfying those needs.

His curiosity was more than piqued. It was on turbo-assisted hyperdrive. He wanted to let this play out a little longer. Who knows, thief, he decided. It might make for an interesting conclusion.

17

Events overtook our plan way too quickly for my liking. Not that I was surprised; that's always been the flaw with our tactic: Murphy's Law strikes again!

It was no longer a case of one-two move on, but a full-on headlong charge for the top.

The man I'd knocked unconscious didn't give me enough to make a considered judgement. There could be as few as three men with Petoskey or as many as a dozen. Think the worst and anything else is a bonus.

It was full on 'balls to the wall', assault time.

We headed for the upper floor with our guns blasting. The intent wasn't to shoot anyone per se, but to cause as much confusion as possible. Petoskey was a rat and everyone knows what rats do on a sinking ship. I ruled out the fire escape at this corner of the building, guessing that Petoskey would make for the one we'd used to gain access.

'I'm going back across, cut off any escape route,' I told Rink. 'You OK with that?'

He racked the pump action. 'As long as I've got ammo, I'll give them hell.'

'When the shooting stops, I want you to come up and join me as quickly as you can.'

'Damn, and here was me thinking it was time for a coffee break.'

'After we're done I'll buy you coffee and doughnuts.'

'Make 'em jelly doughnuts and you've got a deal.'

'Sounds good to me.'

Another volley of fire gained the attention of those on the populated side. I backtracked across the building.

Speed was an issue. Call me cautious, but I made my way through the building as though every nook hid an assassin. Better a minute late than thirty years too early at the pearly gates.

The remains of the door Rink recently blasted were like an open mouth full of jagged teeth. The room beyond exuded the stench of battle on a waft of sour breath. Apart from the stink, the room was now empty. The unconscious man had obviously come to, and he wasn't as ill informed about our chances as he was making out. At least he'd had the sense to get the hell away from the shit storm raging above. The man who had taken a bullet in the shoulder was gone too. A smear of blood on the window ledge confirmed their escape route.

Happy that no one would come on me from behind, I ran along the corridor. Behind me, the boom of Rink's shotgun resonated in the air as he unloaded it towards the upper floor.

On to the other staircase, I headed up. Natural function sometimes takes a back seat when adrenalin shrieks through your veins; I took the full flight of stairs before I remembered to breathe. At the top I paused to exhale, sucked in air, then stepped out into a corridor much shorter than the one I'd passed through below.

A little over thirty feet away, the corridor had been blocked. What appeared to be a new metal door had been installed. It reverberated under the ring of urgent voices from beyond. A background accompaniment of baying dogs and shotgun blasts confirmed I'd found Petoskey's hideout.

Cursory inspection of the metal door told me it was a no-go. There was no handle on this side, no keyhole. The soldier in me said it would be almost impregnable to anything short of heavy artillery. Abandoning the door, I stepped into the office on my left. There was the usual jumble of wrecked furniture and scattered documents.

I made my way to the wall and laid an ear to it. I was quite sure that all the action was at the far end and the possibility of getting hot lead in my ear was pretty slim.

The wall was made of plasterboard and judging by the swollen roar of activity beyond it wasn't as heavily fortified as the door. Immediately I crouched down and took the Ka-bar from my boot.

It was a matter of less than a minute to cut away a torso-sized portion of the plasterboard. Beyond was a second layer of the same substance. Why the Americans called this brittle stuff sheet rock always amused me; using only the tip of my knife, I bored a small circle from the plaster and peered into Petoskey's enclave.

As if on cue, Rink stopped firing, making me wonder if the link we share exceedes mere intuition and laps at the shore of preternatural ability. Then again, he may have been reloading his scattergun. Whatever, the lull in activity was just what I needed.

Through my peephole, I could see an open-plan room running the breadth of the building. A group of men gathered by a second doorway at the far end had to be the hired guns. Their attention was on the stairwell below them. Two more men held pit bull terriers on leashes. The dogs were blood-soaked and torn in a number of places. Unconcerned by the madness of humans they strained at their leashes to continue their own private war. That meant that the final three men standing by a jerry-built arena in the centre of the floor were the high flyers. One of them had to be Sigmund Petoskey.

OK, quick calculation and what did I have?

Ten men in total.

Two dogs.

It wasn't the most difficult summation.

The real question was: could I handle them all?

Whether or not I was capable wasn't an issue. I was going to and that was it.

18

When I was a small child, I grew up in a home poor in money but rich in love. What my parents were unable to provide in fine food and mod cons, they made up for with hugs and kisses and quality time spent with their only child. I don't miss having little in the way of material belongings but I do miss my dad.

After Dad died and my mother remarried, things changed. I still didn't possess the treasures children yearn for, but I did get a little brother. But then it was my brother who got the hugs and kisses. I looked elsewhere for comfort.

My father instilled in me a love of books. Where other kids got stereo record players and portable TVs in their bedrooms, I had a collection of dog-eared novels passed down to me by my dad. Poe, Lovecraft, and R.E. Howard were my favourites. Next in line came the superheroes of the comic books that I progressed on to when a newspaper delivery round gave me the pocket money to spend on treats. Sometimes I wonder if the books taught me about the horrors of our world, while the superheroes taught me how to deal with them. Either way, they gave me a fertile imagination.

Probably this explained why I envisioned myself as the Incredible Hulk when I erupted through the wall. The Hulk had his extraordinary strength with which he thwarted his enemies, but I didn't have that luxury. I came out shooting in a spray of dust and plaster particles.

I didn't aim to hit anyone, firing above their heads. Combined with my Hulk act, it was enough to startle everyone into immobility. Only the dogs responded with panic, circling and ensnaring their handlers with their leashes as they spun.

'No one move or the next bullet will kill you,' I shouted. In reality, if all of them had turned on me at once, I wouldn't have stood a chance. The thing was, without exception, in everyone's mind I was shouting directly at them. No one wants to be a dead hero.

'Guns on the floor,' I shouted as I took a half-dozen paces into the room. The three men nearest me weren't armed. They thrust their hands towards the ceiling.

The dog handlers had too many other concerns with attempting to untangle themselves to pay me immediate attention. Torn between me and Rink, who approached at a gallop, the five at the far end quickly dropped their weapons and kicked them away.

'Inside the room, boys,' I heard Rink shout. His voice jostled them like tenpins, scattering them before him.

My unorthodox entrance, not to mention the demanding muzzle of my SIG, commanded compliance. The three men by the fighting arena moved quickly towards the plastic-shrouded wall, their hands seeking heaven.

A shadow in the doorway morphed into Rink. It was good to see the big guy again. He shot me a wink as he ushered the five goons before him.

'Get your butts in the ring and sit on your hands,' Rink told the men. They crowded into the centre of the fighting area. Space was at a premium as they jostled to be furthest away from the twelve-gauge. Rink turned to the two dog handlers. 'You too.'

One of the handlers, a skinny youth with a huge nose covered in acne, twisted his face at Rink. He was uglier than his mutt. At least the dog had an excuse; it had already gone a couple of rounds.

'Got a problem with your hearing?' Rink demanded.

'The dogs will fight,' he said.

'Then it's your job to stop them, Zit Boy,' Rink said. 'Now get the hell in there. One of you at either end.'

The big-nosed youth entered the ring first, pulling his struggling dog to him. When he was as settled as he could be, the second dog handler entered. Rink pushed the gate to, flipped a catch in place. No one moved in the arena. The tough guys huddled together. Dogs' teeth and a twelve-gauge scattergun respectively provided the proverbial rock and hard place.

Harvey's surveillance shots of Sigmund Petoskey came in handy. Even if I'd never viewed a photo of him, I'd have picked him out by the contempt that radiated from him like the apocalyptic fallout from a mushroom cloud.

'Hi, Siggy!' I said. 'Like to bring your fat arse over here?'

Petoskey's eyebrows rose and he lifted a finger to his chest.

'Yeah,' I confirmed. 'I want a word with you.'

Pointing my SIG at his chest, I indicated the bulge in his breast pocket where ordinary business men would carry a notebook.

'Lose the piece.'

Petoskey pulled a Berretta out of the shoulder rig. Two fingers; like he'd done it before.

'OK. Get over here.'

He stood his ground.

With his eastern European name, you'd maybe expect him to have the stilted accent of a villain from a James Bond movie. You would be wrong. Just as Rink is a contradiction of his ancestry, so was Sigmund Petoskey. He spoke in the cultured tones of an Ivy Leaguer with top honours.

'You are making one hell of a mistake, you fucking asshole,' he directed at me.

Admittedly, his words weren't anything you'd expect from one with such educated standards. Then again, you only have to recall Rink's summing up of Siggy's childhood to imagine where the gutter language came from.

'No,' I told him. 'You're the one making the mistake.'

'Who the hell are you, coming here and shooting up my place? My personal friend, the mayor, will have something to say about this!'

'I don't give a damn what the mayor says,' I told him.

'He'll have your job for this,' Petoskey said. He rounded on Rink. 'And yours, you madman. You can personally mark my words.'

'Like I said,' I told him. 'You're the one making the mistake. We aren't police officers, Siggy. For all I care, your friend the mayor can *personally* kiss my ass.'

For a second time Petoskey's eyebrows sought the top of his head.

'Not the police?'

'Not the police,' I echoed.

'Then you're with Hendrickson. I should have known . . .'

His words faltered at the shake of my head.

'I don't know Hendrickson from Jimi Hendrix,' I told him.

'So, who the blazes are you?'

'Someone who needs answers. And I want them quickly.'

Petoskey looked at his feet, gave a slow shake of his two-hundred-dollar haircut. Something dawned on him and he slowly raised his face to look at me. A scowl broke across his features. 'This is about John Telfer, isn't it?'

John was indeed why I was there, but I'd half expected to have to draw the information from him like rusty nails from a knotty plank.

'Where is he?' I demanded. 'If you've hurt him I'll—'

Petoskey sneered. 'You think I have him?'

'Maybe not here, but you know where he is.'

'Look,' he said, 'I already told your friends: I don't know where he is. The son of a bitch took off owing me a substantial sum of money. Do you think if I knew where he was, I wouldn't have brought him back by now? Jesus Christ, how many times have I to tell *you people* the same damn thing?'

I didn't answer.

This wasn't a put-on. Petoskey's words were ringing true. He really didn't know where John was. Ergo, it was pointless questioning him any further regarding John's whereabouts. Time for a change of tack; his statement had struck me like a blade twisting in my guts.

'You've already spoken to my friends?'

'Twice!' he said. Full of ignominious fury, he held out his hands. An expansive gesture, taking in the entire room. 'And now this?'

'OK, Siggy. Wind your neck in,' I told him.

'I'll do no such thing. You come here shooting and making demands. Now you want me to act reasonably?'

'Unless you want me to start shooting again, you will,' Rink drawled from across the room. For emphasis, he aimed the shotgun directly at the group of men in the dog-fighting pit.

Petoskey wore righteous fury like a dead man's suit. He folded his arms across his chest. Challenged Rink with a sneer. Then he turned it on me. It faltered when I shoved my SIG into the dimple on his chin.

'Tell me,' I said. 'Who are these *friends* that you're talking about?'

'You should know,' Petoskey said.

'Indulge me,' I said.

'Your friends from the government. Who else?'

It was a war to keep my features flat, but the impact of his words must have shown. Petoskey misread the message. Maybe it was the way I allowed my gun to drop from his chin.

'See. I knew it,' he announced. His two friends nodded along with him. One of them opened his mouth to say something. I shot him a warning look. The man clammed up immediately.

To Petoskey, I said, 'You're saying that *CIA agents* have spoken to you about John Telfer?'

'Aren't you listening to me? Twice they've been at my office. Twice they've demanded to know the location of John Telfer. I wish I'd never seen Telfer's goddamn face!'

'These agents actually said they were CIA?' I asked.

'They didn't need to. I can smell a spook a mile off.'

'So you're only guessing?' I said, with not a little hope.

Petoskey shook his head. 'They didn't exactly introduce themselves, if that's what you mean. One of them flashed a badge the first time they came round; they didn't bother the second time. Pretty much the way you haven't now, eh?'

Again I didn't answer. CIA agents, by virtue of their secretive trade, aren't in the habit of flashing badges or announcing their identities. Petoskey had to be confused, must have misread the acronym on the badge. It would be easily done, I suppose, though I doubted that the Child Support Agency would go to such lengths to trace an absent father.

Judging my silence to be guilt, he said, 'You can go back and tell your bosses that they're barking up the wrong tree. For the third time, *I do not know where John Telfer is*. Have you got that?'

We had lost a major advantage, and unless we started shooting again, it was an unsalvageable situation.

On the same wavelength, Rink moved towards me. His shotgun still menaced the men in the arena. No one moved. It wasn't so much the fear of being shot as that they thought we were G-men. Worse than going up against the police, they weren't prepared to risk the ire of the government. They wouldn't make a move. Apparently, neither would we. Not now that we'd been uncloaked as government agents.

Petoskey was wearing a smug look on his face.

'Quite a mess, eh?' he crowed.

Yeah, it was a mess, but not for the reason he thought. We backed away towards the demolition job I'd done on the wall.

'Oh, for pity's sake. Use the door, will you?' Petoskey said.

'We'll leave as we came,' I said as we continued to back-pedal slowly away.

'Do me a favour,' Petoskey called as we stepped through the hole into the abandoned office. 'When you do find Telfer, tell him I want my ten grand. Plus thirty per cent interest. And you can tell him not to show his face around any of my places again. He's not welcome. Tell him he can mail the money to me.'

If he'd let it lie at that, I don't know where the hunt would've taken us next. As it was, like many self-righteous punks, he loved the sound of his own voice too much. 'And tell him my car had better have a full tank of gas when he drops it off.'

I stepped back into the opening. What a difference a couple of seconds had made to the scenario. Tough guys all, the goons in the ring were already fighting their way past one of the dogs in an effort to get out. To win face with their boss, and without exception, they offered to chase us down. Petoskey and the other two suits had moved towards them, and Siggy wasn't a happy bunny.

My SIG rapped a sharp command, shattering the light fixture above their heads.

Did you ever play the children's game called statues? You stand with your back to an advancing group, you turn round sharply and the group has to freeze, as though under a gorgon's stare. Anyone who moves is then out of the game. Well, that's what it felt like then.

My gun was now a useless threat, but I aimed it anyway.

'Telfer took one of your cars?' I demanded.

'Yes,' Petoskey snapped. 'If you'd taken the time to read your friends' reports you would already be aware of that.'

'Must've missed it,' I said. 'What car are we talking about?'

'For heaven's sake! Read the damn report,' Petoskey said.

I took three steps, my anger level rising with each one. Grabbing Petoskey by his lapels, I jammed the SIG under his chin with my other hand.

Petoskey's eyes went wide. That a government agent would actually have the balls to shoot him with all these witnesses standing around was now a definite possibility. Maybe I should have shot him. Undoubtedly, the world would've been a better place with one less scumbag in it.

'Just tell me what fucking car you're talking about.'

'Pontiac.' Petoskey looked to his friends for moral support. All of them were doing their best not to attract my attention.

'Write down the licence plate number,' I ordered.

'I haven't got a pen.'

'Find one.' I pushed him away from me. Petoskey's face was scarlet. He actually stepped back towards me.

'Here,' one of the other suits said, pulling an expensive-looking gold-plated pen from a jacket pocket. Petoskey snatched it, then glanced round looking for paper. Again, the suit came to the rescue, tearing a page from an equally expensive pocket diary. Petoskey quickly scribbled down a number, then thrust it at me.

'Satisfied?'

I snatched the paper out of his hand.

'Thank you,' I said.

'You're welcome,' Petoskey said. Not that I believed him. My spite was reflected by his bilious glare. We were rival wolves meeting on a forest trail. We edged backwards, neither wanting to be seen to give ground, but each recognizing the prudence of doing so.

Rink was at my shoulder. He made a cautious noise in the back of his throat; Rinkese for 'We've outstayed our welcome, Hunter.' How could I possibly disagree? It was definitely time to leave if the clamour of reinforcements charging up the far staircase was anything to go by.

We played it cool as we stepped through the hole in the wall. Then we ran like hell.

19

Mr So-Called-Ambrose wasn't a name that came easily to the lips, so Tubal Cain decided he'd refer to him simply as *thief*. It was all he was, and didn't deserve to be referred to as anything else. Thief, thief, thief.

Names always fascinated Cain. To be named is the achievement of recognition, and he wasn't about to give Ambrose the honour. He was nothing in Cain's estimation. Just a bum. Beneath contempt. Nothing but a sneaking thief.

The thief was back in his room now. Probably wondering what to do about the flat tyre. There was a spare bolted to the rear of the vehicle, but the thief appeared to be the type of man too easily defeated when it came to mechanical contrivance. He was both incpt with a lug wrench and too damn lazy to do anything to fix it. Knowing his kind, the latter was probably the overriding factor. Why go to the trouble of changing a defective tyre when he could go steal himself another car?

Evening was fully upon the hotel now. Way out over the ocean, stars were pale glimmers on a velvet back drop. Here, the light cast through tinted lenses on to the hotel façade was mint green and coral pink. A host of shadows jittered and danced as a faint breeze stirred foliage.

Cain watched as the rosy-cheeked receptionist finished her shift, wandered out into the car park and drove off in an imported Ford Ka. He was tempted to follow her, to act out the fantasy he'd been playing through his mind these past hours. In the end, he let her go. Weighed against the risk of losing sight of the thief, it wasn't worth it. Other opportunities would arise to invite the girl back to his special place.

Cain opened the car door and stepped out on to asphalt radiating the heat of the day. He shrugged out of his jacket, pulled off his tie and unbuttoned his collar. Jacket and tie went in the trunk of the car.

He sauntered round the side of the building to the garden area, savouring the scent of jasmine only slightly tainted by exhaust fumes from the highway. The pool rippled under fluorescent lighting, a vibrant blue now unsullied by the bobbing forms of overfed children and grandmothers floating on inflatable beds.

He carried on to the foot of the winding stairs.

Act furtively and you are done for: another pearl of wisdom from his killer's rulebook. Cain mounted the stairs as if he had the right to be there. He took two steps at a time, almost bounding up to the first landing. He slowed fractionally as he climbed to the next floor, tilting down his face. The thief could be on his way down and he didn't want to be recognized before he could engineer a proper reunion.

At the top of the stairs he turned slowly to the left, surveying. Then, happy that no one was approaching, he walked along the terrace towards the door of the thief's room. His rubber-soled shoes squeaked on the terracotta tiles like angry rodents. He stooped down and pulled them off.

The thief's room was at the corner of the building, the terrace terminating just to the left of the door. If the thief happened to come out now Cain would have nowhere to hide. Immediate action wouldn't be as satisfying as the drawn-out torment he had in mind, but there would be nothing else for it.

At the door, he bent down and placed his shoes on the floor. Minuscule drifts of sand abutted the wall next to the door, blown here on the wind, or maybe it was the remnants of someone walking on the beach and carrying proof of their labour back with them.

'This rule is the one that takes priority above all others, thief,' he whispered. 'Be mindful of Locard's Principle.' That precept of forensic science said that wherever a person was at any given time he left behind a small part of himself; be it hair, saliva, semen, skin cells, clothing fibres, or dirt or plant matter transported on the soles of shoes or in the folds of the clothing. The list was endless. And don't forget fingerprints.

From a trouser pocket, Cain pulled out a roll of plastic baggies and some rubber bands. Cocking an ear towards the door so its opening wouldn't surprise him, he stooped down and pulled a baggie over each foot, stuffed the cuffs of his trousers inside, then sealed them with the rubber bands. That done, he repeated the process, this time with his hands.

The bags were spacious and flopped at the ends of his fingertips like translucent flippers. He looked ludicrous but didn't care. The last thing the thief would think of when folds of flesh were being stripped from his body was Cain's diabolical fashion sense.

Lastly, he pulled a cloth bag from his pocket. He'd prepared eyeholes earlier, singed into the white cloth with the cigarette lighter from the Oldsmobile. The mask made him think of the KKK. Not that he was a racist. He wasn't. Regardless of race, creed or colour, he hated everyone with equal passion.

Low and away from the balcony's edge, he slipped the bag over his head, before standing up and facing the door. The eyeholes took away a little of his peripheral vision, but that was OK. He had a single intent and would be going forwards from now on.

Readiness for the long anticipated reunion required only one more thing. He reached under the tail of his shirt and pulled free the scaling knife. He held it up before his eyes, admiring the rainbow effect along its cutting edge. Sharp, so very, very sharp.

Now he was ready.

He knocked on the door.

20

More than one thing was troubling me about the whole set-up. Louise Blake continued to niggle me like a worm burrowing its way through my cerebral cortex. There was much that woman knew but wasn't telling me. Her reticence, I believed, was linked to the below-the-belt strike that Sigmund Petoskey had dealt us. That the CIA could be involved had jarred me to the core.

'I have to make a couple of calls,' I said. Harvey Lucas extended his hospitality in the manner of a Southern gent, and I was going to take him up on it. The telephone was on a desk across the room.

Harvey watched with an expression that was hard to define. I caught myself mid-stride. In order to gather our wits after such a crushing body blow, we'd returned to his office – a rented unit in an industrial complex on the other side of town. Harvey seemed pleased to see us, as if we did deem him a worthwhile ally, after all. However, once I'd mentioned the CIA he didn't appear to be anywhere near as enthusiastic. Pausing with my hand over the handset, I waited for him to object. Harvey inclined his chin.

'Sure you don't mind?' I asked.

'Go ahead.' He rolled his neck then turned to his computer screen and studied it with way too much intensity.

'When you finish up, I got a call to make too,' Rink said. He was standing behind Harvey and I saw him reach out and grip his friend's shoulder. Rink's never patronizing; his gesture was more one of reassurance. 'Can you find me the number for the Arkansas Humane Society, Harve? Gotta drop 'em a tip concerning illegal dogfighting on their turf.'

Harvey nodded, then bent to the task.

'If you'd prefer I didn't use your phone, I'll go find a pay phone,' I said.

Harvey returned his gaze to mine.

'Go ahead and use it, Hunter. If the CIA is involved, you can bet your ass they're already aware of my involvement.' He rocked back in his seat, resigned. Nerves made him more effusive than usual. 'Makes no difference if you conduct your business from here or anywhere else, they'll have you hooked up in less time than it takes you to dial the number. If you've got anything to say that you don't want them to hear, I suggest you forget about phone calls altogether.'

'Yeah,' I agreed. But I wasn't concerned. Truth is, it didn't matter what the CIA overheard, considering it was one of their controllers I was about to call.

A number I hadn't used in over four years leapt straight from memory to my fingertips. From the handset, I heard the beeping of a long-distance connection as it bounced via service providers and satellites throughout the world. A phone finally rang in a nondescript office in Langley, Virginia.

The call was picked up by an electronic answering machine, gave me options and asked me to key in a twelve-digit number. Again, from long-term memory I typed in the sequence. The line went dead for a split second. In that unfathomably short space of time recording devices kicked in. It didn't matter. Then came a purr as the connection was made. The phone was picked up after only three beeps.

'This better be good,' grunted a man's voice.

'That'll depend on your perspective,' I grunted right back.

'My perspective is always from the bottom of a deep dark place, you should know that by now.'

My laughter was humourless. 'You should get out more. Get a little sunshine on your face. You spend too much time in your little cubby hole for your own good.'

'Tell me about it,' the man said. Over the line came a minuscule shift in the white noise as buttons were flicked. 'You can speak now, Hunter. Line's secure.'

'I've got a favour to ask,' I told him.

'So much for the pleasantries, huh? Straight down to business. Even after all this time.'

'No room for pleasantries I'm afraid. It could be that we're sitting on opposite sides of the fence on this one.'

I heard the creak of leather: Walter Hayes Conrad IV shifting uneasily in his chair. By that subtle movement of his body, I'd struck an unwelcome chord with him.

'Opposite sides of the fence? I thought you were no longer in the game, Hunter?'

'I'm not in your game.'

'So you're still retired?'

'Retired, yeah, but not gone to seed yet.'

'I take it this is a private job we're talking about then?'

'It was private until I heard some of your boys might be involved.'

'Oh?' Walter shifted again, and I could visualize him reaching for the on switch for the recorder.

'Just give me a minute before you make our conversation public,' I said.

'Like I said, the line's secure.'

'Yeah, so let's keep it that way for now, huh?'

'You know I can't promise you that, Hunter. If this concerns one of our operations I can't let it go off the record.'

I sniffed. 'All I'm asking is that you confirm if the CIA is involved.'

'That'll depend.'

'I appreciate that. I'm not asking for specifics. A simple yes or no will do.'

'Then the answer's no.'

'Is that what you term plausible denial?'

'Nah, there's nothing plausible about it.'

'You're right there,' I said. 'Considering I haven't even told you what job I'm involved in.'

'There's no need. I haven't heard your name mentioned, Hunter.'

'Well, there's a surprise,' I said.

'We did wonder what you were doing on our home soil,' Walter said. Walter doesn't offer information for nothing.

'So you knew I was in the country?'

'Of course. What kind of intelligence community doesn't track foreign agents flying in?'

'I'm not a foreign agent, Walt. I'm retired. Remember?'

'Same difference.'

It wasn't overly surprising that my presence in the USA had rung warning bells. Neither would it surprise me if Walter had already made calls to my old commanders at Arrowsake to check I wasn't back on the payroll of the British government. Or – worst case scenario – that I was on *someone else's* payroll.

'You needn't worry, Walter. I haven't turned to the dark side.'

Walter laughed as if he was choking on a bitter pill.

'So what's the deal? I know you hooked up with Jared Rington. Believe me, Hunter, we dropped it there. Not interested.'

'Rink's with me now,' I said. 'He says "Hi".'

'I'm sure he does,' Walter said scornfully. All part of the act.

'I find it hard to believe that you aren't wondering what I'm up to,' I said.

'To be honest, we ain't the least bit interested. Far as we're concerned you're here visiting your old buddy. We're prepared to leave it at that. So long as nothing else comes to our attention.'

'Appreciate it, Walt. But now that I have come to your attention, how are you going to play it?'

Walter sucked air through his teeth. Not the nicest

sound in your ear. 'Depends on the job you're going to tell me about.'

'The one you've already told me you're not involved in?'

'One and the same.'

'Figures,' I said, paraphrasing Rink. 'I take it that what you're not telling me is that you've no one in Little Rock, Arkansas.'

'I don't doubt we've agents there, Hunter, but not on anything you're involved in.'

'You're sure about that?'

'How can you doubt me?' I don't have anyone on your case. OK?'

'OK, that's good enough for me.' I paused, considering my next words. It was a gamble mentioning anything about the job I was involved in, but it was probably too late for that now. By calling Walter, I'd guaranteed that the CIA would indeed be watching me from now on. 'What about my brother, John Telfer?'

Up in his office at Langley, Walter Hayes Conrad IV went silent.

'I take it by your silence that his name means something to you?'

Walter breathed into the mouthpiece. Was that remorse?

'It does, Hunter, but not for the reason you're thinking.'

'I'm thinking you've got guys on him.'

'Nope. It's not that at all.'

Judging by the ache between my eyebrows, my face

was fertile ground begging for a frown. I was afraid to ask. 'What is it then?'

'I take it you haven't looked at the TV lately?'

'No time for TV.'

'Make time. If you're interested in John Telfer, you'd better get yourself acquainted with CNN. Telfer's currently their number-one news slot.'

I turned from the phone. 'You got a TV, Harve?'

'Got one at home. Why?'

'What about your computer? Can you get CNN?'

'The news channel? Sure.'

'Do me a favour and log on, will you?'

Harvey's eyebrows danced towards his shaved head. Rink was watching me expectantly. A shrug was all I offered before turning my attention back to Walter. 'I'm just about to take a look now.'

'Might explain a thing or two.'

'So what's the deal?' I asked him.

'Take a look and make up your own mind.'

'Fair enough,' I said. 'But you're telling me this isn't anything to do with you?'

'No matter how many ways I tell you no, you're still going to have reservations, Hunter.'

'Old habits die hard,' I told him.

'You doubt my honesty, but that's OK, I don't bear any grudges. If I were in your shoes, I'd be the same. For the record, I'll say it again. Then it's up to you . . .' His breath came slow and steady. The pause was not for his benefit. Bad news was coming. 'The CIA is not on your case. We're not on your brother's case. But then again, I can't speak for the rest of the civilized world. Or the FBI in particular.'

'The FBI?'

'Just watch the news. You'll see what I mean.'

'Thanks, Walt. I appreciate your help.'

'No problem,' he said. 'Good speaking to you again, Hunter.'

'Likewise.' I paused, considering. Then, 'Walt, seeing as you've been so open with me, there's something I have to tell you.'

'Go on.'

'I was involved in a job an hour or so ago. Guy I was up against said he'd been visited by some of your boys asking about John.'

'Wasn't us.'

'I appreciate that. But I think you might want to look into who's going round posing as government agents. Might cause a stink for you if something goes wrong.'

'I get it now. That's why you wanted to check in with me?'

'Yeah. Just in case I have to defend myself.'

'They're not mine, Hunter. So . . . *stay safe*.'

Stay safe. This from a sub-division director of black ops. In other words, Walter had just given official sanction to retaliate with lethal force if that situation should arise. What's known in the trade as an executive decision.

'Thanks, Walt.'

Walter isn't big on pleasantries. I was left holding a handset issuing the soft purr of a dead line.

Something popped up on Harvey's computer

screen. I set the phone back in its cradle. All I could think of to say was, 'Shit.'

With equal lack of verbosity, Rink cursed loudly. After a beat, Harvey joined in.

On the screen of Harvey's computer were headlines I could barely comprehend.

FBI CLOSES IN ON MASS KILLER

THE HARVESTMAN FINALLY NAMED

Beneath the headlines was a photograph of my little brother.

21

Tubal Cain knocked again.

Louder this time.

Again, there was no answer. Frowning beneath his impromptu hood, he stepped to the side of the door. By pressing close to the glass, he could make out any movement from within. Or, in this case, the lack of movement.

No one home? How unbelievable was that?

Letting out a sigh, he pulled the hood free and stuffed it into his trouser pocket. His palms were sweating inside the baggies, but he didn't take them off yet.

'Where the hell are you?' he wondered aloud. There was the possibility that the thief had given him the slip but he didn't give it much credence. He'd been parked in a position where he could watch the major exits from the hotel and, unless the thief had come down the back stairs and scaled the nine-foot perimeter fence, he was still here.

What are the chances of that happening? Slim to zero.

There was the chance that he'd gone down to the restaurant to take an evening meal, but again it was highly unlikely. From the furtive manner in which the thief acted when he was in the car park, he was hiding from someone. He wouldn't eat out in plain sight in the restaurant, not when he could order food from room service.

That left two or three possibilities. The thief was asleep and hadn't heard him knock. Or he was in the bathroom, and had again missed the knock. Or he'd slipped out while Cain had made his way round the back of the hotel and was even now in the parking lot looking out another vehicle to appropriate. Maybe an Oldsmobile.

Vacillation danced a quickstep through his mind. He could run back round front to check on the state of play, or he could gain admittance to the hotel suite and check out his other theories. In the end, he chose the latter.

As quietly as possible, he tested the door handle. The door didn't open. Not a problem. He inserted the tip of his scaling knife between door lock and frame and twisted. The lock snicked open with barely any pressure.

The door swung open to reveal a short vestibule bordered on one side by two closed doors. At the far end, a door was open and he could see part of a combined sitting room/bedroom apartment. Next to a recliner was a pair of running shoes and a denim jacket was slung over the arm of a chair. Looked like the thief hadn't packed to leave.

Inside the vestibule, Cain listened. He could discern neither running water nor snoring. He took another step, the plastic bags making a faint sucking noise on the tiled floor. Watching the open room at the end, he pushed the front door closed, then turned to the first door to his right. Slowly he pushed down on the handle, allowing the door to swing open of its own volition.

He sneaked a glance into the room. It was a tiny kitchen area. A couple of buzzing flies bashed their skulls against a window in an effort to escape the stifling heat. There were a few dirty dishes piled in the sink, and a ring-stained coffee cup on the draining board. He reached out and touched a kettle. Through his plastic shrouding, the kettle still bore the heat of being boiled. Proof of recent or current occupancy, Cain decided.

Leaving the kitchen, he moved along the vestibule. He held his breath. Anticipation building. If his assumption proved true, the next door would open into a bathroom, the most likely place to find the thief. Cain smiled to himself, imagining surprising the thief sitting on the WC with his trousers round his ankles, a shocked look on his face. How ignoble!

He pressed an ear to the door, listening for the telltale sounds of an industrious man at work. Nothing. No soft grunts, no delicate splashes, no sighs of relief or rustle of newspaper. Neither was there the sound of shower or faucet trickling, but it didn't mean the thief wasn't prone in a tub and taking a moment of silent reflection.

By habit, Cain always bolted the door to his bathroom, even when he knew he was alone. But the door swung open as easily as had the kitchen door. Cain stepped into the cooler confines of the bathroom, a delicate waft of lavender invading his senses. The lid on the toilet was up. The bath was empty. Unfortunately, the shower curtain was pulled to one side, so there was no chance of a Hitchcock moment presenting itself.

He fought down the impulse to swear. Swearing is for the uncultured killer; he of the chainsaw or machete and lampshades made from human hide. Turning instead to the vestibule, he walked along it with the stealth of a ninja assassin. His blade led the way, lifted like that of a matador poised for the *coup de grâce*.

The open room remained constant. He attempted to attune himself to the still air, to feel the subtle draughts and eddies of the atmosphere around him. Those restrained hints that human life stirred in the space out of his sight but not beyond the reach of his other senses.

At the threshold, he once more tugged the hood from his pocket and pulled it over his head. The shock of seeing a hooded man would have the desired effect of halting the thief in his tracks. All he required was a second or so of addled wits for Cain to take charge. He took a deep breath and stepped into the room.

'Damn it!'

The room was sterile.

Sighing now, Cain looked back over his shoulder.

Perhaps he should've checked the parking lot first. He shrugged. There was nothing he could do about that now. Might as well search the room.

The thief could have left his precious Bowie knife behind in his need to move on.

Cain checked the layout of the room. The recliner was off to his right, but all that remained over there were the denim jacket and the training shoes. On a coffee table lay a yachting magazine with photos of an exclusive club over at Marina Del Rey.

Cain moved over to where a bed and chest of drawers took up the far wall. The bed was unmade. A pair of boxer shorts lay crumpled on the floor at its foot. Cain walked over and kicked the boxers until he could read the label inside. They confirmed the thief's nationality. Definitely an Englishman. Marks and Spencer, the provider of many a conservative Englishman's underpants.

He next tried the drawers in the chest unit. T-shirts were pushed into the top drawer along with more underwear and wadded socks. The next drawer down held a pair of folded sweat pants but nothing else. The final drawer held nothing belonging to the thief, just a stack of well-fingered brochures and menus for local businesses as well as the obligatory 'Welcome' message from the hotel manager that no one ever read.

Cain made a scornful noise in the back of his throat. He cast his gaze round the room. A pay-per-view TV rested on a table next to the recliner, but there was nothing of the thief's sitting on top of it. He turned instead to the built-in closet that made up the wall next to the entrance door.

He stared at the double doors. If the thief had fled the apartment then he would surely have taken his clothing with him? If the cupboard contained his coat and other belongings then it was apparent that he'd be returning some time soon.

Cain approached the closet with a new idea in mind. It made the ideal hiding place. Concealed inside, he could wait for the thief to return and spring out when he was least expecting it. Smiling at his wisdom, he pulled open the doors.

'Ah,' he said.

The thief's coat was still there. But something else assured Cain that the thief hadn't fled as he'd first worried.

The barrel of the gun pointing directly at his face.

22

'You OK, Hunter?'

No. I was . . . numb.

The face on the screen was unquestionably that of my brother. His hair was shorter than I remembered, and there were a couple of new lines at the corners of his eyes. But it was definitely John.

'This can't be right,' I said.

The accompanying story wasn't helping. I couldn't concentrate for glancing at the photograph to remind me that I wasn't reading an unconnected piece of hack journalism. My heart drummed in my chest like a volley of cannon fire. Even the adrenalin rush of battle didn't affect me in this way.

'I don't believe it,' I said for what must have been the umpteenth time. 'There must be some kind of mistake.'

Rink wasn't so certain. He didn't know John the way I did. True, John was a self-centred, lying, cheating, thief who'd run out on his wife and kids. But there was one thing I was certain of: my brother wasn't a depraved psychopathic killer taking the bones of his victims as trophies. Rink was taking things at face value. He tapped the screen to prove his point. 'You can't argue with the forensics, Hunter.'

I shook my head like there was a wasp in my ear. 'No, I can't accept it. Something's wrong here.'

'How do you explain it, then?'

'I don't know, but I'm sure as hell going to try.'

Reading the news release once again didn't calm my racing heart.

The FBI had been searching for the perpetrator of a number of brutal murders that spanned the country from coast to coast. The deaths had reputedly occurred over a three-year period. The FBI was unwilling to divulge the quantity dead at this man's hands, but would confirm that the killer's signature was the removal of skeletal parts. The killer had finally been named as John Telfer, a British subject living in the Little Rock area.

'It's all a load of bollocks,' I told the screen. Rink threw up his hands.

Fair enough, John had been in the country during the three-year period, and had, by Louise Blake's admission, been employed as a delivery driver some of that time. This gave him the opportunity to have visited the places listed. But, according to Louise, John had gone missing less than a month ago. Surely if he'd been involved in these random killings, he'd have left town much sooner?

Experience dictates that a serial killer starts slowly, the interval between his kills narrowing with each attack as he craves further and more depraved satisfaction, until he reaches a point where he can no longer restrain the murderous urge. I suppose, with that in mind, John could have been carrying out the slayings, and it was only now that he'd spiralled out of control and gone off on a final rampage.

Not that I was about to admit that for a second.

I read about a man and woman found murdered in a motel at the fringes of the Mojave Desert, how they'd both had fingers removed as trophies by the maniac the press had dubbed the Harvestman.

A witness related how the murdered couple were seen picking up a stranded motorist the previous morning. The police examination of a vehicle found abandoned a little distance from where the motorist had got his ride showed it was registered to one Sigmund Petoskey of Little Rock, Arkansas. Mr Petoskey had only this evening informed police that a previous employee, John Telfer, had stolen the vehicle. Tests of fingerprints inside the car confirmed that the driver had indeed been John Telfer.

Police and FBI agents were now searching for the location of a yellow Volkswagen Beetle, stolen by the killer after murdering the young couple found dead at the motel. There was no corroborating forensic evidence at the murder scene to tie Telfer to the motel, but on the balance of probabilities, the FBI felt naming him as the chief suspect was justifiable under the circumstances.

'Justifiable under the circumstances?'

'It's a logical assumption when you think about it,' Rink argued. 'John breaks down, he's picked up by these motorists, they go to a motel together. John then kills the couple, steals their car and carries on his way, headed God knows where.'

I wasn't having any of it. 'No way. They say here that the car contained John's fingerprints. Why wouldn't he wipe down the car the way he's supposedly done at the motel?'

Rink shrugged.

'Maybe he didn't think about wiping down the car before he was picked up,' Harvey offered.

'According to the FBI they've been searching for this Harvestman character for the past three years. Never once have they found any evidence of fingerprints before. Isn't it a stretch to think he'd forget to wipe down a vehicle he was driving if he was on a killing spree?'

'Maybe,' Rink offered. 'You know how these crazies are. They get to a point where they don't give a damn any more. They believe that they're indestructible, that the police can't catch them. They start taking chances, dropping the Feds the odd clue. Makes it all the more exciting for them.'

'So why be so meticulous at the motel? If you want to drop the Feds a clue, why not leave your prints at the scene of the crime?' I sat back, crossed my arms over my chest.

'That'd probably be too blatant,' Harvey offered.

'And leaving a car full of evidence isn't?' I asked.

'Not if you never suspect the car and the killings are going to be connected,' Harvey said.

'Yeah,' said Rink. 'It was only by chance that John was seen getting picked up by the couple. Maybe he didn't think the abandoned car would ever be tied to what happened at the motel.'

It was a fair assumption, just not one that I shared. John was no killer. I'd have staked my right hand on it, if only the wager wasn't inappropriate under the circumstances. I rubbed my hands over my face, groaning in a mix of frustration and fatigue.

'What time is it?' I finally asked.

'Late,' Harvey replied.

'Does that mean it'll be morning in England?'

Both Rink and Harvey glanced at each other, made faces. Rink finally turned to me and said, 'It'll be *early* morning. Who are you thinking of calling? Jennifer?'

'I'll have to ring her at some point. But that's not who I was thinking about,' I explained.

'Who then?' Rink asked.

'Raymond Molloy,' I said.

'Detective Inspector Molloy?' Rink asked. 'The cop you did that job for? Why do you want to call him?'

'I need to check up on any similar murders back home. See if there's a pattern. To show if John's involved or not.'

'What if he won't speak to you? It's not as if you're still on the government payroll, Hunter.'

'He'll speak to me. He owes me a favour.'

DI Molloy did indeed owe me a favour. I 'sorted' a little problem for him concerning a pimp who'd tried to extort money from him after Molloy dallied too often with some of his girls. It wasn't a problem his own resources could handle without his indiscretion becoming public knowledge. It took only one visit to the pimp for him to see sense – and to hand over the incriminating evidence of Molloy getting very creative and athletic on a waterbed.

That didn't mean Molloy was pleased to hear from me. I'd saved his professional reputation, but I'd also made it very clear that rough treatment of a woman – paid or not – might just make me forget about helping him next time. He answered my queries curtly. Little more than yes, no and kiss my arse.

'Thanks for nothing,' I said as I placed the phone back in its cradle.

'Well?' Rink asked.

'As ever, Mr Molloy was his charming self.'

'But did he give you what you wanted to know?'

'Yeah,' I said. 'There are no cold investigations into murder victims subject to post-mortem mutilation. Rules out the chance that John was killing before he came here.'

Rink hiked his shoulders. 'Doesn't mean that he's innocent. Just that he didn't start killing until he arrived in the US.'

I shook my head as I got up and paced the length of Harvey's office.

'You don't go from being totally inexperienced to hacking up bodies and taking skeletal remains as trophies. You build up to something like that. There's nothing in John's background that hints that he was even violent. Christ, he was a number one arsehole towards the end, but that was because of the problems he was having. In all that time though, he never lifted his hand to anyone. Not Jennifer, not his kids. He wouldn't even stick up for himself when Shank threatened him. Does that sound like someone who is capable of murdering people?'

'Most murderers are nothing but low-down cowards,' Rink reminded me. 'It doesn't take a brave man to take a woman hostage at knifepoint.'

'I agree,' I said. 'But it takes some balls to take out a man and woman at the same time.'

'Unless he took out the man first,' Harvey said. He peered up at me from his swivel chair. 'Sneaked up behind him and slit his throat or whatever. Then he could have done the woman.'

Rink said, 'Regardless if John's their man or not, the FBI is searching for him. Kind of complicates matters a bit, don't it?'

'Yes and no,' I countered. 'They've more resources than we have. They might be able to find him for us. When he's cleared from their enquiries it could be as simple as going and picking him up.'

'You think they're simply gonna let you walk in and take him home?'

'If he's innocent, yes.'

'And if he's not? If he does turn out to be this punk Harvestman?'

'Then they're welcome to him,' I said. The words felt cold in my mouth.

'You think Jennifer's going to be happy with that?'

'Jennifer isn't going to be happy whatever the outcome,' I told him.

'And what about you, Hunter? What if you don't take him home? How will you feel?'

'How'd you think?' I pondered for a moment. 'What about my family? How'd you think they'll feel when I have to tell them that my brother's locked up in an American prison?'

'Won't be good.'

'No, Rink, it won't.'

Harvey swung his chair side to side. The machinations of thought whirred away behind his furrowed brow. In the end, he looked up at the two of us and said, 'Neither of you boys thought about it yet?'

'Thought about what?' Rink asked.

'The obvious,' Harvey said.

'Obviously we haven't or we'd have mentioned it already.'

Christ, it was like working with Abbott and Costello.

'Thought about what?' I asked.

'When you spoke with Petoskey earlier . . . Why didn't he mention that the FBI had been in contact with him? That they'd already talked to him about his car? That John was a suspect in the biggest hunt since the Unabomber?'

'Son of a bitch was lying to us,' Rink said. 'Unless he got mixed up when he said the CIA had been on his back.'

'Bit of a difference between the Feebies and the Spooks,' Harvey said.

'It doesn't make any sense,' Rink said.

'No, it doesn't,' I said. 'And John as a serial killer doesn't make any sense either.'

'I'm beginning to think that nothin' about this case makes sense,' Rink said.

'Me too,' I admitted. 'Petoskey knows more than he's saying, that's for sure.'

'What about Louise Blake?' Harvey offered. 'You want me to set up another meeting with her?'

'Yes,' I said. 'I'd like to speak with her first thing in the morning.'

'We'll have to be careful, Hunter,' Rink cautioned. 'With the heat on John over this Harvestman thing, you can bet your sweet cheeks that the FBI is staking out her home.'

I nodded, ruminating.

'Harvey, you mentioned spotting someone watching Louise's place . . . you think they were Feds?'

Harvey shook his large head. 'No. They've been watching her since before Telfer became a suspect in these killings.

'Any ideas?'

'All I can say is they're not from round here. They look Mexican or Puerto Rican, could even be Cuban. I spotted two of them, but there could be more; looked like backing singers for the Kings of Mambo. Slick dressed muthas.'

Whatever involvement these two had, it wasn't good.

'We have to find these guys,' I said.

'Shouldn't be too difficult,' Rink said. 'Ain't too many homeboys hanging around Louise's hood.'

'Unless,' Harvey reminded us, 'the FBI are already there and they've beat a hasty retreat.'

Rink sniffed. 'You want to have a run over and see if we can round them up now?'

I glanced around, looking for a clock. Other than *late* I hadn't a clue what time it was. Finally, I said, 'We'll wait for morning. I don't know about you boys but I need a couple of hours' sleep. Jet lag's got to me, I think.'

Rink shook his head sadly.

'Jet lag, my ass. Admit it; old age is finally catching up with you.'

I gave him a weary smile. 'No, I just think it'd be better if we speak to them at a more civilized time.'

'And,' Rink asked, 'in a more civilized manner this time?'

Only thing was, there's no such thing as dealing with scum in a civilized manner.

23

'Son of a bitch.'

Cain sighed as the barrel of the gun pressed to his forehead. Even cultured killers let a little profanity slip now and again.

'You've got that right,' said the thief as he stepped out of the closet. Pressure from the gun made Cain step back. 'Now drop the knife or I'll shoot you where you stand.'

Cain dropped the knife. It landed with a faint thud on the carpet.

'Kick it away,' the thief ordered.

Cain glanced at his bagged feet.

'I might cut myself.'

'I don't give a rat's arse if you cut yourself. Kick it away *now*.'

Cain used the edge of his foot to do so.

'Satisfied?'

The thief grunted.

'Sit on the bed.'

Argument was pointless. He sat down.

'Sit on your hands,' the thief said.

'What for? You have a gun. You think I'm crazy enough to come at you?'

'Humour me.'

Cain sighed expansively. Could things get any worse? Of course they could, the thief could shoot him. He was no killer, but a nervous finger could slip. Cain pushed his hands beneath his thighs.

'If you take your hands out I'll shoot you.'

'Fair enough.'

'You think I won't?'

Cain shrugged. 'I have to give you credit. You got the drop on me.'

'Good. It's best you remember that. Now . . . tell me. Who the fuck are you?'

'You could call me a concerned member of the public.'

'Bollocks.'

'Honestly. I'm simply a member of the public attempting to right a wrong.'

'So you say. Who the hell do you think you are? Dressed up like friggin' Batman?'

Cain tilted his head.

'You don't like my costume?' he asked.

'You look like a reject from a bee-keepers' convention. What's the deal? Your employers can't afford to buy you a ski mask or decent gloves?'

Cain frowned. My employers? Now what's that about?

The thief continued, 'Who's with you?'

'No one.'

'Bollocks! You assholes always hunt in packs. You're like a bunch of fuckin' hyenas.'

'I'm telling you,' Cain said slowly. 'I'm alone, so you

needn't worry. You can stop waving that gun around if you like. I won't make a move against you. I only want what is rightfully mine, then I'll walk out of here and leave you alone.'

The thief made a sound of scorn deep in his chest. 'Do you think I'm a fucking idiot or something?'

'No, like I said, I've a healthy respect for you. You got the drop on me. In fact –' Cain laughed in good humour – 'you ambushed me in exactly the same way I was planning for you.'

The thief sniffed. There was a hint of conceit in his eyes. He was proud of his accomplishment and equally pleased at its acknowledgement. Conceit and vanity, both were weaknesses Cain could exploit.

'You're too good for the likes of me. I should've known better than trying to sneak in here.'

'Don't patronize me,' the thief warned.

'I'm patronizing no one. Just showing my appreciation of your skills.'

'Just cut the shit, will you? Tell me why you're really here?'

'To regain something that belongs to me. I told you.'

'Something that belongs to Hendrickson you mean?'

Hendrickson? Who the heck was Hendrickson?

'I've no idea who you're referring to,' Cain told him. 'I think you're confusing me with someone else.'

'I'm not confusing you with anything but a piece of lying shit.'

'Oh, but you are,' Cain said. 'And if you would only let me take off my hood, you'll see.'

The thief paused. Considering. Then he shook his head.

'No, I don't want you to move.'

'Then you take off my hood. It'll explain every-thing.'

The thief considered a moment longer, then he pointed his gun at Cain's head as he snatched the hood away. His look was testament to the confusion Cain's face brought.

'You're that weirdo from the desert?'

'Got it in one.'

'What the fuck are you doing here?'

'I've told you.'

'You're trying to regain something belonging you. Yeah, you already said. But that's—'

The thief shook his head.

'You want your SUV back. Is that it? You can have it and you're welcome to it. Piece of shit has a flat tyre anyway.'

'I'm not bothered about the car,' Cain said. 'It's something personal to me that I want.'

'If you're after revenge you can forget it. I'm the one holding the gun remember.'

'Not revenge either,' Cain said.

'What the fuck is it then?' The thief's face was a picture of consideration. If only for a second or so. 'Oh, I get it: you want your knife back.'

Cain smiled.

'Well, you're wasting your time. I threw it away. All this has been for nothing.'

Cain shook his head.

'I don't believe that.'

'Believe what you want.'

'Why'd you throw away a perfectly good Bowie knife?'

The thief shrugged. He'd be useless in a game of poker; deceit was painted across his features as plain as a billboard advertising Honest John's quality used cars. 'What good was it to me? I've got a gun; why would I need a knife?'

'If that's the case, why did you take it?'

'Because I wanted to,' the thief said. 'And anyway, I don't need to explain myself to you. You're the one who needs to start giving me answers.'

'There's nothing more to say. You stole my knife, I followed you, and I want it back. End of story.'

'Can't help you.'

Cain shrugged. 'You could at least tell me where you left it so I can go and find it.'

'Who says you're going to walk out of here alive?'

'Oh, come on,' Cain said. 'We both know you're not going to shoot me. If you were any kind of killer you'd have left me for dead out in the Mojave.'

'I did leave you for dead,' the thief said with no conviction. 'I didn't think a soft arse like you would survive more than a few hours.'

Cain laughed. 'Next to a major highway?'

'I made a mistake.'

'You made more than one,' Cain told him. 'Haven't you wondered how I found you so easily?'

The spark in his eye told Cain he was intrigued. Maybe more than intrigued, perhaps a little concerned.

Cain sat back on the bed, resting his shoulders against the wall. The inconspicuous movement had a twofold reason. He was attempting to disarm the thief by appearing relaxed, and simultaneously subtly relieving the pressure from his hands. 'It's obvious that you're on the run from someone. This Hendrickson guy you mentioned. You're afraid of him, right?'

As ebullient as a piece of driftwood, the thief sniffed.

Cain went on, 'When you're trying to lose yourself there're a number of things you don't do. For one, don't use any credit cards or ATMs.'

'I know that.'

'I believe you do,' Cain said. 'Next, don't use an alias that's anything like your real name. For instance, if you're called David Johnston, don't go calling yourself John Davidson. It's too easily spotted.'

'Yeah, I know that too,' the thief snapped.

'Thirdly, never write anything down that'll give away your hiding place.' Cain paused, waiting for the truth to dawn on the thief. 'Or if you do, you make sure it's destroyed.'

The thief nodded. 'I wrote down the telephone number for this shithole.'

'Uh-huh.'

'But how did you find it? I threw the fucking thing out the car window.'

'The wind must have blown it back in.' Cain shrugged his shoulders, imperceptibly loosening his hands. 'Hey, don't be so disappointed. We all make mistakes. I made a mistake by underestimating you, didn't I?'

'Yeah, you did,' the thief reminded him. 'But don't think I'm gonna underestimate you. I know what you're trying to do. Trying to get me to think of you as someone with my best interests at heart. I can smell the bullshit from here, so you may as well give up now.'

Again, Cain shrugged his shoulders. He wasn't at a loss, the way the thief was. He'd just slipped one hand out of its plastic shroud. His palm was slick with perspiration and he gripped the bed sheets beneath him to dry it off.

'I'm only trying to help,' he said.

'Bollocks,' the thief snapped. 'Why would you want to help me?'

'Because I want to.' Cain shook his head. 'Another lesson for you, my friend. Never turn down help, it may save your skin.'

'Two things. First, I'm not your friend. Second, I don't need any lessons from you.'

'You're partly right,' Cain agreed. 'You don't need any lessons from me. You're the one with the gun. I'm the one made the mistake. But you might want to reconsider the friend part.'

'Yeah, right. What the fuck do you take me for?'

'Someone in need of help,' Cain said.

'I don't need or want your help.'

'Shame,' Cain said. 'Because, from where I'm sitting it looks like you need all the help you can get.'

'There you go again, patronizing.'

'Take it as you will. I only want to help.'

'I don't need your help.'

'I beg to differ.'

'You'd be better off begging for your life.'

'Nah,' Cain said. 'Why bother? We've already established that you aren't going to kill me.'

The thief lifted his gun, pointing it directly at Cain's face. 'Maybe not in cold blood. But who knows what I'll do in self-defence?'

Cain smiled up at him. 'Like I've already said, though, I'm not going to make a move on you. So you won't get the opportunity to test your theory.'

The tableau held for the best part of a lifetime. At least a lifetime counted in seconds. Finally, the gun barrel wavered and dropped away from Cain's face.

'So what have we got then? Stalemate?' the thief asked.

'More like an impasse,' Cain offered.

'Same thing isn't it?'

'Depends on your perspective,' Cain said. 'A stalemate's when two enemies are at a deadlock. If we look at our situation as companions with a shared problem then we can resolve it together.'

'Only problem I can think of is how to get rid of you,' the thief said.

'You can't very well call the police, can you?' Cain asked. 'Fair enough, you could say I was an intruder, but what happens when I explain I followed you here because you hijacked my car? Two wrongs don't make a right, my friend.'

The thief pondered a moment.

'I could tie you up and leave you here, though. Then I could make an anonymous call to the cops.'

'They're still going to ask questions. They'll identify you in no time. I take it your fingerprints are all over this room? Not to mention the SUV – which I'll remind you is not going anywhere soon. And, before you consider wiping everything down, may I remind you about the front desk downstairs? Are you positive you didn't leave your fingerprints there when you signed in?'

The thief sniffed again. 'You're assuming the police are after me. I'm not on the run from the cops.'

'You will be if I tell them you kidnapped me.'

The thief watched him and Cain smiled.

'Impasse,' Cain said.

'No,' the thief replied. 'Stalemate.'

'Look,' Cain said. 'We could go on like this all evening. We've both wronged each other. I'll admit that. If you're prepared to let bygones be bygones, so am I.'

'I can't trust you,' the thief said.

'But can I trust you?'

Now it was the thief's turn to smile. Honest John's quality used cars had a new head sales clerk.

Cain closed his eyes. 'If I tell you something, then you're going to have to trust me. I don't want the police involved any more than you do.'

The thief shook his head. 'I don't want to know anything about you.'

Cain opened his eyes slowly. 'You did earlier.'

'That was then. That was when I thought you were one of Hendrickson's men.'

'And you believe now that I'm not? Well, that's a start.'

'Something's bothering me, though,' the thief said. 'You're not here on some stupid quest to recover a stolen knife. What's the real reason?'

'I was telling you the truth,' Cain said. 'I do want my knife back.'

'What the fuck for?'

'Sentimental value,' Cain explained.

'You follow me hundreds of miles, sneak into my room like some psycho from a cheap horror movie, just to get a knife?'

'Yes.'

'That's it?'

'Well,' Cain said. 'If you want the full truth, I did intend making you pay for putting me to the trouble.'

Glancing down at the discarded scaling knife, the thief laughed, shaking his head in disbelief.

'But now you want to help me?'

'Yes,' Cain said. 'Believe it or not, but I like you. You're a man after my own heart.'

'You like me? You're so full of shite I can't believe it,' the thief said.

'Of course, if I'm going to help you, there are conditions attached.'

'I give you back your knives so you can stick them in me first chance you get?'

'Exactly,' Cain agreed with his most disarming grin. 'And one other thing. If I keep your secret, you do the same for me.'

'You don't know my secret.'

'But that's part of the bargain. It's the only way we can work together. You tell me why you're on the run, and I'll do the same. Call it leverage against one another. We have to work together to keep both our secrets. That way we can't afford to betray each other.'

'No, I'm not having any part of it,' the thief said. 'This is all just a trick so that you can escape. You'll drop me in it first chance you get.'

'Not if I tell you my secret first,' Cain offered.

'So what's the big secret you're hiding?' he demanded.

'We have to make a deal first,' Cain said.

'Uh-uh, not until I know what the hell you're talking about,' the thief said.

'OK. But first, you have to show a little faith. Put the gun down.'

'No.'

'At least point it at the floor, then. I don't want it going off by accident.'

'Don't worry, there's nothing you could tell me that'll surprise me that much.'

'Want to bet?' Cain asked.

The thief shrugged, but there was something in Cain's face that made him lower the gun.

'Come on, then,' he said. 'Tell me.'

'OK,' Cain said. 'Drum roll please.'

'Just get on with it.'

'Fine, but it is a little dramatic. You could at least allow me my big moment.'

And then the thief made *the* mistake. He sighed, glancing up at the ceiling as if in search of spiritual guidance. It was the moment Cain had been waiting for. He erupted from the bed in a blur of motion. Cain had hold of the thief's gun hand before he could snatch it up. Then Cain's other hand was at the thief's throat as he snaked a leg round the back of his ankles. In the next instant Cain was standing over him as he sprawled on the floor. And the gun was now pointed at his chest.

'My big secret,' Cain said, with a look of triumph, 'is that I'm a killer, and, unlike you, I'm prepared to prove it.'

24

Once I was pursued through a rainstorm that did little to dampen the fires raging through Grozny. Rebel Chechen soldiers were nipping at my heels. It was unfortunate; I wasn't their enemy. Trouble being I was in the wrong place at the wrong time, on a mission to take out a rogue Russian *Spetsnaz* – Special Forces – soldier who was just a little too fond of prepubescent girls. To infiltrate his position, I'd gone disguised in Russian uniform, and now the Chechens were after my blood. Ironic, you might say. I was there to kill their worst kind of enemy, and yet here I was being hunted like a rabid dog.

I had no intention of returning fire, so I chose to run. They were persistent. To elude my pursuers I lay up beneath the corpse of a bullock. The poor thing had avoided slaughter to feed the invading Russian troops by haphazardly wandering into a pasture sown with landmines. The bullock's folly was my salvation. Even so, it was about the most miserable twenty-eight hours of my life. The stench was bad enough, but the crawling infestation of maggots made it almost un-endurable. Believe me, on that occasion I came close to surrender.

Yes, I've slept in some pretty grim places in my time. But even a bullock's belly can be comfortable when compared to an office chair.

I slept fitfully, waking with the dawn with a stiff neck and the feeling of an intense hangover.

Harvey had invited us back to his split-level ranch out beyond the suburbs, but we'd declined, wanting an early start and knowing that the tranquillity of a remote farmhouse and a soft bed wasn't conducive to an early rise. Struggling out of the chair, I knuckled my lower back, blinked around the small office. Rink was gone. Probably a good job. I wasn't a pretty sight. I scrubbed the balls of my thumbs into my eye sockets, yawned.

I pushed into the washroom, yawning again. Rink was standing by one of the two small sinks, his upper torso bared. The tattoo on his left shoulder was stark even against his tawny flesh. I have an identical tattoo on my shoulder. The tattoos are testament to our time in the joint Special Forces Unit we'd both been part of for all those years. It was a tattoo sported by only a handful of living men, and not one we ever wore when we were active in the field.

Mid-stroke with his razor Rink paused, glancing at me in the mirror. 'Boy, you look like shit this morning.'

'Gee, thanks,' I said. 'I feel like shit, too, if it's any consolation.'

'There's a spare razor if you want to use it?'

I sniffed, ambled over to the sink and picked up the disposable razor. 'Courtesy of Harvey?'

'Yup,' Rink said, taking another stroke at his chin. 'Keeps a stock of them for shaving his head.'

I grimaced at the blade, checking for short bristles caught between the twin blades. 'He hasn't used it already?'

Rink laughed. Didn't answer. I shrugged, ran the blade under the tap. Rink tossed me a can of shaving foam. I nodded my thanks at him, then stopped.

'Problem?' Rink asked with a twinkle in his eye.

'You've shaved off your moustache?'

'Can't hide anything from you, can I, Hunter?'

I grunted. 'That's what makes me a damn good detective.'

Rink slapped me on my shoulder as he brushed past, heading back to the office. I washed and shaved, dried off. When I returned to the office, Rink was on the telephone to Harvey.

'Harvey's over at Louise Blake's place. He wants us over there,' Rink said. 'He just watched a couple of guys go inside. Didn't look like they were selling home insurance.'

'How slick did they look?'

'Like eels in a bucket of sump oil.'

25

John Telfer sat on his hotel recliner and stared at a blank canvas just past the end of his nose. Light from the overhead bulb filtered through the cloth and if he stared closely enough he could make out the minute nuances of texture and pattern of the cotton weave. It was all he'd had to focus his eyes on for the best part of five hours. His other senses hadn't been given many stimuli either, not since the man had forced the bag over his head and tied his hands behind his back with an electric flex torn from a desk lamp.

He sat mute, listening for any telltale sign that his time was finally up, that the maniac was approaching stealthily towards him, knife or gun ready to take his life. But all he heard was the occasional shifting of body weight on the bed across from him. Not for the first time he wondered if his captor had fallen asleep.

He heard a soft grunt. Was it the sound a man makes as he slips into dreamland? Or, more likely, the sound of one coming to a decision. Fearing he was about to find out, he straightened, craning his neck to try to shift the hood enough that he could see beneath it.

'Sit still,' the man commanded from across the room.

'What are you doing?' Telfer asked. His own voice was strained and distant.

'Thinking,' answered the maniac. 'Now please be quiet and allow me to do so.'

Telfer nodded beneath the bag. Show that I'm not a threat, he thought. But he couldn't help asking, 'What're you going to do with me?'

The man snorted in derision. 'What do you think?'

Telfer's shoulders slumped. He felt like asking why didn't he just get on with it then? But that would be suicidal. He didn't want to die, and every second of life he could hold on to, he'd do so with all his might. He kept quiet.

The minutes passed and Telfer went back to scrutinizing the inside of the cloth bag. It was similar to a cinema screen, but a three-dimensional one that wrapped round and out of his peripheral vision. He could almost imagine his life, with all its scant joys and magnitude of woes, played out upon it. Almost was as far as he got. His memories remained scattered and disjointed, and in the end he gave up and simply stared at the blurry cloth, lost in some still, Zen-like place. After a while, he began to rock back and forth.

'Will you please be quiet?'

'Unh?' Telfer asked.

'You're humming again,' said the man. 'That same god-awful tune that has no harmony.'

'I didn't realize,' Telfer said. Below his hood, he blinked slowly. He was unaware that he had been humming a tune.

'It's getting right on my nerves. Maybe I should just cut out your voice box so that you can't do it any more?'

Telfer shook his head. 'I won't do it any more. I'm sorry.'

'Good. Now if you'll just give me a little peace and quiet, I can come to some sort of decision.'

'Are you going to kill me?'

The man sniffed in reply. 'Probably. Only thing is, I haven't decided how yet.'

'Thanks for being so honest.'

He heard the man get up from the bed and walk over. Telfer's whole frame tightened in response. He made a short wailing sound, before something made him stop. He didn't want to die, but if he had to, he didn't intend shrieking like a lost soul. In defiance, he lifted his chin, exposing his throat for a quick slash. Then he blinked at the sudden intrusion of light as the hood was snatched away. The man wasn't holding a knife, but Telfer's own gun was pointed at him.

'I've asked and asked for you to be quiet,' said the man, 'but you just can't seem to keep your mouth shut. So I've decided. What I want you to do is keep right on talking. OK?'

Telfer squinted up at him. 'What do you want me to say?'

The man gave a sigh of exasperation. 'I want you to tell me who you are and how you wound up here. And I want the truth. No lies. Believe me, if you lie to me, I will know. And I will hurt you. Understand?'

'Yeah, I understand.'

'Good. Now go ahead. But don't go raising your voice. We don't want anyone eavesdropping on our conversation, do we?'

Telfer glanced at the wall over his shoulder. Like most hotel walls, these were about as porous as a sponge. He couldn't be sure if anyone was in residence next door, and he couldn't take the chance that their conversation would be overheard. A bit of a strange notion, considering a psycho was holding him at gunpoint. He looked back at the man and saw a faint smile playing about his lips. He seemed amused, as though he knew that Telfer could not shout for help.

'My name isn't Ambrose,' he began.

'I know that. So what is your real name?'

'John.'

'Mmm.'

'Honestly. My name's John Telfer.'

The man nodded as though he was confirming something he already knew.

'I'm from England.'

'We've already established that.' Again the nod of the head, the wistful smile.

'I came here on a work permit,' Telfer said.

'That has since run out?'

It was Telfer's turn to nod. 'I haven't been able to get a full visa yet.'

The man shrugged. 'You and about a couple million others.'

'So,' Telfer said, 'I've had to move on. If I stayed put, I'd have been deported back home.'

The man watched him steadily for more than half-a-dozen heartbeats. Then he moved closer, pushing the gun down the waistband of his trousers. He took out the curved knife and held it below Telfer's nose. Telfer edged back from it, the cords in his neck tightening.

'I told you not to lie.' The man placed the blade so that it lay flat on Telfer's cheek, the point millimetres from his right eye. 'That also includes half-truths. Now I don't doubt that you have no visa, but that's not the reason you're running. I want the full truth. Take this as your last warning.' He turned the blade on its edge and sliced through the flesh. Not a deep cut, just enough to part the outer dermis. Still, blood flowed warm and itching down Telfer's face to pool at the corner of his mouth.

'Jesus . . .' Telfer hissed.

'Hurts like a bitch, doesn't it?' said the madman. 'But you know that's just the start, Johnny boy. No more lies?'

'No more lies,' Telfer echoed.

The man retreated a couple of steps, wiped the tip of the knife on Telfer's knee. He placed the knife back in his trouser pocket. Then the gun was back in his hand and pointed at Telfer's face.

'I've done something wrong,' Telfer began.

The man nodded, sitting on a corner of the coffee table.

'I'm on the run.'

'Also already established. Get on with it.'

Telfer twisted his mouth into a knot. He didn't want the knife coming out again. 'I stole something.'

'Yes,' said the man.

'I'm not a thief,' Telfer began.

'Oh? What about my car? My knife?'

Telfer shook his head. 'OK. But I'm not *normally* a thief.'

'You're not? You do a good impression of one.'

'Until four weeks ago, I never stole a thing in my life.' Telfer stopped. He knew he was lying to himself. There was the small matter of the money his brother Joe gave him to clear off a debt. Money he'd immediately lost on another hopeless bet. In one sense that did make him a thief. Then there was the matter of Jennifer and the kids. He'd stolen their hearts. Broke them into little pieces and snatched a random handful that could never be returned.

'What are you crying for?'

'Uh?'

'You're crying,' the man pointed out. 'Was this theft so dreadful that it brings you to tears?'

Telfer sniffed. 'No. Not the theft.'

'Oh. I see. There's more to it than that? Go on. Tell me.'

'I have a wife and kids.'

The man nodded slowly. A shadow passed behind his features. 'Haven't we all?'

'I wronged them,' Telfer went on. 'I wanted to make things right for them again.'

'Which is why you stole this thing?' The man bent down and pulled Telfer's rucksack from beneath the coffee table. Telfer jolted as if he'd sat on an exposed electrical wire. He watched, eyes intense, as the man fished in his rucksack and pulled out an oblong package wrapped in black tape. He placed it on the coffee table next to him, then he upended the bag and thick wads of cash thudded on to the carpet.

Telfer had no words. He simply sat looking at the taped package. The money was of no immediate interest, though there had to be upwards of $600,000. Likewise, the man paid it scant attention. He nudged the package with the muzzle of the gun. He said, 'I've a feeling I know what this is.'

26

Louise Blake's house was modest when compared to some in her neighbourhood, but a palace compared to the flat John left his wife and kids in back home in Manchester. It was a single-storey clapboard cape, with a porch and adjoining garage. The lawn and shrubs were well tended. A ginger tom cleaned itself on the front stoop.

The scene was the epitome of suburban tranquillity. But that was about to be shattered.

Rink parked the rental a block away and we rushed towards the house. Dawn in Arkansas can be cool at this time of year, but that wasn't why we wore coats. Rink's Mossberg was slung from a harness beneath his armpit. I had my SIG holstered in a shoulder rig.

Harvey was waiting for us, standing in the shadows of a garden shed of a neighbouring property. He gave a low whistle and we angled towards him.

'What kept you guys?' he hissed. 'I thought I was gonna have to start the party without you.'

'What's the deal?' I asked. 'They still inside?'

'Yup. Two of them.' He nodded up the road. 'Third muthafucka in a Chevrolet parked a block over.'

'Same guys as before?'

'Yeah.'

'Any movement?' Rink asked. Our view of Louise's house was partially blocked by a topiary hedge. Between the swooping wings of a shrubby eagle, her kitchen windows reflected the early sunrise. Our vantage didn't offer a view of the front, but as we'd approached, I'd noted that the blinds were drawn.

'Haven't seen anything since they went in. Heard raised voices just before you got here, but it's been quiet since.' Harvey held my gaze. There were the beginnings of a cold sweat on his brow. 'We going in or what?'

'We're going in,' I told him.

'Good,' he said. He pulled a Glock from within his leather coat, racked the slide. 'They've touched the girl, I'm gonna rain some hurt on the muthas.'

'We don't know what we're going in to,' I cautioned him. 'Could get nasty.'

'Believe me, Hunter. If they've hurt her, you can bet your ass things *is* gettin' nasty.'

'Just so long as you know things're going to get hot in there.'

He winked at me. 'Don't you worry. I'm up for it.'

'OK.' That was the prep done. Now all that was left was the hard part.

We fanned out. No preamble, just instinct sending us on our merry way. Harvey headed for Louise's backyard, Rink and me to the front door. Best tactic? In fast and noisy, shoot anything that wasn't wearing lip-gloss.

The ginger cat was wise enough to flee.

From within, I heard something crash to the floor. Before it stopped echoing, I rammed through screen and door and into a scene straight out of *Goodfellas*.

It was one of those snapshot moments where everything is so vividly imprinted on the optic nerves that you don't have to actually look to see even the minutest of details.

It was like this:

Louise Blake on her knees, flowery skirt rucked up round her thighs. Streaked mascara. Smear of blood on her lips.

First Latin male holding her bunched hair and her two hands in one of his. Stretching her up. Exposing her ribs.

Second Latin male lifting a rolled telephone directory for another whack at her side.

These guys weren't CIA or FBI. Even if they were, they still deserved to die.

I fired.

The report of the SIG set the world back in motion.

The man with the impromptu torture device took my nine-mm slug high in his shoulder. The directory spun from his hand, pages fluttering on the breeze of his agony. He staggered away, crashing up against a dresser. Stacked dishes slid and exploded on the floor.

My next step was followed by another shot. We all have imperfections; this bullet missed, drilling a hole in the plaster behind him.

Rink burst into the room all spit and venom. His scattergun remained silent. The second man had the sense to place Louise in the way of Rink's attack.

Shielded by her body he back-pedalled. From his hip he snatched a semi-automatic that flashed blue in the sunlight pushing through a gap in the curtains.

I leapt and rolled, putting a chair between us. It wasn't any protection from a high-velocity round, but that wasn't my purpose. I threw myself into the room to draw the man's attention to me. Away from Louise.

Sure enough, he shot at me. I kissed the carpet and tatters of upholstery sifted down on me. Then I was up and moving. So was Rink. The man was caught in a pincer move and there was only one way out. He spun Louise into Rink's arms. His gun came up. And for one second I feared he would put a bullet in her spine. My response was to fire.

Lucky son of a bitch jerked aside at the exact same moment and my round nicked only a small portion of his ear – instead of a large chunk of skull. The slippery bastard lurched away from me and now Louise and Rink were between us. Encumbered with Louise, he couldn't bring the Mossberg to bear on the man.

The man took three running steps and dived head-long at the nearest window. Drapes tangled him, glass wedged in his deep blue suit, but then he was crashing out into sunshine. I charged across the room, leant through the window. The man vaulted through the topiary hedge we'd so recently stood behind. That suit of his was going to be a mess.

As he bolted through the neighbouring garden in the direction of the street, a pale blue Chevrolet squealed along the asphalt towards him. I got a bead on him. I squeezed. His suit was going to get messier.

A bullet cracked the window frame next to my head. Splinters of wood jabbed into my cheek. Automatically I flinched, the action transposed on to my trigger finger and my bullet went wide.

Only one person could have fired on me. The guy I'd already winged. Move, Hunter, or die, my mind screamed at me. I dropped, spinning on to my haunches. My gun began its rise, but I was again caught in a snapshot moment.

The injured man was coming towards me. His mouth was wide with a silent curse. The muzzle of his handgun was a yawning black hole about to suck the life out of me. John's face flashed through my vision. Eyes sad.

There was a single crack.

Despite myself, I jerked against the pain.

Above me the man swayed. His anger-torn face elongated, eyelids shuddering. I saw a deep red blossom on the breast of his silk shirt. His knees folded and he fell towards me. He was limp as I shoved him aside. Beyond him, Harvey Lucas was like an angel with a Glock in his fist.

'Welcome to the dance,' I said to him.

Harvey stepped forwards. He gripped the shoulder of the man and pulled him over on to his back. Air sighed between the man's lips. A grunt. A spark remained in his eyes. He made a futile attempt at lifting his gun. Futile because Harvey's size twelves ground his wrist into the floor.

'You like hurting girls?' Harvey asked him.

Then he placed a single round in the man's open mouth.

It was a classic hit. One in the heart, one in the head. It's the only way to make sure your enemy is dead.

Harvey stretched out a hand to me. I took it and he hauled me up.

'Thanks, Harvey,' I said. 'I owe you.'

'Was nothin'.' His eyes were a reflection of my own. As a Ranger, he'd known action. But not up close. Eye-to-eye. Harvey now belonged to the exclusive club of which Rink and I held lifetime membership.

27

There was no time for clean up.

We had to move fast.

Priority was getting Louise away from any backlash following the turmoil at her house Harvey was up to the task. He took Louise one way with instructions to meet us in an hour. Rink and I streaked away from the house with the rising wail of sirens approaching.

A telephone call on my part was enough to ensure police action would be in our favour. Walter has that effect. It's the weight a sub-division director of the CIA wields.

We met at the same café as last time. Louise was dressed as before. Still good-looking. Still worn around the edges. But she was different now. She held herself tentatively, like every muscle in her body ached. Fear haunted her eyes.

She was hurting from the beating she'd taken and scared half to death by what she'd witnessed. I sympathized with her, but that wasn't why we were there. The men who'd tortured her did so for a reason. She knew more than she was admitting to.

She'd already swallowed a cup of black coffee and was indicating for more when we walked in. Harvey, playing chaperone, was sitting opposite her in the same booth. He looked as sharp as Samuel L. Jackson did in the remake of *Shaft*.

In contrast, I felt, and probably looked, like someone who'd slept in his clothes and tended to his ablutions in a tiny bowl in a cramped bathroom. Though washed and shaved, my body felt gritty and as rumpled as my shirt. The splinters of wood in my cheek itched like hell.

I sat down in no mood for wasting time.

'So what've you got to tell us, Louise?' I asked.

Louise shrugged, reaching for her coffee. I put my hand over her cup and she snapped her face to mine. There was fear there, but not a little anger. Good. It was the ideal mix.

'You haven't come up with anything that'd help us find John?' I said.

'No,' she said. 'I haven't exactly had the time, considering I was held captive all morning.'

'Have you seen the news?'

From the tight grimace on her face, I could tell that she had.

'Have you spoken to the FBI yet?'

'Yes. They were at my place half the night. Another reason I didn't get round to looking for *clues*.'

'So what did you tell them?'

'Just what I told you.'

'Which is just about nothing,' I said. Sarcasm was heavy in my voice, but I was in no frame of mind to worry about hurting her feelings. In my estimation, she wasn't the sensitive type anyway.

'I don't know anything.'

'Bullshit!' I said a little too loudly. The waitress behind the serving counter shot me a concerned glance. I raised an apologetic hand. The waitress nodded and went on about her business. She knew when to keep her nose out of other people's affairs.

'The men who were in your house,' I said. 'What did you tell them?'

'Nothing,' she said. Her voice was strident. She pawed at the tail of her blouse, hitching it up. Her ribs were red and swollen from repeated whacks of the Yellow Pages. 'Why do you think they were hitting me?'

She did have a point.

She didn't tell them anything. But it didn't mean there was nothing to tell.

Her hands were icy cold when I took them in mine.

'Now, Louise. We're going to start all over again. This time you tell me what you know. OK? You asked me here to help find John. I've travelled thousands of miles to do so. The least you can do is tell me the fucking truth.'

Louise prised her hands free, then sat looking down at the table. I thought I detected a tear at the corner of one eye, but I could have been mistaken. She pushed her hair off her face, maybe surreptitiously wiping away the tear. When she looked up at me, it was with clear defiant eyes.

'John's no killer,' she said. Her voice was like wind frosted with a veneer of ice-crystals.

'I know that,' I told her. 'But he has been up to something illegal. And you know exactly what it is.'

She shook her head, a lock of hair breaking loose and floating across her features. 'If I say anything, he could go to prison.'

I snorted. 'If you say *nothing* he'll be going to prison for a damn sight longer.'

'If he doesn't go to the gas chamber, that is,' Rink added for emphasis.

'He didn't kill anyone,' Louise said. She was adamant, but chose to display her feelings by clawing at the table with her fingernails. 'He was with me when some of the murders took place. I can swear to that!'

'You have to prove it, though,' I pointed out. 'Your solemn word isn't worth shit, Louise. Can you alibi him for when the other deaths happened?'

'That's the problem,' she said. She glanced over at the waitress, checking she wasn't listening. She leant towards me, whispered, 'If I say where he really was, he'll get put in prison anyway.'

I looked at Harvey, then at Rink, for support. Both sat with frowns on their faces. It was helpful having such sage counsel at hand. When I spoke, I'd lost the hard edge to my voice. 'Tell me what he's been up to, Louise. If I'm going to help John, I need to know.'

She chewed at the corner of her lower lip. Any other time it would have looked as sexy as hell. Not now, though. It simply looked like a woman terrified of the consequences of her next words. 'The delivery job,' she said.

'Oh,' I said.

She shook her mane of hair. 'It's not what you think.'

'Not *drugs*?' I asked.

Louise looked like I'd just thrown salt in her face. 'No. Not drugs. Do you think I'd stand by him if he *ever* went near that shit?'

I shrugged. 'Depends on how much you love him.'

Louise snorted, gave me the dead eye.

'Sorry. I don't doubt that you love him.'

'It wasn't drugs,' she stated.

'OK,' I said, relieved. 'So what was he doing?'

Louise picked up her coffee in defiance, drained it, placed the cup back down. A stall while she ordered the words in her mind. 'He was couriering.'

'Couriering what?'

'It wasn't so much what as who he was doing it for.' She glanced around again. 'Like I said, if the police find out, he'll be in deep shit.'

'Let's worry about finding John first,' I said. 'We can worry about the police later.'

Louise jerked her head in acquiescence.

'He stole something. Something big.'

I blinked. 'Something big?'

'That's all I know. He wouldn't say what it was.'

I pushed my hands through my hair, back down over my face, then propped my elbows on the table. 'You've got to be kidding me?' I finally asked. 'Though I knew she wasn't. John had got very good at hiding secrets towards the end.

'Honestly. He wouldn't say, so I didn't ask. Whatever it was, he said he could sell it, to make life better for everyone' she said. As if that made things all right.

I swore under my breath. I knew exactly where this was taking us now, who the fake CIA agents probably were. 'Who was he working for?'

'Sigmund Petoskey,' she said.

'Uh-huh,' I said. 'But who was he collecting from?'

'I don't know for sure. A gangster from up north. Henry-something-or-other.'

'Hendrickson?'

'Yes. That's it.'

'The men who were beating you this morning,' I said. 'They work for Hendrickson, huh?'

'They're the ones that John's running from,' she agreed. She turned her face to the table, began playing with her empty cup.

'Have they been pressuring you for John's whereabouts?' I asked. 'Before this morning, I mean.'

Without answering, she leant back, lifted up her blouse. I saw a toned abdomen. She pulled down the waistband of her skirt and there were three definite cigarette burns peeking above her panty line. 'I'd show you more,' she said, 'Only I don't know you as well as my gynaecologist.'

I bit down on my lip. One thing I was sure about: there was going to be a reckoning with the two who'd escaped us this morning.

'Why didn't you say something, Louise? We could've stopped them from hurting you again.'

Her downcast eyelids trembled. 'I was trying to protect John.'

I looked at Harvey. 'Any word on the street about the two who got away from us?'

'Nothing, Hunter,' he replied. 'You ask me, they heard the news and took off to the Mojave to try an' pick up John's trail. Which, I suggest, is probably your best play, too.'

'I've been thinking the same thing,' Rink told me.

Yeah, me too. But there were still a few loose ends I wanted to clear up first. When we'd raided Petoskey's building, I'd always thought he'd been too ready to talk. Made me wonder if he'd been hiding something else about John. His anger at my brother had never been about a gambling debt. It had all been about this *something big* Louise mentioned. 'Louise, what involvement did John have with Petoskey?'

She scrunched her hair in her hands. 'Petoskey was paying him decent money to drive up country. I don't know where he was going, but he was gone about three days each time. He'd come back with his van loaded with packing crates and he'd drop them off at a warehouse Petoskey owns. That was his only part in it.'

'What happened to the packing crates after they were dropped off?'

'I don't know, John didn't tell me.'

'And you've no idea what was inside them?'

'No.'

Rink asked, 'Any word about what Petoskey is up to, Harvey?'

'Nope,' Harvey said. 'Petoskey's probably only playing the middle man. Likely, whatever's in the crates are getting shipped out of country.'

'Where to?' I asked.

Harvey shrugged. 'Beats me, man.'

I had my suspicions but let them lie for now.

'What do you think?' Rink asked me. 'Petoskey, Russian mob? The Mambo Kings, Cuban? You think there's some kind of communist connection? You know where I'm going with this?'

'Could be. But it's not our concern just now. I'm more interested in finding John before anyone else gets to him.'

Rink exhaled. 'You want me to wait before I call this in?'

'Yeah, Rink. The last thing I want is more involvement from the government. It's bad enough we had to call in a clean-up crew for this morning. As far as Walter's concerned, we offed a hitman. That's all.'

Walter had come through for us on this one. However, just the sniff of foreign involvement would mean the entire weight of the Central Intelligence Agency coming down on us like an avalanche. At best our movements would be severely hindered, at worst we'd be locked in a small dark place for fear we'd jeopardize their mission. Our suspicions had to remain just that.

'Don't worry, Rink. If things do turn out as we suspect, Petoskey will be made to pay when this is over with,' I told him.

Louise watched us with dawning horror. Panic was building in her and I snapped a look at her to stop her raised voice. Nonetheless, she did blurt something out, fortunately in a frantic whisper. 'Are you saying those men at my house could be *terrorists*?'

'No, I'm not saying that,' I told her.

'They could've killed me.'

'Of course,' I said. It was pointless lying. If the beating didn't finally get what they wanted from her, who knows what they would have done next? Louise's face crumpled in despair.

I felt shitty. After all she'd been through, I wasn't coming across as the sympathetic type. Sure, she'd been lying . . . at first. But what woman wouldn't do that to protect her man? It was probably the ideal time to give her a little hope.

'Now that they've got a lead on John, I guarantee you won't see them again,' I said.

'But what if they don't find John? Won't they come back?'

'They won't,' I promised. Not if I stopped them first.

Louise was growing despondent once more. She snatched a lock of hair into the corner of her mouth and began gnawing on it.

'At least we've got a starting point,' I said. 'We'll leave for Los Angeles this afternoon, try and pick up John's trail from there.'

'Why Los Angeles?' she asked.

'It's obvious that John was headed west. His car was found abandoned only a few hours from Los Angeles; I'm betting that's where he is now.'

'Some big-time players out on the west coast,' Rink put in. 'You think John's out there looking for a buyer?'

'Yeah,' I agreed.

If John wasn't the killer of those people at the motel, something had suddenly become very obvious to me. The real killer and John had crossed paths. Maybe John was already dead, buried somewhere out in the Mojave

Desert. In all likelihood, the killer now had what John stole, which probably meant he'd be looking for a buyer for it. That meant the killer was probably in the LA area trying to hook up with one of these big-time players. Whatever this *something big* turned out to be, it was a curse; he was welcome to the damned thing. But if he had killed John, then he'd just made himself one terrible enemy.

28

'Ken Bianchi and Angelo Buono,' Cain whispered to himself.

As far as serial killers go, their names aren't easily recalled. Not like Bundy or Gacy. Not until their singular epithet is apparent: the Hillside Strangler. Now that's a name that's familiar to every American citizen over the age of puberty.

Cousins Bianchi and Buono terrorized the western states in the 1970s. Raping and killing in unison, the law only caught up with them after Bianchi's lust became too great. Without the aid of his partner in crime, he'd botched the abduction of two women, and gone and got the Hillside Strangler caught.

It isn't often that killers work in tandem. As far as Cain was concerned, they were the only true serial killer combo to do so. Which was why he'd been toying with the notion that the world was overdue another terrible twosome.

The thought hadn't appealed for long. For a number of reasons. John Telfer didn't have the gall to pull the trigger when he'd had the opportunity. He was no killer. He was a thief who deserved only to be punished.

But mainly: why the hell should John *freaking* Telfer share any of his glory?

No, any thought of a fledgling partnership was out the window. Telfer had to die. Perhaps he'd even be Cain's magnum opus, his announcement to the world. The death that would make him famous.

However, there was still a task or two to be completed before Cain allowed himself the satisfaction of flaying the hide from Telfer's thieving hands. First off there was the subject of what he'd discovered in Telfer's backpack.

Last night's denouement had come as a surprise even to him.

'I've a feeling I know what this is,' Cain had said.

Telfer sighed. 'They're plates.'

'Litho plates? For printing counterfeit money?'

Telfer sighed again.

Cain had slowly bent down and picked up one of the wads. As Telfer eyed him expectantly, he peeled one of the bills loose and held it up to the light fitting above his head. The watermark was there.

'Not bad,' Cain said. 'Though if you look closely, there's a little merging of the whorls along the edge. It wouldn't pass the scrutiny of a Treasury agent.' He'd been lost momentarily as he studied the note, turning it over in his hand. The gun was no longer pointed at Telfer and for a split-second the opportunity was there for Telfer to leap at him. Even with his hands bound, he possibly could have wrenched the gun free, turned the tables on his captor. But the moment had passed. 'This paper stock. How did you get it?'

'I don't know. I had nothing to do with the printing of the money. I was just a courier.'

Cain had nodded to himself. 'Apparently the paper's the hardest to come by. It's all produced up at a mill in Massachusetts. Under guard of the US Treasury Department, no less. It's some sort of high-grade cotton and linen mix, extremely hard to duplicate. And see these little blue and red lines; they're rayon fibres mixed in to make the paper even more difficult to fake. Most counterfeit bills don't have these. Oh, wait, I see it now.' He'd held the note very close to his face. 'The security marks aren't actually in the weave of the paper. They've been added at the printing stage. Still, it's a very good copy.'

Telfer looked at him as though he was mad – which in effect he probably was.

Cain had laughed to himself. 'I've a keen eye for detail, that's all.'

'You sound like you know what you're talking about.'

Cain waved down the flattery.

'I just know these kind of things.' He'd laughed in a self-conscious manner totally out of character. 'I suppose you could say I'm well read. A mine of useless information, huh?'

'Or you do work for the people who are after me?' Telfer had asked. He made it sound as though he was joking, but the idea had obviously invaded his thoughts.

Cain had twisted his mouth. 'No. I work alone.'

By the look in his eyes, Telfer had believed him. But it didn't make his predicament any less dangerous.

Cain had dropped the bill on the coffee table, reached for the litho plates. 'These can't be originals?'

'I don't suppose they are,' Telfer replied. 'But they're still worth decent money to the right person.'

Cain gave him a shallow smile. 'Are you attempting to bribe me, Mr Telfer?'

'If it's going to save my life, yes.'

Cain's smile had turned into a full grin. 'At last! We're being fully truthful now. That's more like it.' He'd pulled the tape free from the stack of four litho plates, and held one of them up. 'They're not real plates. They've been etched from a copy after a hundred-dollar bill has been scanned into a computer. That's why there's no clarity on the scrollwork. Still, like you say, they'll be worth good money to the right buyer.'

Telfer had grinned along with him. 'So what do you say we make a deal? My life for the plates?'

'Nah,' Cain had said, dropping the litho on the table. 'It's not as simple as that. Why would I let you go when I can kill you and then take the plates for myself?'

Telfer inclined his chin. 'You seem to know a lot about the process of making counterfeit notes. Do you also know who is in the printing game? Who'd be prepared to buy the litho plates from you?'

Seesawing his head, Cain had said, 'Well, I have to admit . . . You've got me there.'

'I've already set up a deal. I'm supposed to meet the buyer tomorrow.'

Cain had snorted.

'It's the truth. Why would I lie to you?'

'Who are you meeting with?'

Telfer shook his head. 'Christ, man. Give me a little credibility will you? I'm trying to save my life here. You can't expect me to tell you who I intend selling the plates to?'

'I could cut the name out of your throat,' Cain had pointed out.

'Yes, you could. But it wouldn't do you any good. My buyer won't deal with anyone but me. He's too afraid that the FBI is on to him to deal with anyone he doesn't know. If I don't show at the meet, he won't show.'

'Touché.'

'So that means that you need to keep me alive, or the deal will be off.'

'How much money are we talking about here?'

Telfer had exhaled. Indicating the pile of money, he said, 'About two hundred grand for that.' He'd paused. 'Maybe half a million for the plates.'

Cain raised an eyebrow. 'Seven hundred thousand?'

'Three-fifty apiece.'

Cain had shook his head. 'Seven hundred for me. You get to stay alive.'

The corners of Telfer's mouth had turned down.

'That's the deal,' Cain had told him. 'All or nothing.'

'OK,' Telfer had said after a beat. For the first time in hours, he appeared to have relaxed into the seat. 'You've got yourself a deal.'

Cain smiled as well, restacked the litho plates. 'Yes,' he'd said. But his voice had held all the promise of a serpent.

It had been a long night. And he'd done a lot of thinking.

He wasn't a greedy man. Sure, if he wanted something he just took it as his own. Appropriated the chattels of his victims as if they were the spoils of war. He'd never found it difficult to finance his lifestyle before, but he had to admit that the thought of a cool seven hundred thousand bucks rang sweet even to his ears. Especially when enunciated slowly.

Seven. Hundred. Thousand. Dollars.

Undeniably, the subject of the money was a distraction. He'd pondered taking what was already available and making do, but the thought that the bogus money could spell his downfall made him hold back. Why risk blowing his cover passing a fake note at a goddamn McDonalds when he could have as much of the real thing as he'd ever require?

Not only that, but the thought of playing Telfer like a pawn appealed to his sense of the grandiose. He'd allow Telfer to touch the money, hold it in his hands, let him sniff the stench of riches beyond his dreams, before finally snatching it away from him. That would be just punishment for the trouble he'd put Cain to.

Then, of course, it would be a pleasant trip out into the desert for the final reckoning.

Yes, the subject of the money was a distraction. But so was what he'd just witnessed on the motel's TV set. He wasn't one for watching the television. Never had been. The only reason he'd switched it on was to mask their conversation from guests in the adjacent rooms.

He wasn't averse to seeing his handiwork on the screen. But there was a major difference this time. He had a good mind to telephone the freaking FBI and put them right about a thing or two, particularly the point regarding Telfer's part in the slaying of the two drifters he'd appropriated the VW from. Why the hell should Telfer get any of the glory from that?

'Don't you be getting any big ideas,' he said. 'We both know who killed those two wasters, and before long *everyone* will know the truth. How anyone could even think you were responsible beggars belief.'

He turned from the TV to observe the trussed form lying on the recliner. Telfer hadn't the faintest idea what he was referring to. He was asleep, fatigue finally overcoming his fear and discomfort. Cain raised an eyebrow. He listened to Telfer's breathing patterns. Not feigning then? Definitely asleep.

Cain made a noise deep in his throat, the call of a quizzical owl. He switched off the TV. Then he walked over to the recliner and nudged Telfer awake with his foot. It was Telfer's turn to make owl noises, this one startled and ready to take flight.

'Chill out,' Cain told him, 'I'm not going to harm you.'

Stiffly, Telfer squirmed up to a sitting position. It wasn't an easy task with both his hands and feet bound. 'What's going on?'

'Almost time to go,' Cain told him.

Telfer sucked in a couple of breaths, exhaled long and loud. Then he rocked forwards so that he was on

Matt Hilton

the edge of the recliner. He nodded at his bonds. 'You planning on carrying me out of here?'

'No,' Cain said, 'I'm going to allow you to walk. But remember that I'll be holding a gun. Shout or try to run and I'll kill you. I don't care how many people are around, I'll do it. The truth – as they say – will out.'

Telfer gave him an odd look. He had no idea what Cain was referring to. Cain smiled to himself. Let him wonder. Let him fear.

Cain indicated Telfer's feet. 'I'll cut you loose in a moment. Your hands'll stay tied until it's time to leave.'

'OK.'

'If you want to use the bathroom I'll let you.'

'That's good of you,' Telfer grunted.

'Don't want you thinking I'm a total bastard.'

'The thought never crossed my mind,' Telfer said. He watched Cain. The ghost of a smile played across Cain's lips.

'What've you got in your fridge? Anything cold to drink?' Cain asked.

'Nothing. Unless you like milk.'

Cain made a face. Then hopefully, 'Chocolate milk?'

'Cow's milk.'

Again the face.

'There's always tap water,' Telfer offered.

'I'll pass,' Cain said.

'You know, I think I do need to go to the toilet.'

Cain tsk'd. 'Better only be a number one. I refuse to wipe your ass for you.'

'You could always loosen my hands,' Telfer suggested with a smile.

'Your hands stay tied 'til I'm good and ready.'

Telfer shrugged. 'Do you want to unzip me?'

'Forget about it,' Cain said deep in his throat. 'You can go just before we leave.'

Telfer gave him a wink and a jerk of his head.

'What are you so goddamn happy about?' Cain demanded.

'It's good to be alive,' Telfer said.

'Yeah,' Cain said. 'Keep that thought in mind and we'll do just fine.' He glanced at his wristwatch. 'OK, time to cut these ropes. And no Bruce Lee stuff. You try to kick me and I'll shoot your feet off.'

If Telfer could have raised his palms, he would have. 'I thought we'd made a deal. I'm not going to try to escape. I've promised you I'll do the deal for the litho plates. You've promised that you'll let me live. I'm happy with that.'

'I'll only be happy when you're out of my frigging hair,' Cain grunted.

'You could always let me go now,' Telfer offered.

Cain snorted. There was something disarming in John Telfer that appealed to him, something that made him smile. Maybe killing him was a little extreme? No, it was just. An eye for an eye. Telfer had stolen his Bowie knife and thrown it away. It would be fitting that a knife would be used to punish him in turn.

Cain made Telfer push out both feet. Then, in a swift draw that would have shamed a gunslinger, he brought out the scaling knife and swiped down in a shallow arc. The cord from the Venetian blinds he'd used to tie Telfer's ankles gave with a twang and

Telfer's legs sprang open of their own volition. Before Telfer could control his wayward feet the knife was back in Cain's waistband. Cain gave him a tight smile. The quick draw display was for more than the purpose of loosening his prisoner's legs; it was a show of his skill with a blade. Something for Telfer to dwell on while they travelled together.

'So, how're we going to do this?' Telfer asked.

'We're going to go out to my car. I'll have the gun. Simple as that.'

'Do I get to put my shoes back on?'

'Obviously,' Cain said.

'What about my rucksack?'

'I'll carry it.'

'My spare clothes?'

'Leave them,' Cain said. Again, he smiled, but this time there was a cold edge to it. 'If you wish, you can always come back for them afterwards.'

Telfer sat back, lips pursed. 'Do you want to pass me my shoes or can I fetch them myself?'

'Here,' Cain said, slinging his shoes to him. Telfer scrunched his feet in without the benefit of untying the laces. 'Ready?'

Telfer squeezed out a smile of affirmation.

Cain came forward. He held the gun in his left hand, and again drew the scaling knife with his right. This time the motion was languid. He pressed the gun to Telfer's forehead. 'Easy now,' he warned.

Telfer didn't move, apart from to raise his bound wrists. Cain snicked apart the electrical cord. Telfer dropped his hands but continued to work his wrists in small circles, attempting to get the blood flowing once again. Cain backed away.

'Now,' Cain said. 'We do this nice and easy. We go out the room and down the back stairs. You'll lead the way. When you get to the ground floor, go to the right, go round to the parking lot. When we get there, I'll tell you which my car is. OK?'

'Got it,' Telfer confirmed.

'And remember, try to alert anyone . . .'

'And you shoot me.'

'Got it,' Cain mimicked.

Telfer rocked his weight back in the recliner, using the coiling motion to bring himself to his feet. As he came up his right hand remained behind him, hidden momentarily from Cain's view.

Cain was ready for Telfer making a break for freedom, but not at that instant. Not when the stalemate still presented itself. Not while Cain still held the weapons. He was totally unprepared for Telfer whipping his arm towards him, the blade of his very own Bowie knife scything the air before him.

'Whoa!' Cain yelped, taking a step back. His reaction wasn't to bring up his gun, but to snatch up his scaling knife. If Telfer wanted to, he could have sprung in close and gutted him in one motion. But, to Cain's dazed surprise, Telfer never followed through. Instead, with a smile on his face, he twirled the knife over and presented the handle to Cain.

'What the hell?' Cain demanded.

Telfer said, 'This the knife you were so concerned about?'

Cain gaped at Telfer for the best part of a minute. Telfer returned his stare, watching him steadily. Finally, Cain gave his head a little shake, seemed to come out of his daydream. 'So you didn't toss it away? You had it all along?'

'Down the back of the recliner,' Telfer said. 'A trick I learnt back home. You never knew when you'd get a visitor with less than your best interests at heart. Not that I ever needed to pull a knife before, but I was always prepared. Just in case.'

'You could've killed me. You could've escaped.' Cain appeared to be mildly impressed. 'Why didn't you?'

'I'm not a killer,' Telfer said.

Cain stared at him.

Telfer sniffed. 'Just call it an act of faith, OK?'

Cain's eyebrows shot heavenwards.

'I've given you back your knife.' Telfer paused. 'All I ask is that you stay true to your word.'

Cain bobbed his head in answer. Slowly he reinserted the scaling knife in his waistband, then tentatively reached for the hilt of the Bowie.

Taking it, he withdrew it slowly from Telfer's grasp. 'I've done you an injustice, after all. Perhaps you're more dangerous than I thought. Maybe I should kill you now and get it over with, huh?'

In answer, Telfer raised his shoulders. 'If that's the way it's going to be, there's nothing I can do about it. Not now *I've given you back your knife.*'

His head quirked to one side, Cain beamed a smile. 'You know something? For a thief, I think I'm beginning to like you, John. Maybe I will let you live after all.'

'Just maybe?'

It was Cain's turn to shrug. 'Let's not attempt to fool each other John. We're both the same in many respects. One thing is obvious: we're both able to lie convincingly. If I told you that I promise not to kill you, would you believe me? Perhaps it's best I simply say "maybe". At least then you can't be sure. Does that not give you a modicum of hope?'

Telfer shook his head in bemusement.

'When you put it that way, I suppose it does. Can I ask you one thing before we leave?'

Cain raised his chin.

'Can't we do this in a civilized manner? Without the threat of a gun constantly pointed at me?'

Cain agreed. 'As an act of faith?'

'Precisely.'

'Lead on, then, John. You know the way.'

Telfer turned towards the vestibule. Cain slipped the gun into his trouser pocket and followed, the Bowie held like a baby across his palms.

'Where are we going anyway?' Cain asked.

'Marina Del Rey,' Telfer said over his shoulder.

Cain glanced down at the magazine spread out on the coffee table. All the beautiful yachts. He snorted out a laugh. 'I should have known.'

29

We walked out of LAX into brilliant sunshine tinged with smog.

'Welcome to Los Angeles,' Rink said.

I clamped down on the urge to cough.

Rink laughed to himself. 'You get used to it, Hunter. Just try not to breathe for the next week or so and you'll be fine.'

We hailed a cab and followed Route 405 north. Off to our left stretched the vastness of the Pacific Ocean. We only saw snatches of the blue expanse, but I was constantly aware of it: something about the sky above the water, like it hovered over a magnificent precipice. Signposts over the highway indicated Marina Del Rey, Venice Beach, Santa Monica, all off towards the sea. All places I'd have loved to visit given the opportunity.

To our right, Hollywood and Beverly Hills beckoned, but we continued north past the Getty Center until we hit the 101, then joined the flow of traffic heading east. We passed Universal Studios and, like most, I craned my neck hoping to see someone famous. Then we were fast approaching Pasadena where Rink had set us up a place to stay.

We had to speak to a house manager, something like a low-rent concierge, who had an apartment on the lower floor of the accommodation block we were to stay in. He gave Rink a key card and directed us to our apartment with gesticulations of the ham sandwich he held in his hand.

When we found our apartment, it turned out to be bigger than you'd expect for the fee we paid. We chose a bedroom apiece then convened in the lounge area. It was clean and roomy, and the air conditioning was a blessing after the sweltering drive. Still, neither of us wanted to remain cooped up here too long.

'Want to hit the shower, then go out and get a bite to eat?' Rink offered.

'Sounds like a plan,' I admitted. 'But I think the shower can wait, my stomach thinks my throat's cut.'

'What do you want?' Rink asked. 'Silver service or burger an' fries?'

'Burger and fries all the way, big guy,' I said.

'I know just the place,' Rink said.

He took me to a diner with the unlikely sobriquet of Spicy Johnny's – I couldn't stop myself laughing, the name conjuring the image of the kind of advert you see emblazoned across those coin-operated machines in men's public toilets back home in England. I have to admit though, Spicy Johnny flipped a mean burger and his Caesar salad topped off with breaded onion rings and mayonnaise was to die for. A side plate of Cajun spiced potato wedges and a huge banana shake finished me off.

Back in our rooms, we fell asleep almost instantly. Even my worry for John was shoved to one side for the more urgent need for quality rest. I slept for the best part of two hours, waking when the sun was at its zenith and its most intense.

My body was lathered in perspiration and I could put off my shower no longer. Coming out of the stall feeling almost human again, I could hear Rink pottering about in his own room. Vacating the bathroom, I went into the lounge, popped a bottle of mineral water I found in the fridge and sat back on a comfy chair in front of the TV. The news was on, so I let it play.

When Rink was finished sprucing himself up, he joined me in the lounge. We'd already discussed local contacts and Rink was going to set us up with an LAPD officer named Cheryl Barker to get a feel for the local buzz. Before that could be done there were still a few things left over from Little Rock that I wanted to lay to rest.

'I feel a bit of a shit leaving Harvey to pick up the pieces we left behind.'

'Harve'll be fine,' Rink assured me. 'If we hadn't allowed him to do something for us, it'd have hurt his feelings. He's a sensitive guy, you know.'

I gave a laugh. To look at him, Harvey looked impregnable. You would blunt an axe trying to mark his shiny dome. But Rink was right; I'd seen Harvey's vulnerability when he had to take a step back from the assault we made on Sigmund Petoskey. It didn't rest easy with him having to sit on his haunches while the rest of us went out into the thick of it.

Then there was the other side.

The cool way he'd shot the hitman in the mouth.

'He'll get Louise Blake to a safe place,' Rink went on. 'Don't worry about that.'

'As long as nothing happens to them before he gets the opportunity,' I said.

'What's goin' to happen? You ask me, the homeboys who were putting the heat on Louise are out this way now. I don't think Harve's got anythin' to worry about.'

'You think the FBI is going to let Louise go? She's a direct link to John; they'll be watching in case he tries to make contact.'

'Harvey's good. He'll get her out safely. Whether the FBI like it or not.'

I took Rink's word for it. He knew Harvey. Rink told me prior to my first meeting with Harvey that he was a good soldier. Now I'd witnessed his skills at first hand, and I'd no doubt that Rink knew what he was talking about.

'So what do you make of what Petoskey told us?' I asked.

Rink shrugged, made a clucking noise with his tongue. 'All bullshit.'

'In particular what he said about CIA agents?'

'Bullshit. He knew full well who those other guys were. He was just spinning us a line because he thought we were Federal agents.'

'You remember the name someone shouted when we were in the building?'

'Yeah. Hendrickson's men are here,' he said. 'They were shouting like we were from a rival gang.'

'Yes. A *rival* gang. I think Hendrickson sent them to mess with Petoskey. I get the feeling Petoskey and

Hendrickson aren't on good terms any more. Shit, we went in there and blasted the hell out of some of his guys, shot up his building, probably ruined his evening. But, he hasn't made one word of complaint to the police. If he believed that we were government agents, don't you think there'd have been a massive lawsuit lodged by now?'

'Unless he knew we weren't with the CIA and was only playing out a scenario for the benefit of his guests.'

'Nah, too slim.' I mulled it over a little longer. 'Could be he thought we were sent by Hendrickson, and he mentioned the CIA to put the frighteners on us. You know, like a subtle threat?'

'Unless these Latinos *are* government agents?'

'They're not CIA. Walter confirmed that.'

'He could've been lying.'

'No, Rink. He wouldn't've given me approval to shoot to kill if they were any of his men.'

'So why all the bull from Petoskey about the CIA?'

Back to square one.

'We can only wait and see,' I said.

30

The sun was warm on Cain's face. Above him, a yellow-and-white-striped awning dotted with dried insect carapaces flapped on a lazy breeze. He was quite at home sitting outside a café overlooking the boardwalk of a private mooring point in Marina Del Rey. He could see himself living in a place just like this. Then again, even seven hundred grand wouldn't buy him a tool shed here.

Beyond a six-foot wall of preformed concrete was a yacht valued at more than five million bucks. In keeping with the area, even the concrete wasn't tacky. For its entire length, there was a bright mural lovingly painted in azure, emerald, and stark, brilliant white. Beyond it, he could hear the lapping of the water, the groan and heave of boats as they susurrated against the pilings of the dock. Gulls wheeled above the masts that heaved like a forest in a gentle breeze.

Against his better judgement, Cain had allowed Telfer to enter the private harbour alone. Before agreeing, he'd first made guarantees that the only exit – apart from the open sea – was through the wrought-iron gate thirty metres to his right. It was of course the only way that the deal could be struck. Telfer had argued that his buyer would panic if he saw a stranger tailing him on to the boat. The likely assumption would be that Telfer had set him up and one of two things would happen. He'd refuse to negotiate. Or worse, he'd have Telfer and Cain sunk to the bottom of the sea following the next high tide.

Cain had to agree. Though he wasn't happy about relinquishing either the bag of goodies or Telfer, had he walked aboard the yacht with a gun trained on Telfer, he could say goodbye to the promised riches and to the reckoning he still planned for the thief.

A waitress brought him an espresso coffee in a cup hardly bigger than a thimble. He drank it in one gulp and ordered a second. The woman gave him a look that he greeted with a sour expression of his own. She went off to fetch another.

'Make it a double,' Cain called after her, as though ordering whisky at a Wild West saloon.

When she returned, she placed the cup – more like a teacup this time – down on his table, then hurried off before he could tie up any more of her precious time. Service, it appeared, was not customary for the trash who came to ogle the rich dudes' yachts.

Fifteen minutes passed without any activity. Cain was sure that Telfer hadn't slipped away undetected, unless he'd snorkelled his way to freedom beneath the waves.

Still, he was beginning to grow uncomfortable.

Fifteen minutes wasn't a long time for someone to make a deal for seven hundred thousand, but it was fifteen minutes too long for Cain. Scenarios were beginning to play out in his mind and he knew he wouldn't last another five minutes. His inner pessimist was working overtime.

What if Telfer had done the deal, but then appealed to his business partners to help him escape? What if they'd already called the cops, telling them that a self-confessed killer was sitting outside, sipping bitter coffee on the harbourside? What if, even now, plain-clothed detectives were creeping up on him, disguised as rich men in Armani suits?

He surreptitiously scanned the boardwalk. Could there be police posing as tourists who, like him, feigned interest in the elegant yachts? Are they moving on me now? he wondered.

It was enough to make him squirm. Cain didn't like squirming. He made others squirm.

Enough is enough, he told himself.

Telfer had too much to lose if the police became involved. His lifespan would be back in his own hands, and likely he would get the money, but chances were that the police would be on to him and his business associates as thick as stink on a mangy goat.

Knowing the way a thief's mind worked, Cain believed that Telfer would do the deal, then return to him with the hope of escaping and relieving him of the money when a healthier opportunity presented itself. If the tables were turned, that's exactly what he'd do. So, he could only wait, bide his time, take charge again when Telfer returned with the money.

He might as well enjoy the sunshine. And his coffee.

Then he saw the two men.

They were both dark, with wavy hair and thin moustaches. Both wore silk suits and tooled leather loafers – without socks. They were alike in so many ways that they could be brothers. The only thing that differentiated them was that the slightly taller of the two wore a gauze dressing on one ear. The bandage stuck out like a blind cobbler's thumb.

Something else: they carried guns. Not out in the open, but pushed down the backs of their trousers. He could see the telltale bulge in their lower backs as they sauntered past. He couldn't make out what they were saying; not only were they conversing in hushed tones but they were speaking in Spanish or Portuguese. Cain could speak five languages, but – unfortunately – none of them was of Mediterranean origin.

Ordinarily the men's presence wouldn't have alarmed him. It wouldn't be unusual for armed security to prowl the harbourside. But there was something about these men that jangled his inner alarms. Their furtive approach to the gate was untoward, as was how they glanced up at the rigging of the yacht Telfer had boarded and nodded at each other in affirmation. Then there was the way they sauntered along while unconsciously glancing over their shoulders every couple of steps. They were so obviously trying to remain inconspicuous that their presence here screamed out at high volume.

Cain sniffed. He couldn't sit on his thumbs any longer. He rattled a handful of coins down on to the table and stood up, gulping the remains of his espresso. Then, after he'd stretched and rolled his neck, he fell into step behind the two men. Unlike them, he stayed near to the entrances of the cafés and boutiques lining the harbour, using his cover as a browsing tourist to mask his interest in the pair. Undetected, he got to within five meters of them.

They still conversed in whispers, but one word stood out. He heard it mentioned twice. A name: Telfer. And he knew that the men Telfer was running from had finally caught up with him.

Oh, such a dilemma. But, oh, what a challenge. Cain smiled to himself, slipped his hands into his pockets and caressed his keepsakes. Pretty soon, he decided, more bones would be joining his collection.

Happy with the thought, he watched as the two men approached the gate and hailed the security guard sitting in a booth on the other side. The guard walked over, looking ridiculous in pale blue shirt, knee-length Bermuda shorts and deck shoes, with a peaked cap perched jauntily above his sun-weathered face.

One of the men flashed something at the guard. Just a brief glimpse, but Cain gathered the impression of a badge in a leather wallet. The guard looked impressed, and not a little excitable. He nodded vigorously as he bent to unlatch the gate. All that was missing was a tug of the forelock.

Cain's smile grew sour. Anyone worth their salt could get hold of fake credentials; the guard needed a good kick in the ass for not paying more attention to the man's ID badge. Likely, he was a frustrated wannabe cop who couldn't help but worship those who carried the badge for real. His fawning was almost sickening.

The two Latinos were admitted to the inner compound. One of them rewarded the guard with a pat on the shoulder and the guard looked like he was ready to salute. He was still standing with a hand on the open gate, watching the two men walk along the pier towards the moored boats, when Cain stepped up behind him.

'Excuse me,' Cain said, and the guard turned to him with the light of a sycophant bright in his face.

'Yes, sir, how may I help you?'

'I'm Special Agent Kennedy. FBI. First off, you can keep your voice down,' Cain said. He used a confidential tone as if about to reward the man with a message of great importance. Hooked, the guard looked at him expectantly. Cain leant in close and whispered, 'This is a matter of extreme sensitivity.'

Cain steered the guard back towards his booth. 'Can we speak inside?'

Caught up in the mystery of the moment, the guard even opened the door and allowed Cain to press inside the booth with him. The enclosed space was redolent with the locker-room smell of sweat.

The guard was jammed up against the single chair, almost buckling at the knees. He didn't object, as if he accepted this invasion of his personal space as a factor of the clandestine encounter.

Cain asked, 'The two men who just entered, what did they say to you?'

'They said they were with the government,' the guard answered quickly. 'Agents Ramos and Esquerra.

They wanted to know the location of Mr Carson's boat. Why do you ask, sir?'

'Because I'm a real government agent and those two aren't,' Cain said. He tipped a nod towards Carson's boat.

'You mean their badges were fake? Damn.'

'As fake as Pamela Anderson's breasts,' Cain told him.

The guard appeared stunned at Cain's choice of words. 'I didn't know,' he finally said, as though in apology. Cain couldn't decide if he meant the men's badges or Pammy's main assets, but he let the notion pass without smiling. He said, 'They're a pair of international drug traffickers, and I'm about to bust them wide open.'

'You are? All alone? Don't you have back-up or something?'

Cain shook his head in mock remorse. 'Me and my partner got separated. I don't even have my goddamn walkie-talkie with me to get in touch with him. These guys are real good. We've been after them for months. When I spotted them, I had no option but to follow them.'

The guard was nodding along with each new nugget Cain fed him. 'You want me to phone for help?'

'I'd appreciate it if you would,' Cain said.

'No problem,' said the guard as he turned to sit in his chair. As he picked up the receiver and brought it to his ear, Cain was happy that the guard was sufficiently distracted. Plus, sitting in the chair, he was out of sight of any passers-by. Pretending to spy out the window at the receding men, Cain leant over him. He pulled out his scaling knife.

'Who should I call?' the guard asked. 'The FBI?'

'Nine-one-one will do,' Cain told him. 'Maybe you'd best call for an ambulance.'

The guard didn't detect the change in tone, nor the loaded statement. In fact, he didn't detect anything more than the pressure of Cain's hand on his shoulder. He glanced up and back, and as he did so, Cain drew the knife across his exposed throat. Reflexively the guard dropped the telephone receiver, reached towards his throat, but already he'd lost control of his extremities and his palms flopped uselessly against his upper chest. Blood spurted from his severed arteries. Cain held him, steady pressure on the guard's shoulders to stop him rising out the chair. The guard's feet kicked and skidded in the blood pooling beneath them.

It didn't take long.

He was dead before the two Latinos made it to Carson's yacht.

'Totally inept,' Cain told the unhearing guard. 'No wonder your application to the LAPD was denied.'

No time for keepsakes, he paused only to pull down a screen that closed off any view into the interior of the booth. He felt around in the guard's pocket and found a bunch of keys, which he used to lock the door behind him.

The two bogus agents were poised at the base of a gangway giving access to Carson's yacht. There was a third man on the boat itself, and he had a radio pressed to his ear. As Cain went towards them, he saw the third man nod, and the two Latinos began an ascent of the ramp.

'What's going on here, then?' Cain wondered aloud. He thought, from what Telfer had explained, that the man whom he'd stolen the litho plates from employed the men following him. The guy on the boat, Mr Carson, was a rival of their employer. So how come the two Latinos were given unchallenged access to the boat?

Only one conclusion: double-cross. Couldn't be anything else. Telfer had been set up. And by association, so had Cain. And that made him angry. He began to walk faster, his shoes squeaking on the boardwalk. He slipped his hand into the back of his waistband, came out holding the gun. With his other hand, he drew the Bowie.

Only twenty yards away he heard raised voices and began to hurry.

Ten yards from the yacht he heard harsh laughter, then, 'You think I'm about to go to war with Hendrickson over you, you goddamn asshole?'

Then Telfer's voice: 'You bastard, Carson. I trusted you.'

'Shame,' said Carson. 'Let that be a lesson for you. Money talks and shit walks, my friend.'

'You—'

'Quiet!' barked a voice. One of the Latin men. 'You're coming with us, Telfer. Dead or alive, I don't really give a shit.'

Then Cain was at the bottom of the gangway. Without pause, he mounted it in two bounds. Stepping on to the deck, he saw the man with the radio. Minder, Cain decided. Probably one of a number of guards on the boat. Cain's arrival caused the man to turn. Before the surprise could even register in his face, Cain was chest-to-chest with him. The man grunted, looked down and saw the handle of the Bowie knife jutting from beneath his breastbone.

'Quietly does it,' Cain hushed him as he tugged down on the handle. By the law governing leverage, the tip sawed upwards. Eight inches of honed steel easily found the lower chambers of the man's heart. He was dead before he could make a further sound. Cain supported his weight to the deck, then tugged loose the blade, wiped it clean on the man's trousers and turned towards the cabin.

The yacht was huge, and the living area was about as plush as any five-star hotel Cain had ever seen. Wide sliding doors led into an elegantly furnished sitting area. It was all cut glass and sumptuous leather. Even chandeliers. A massive plasma screen satellite TV dominated the near wall. Then there were the six men.

John Telfer was sitting in a chair across a glass table from an older man in open-neck shirt and tan slacks. His hair and the tufts that poked from his chest were white, anomalous against his deep tan. That'll be Carson, then, Cain decided.

On the table was Telfer's backpack, open to show the spurious treasure within, and a briefcase that was shut tight. Inside it, Cain guessed, was the seven hundred grand. The two Latinos were there, their backs to Cain. He noted that they hadn't yet drawn their guns, but the two other men in the room had. These were minders, like the man Cain had just stabbed. Hard-faced men who crowded Telfer yet wore cautious expressions in front of the Latinos.

Cain detected movement above him. He glanced up, ready to lift the gun, and saw a young bikini-clad woman move hurriedly away.

One of two things was about to happen. The bitch would have the good sense to get the heck off the boat, or she was going to set up a racket to alert her sugar daddy in the cabin. Cain couldn't take the chance it would be the second option. He had to act now, while he still had surprise on his side. With the decision came action. He only had six bullets and he had to make them count. The minders first, then.

Cain stepped up to the door. One of the sliding partitions was open. He went inside. He was only ten feet away from the first minder when he lifted the gun and fired. The man's head erupted in cherry-red fragments.

Then chaos ensued.

Chaos was fine with Cain. He existed in the realm of chaos.

Telfer's face came up, registering shock, and not a little relief in a mad sort of way. The Latinos were spinning, both going for their guns, the second minder already rounding on Cain. Only Carson had the good sense to throw himself to the floor and attempt to escape beneath a nearby counter.

Cain snorted, and shot the second minder. He hit the man in the right arm, the bullet passing through into the flesh of his thick chest. The man went down, though Cain knew immediately he wasn't dead. Didn't matter, he'd dropped his gun, and he saw that Telfer had the presence of mind to snatch it up.

The two Latinos were next. Cain shot the one with the bandaged ear, hitting him in the thigh as the man leapt away. The bullet spun him and the man went to the floor at the feet of his friend. The second Latino was already bringing up his gun to fire, and Cain realized it was time to move. But instead of bolting for cover he charged further into the room, shouting, 'Move your ass, Telfer!'

The second Latino fired. Not at him, as Cain had hoped, but at Telfer. The bullet struck the back of Telfer's chair, directly where his head had been an instant earlier. Telfer was already bent double over the glass table reaching for the briefcase. As the Latino tried to draw another bead on Telfer, Cain shot him. Twice, once in the gut, then higher up at the jawline. The man went over backwards, trailing a ribbon of blood that showed stark against the chandeliers' twinkling lights.

Cain turned on Telfer. 'Get a freakin' move on!'

Telfer snatched the briefcase to his chest, rising up at last. Cain approached him, the gun trained on him. 'Give me the gun.'

Telfer shook his head. Lifted his own gun and pointed it at Cain.

'We haven't time for this now,' Cain warned him.

'No,' Telfer said. 'We haven't.'

They eyed each other over the ends of their guns.

'Let's get the hell out of here and worry about the rest later,' Cain offered.

Before Telfer could accept or decline the invitation a door burst open at the front of the cabin and another man skidded through with a compact Uzi sub-machine gun in his hands. He made a quick scan of the living area. To give him his due, the chaotic scene didn't appear to faze him too much. He lifted the Uzi and let loose an arching stream of bullets as he thudded over to cover Carson. In the same instant the injured Latino rolled over, grabbing at the gun he'd dropped on the floor. Two targets, one bullet, more coming his way, Cain decided the best course of action was to get out as quickly as possible.

As bullets churned the decor behind him, he flung himself through a side window, crashing through glass to sprawl on the deck. From inside the cabin came shouts, then Telfer was sprawling on the deck beside him, the briefcase clattering away from his grasp. Blood was visible on Telfer's shirt and he groaned as he rolled to his knees. Cain grabbed him, checking his hands.

'What the hell're you doing?' Telfer demanded.

'Where's your gun?' Cain snapped.

'I threw it at the maniac with the machine gun,' Telfer said.

'You threw it?' Cain said, incredulous.

'I couldn't get it to shoot!'

'Jesus Christ,' Cain said. He slapped Telfer's shoulder. 'Get the briefcase. We're out of here.'

Telfer went on hands and knees, grabbing at the Samsonite case. He came back to Cain, the case against his chest. 'That better be *real* money,' Cain said.

'Course it is. I'm not a friggin' idiot.'

Cain nodded, indicated the front of the boat. 'That way. Now.'

They both lurched up as the fourth minder appeared at the window they'd recently crashed through. He gave an angry shout, twisted so he could bring the Uzi into play. As he did, Cain sprang towards him. Left-handed he struck down with his Bowie knife. The knife connected before the man could depress the trigger, severing his thumb. The man screamed, the gun flopping sideways, bullets splintering the wooden deck next to Telfer. Cain chopped again, this time deep into the man's wrist, and the man withdrew his seriously wounded arm from further harm.

Telfer was up and running. Cain glanced at him, then down at the deck. He paused in his flight to retrieve the severed thumb, slipping it into his pocket alongside his other mementoes.

The bodyguard was back at the window again, but only to scream in abstract terror while he attempted to manoeuvre his drooping hand into its rightful place. Cain grinned at him, then charged after Telfer.

He caught up with Telfer at the helm of the yacht. Telfer was wide-eyed as he looked down at the seemingly bottomless gulf below them. The water had that turquoise sheen common to harbours, a thin layer of diesel oil on its surface.

'Jump,' Cain told him.

'No,' Telfer said, the briefcase clutched tightly to him.

'Jump, Telfer.'

'No way. I can't swim.'

'Jesus Christ on a freakin' bike! You can't swim?'

Again Telfer shook his head.

'I don't believe it,' Cain said. He grabbed at Telfer and propelled him towards the rail. 'Get the hell over the side. If you think I've gone to all this trouble to let you drown . . .'

Telfer resisted, but he knew it was his only chance at survival. Even as he dithered, he could hear the slap of feet echoing from inside the cabin.

'One of them spics is still alive,' Cain snapped at him. 'So are two of the guards and Carson. Any second now, they're going to be out here and we'll be dead. You got that?'

Telfer nodded, but he still held back from jumping.

'Oh, Holy Christ!' Cain said as he grabbed him and flung him bodily over the railing. Telfer hit the water like a stone and sank immediately. Cain lifted a leg to the railing, just as the minder he'd shot in the arm rounded the deck. Blood made a patchwork of his chest but he was still in the game. He had the Uzi and was already searching for a target.

Cain lifted his gun and fired.

Not at the man, but at the scuba-diving tanks he saw stacked neatly along one wall of the cabin. It was a desperate shot, one he hadn't time to calculate, but even as he plunged headfirst into the sea he felt the force of an explosion send shock waves through the water around him. Cain swam deeper, his ears thrumming with the concussive blast, until his clawing hand found Telfer's shirt. Telfer twisted and tugged, in the throes of panic.

Cain cursed, letting loose a stream of bubbles. He couldn't get a grip on Telfer for the handle of his Bowie. All the trouble he'd gone to in order to regain his knife and now this? He let the blade drop from his hand, watched it sink with a wistful look on his face until it was lost in the murk. Then he angrily snatched at Telfer's clothing and kicked upwards.

They broke the churning surface, Cain behind Telfer with an arm looped round his neck. Telfer gagged, spat, and sucked in great lungfuls of air as he cradled the briefcase to his chest like a baby. Cain guessed his death grip on the case had nothing to do with what was inside, but rather that the sealed case was a handy floating device.

A short distance away, the yacht was on fire. When the tanks had gone up, they'd taken the minder with them, not to mention a good portion of the deck and cabin. Cain spied a bikini-clad figure leap from the boat into the water. Another figure hobbled down the steps onto the harbourside, a white patch on the side of his head. Even from here, he could tell it was the remaining Latino.

Of the other minder and Carson, there was no sign. Perhaps the Latino had turned his gun on them before making his escape? But no, even as he wondered, Carson staggered to the railing and fired a handgun towards the limping Latino. His aim was useless, and the Latino made it to the shelter of a second boat. The Latino proved a better shot, firing back three times in quick succession. Carson folded, somersaulted over the rail and sprawled face first on the boardwalk. Didn't look like he'd be getting up again.

Cain paid them no further heed. He kicked with his feet, dragging Telfer and his precious cargo behind him. They'd just made it to the ladder of a second berthed yacht when the air turned inferno-hot around them. Cain held Telfer down, following him beneath the water as Carson's yacht erupted into a churning fireball that scattered steaming chunks of metal and wood across the harbour.

31

'You've gotta be yanking my goddamn chain?'

Rink was standing with his knuckles on the bonnet of Cheryl Barker's squad car. His bowed head emphasized equally the breadth of his shoulders and his dismay.

I wasn't feeling much better. I was thinking much the same thing as he was.

We'd both caught the TV news earlier.

A man with a hangdog expression related the disaster that had struck an exclusive yachting club only minutes earlier. The scene cut from the studio to an on-scene reporter who was standing amid crowds of stunned onlookers as a huge pall of black smoke breached the heavens behind them. I'd grimaced at the screen. The world was full of doom and gloom. Even, I'd decided, in exclusive rich men's playgrounds like Marina Del Rey.

Uninterested, I'd switched channels. Then we'd driven out here to meet with Cheryl Barker.

We were parked at the ridge of a shale embankment, at the head of a valley in the bottom of which the roofs of houses could be glimpsed amidst lush greenery. Palm and pepper trees dominated. Birds called and flapped in the skies above us.

Cheryl had chosen this place for an impromptu meeting, simply because it was a halfway point for us all. I could hear the disjointed chatter and squeals of children and guessed it was playtime at some park hidden in the trees. It was a surreal moment, us talking about death and destruction while dozens of kids laughed and whooped with delight below us.

Barker, a freckled-faced woman with short but unruly red hair, shook her head. 'I ain't the one yanking chains, Jared. It's just come over the air. The fireball down in Marina Del Rey is down to your good buddy, John Telfer.'

Rink glanced my way, and I lifted my shoulders in a non-committal shrug. Since the nonsense I'd read on Harvey's computer, not to mention the subsequent newscasts I'd caught on TV and our rental car radio, it didn't surprise me that this latest atrocity was being laid at John's feet as well. It seemed that John had superseded Osama bin Laden as the most notorious felon in the western hemisphere.

Barker was almost as tall as Rink, but she had a spareness to her that made her appear diminutive next to my friend's bulk. She stood with her thumbs hooked in her belt like some Wild West gunslinger: Annie Oakley in the flesh.

Rink turned from bracing himself on the bonnet of the LAPD mobile. He looked Barker up and down. He took in the officer's pristine uniform.

'You ain't made detective yet?'

'Nope.'

'Someone has to see sense soon,' Rink offered.

'Tell the truth, I'm in no great hurry. I'm as happy swanning around in a squad car as steering a desk. If I get the promotion, all well and good. If not, well, I'm as happy busting the balls of gangbangers and writing misdemeanour tickets for little old ladies driving the wrong way up the freeway.' Barker glanced down, brushed an imaginary piece of lint off her black shirt. 'Anyways, I'm partial to the uniform. Can't see as why there's such a big deal about getting back into civilian duds.'

Rink gave Barker a tight-lipped grin. 'Plus you get to drive a cool car, huh?'

'Yep, beats the hell outa the pool cars the detectives limp around in. More power under the hood for one thing.'

'You'll need it when you're chasing all these rogue grandmothers in golf carts.' The small talk out of the way, Rink asked, 'You placing much credence on it?'

'What? The fireball? No doubt about it, Jared. Eyewitness testimony places your boy at the scene.'

'They sure it was John Telfer?' I asked, stepping into their circle.

Barker turned and squinted at me.

'Joe Hunter,' I introduced myself. I stuck out a hand and Barker accepted it, shaking it languidly. 'John is my brother.'

Barker's face pinched. She glanced at Rink, who said, 'It's cool, Cheryl.'

Rink's word was enough for Barker.

'Your boy's been on every network and newspaper

in the country. Witness swears blind Telfer was the one brought hell to that boat.'

I still wasn't convinced. It obviously showed in my face.

'Before the boat went supernova the witness managed to get off unscathed. She says that John Telfer must've brought a bomb on board with him. He was carrying some kinda backpack when he arrived.' Barker sucked air through her teeth. 'Mind you, we ain't giving the bomb part much weight. More than likely, something on the boat went bang. Apparently there were a lot of guns going off prior to the explosion.'

'It's not like John,' I said, speaking my thoughts aloud.

Again, Barker shrugged her knobbly shoulders.

'Just telling you the way it's been said.'

'Was there any mention why John was on this boat in the first place?'

'Nothing the witness will admit to.'

'Who is the witness?'

Barker said, 'A hottie Rhet Carson picked up over on Catalina Island. You know how these old rich guys are. They like a touch of eye candy draped over the rails of their yachts when they pull into dock. Gives them, whaddaya call it? Esteem?'

'Are you saying your eyewitness is a hooker?'

'Hookers have eyes the same as anyone,' Barker replied. 'She says that Telfer wasn't the only one to come on board. Two guys in sharp suits turned up. Then some other guy. She seems to think that the last guy on board was with Telfer. The shooting started just after he got there.'

Rink and I looked at each other.

'Did she give a description of any of the three that turned up after John? The two guys in suits, for instance?'

'Let me see.' Barker pulled a notebook from her shirt pocket and thumbed through to a page marked with an elastic band. I doubted she needed the prompt. 'Yeah, here we are. An APB was put out for them. Both guys are in their thirties, medium build, dark-haired. Kinda swarthy-looking. Dressed in designer suits by all accounts.'

'The Mambo Kings.' I nodded to Rink.

Barker quirked the corner of a lip at my remark. 'You know these two?'

'Not personally,' I said. 'But I intend to.'

Barker looked off across the valley. 'Whatever your intentions, you can scratch one of them from your "to do" list. Got another dispatch through not ten minutes ago saying one of them was amongst the dead found in the burnt-out wreckage. The other could be at the bottom of the harbour for all we know. They're sending divers down as we speak.'

'What about the third man? The one she thought was with John?'

Again, Barker scanned her notebook. She made an exasperated noise as she puffed out her cheeks. 'White guy. Late thirties to early forties. Cold eyes. That's about it.'

'Nothing about his clothing? His hair colouring?'

'Nope. The witness said she only got a quick glance at him. Something about the way he looked at her was enough to send her scuttling for cover.' It was apparent Barker didn't like what she was reading. 'Not to mention the fact he'd just gutted one of Carson's bodyguards with a knife.'

It was my turn to puff out my cheeks. I looked at Rink and saw him staring back. Turning back to Barker I asked, 'Did the witness say anything else about him or John? Did they make it off the boat before it blew?'

'She says they jumped in the harbour just before the boat went up. She didn't see them after that. Chances of them surviving that kind of explosion would be pretty slim.'

'John can't swim,' I said, a feeling of dread gnawing at my vitals. Burnt or drowned, neither would be pretty. I had the fleeting impression of John's bloated face peering up at me from some infinitely deep place. Shaking off the disturbing vision wasn't easy but I had to remain optimistic. I wasn't prepared to admit defeat just yet. Neither was I ready to give up looking for him until the police divers dragged his lifeless corpse from the murky water.

'He could've made it out,' Rink offered. 'Boats are generally moored closely together. It's likely he made it to another one and climbed out the water.'

'I hope so,' I said.

'Funny thing is,' Barker said. 'This other guy, the one who was with Telfer. Apparently he did something extremely odd while he was on the yacht.'

'Apart from gutting someone with a knife?' I asked.

'Yeah. One of Carson's bodyguards survived the explosion. He was pretty mangled up and not making much sense. He was off his head with pain and blood loss, but he kept on saying, "He stole my thumb."'

I glanced sharply at Barker, who gave me a wry smile in return.

'Apart from burns over much of his body, his wrist was cut open and he was missing a thumb. Of course, his injuries could've been because of flying shrapnel from the explosion. Thing is, he was adamant that this mystery man picked his thumb up off the deck.'

'Jumpin' Jesus,' Rink said and I could only agree with him.

My theory about John crossing paths with this Harvestman was beginning to take greater shape. Only thing I couldn't fathom was what that meeting meant to them. What was John doing accompanying a murderer? Were they acting as allies, on some mad spree where they were working together? Or was John being compelled to work with this beast? I could only hope it was the latter. For everyone's sake.

I didn't realize I'd fallen silent, caught up in my own thoughts, until Rink nudged me. 'You hear that, Hunter?'

'Uh? Hear what?'

'Rhet Carson? The guy who owned the yacht?'

I squinted at Rink in incomprehension.

'I knew we'd lost you there,' Rink said.

'Sorry,' I said. 'I was just thinking.'

'Yeah,' Rink said. 'I could hear the cogs turning from here.'

I shook myself into the here and now. 'So what did I miss?'

'Rhet Carson's a major player. Head man of one of the outfits out here.'

'What? Like the Mafia?'

Barker gave a little giggle. 'The Mafia doesn't hold much sway any longer. Not if you're looking for the old-time Godfather type you're thinking of. But you could say he was a key player in the local underworld. Nowadays, your most successful mobsters shun the old style Cosa Nostra methods. Carson's a top-flight business executive. Runs his business from a down-town commercial centre, even advertises on the cable networks.'

'His business being?' I asked.

'Banking,' Barker said. 'But more specifically, moneylending.'

I said, 'You telling me he was money laundering? What better front than to use your own bank?'

Barker snapped her fingers. 'You've got it, my friend. There have been a number of high-profile investigations into his business, lots of supposition, but nothing that would stick. There was the rumour that he was laundering counterfeit dollars for some outfit from the east coast, but the case never really got off the ground. He's laid low for the last coupla years, kept his nose clean, spent more time on his boat. I'm thinking Carson was maybe about to get back in the business again.'

I'd had my suspicions since our last talk with Louise Blake. What the *something big* was she'd referred to.

Forged money has never been a big problem in the US, obtaining decent paper being just about impossible. But I also knew that it was a ploy of some terrorist groups to flood countries with fake currency, in order to destabilize the value of the dollar, bringing down the almighty American Dream. What they couldn't achieve with bombs, they made up for in Mickey Mouse money. Petoskey and Hendrickson would have been making top dollar, selling to the enemies of the USA.

And Rhet Carson had wanted in on the action.

I asked Cheryl Barker, 'But without the drawback of being the middle man this time?'

'It's a fair assumption,' Barker said.

'This outfit he was working with, do you know who runs it?'

'Not personally,' Barker said. 'I suppose I can find out.'

'I might be able to give you a couple of names.'

'You already have your suspicions?'

'Yeah. A few. Could be a guy called Sigmund Petoskey. He has his base in Little Rock, Arkansas.'

Barker shook her head at that. 'Nah. The mob I'm talking about was rumoured to be up in Virginia, maybe Georgia, I can't recall.'

'How about Hendrickson?' I asked.

'Like I said, I don't know the names personally. Hendrickson? Sounds familiar. I'll find out.'

Rink gave Barker his mobile phone number.

Barker, looking every bit the cowgirl, tipped the brim of an imaginary stetson our way. 'I'd best be on my way. Dallied a little too long. Dispatcher's probably wondering if I've got myself shot dead and is already planning a search party.'

I shook hands with Barker, wondering if ever we'd cross paths again. Probably not. Then Barker and Rink hugged as if they'd been intimate once. I didn't ask. Barker turned to her car and slid behind the wheel, giving us both a theatrical wink as she did so. 'I'll be in touch.'

We watched her drive off, her vehicle almost concealed by the plume of road dust churned up by her wheels. After she was gone, we stood kicking our heels.

'So what's the plan of action?' Rink finally asked.

'Marina Del Rey's about as good a place as any to start,' I suggested.

32

John Telfer was leaking blood. Ordinarily that would have been good. But not under these circumstances. Not when the bleeding was extraneous to Cain's plans. Not when it could alert a nosy observer to Telfer's plight. Anyone with an ounce of brains would immediately tie a bleeding man to the recent events at the not-too-distant harbour.

'We have to do something about your wound,' Cain said.

Lying flat at the bottom of the dinghy, Telfer grimaced up at him. Cain sat at the rear, guiding the outboard motor with one hand. With his other, he held the now-empty pistol aimed in Telfer's direction. The sea was choppy, causing the rubber boat to lurch as it breasted each successive wave.

'Feeling nauseous?' Cain asked.

'What do you care?' Telfer grunted.

'I care. Isn't that enough?'

Telfer twisted his face. 'The only thing you care about is getting your hands on the money.'

'Not true. I also care about your well-being.'

'Yeah. Right.'

Cain shrugged. 'Think what you will,' he said. He

made another scan of the horizon. Off over his right shoulder the distant Catalina Island was wreathed in sea haze. He could see the ferry to the mainland chugging towards harbour, and there were other vessels on the water: a couple of yachts, a speedboat, and half a dozen chartered boats hauling groups of men off to favourite fishing sites. Thankfully, none of the boats appeared to belong to the coastguard or LAPD. Equally thankfully none of them was near enough for anyone to see Telfer lying in the bottom of the dinghy.

'Were you shot?' Cain asked.

Telfer ran a hand up his chest. He was tentative, expecting the worst. Finally, he shook his head. 'I think it was more of a ricochet. Luckily whatever hit me didn't go all the way in, just scored along my flesh. Hurts like a bugger, though.'

Cain nodded solemnly. Inwardly he was relieved. He didn't want Telfer dying on him before he was ready. Still, he didn't want Telfer to know that. The last thing he needed was for Telfer to start kicking up a commotion out here on the water. If Cain had to kill him, it could attract unwanted attention. And he didn't relish attempting to outrun the coastguard in this paltry boat.

'As soon as we make land I'll take a look at it for you,' Cain offered. 'I know it's only a couple of hours since, but it shouldn't be bleeding now.'

Telfer rolled his shoulders. 'It'll be OK. I think I just opened the wound crawling in here.'

'Maybe so, but it won't harm you if I take a look.'

Telfer sighed. 'Why're you bothering?'

'Bothering? Because it's important to me.'

Telfer shook his head. 'You don't give a shit about me. I know that you've got no intention of upholding our bargain.'

'You can think what you like. Just ask yourself one thing. If I intended killing you, why would I bother saving you when I could have as easily left you on that yacht back there?'

'That's easy. You needed me to carry the money.'

'So what about when you were in the water? I could've let you drown. It'd have been easier for me to take the briefcase than hauling your sorry ass to safety.'

Telfer thought about that one. In the end, he had no reply. Instead he asked, 'So what exactly do you intend doing with me?'

'First things first, huh? First, we get to dry land. We clean you up. Then I'll decide what happens from there.'

'What about this?' Telfer reached behind him and touched the briefcase he was using as a somewhat uncomfortable pillow.

Cain gave him a smile. 'I'll unburden you of that. You're injured. It would be unfair of me to expect you to haul it around with you.'

'I've still got one good arm. It'll be no problem, really.'

Cain laughed. 'I like your sense of humour, John.'

'I'm not joking.'

'Regardless. You're still a funny man.'

A smile quirked Telfer's lips. Even under the circumstances, he felt strangely pleased with himself.

'You should see me when I'm happy; I'm the life and soul of the party.'

Cain shook his head, as though at the amusing antics of a toddler. He adjusted the outboard so that they began angling towards land. Here there was a stretch of golden shore, where beach houses on stilts crowned the low horizon. Beyond them loomed mist-shrouded tower blocks where the urban sprawl of south LA crept past Redondo Beach towards Long Beach. At random, he selected one of the beach houses and headed for a wooden jetty that nosed out into the waves.

Beyond the jetty was a summer house; a playground for the not so rich judging by the way the paint flaked from the window frames. There was only one car, a battered Dodge sitting under the porch that abutted the southern side of the house, and no speedboat at the mooring point. The house had a semi-dilapidated air, as though it was used infrequently, and maintained even less. There were no kiddies' swings or toys strewn along the edge of the beach, and no sign of recent use at the stone-built barbecue that contained only ashes and a lingering scent of burgers gone by. If anyone were home, it would be one person, two at the most.

He deftly steered the dinghy up to the pilings, a lasso action snaring the boat to a stanchion. He used the threat of the gun to motivate Telfer. 'Bring the brief-case,' he ordered. 'I'll take it off you when we get inside.'

'What if there're people home?' Telfer asked.

'Then we impose on their generosity to get you fixed up.'

'That's all?'

'What else?'

Coming to a painful crouch on the jetty, Telfer studied the empty windows. 'You won't hurt them, will you?'

Cain looked pained. 'I thought you were beginning to understand me by now.'

'I am,' Telfer said. Then to himself, 'That's the trouble.'

'I heard that,' Cain said in singsong fashion.

'You were meant to.'

Cain's features went from night to day in an instant. 'I suppose it all comes down to whether or not they're willing to be of assistance. I don't care for selfish people. What about you, John?'

'I don't suppose they have much choice when you're pushing a gun under their noses.'

Cain shrugged.

'What if there are children?' Telfer implored.

'I haven't killed a child lately,' Cain said.

Telfer didn't reply, concentrating on shuffling by his nemesis to conceal his disgust. Cain allowed him to take the lead. He glanced down at the empty gun, considered its convenience as a tool and decided that as long as no one suspected it was empty then it was still worth the effort to take it along with him.

Telfer shuffle-walked the length of the jetty, the briefcase stuffed beneath one armpit. Behind him, Cain grinned to himself; Telfer reminded him of a shambling mummy as he clawed at a railing to help him up the steps to the house's front yard. Beyond them the summer house presented a skull-like visage, dark empty sockets for windows and a grinning jaw of picket-rail teeth. It was an image that appealed to Cain but only added to Telfer's apparent foreboding. He turned and gave Cain an imploring look.

'On you go, John. You've got nothing to worry about.'

Telfer shook his head. He set his shoulders, unresigned to the prospect of further violence. Cain nudged him in the small of his back but he resisted the push.

'You don't have to kill anyone,' he whined.

'No,' Cain agreed. 'I don't have to.'

Telfer still refused to move.

Cain coughed out a grunt. 'But I might just start here and now if you don't move your ass.'

A propane blaze of anger flushed Telfer's face. Slowly he turned and faced his captor. Cain glared back. The tableau held for half a dozen heartbeats. It was finally Telfer who spoke. 'You know, the more you threaten someone, the less those threats mean.'

Cain grunted, but this time in humour. 'You should know by now that I don't make threats idly, John.'

'I'm fully aware of that. All I'm saying is that maybe you should take care who you threaten. Sooner or later you're going to have to do something about it.'

'Now who's making threats?'

'No. Not a threat. Call it friendly advice.'

Cain winked. 'OK, John, I get you. Now do me the honour of getting yourself inside on your own two feet before I have to plug you and drag you in by your ears.'

'Another threat?'

Cain shrugged. 'Call me Mr Predictable.'

Telfer shuffled on ahead and Cain glanced down and saw a pattern of dark splotches on the wood planks. Telfer was bleeding worse than he'd first thought. Probably the reason for the bravado: a last-ditch attempt at showing he had a backbone after all. Following the trail he cast his gaze once more on Telfer's shuffling form. Maybe patching him up was a waste of effort; maybe he should just end it now. Dead, he'd no longer be a hindrance. And he'd be more manageable stuffed in the trunk of the Dodge than up front riding shotgun. But that would mean changing the plans he'd fantasized over these past hours. Killed here with little fuss or later at the designated place with all the pomp and ceremony the occasion demanded? It wasn't too difficult a choice. He followed on behind, his mind made up.

Although the house looked uncared for, the tiny garden was a different story. Bougainvillea in terra-cotta troughs made a pleasant border along the final approach to the front door. He curled his lip. Kind of spoiled the overall ambience. So, too, did the tinkle of piano music coming from beyond the screen door.

Exhaling at the domesticity of it all, Cain hurried so that he came to the door just as Telfer raised a hand to rap on the door frame. He was about to halt Telfer when the crunch of feet on gravel achieved that for him. Synchronized, they turned and greeted the man rounding the side of the house. Then they both glanced down at the Rottweiler that strained at the leash in his grasp. Telfer's mouth held the ghost of a smirk as he looked at his captor.

'Help you gentlemen?' the man asked. He appeared to be about sixty years old, sunburnt and paunchy. An early retiree on a short break. Cain would bet his right testicle that this man would prefer to take his holidays in a mobile home. The massive dog continued to tug at the leash, tongue lolling in anticipation of a couple of tasty morsels.

In another piece of sleight of hand, the gun was spirited into his waistband and Cain's hand clapped down tight on Telfer's shoulder to halt any telltale movement. 'Hopefully you can, brother,' Cain said, stepping past Telfer. 'My friend here is injured. I'd appreciate it if you'd call nine-one-one for us.'

'Need an ambulance?' the man asked, craning to see past Cain as though attempting to ascertain the severity of Telfer's injuries. Subtly, Cain shifted on to his other foot. The blood on Telfer's shirt was like a flashing light to the man. Eyes wide, he lurched forwards, aided by the pull of the heavy dog. 'My God,' he spluttered. 'You're bleeding!'

Cain held up a hand. 'Don't worry, brother. It looks worse than it is. But we'd appreciate your help nonetheless.'

'Yes, yes,' the man said, coming towards them at a trot. The dog jounced along at his side, no longer tugging at its leash. Cain gave the dog a nanosecond of perusal before he feigned alarm and edged away. The man saw the movement, gave a shake of his head. 'Oh, don't be worried about Popeye none. He looks scary but really, he's a big old softie. More likely he'll lick you to death than bite you.'

'Wow. That's a relief,' Cain said. For Telfer's benefit he raised an eyebrow, gave a lopsided smile. Telfer gave a short cough, but already Cain was dropping to a knee as if to greet the dog.

As the dog brushed past, Cain swiped his hand under its muzzle. A seemingly innocent pat of its broad chest. It took only two further paces before it collapsed, not even offering a startled yelp before it died. Stunned, the man stared down at his dog. Eyes pools of bewilderment, he looked back at Cain who was rising from his crouch.

'Don't like dogs,' Cain said.

The man's gaze travelled the length of Cain's arm, fixed on the ultimate point. The scaling knife was almost devoid of blood, so quick and easy was its entry and exit.

'They're competition,' Cain said. 'For your bones.'

'Oh,' the man said, his knees rebelling at the same time.

33

The last time I was on a motor launch it was at night, and I was being deposited on a deserted beachfront in the Indian Ocean. I was part of an eight-man team sent to extradite suspected terrorists who'd been holed up there since a pre-dawn attack on a village full of women and children.

On that occasion, I didn't take too much notice of my surroundings. It was a case of in and out, a smash and grab mission that left no time for sightseeing.

Now, standing on the prow of the launch, I took the time to savour the spray of the ocean on my face, to smell the tang of brine in my nostrils and feel the wind in my hair. The Bailey motorboat was riding high on the ocean, lifting majestically with each swell, dipping down with each trough. I stood with my legs braced against the motion, but neglected to reach for the handrail.

'If you close your eyes and hold out your hands it feels like you're flying,' Rink quipped from behind me.

I snorted at the image.

'Start singing like Céline Dion and I'll throw you overboard,' I promised him.

Rink grunted, moving up next to me. He rested his meaty forearms on the guardrail. 'What makes you think they've headed south?'

'Just a feeling.' I said.

'A feeling? What? Like a sixth sense or something?' Rink wasn't kidding. Like most soldiers, he knows that there's a force out there that isn't tangible. Many a soldier's life has been saved by an enhanced instinct that borders on the supernatural. Something that warned him about the concealed tripwire or sniper lying in ambush. Some argue that it's simply a product of supercharged adrenalin and a keenly trained eye, but I believe there's more to it than that. It's more than the creeping flesh sensation that unseen eyes are watching you. But the feeling I was referring to had nothing to do with that or any other power. Simply, it was to do with deduction.

'No, a feeling that if I was in their shoes I'd've headed south, too.'

'If they survived.'

'There's no doubt about it, Rink. Whoever this guy is that John's with, he knows his stuff. Only someone with training goes on to a yacht full of armed men and ends up blowing it and everyone aboard to shit.'

'Unless he's got the other important ingredients: he's as crazy as a bag of weasels, has more balls than sense, and he's the luckiest goddamn son of a bitch on the planet.' Rink raised his shaggy brows, inviting disagreement.

I shrugged, moving to join him at the guardrail. Below us, the bow wave split like blistering phosphorous against the deep aqua of the ocean. 'Maybe he has both,' I said. 'The training and the other ingredients. He had a get-out plan. You can bet your life on it.'

'So, it stands to reason,' Rink acquiesced, 'he heads out to sea to avoid the cordon of blue lights converging on the harbour.'

'Coastguard have their base to the north. It's what I'd've done,' I told him, and Rink nodded in agreement.

'So, who is this guy? You think it really is this Harvestman the media's screaming about?'

'Has to be,' I said. 'It'd explain why John's fingerprints turned up in connection with the killings of that couple at the motel. Somehow, John's got himself into something way beyond his ability to get out of. Only thing I can't fathom yet is what part he's playing in all this. I can't believe he'd be a willing participant in murder.'

Rink sucked air through his teeth. 'Maybe you don't know John the way you think you do.'

'You keep saying that. Maybe you're right, Rink, but until I'm proved wrong, I prefer to give him the benefit of the doubt.'

'Fair enough,' Rink said. 'But what if he has turned, Hunter? What if your brother has acquired a taste for blood? What if he's a goddamn willing participant?'

I didn't answer for a moment, my gaze fixed on the horizon. Like the point where the sky and ocean met, my whole reason blurred into a haze of nothingness. Finally, I turned to Rink and saw that he was studying me with an intensity he often employed. I blinked slowly, breaking the connection. 'If that's the case, it puts a whole new slant on my purpose for finding him.'

Rink nodded sagely, lifted a hand and placed it on my shoulder. 'Let's hope it doesn't have to come to that, huh?'

A shout from behind us broke my melancholy and I turned to squint back at the skipper who was at the wheel of the boat.

He was pointing with ill-restrained excitement towards the shore. A little more than five hundred metres away I saw what he indicated. To me, it was nothing more than one more boat tied to a boardwalk jetty.

Together, Rink and I made our way back to the skipper's cabin. He was grinning. 'The dinghy over there,' he said with an exaggerated nod of his head. 'It's from the *Morning Star*.'

'The *Morning Star* being one of the yachts moored in the harbour?' I asked.

The skipper snapped his fingers then pointed a gnarled digit at me. 'Got it in one.'

'How can you be sure?' Rink asked.

The skipper's eyebrows did a little jig. 'I've been around them boats all my working life. I know what skiffs belong to what and to whom. Not only that, but if you look at the painting on the outboard, you can see that it's a five-pointed star coming up over the sea, not the sun as you'd expect.'

I squinted across the waves. I could barely see the outboard motor, never mind the motif on it. I looked back at the skipper, and he grinned again.

'I'll trust your better eyesight,' I told him. 'But couldn't there be an ordinary reason why a dinghy from the *Morning Star* would turn up here?'

'None that I can guess at,' the skipper said.

'No. I suppose not.' I looked back at the dinghy. 'Can you bring your boat in close to the same berth?'

'Tide's a bit low for my girl. I'll get in as close as I can but you might have to wade to shore.'

'OK.' I turned to Rink. 'You ready for this?'

Rink patted the bulge under his armpit. 'Ready, willing and able.'

Returning my attention to the skipper, I indicated the beach house a short way up from the jetty. 'Do you know whose place that is?'

He shook his head. 'I'm good with boats, haven't a clue about houses.'

I shrugged. 'OK. Can you get the emergency services on your radio?'

'Yeah. Of course.'

'Yeah,' I agreed. 'Once you've put us ashore, shout up for help, tell the cops to get to this location as fast as they can.'

The skipper was no naive old fool; he knew we'd chartered his boat for the strict purpose of hunting someone fleeing the scene of devastation up at Marina Del Rey. What he didn't know was exactly who we were chasing. Or why.

'You expecting trouble, son?' he asked.

'Maybe of the worst kind,' I told him.

'So why don't you wait till the cops get here before you go ashore?' he asked. For the first time, I noticed a hint of something less than his ordinary ebullience.

'We could have some kind of hostage crisis. I can't wait for the cops to get here before any innocents are harmed.' The first was for the old man; my next was directed at Rink. 'If the men we're after have already been and gone, I've a horrible feeling that there'll be some cleaning up to do. Best we leave that to the authorities this time.'

Rink nodded in understanding, while it was the skipper's turn to squint at the rapidly approaching shoreline. He didn't ask for an explanation and I offered him none. The skipper guided the prow of the Bailey towards the jetty, and as he'd predicted we were more than five metres short of the boardwalk when we felt the judder of sand beneath us. The skipper threw the boat into reverse, edging back until we were in clear water. From the front of the boat, I gave him a thumbs up and he nodded at me.

'You want me to wait for you?' he called from the cabin.

I shook my head over the sound of the idling engine. Whatever the outcome, I didn't believe I'd be boarding a boat again any time soon. 'Maybe it's best you pull back from the shoreline. Could be bullets flying around before long.'

'I appreciate the warning, son, but you don't have to worry about me. Completed two tours in Vietnam, so the prospect of flying bullets means nothing.'

'Fair enough, but I don't want your death on my conscience.'

The skipper winked, dipping the peak of his cap. 'It's your mission, son. Keep safe. An' tell your big buddy to do likewise.'

'Will do,' I said, glancing Rink's way. He was standing at the prow, scanning the beach for movement. His shoulders twitched, adrenalin searching for release. As I walked towards him, I placed my hand under my armpit and felt the reassuring bulge of the latest SIG Sauer supplied only an hour earlier by Cheryl Barker. It was the older Swiss P230 model, with no manual safety button so that the weapon could be brought into action very rapidly. The feel of it brought back memories from my Point Shooting days.

We went over the side of the boat together, splashing waist deep in the foam. Sand immediately invaded my shoes and my trousers clung to my skin. I forgot my discomfort as we pushed towards the dinghy.

'Blood,' Rink observed even as we approached. It was smeared over the edge nearest the jetty as though something limp and lifeless had been dragged on to the walkway. I pressed up to the boat. More frothy blood was pooled in the bottom. Rink and I shared a disconcerted glance. All this blood wasn't a good sign we'd find John alive, but it meant my hunch was correct after all. There couldn't possibly be a more likely explanation for this boat to be here than that it had carried escapees from the carnage at Marina Del Rey.

Pulling my SIG out of its holster, I chambered a round. I heard a similar *kachunk!* as Rink followed suit with his Mossberg. We followed the line of the jetty on

to the beach. Rink peeled off to my left. Before us was a
wooden house with a well-tended garden. A dust-
streaked Dodge was parked alongside the house. There
was no further room in the lot for another vehicle so I
guessed that John – if he was still alive – was inside the
house. Not good in one sense, it added to my app-
rehension of a possible hostage situation escalating
beyond my power to control.

Rink was well ahead now, moving towards the
house. I sucked in a deep breath and moved on to a
gravel path that led to the door of the property.

Spatters of blood on the doorstep confirmed my
fears. Hearing the sputter and roar of an engine, I
swung my gaze towards the launch and saw that the
skipper was heeding my warning. I wondered if he'd
already called for back-up, searched the sky for any
swooping helicopter rushing towards us.

Nothing.

Just a single speedboat hurtling along about quarter of a mile to the north. Even from here, I could tell
it was a private boat, so I gave it no further mind.
Even if the skipper had immediately called through
to the authorities, they were still many minutes away.
This meant I had no time to waste: if John was
inside, especially accompanied by the Harvestman, I
had to take decisive action before any innocents were
injured.

Given the opportunity, I'd have scoped the place
and gained a better understanding of what it was we
faced. Rink and I would've devised a plan of approach,
but like always, Murphy's Law took precedence here. I

could only hope that the chaos rule would favour us as it had done innumerable times in the past.

With this in mind, I'd no recourse other than to charge the screen door, lift a foot and crash through; hurtling into whatever hell storm would follow.

Which is exactly what I did.

34

Snapshot.

On first perusal, it was a nice home.

Reminded me of my grandparents' bungalow.

On deeper reflection, the memory of their home told me everything I was afraid of.

There was a cancer at this house's core.

To maximize the sunshine, all these beach houses had been built so that their fronts faced the ocean. Therefore, through the door I shattered lay a vestibule leading directly to an open-plan living area on one side and a bedroom on the other. Towards the back of the house would be a kitchen and perhaps a utility room, but these were of no interest to me at the time.

Kick-start the world.

I moved.

My entire attention was skewed to the left as I swung into the living area. I say living area; I could already see the corpse of some hulking dog lying alongside its ceiling-staring master. The man was indisputably dead judging by the mess of his throat and the cataract-glaze of his eyes. His mouth hung open in shock and pink spume clung to his contorted lips. Another thing I took in during that nanosecond of horror: his left hand was missing, shorn off at the wrist. The Harvestman had been up to his old tricks.

Apart from the corpses, the room was as ordinary as any in a home supported by a modest income. There was the obligatory TV, settee and furniture, trinket-type ornaments and photographs in frames. What stood out was the large piano that took up most of one side of the room. Then there were the three people standing round it.

Perhaps 'standing round it' isn't the most apt way to describe the scene.

One figure, an elderly woman, was being helped off the piano stool by the tug of a man's arm across her throat. As she stood in an awkward spasm, her fingers clawed at the piano keys and a deep-throated note vied for dominance over an equally harsh one. The man pulling her backwards stared at me over the woman's shoulder, his lips split in a feral snarl.

My SIG came up. Ordinarily I'd have fired, but the man placed the muzzle of a gun to the side of the woman's face and I stayed my hand. My gaze flicked to the nearer side of the piano. Immediately I saw my brother.

At the time, I can't honestly say if I was pleased to see him. I think, deep down in my soul, I'd secretly hoped that John was dead, that the possibility that he'd become a monster had been removed.

John turned his face to mine, and shock struck his dull expression. Then hope flared. That look was all I needed to confirm that John wasn't a consenting player in this game. Immediately my attention skipped back to the man holding the woman.

'Drop the gun,' I shouted.

The man's snarl broadened ever wider and I saw ice behind his pale green eyes. Using the woman as a shield, he pressed the gun under her jaw.

'I think it's you who'd better drop yours,' he said.

My SIG didn't waver. I took a step closer. Finger pressure increased on the trigger. Calmer, I repeated, 'Drop the gun.'

In answer, he thumbed back the hammer. 'Think you can drop me before I kill this old bitch?'

'Yes.' I stared at him along the barrel of my gun.

He shook his head. 'I don't think you're as confident as you're making out. If you could do it, you would've by now.'

'You've got another five seconds to comply,' I told him.

The man laughed. His captor whimpered in terror. Her arthritic knees threatened to dump her on her backside and only the dragging arm around her throat held her up. She was no lightweight, but the man didn't seem to be struggling to control her. The arm looped around her throat bulged with lean strength.

'One,' I counted.

'Aw, cut the dramatics, will you,' he taunted. As he did, he shuffled sideways, putting himself in a corner of the room. It wasn't an attempt at finding an exit, but to ensure he couldn't be triangulated. His back to the corner, he took away any opportunity for Rink to get a bead on him. I glanced to my left and saw Rink standing outside the open window, his shotgun trained on the man. My friend gave a subtle shake of his head. No line of fire.

'You're cornered,' I told the man. 'Let the woman go and you'll live. Harm her and we'll shoot you like a mad dog.'

'No. What you are going to do is put down your weapons. I leave with the woman.' He glanced over at a briefcase I only now noticed on the lid of the piano. 'And that.'

'No deal. You let the woman go first.'

'Uh-uh. Maybe I'll just shoot her face off and take my chances, huh?'

He pressed the barrel of his gun into her left eye socket, eliciting a shriek from the woman. Again, my finger tightened but didn't follow through.

Think of damp ashes: that was the colour of John's face as he turned to me. He supported his weight against the piano, body racked with pain, weak and hurting. 'He means it, Hunter. He'll do it.'

My gaze jumped between him and the gunman. A smile flickered at the corner of his mouth, a tensing of his eyes. Was that recognition of my name? Shouldn't be, I told myself, it's not as if I'm James Bond. To John I said, 'Get over here behind me, John.'

The gunman grunted. 'You two know each other?'

Neither of us answered but the silence was palpable.

'Wait a minute. Hunter?' The man searched my face. Lines crinkled at the corners of his eyes as though something amusing had struck him. 'Not Joe Hunter?'

Unbidden my face pinched. My teeth ached as my jaw tightened. Some secret I turned out to be; maybe I should have worked under a code name, after all.

'Well, for the love of all that's holy! Who'd have thought they'd put *you* on my trail?'

Again, I didn't answer, and the man turned his attention on John.

'Wait a minute . . . I see it now. The family resemblance. You're so full of surprises, John. You didn't tell me that you were related to such a notorious assassin as Joe Hunter . . .' He squinted across at Rink who remained statue-solid at the open window. 'And, don't tell me . . . not Jared Rington as well?'

John's face puckered. It can't have occurred to him before just who – or what – his big brother really was. He was aware that my work involved hunting terrorists, but I don't think he appreciated what that actually entailed. To him, I was just a soldier killing other soldiers. Now he was wondering: Aren't assassins the bad guys?

I don't appreciate the term assassin, but I suppose, at the end of the day, it's all down to your perspective: Rink and I were either saints or sinners. At that moment, I saw myself as the saint; the man with the gun shoved in an elderly woman's eye socket assured me of that.

'Let her go,' I commanded again.

The man wasn't interested. My identity seemed to please him in a way I found troubling. His next words did go some length to explain his apparent pleasure. 'I guess I should be honoured. Does that mean that I've finally being given the level of notoriety I deserve? Huh? I suppose that means you know who I am now?'

'I don't give a shit who you are, or what insane reason you have for murdering innocent people. All I'm interested in is you dropping your gun before I put a bullet in your head.' To assure him of my intentions I took another half-step towards him.

In return, he giggled. Said, 'If I'm going to die, I'm taking her with me. Maybe one or two of you, as well.'

I drew back again. Inwardly I cursed myself. I'd just made the mistake of showing him that I wasn't in charge of the situation. One up for the *real* bad guy. He moved the barrel of his gun so it was under the woman's ear now. Once more, the woman squeaked out her fear. Her eyes rolled my way, beseeching. I had to do something to even the score.

'John,' I snapped, this time. 'Get yourself over here.'

He staggered over, one arm tight against his chest where his sodden shirt clung as tenaciously as did my soaked trousers. The only difference was the blood. I moved to my right, giving him clearance to gain the doorway. At my shoulder, John came to a stumbling halt. Something bothered me about the abruptness.

Without thought, I pivoted on my right foot, smacking against the near wall, eyes still on the gunman to my right, but my peripheral vision searching out what had stopped John. I saw the gunman's eyes widen in surprise, saw him flinch, and I knew that there was new danger in the house. Danger to us both. I was caught between two equally vicious enemies and it was a split second's decision as to my response. Even as I swung to my left, I gave a silent prayer that Rink would cover the killer I couldn't keep my eyes on. My gun swept the air, and I fired without pause.

Even as he was stepping into the living room, my first bullet caught Hendrickson's hitman in his right shoulder, spinning from his fingers the gun he pointed at John's head. I'd seen this man before, testament to that was the wound on his ear. Even if I'd never had the privilege, I would've recognized him for what he was: a stone-cold killer. Moreover he was an apt stalker in his own right, and he'd used Rink and me to lead him to John. The memory of the speedboat racing towards us after we'd disembarked from the skipper's launch came fluttering into my memory.

Injured, the Latino dropped low, already reaching left-handed for a second weapon concealed in an ankle holster. My gun boomed again, but even as I fired, I snatched the barrel up so that the bullet swished above his head to splinter the door lintel. I'd missed him, but it was a good job I did. It meant I also missed John who'd chosen that moment to stagger into my line of fire.

Things were rapidly turning to shit.

I swerved round John, expecting the killer at my back to put a bullet in my spine.

I cleared John just as the hitman came up from his crouch. His gun fired. Instinctively I'd already twisted, but a searing coldness snapped alongside my ribs. Wind whooshed out of me, but I couldn't allow the thought of the hit to stop me.

Before he could fire again, I struck his gun hand with the barrel of my SIG, knocking his aim wide. His bullet lifted keys from the piano amidst a tympani of discord. Moving unhaltingly, I swept my gun under his forearm as though it were a rapier and snaked my arm up his back.

In close and dirty, we went to town. I ground him against the wall, both our guns momentarily scraping and rasping against wallpaper. His gun went off, further marking the wall. With his free hand, he grabbed at my testicles. I stabbed my fingers into his eyes, tore at his damaged ear and he forgot all about squeezing my balls. Instead, he punched me in the mouth. The tricky bastard. Right back at you, dickhead, I thought, as I smashed his nose into a new position on his face.

He was slippery, even though shot in three different places – he had a wounded thigh that I was only now vaguely aware of, plus the two I'd given him. His nose was broken and he was bleeding, but the adrenalin-charged flood of endorphins gave him the strength of desperation.

He fought back, tried to headbutt me, but instead found the point of my elbow as I rammed it into his cheekbone. His eyes rolled upwards. Before he could recover from the ringing concussion, I snatched down his head, straight into the path of my uprising knee.

It was like a mallet pounding a watermelon and the tendons in the backs of both knees failed him.

As he dropped, my gun followed him, and even as he sprawled out, I put two bullets into the rear of his skull.

'That's for Louise Blake,' I hissed through my teeth. Then I shot him again between the shoulder blades.

Touching my ribs where I could feel the first sting of contact, I added, 'And that one's for me.'

Captain Fairbairn once famously wrote that the average armed affray is over in seconds, literally a matter of *the quick and the dead*. I had acted instinctively, relied on speed and the extension of the gun in my hand. Now the hitman was dead. Once again, my mentor's ghost spoke in volumes. But, it wasn't over.

No other guns had barked during the few seconds it took to dispatch Hendrickson's man. It was safe to assume that the threat of Rink blasting him had stayed the Harvestman's hand. Allowing the Latino to lie in his own blood, I shifted again, reaching down and clawing John from the floor even as I swung my gun to find its next target.

Coming up with John clutched beneath one arm, my gaze struck sparks off the murderer's. He still coddled the elderly woman as a shield, but some of the force with which he pressed his gun to her had gone.

'I couldn't have done a better job myself,' he said.

'I'm not interested in what you think,' I snapped back at him.

'I remain impressed nonetheless. If my hands weren't so full I'd applaud you. I'm leaving now. I'm taking the woman as insurance. If you stay put, I promise you she'll be released unharmed. If you follow me she will die.'

The deal wasn't an option. I knew the only way the woman would be returned to us would be sans significant portions of her anatomy. I slowly shook my head. Prodding the dead assassin at my feet I said, 'You know what I can do. You've seen it with your own eyes.'

'I don't doubt that you're good. But are you really prepared to put this dear old lady at risk?' His smile was that of the Anti-Christ. 'Even if you shoot me now, are you certain that the trauma of a bullet in my skull won't make me jerk this trigger? Are you willing to take that chance?'

Reluctant to give him an edge, I said, 'We'll just have to see.'

Again, the old woman mewled and a torturous pain shot through me at having to subject her to such terror. Unfortunately, I had no other recourse. To allow the Harvestman to take her was out of the question. If she didn't die now, she would certainly die later. And it wouldn't be via a quick and painless bullet through her brain.

On the grand scale of things, if this woman were to die, then it would be best if the murderer died along with her. It would be a supreme waste of life, but her sacrifice could mean the difference between life and gruesome death for so many others if the bastard was allowed to live.

Surprisingly, John came to my rescue.

Cradled in my armpit, I felt him shift; he clawed at my shirtfront, as if drawing himself upright. Momentarily he blocked my view of the Harvestman, and I had to lean my gun hand over his shoulder to avoid losing a line of fire. John plucked at my shirt again and my face pinched in understanding.

'Let me go with him,' John said. His voice was as brittle as month-old crackers.

I shook my head.

'You have to let me go, Joe,' he said. Again, I felt his hand on my shirtfront, a quick rummage of his fingers. 'Cain, let the woman go and I'll be your hostage.'

The Harvestman's brow furrowed.

'John?' I said, snatching at his collar, but my brother pulled himself loose. He took a faltering step towards the murderer, hands wrapped round his torso in an effort to subdue the pain evidently flaring through him.

'Let the woman go, Cain. Take me instead.'

The murderer looked beyond John, staring at me. I didn't move. Scowling my hatred at him, I conceded, offering this arrangement as a way out for him. Complex emotions were fluttering behind his cool façade.

Taking another step, John said, 'We have unfinished business, Cain. We both know that. If you let the woman go, I'm willing to see it through to the end. I'll sacrifice myself for her.'

'What do you say, Cain?' I asked. 'Do we have a deal, or do we start shooting?'

Cain gave me a serpent's grin. 'Bring the briefcase, John.'

Cain removed the gun from the woman, waved me aside with it. 'Back off, Hunter. Go over there next to the window with your friend.'

Rink gave me a subtle shake of his head, not for a second taking his aim from Cain. His features were set in bronze. 'I think we can take the frog-giggin' son of a bitch,' he hissed.

'No, Rink. Stand down,' I said. Without lowering my own gun, I crabbed over to the window, blocking Rink's line of fire.

'What you doin'?' Rink whispered harshly. 'I can take the bastard.'

'Just let it go, Rink,' I whispered back. 'For now.'

Behind me, Rink's curses were blasphemous, whatever Good Book you follow.

'Hunter?' he pleaded, but I'd already refocused my attention on Cain. John had grasped the briefcase to his chest and was nearing him. As he blocked my view of Cain, the woman was unceremoniously shoved to the ground, then Cain had John by the shoulder and was spinning him round. Without pause, Cain used him as a shield as he moved away. At the door, Cain issued a final warning. 'Don't try to follow us too soon. If you do, John dies in more agony than you could ever imagine.'

I stayed put. Rink was as itchy as a flea-bitten dog, and without taking my eyes off Cain I whispered, 'Just wait.'

From behind me I heard the answering response, indicating Rink understood. 'I'm waiting.'

Cain didn't hear the whispered exchange. He was as nutty as squirrel shit, but he was no fool. He paused in his tracks. 'I guess this won't be the last time I lay eyes on you?'

'Count on it,' I told him.

'Don't worry, I will,' Cain said. 'In fact, I kind of look forward to it. It'll look good to have such a formidable trophy as Joe Hunter on my résumé.'

Cain held my gaze a moment longer, then, in an act I should have expected from one with such a depraved mind, he waved goodbye. It wasn't his hand he used. It was the bloodless souvenir taken from the old woman's husband.

Then Cain and John were gone.

Before I could move, the old woman wailed and began scurrying across the floor on hands and knees. The object of her quest was the still form of her husband. Her sobs were pitiful.

Grief is a savage torment, especially when so raw as this. It can leave a person insensible to what is happening around them, and totally unaware of consoling hands. My softly spoken words were likely pure gobbledygook to her.

While she wailed, I gave her the quick once-over. Her injuries were minimal, a little bruising on the throat, a bumped elbow. Searching for any broken bones, I traced the folds of her blouse with my fingertips. Bodily she was intact, but there was a narrow rent in the fabric. I studied the slashed cloth, noting that a patch about the size of two fingers was missing, stripped away, wondering what in hell that was supposed to mean.

I shook off the thought as Rink charged into the living room. 'They've taken the old lady's car.'

I nodded at him.

'So what're we doin' standing around? Let's get after the son of a bitch,' Rink said.

'There's no rush,' I told him.

Rink inclined his head. 'What's going on?'

'Like I said, we only have to wait.'

Rink wasn't aware that John was laying down a trail for us.

'When John was holding on to me,' I explained. 'He took my mobile phone out of my shirt pocket.'

'I can't see him getting the opportunity to call in his location,' Rink said.

'Doesn't need to,' I said.

'No. Of course. We can have the phone pinged and triangulated. It'll lead us straight to him.'

'I trust you have someone in telecommunications that can do it for us?' I asked.

'I might know a woman who does.'

'Cheryl Barker? It's OK, Rink, I've had another thought.'

The sirens came.

It was only minutes before Rink and I were kneeling with our hands behind our heads as we were frisked for concealed weapons.

'Get me Walter Conrad,' I told a stern-faced special agent from the FBI's Hostage Rescue Team. 'He's a sub-division director with the CIA.'

On reflection, I was in no position to make demands but if anyone could put a trace on the phone John was carrying, it was Walter.

To my surprise, he said, 'Don't worry, Mr Hunter. Your boss is already on his way.'

35

Your *boss* is already on his way.

It's not often that Walter Hayes Conrad IV travels in the field these days. As a handler of undercover agents, most of them up to their elbows in wet work, he has to maintain a degree of anonymity, distance himself from the dirty deeds performed by his government in the name of national security. On this occasion, however, it had been necessary for him to fly out to this place marginally north of Long Beach. Orders were to contain what was rapidly escalating into a massive embarrassment for both him and the security community at large.

He walked into the bedroom where I'd been confined for the last twenty minutes. All that was missing was the fanfare blast of trumpets to announce his arrival.

Walter greeted me with a tight-lipped smile, and an unlit cigar jammed between his fingers. Without preamble, he dismissed the two Hostage Rescue Team troopers who'd been my uneasy jailers. Funnily enough, the FBI agents deferred to his authority.

'Walter,' I acknowledged with a nod. I stood up from the bed that had been my perch, smoothing out the rumpled comforter with a tug.

Walter's cigar exchanged hands. Gripping it as though it were a lifeline, he offered his other damp palm. I shook hands with him, regarding him solemnly. He didn't say anything.

'You must have hot-footed it out here, Walter,' I said, 'seeing as it's less than half an hour since the call went in.'

Walter bunched his prodigious cheeks in what was supposed to be a smile. 'Got my very own Lear.'

'You're telling me,' I said. But he didn't get the joke. When he didn't respond, I added, 'Even a jet couldn't have got you all the way across country in that time.'

'It's a very fast jet,' Walter said, and now the smile was genuine. 'Nah, I've been in LA since the early hours of this morning.'

'Can I ask the reason why?'

'Of course not,' he said.

It was a game. His game; one that Walter loved to play.

I offered my deduction, to see what lies he came up with.

'When we talked on the phone I piqued your interest. Got you thinking, huh?'

'Pure speculation.'

'So tell me, Walter, who is the Harvestman?'

'What makes you think I know that?'

'Don't play with me, Walter. You haven't flown all the way across the country for nothing. You're here because you know who he is. You're on a containment mission.'

Walter jammed the unlit cigar between his teeth.

'I gave up smoking eight months ago,' he said. 'Still carry a cigar around for moments just like this.'

'I take it you're not referring to a moment of celebration?'

'No, I'm talking about a reminder of how much I've fucked myself up in the past.' For the first time I honestly believed him. 'There's a lot of truth in that concept, Hunter. That your past always catches up with you in the end.'

'Yeah,' I agreed. His words echoed precisely my own feelings. He sat down on the bed I'd recently vacated, clenching his fists on his ample thighs.

'The Harvestman knew me,' I told him. 'He also knew Rink. Makes me think that he has to be a member of the security community.'

Walter nodded but didn't volunteer anything.

'Is he one of yours, Walter?'

Walter shook his head. 'Not CIA.'

'Secret Service?'

He wagged a fat finger, pleased with his top student.

'So how's it you're involved?' I asked, 'Last I heard the CIA and Secret Service were separate entities.'

'Like you said, Hunter. Your call got me thinking, made me pull a few loose strings together. It's a joint agency decision that I step in as SAC.'

'Special agent in charge? You pulled rank?'

'Of course.' He smiled.

'Figures,' I said. 'So what happened? What makes a bodyguard turn into a killer?'

'Is there a difference, Hunter? Isn't the purpose of a bodyguard to kill or be killed? We're talking brass tacks

Matt Hilton

here, none of that ethical bullshit you see in the movies.'

'There's a huge difference, Walter,' I reminded him. 'Bodyguards protect the sanctity of life; they don't take fucking trophies to display on their dining-room wall.'

'Not in the classic sense,' he demurred. 'But they take trophies nonetheless. You just gotta speak to any long-serving agent and they wear their trophies on their sleeve. Metaphorically speaking.'

I shook off his comment. I sat down on the bed next to him.

'So, are you going to tell me?' I pressed.

'Situation's kind of delicate, Hunter,' Walter said. He shifted uncomfortably and the bed creaked in protest.

'Everything you touch is delicate. What's so different this time?'

'Do you realize the extent of the scandal if it gets out that a former Secret Service agent's responsible for murdering upward of twenty people?' He turned his large head to me, and I could see the pain wriggling behind his slick brow. 'Christ, Hunter, it'll be ten times worse than all the screaming over the Iraq campaign. It'll lend weight to the naysayers who're preaching that our government is allowing the murder of innocents in order to justify the invasion. Hell, if they find out the Harvestman has had free rein for over four years, do you think for one moment they'll believe it wasn't with the blessing of the government? Next thing you know the crazies will be swearing that he's still on our payroll and has been taking out people who knew the truth behind JFK's assassination.'

'Are you telling me that you've been aware of him for four years? That nothing's been done to catch the crazy son of a bitch? Makes *me* wonder if he's still on the payroll.'

'He's only recently come to our notice,' Walter said. 'The FBI have been investigating a number of random killings spread the length and breadth of the country. It hasn't been an easy task, simply because most of the bodies have never been found. People were reported missing, presumed dead. Others, well, you know the headlines, they've turned up missing body parts. Other than the MO nothing could tie the murders together.'

'What? No forensics? I find that a little hard to believe.' Frustration made me lurch up and stomp the length of the bedroom. A dressing table that wouldn't have looked anachronistic in the 1970s became my resting place. With my hands on the cabinet, I stared at my reflection in the mirror. It wasn't a face I recognized. Or liked. 'This is all bullshit, Walter!'

Walter eyed me with not a little annoyance. 'It's the truth, Hunter.'

I craned round so I could hold his gaze. 'Walter, you wouldn't know the truth if it sneaked up and bit you on the arse.'

'I'm telling you the truth,' he insisted.

Returning to the bed, I sat down with the petulance of a bored teenager. I adopted the fists on thighs posture of the man next to me. 'So what alerted you to the Harvestman's identity? I mean, considering that you haven't found any forensics? Did he start sending you taunting letters challenging you to catch him?'

Walter made a noise in his throat.

'There's no need for sarcasm. And anyway, I didn't say there weren't any forensics. You said that.'

This time I didn't bite.

'Only thing was, the forensics have only just recently come to *our* notice,' Walter went on. 'The FBI didn't have access to the USSS DNA records. We did. We only became aware of the Harvestman's identity following the murders of the couple at the motel out in the desert.'

'You mean the murders that my brother's been blamed for?'

'Exactly.'

'Yeah, but you know it wasn't John,' I said.

'Right. But it served our purpose to put that story out.'

'Served your fucking purpose? Walter, you know I love you, but sometimes you're a fucking arsehole!' My stare challenged him to disagree. In reply, he could only shrug.

'Comes with the job,' he said.

Yes, I suppose it did. It was my turn to shrug. What else was there for me to do? 'So you tipped off the media about John? What for? To draw out the real killer? You thought his ego would get the better of him and he'd show himself in order to snatch back the glory? Or was it a ploy in order to conceal the Harvestman's true identity?'

'A bit of both, I suppose,' Walter said.

'Christ, Walter! Even when you're being truthful I can't get a straight answer out of you.'

'OK, Hunter. Let me explain. That way you'll have everything I know and maybe you'll believe me for a change.' With a grunt he rose and walked away from me, fumbling the cigar to his lips. Like an evangelist preacher, he raised a stubby finger to signal the sermon was in session. 'Are you familiar with the book of Genesis?'

'I've read it, don't necessarily believe it,' I answered.

'It's not necessary that you believe it, only that you have some idea of its content.'

'I remember there are a lot of people with odd names begetting one another. Everything else I know I learned from Charlton Heston movies.'

Walter shook off my sarcasm. 'You've heard the story of Cain and Abel?'

'Who hasn't?' That was my last sarcastic quip. I remembered John referring to the Harvestman as Cain.

'It's nothing new for some demented bastard to take on the name of Cain,' Walter said. 'In fact, the psych of a murderer is often referred to as the Cain complex. Murderers often look up to the great grandpappy of all murderers as some sort of godhead in his own right. They think they're continuing his work on Earth and all that bullshit.'

'And your sicko is no exception?' I asked.

'No, no, no. Not *the* Cain.'

'Who then?'

'I'll come to that in a while. First I'll give you a little background on our man.'

I gave him the go-ahead, but he wasn't ready. He searched his pockets for a lighter. When he didn't find one, he looked at me expectantly.

'Can't help you,' I said.

In annoyance, he chewed on the wedge of tobacco leaves between his teeth. Not for the first time I saw him as Edward G. Robinson in one of those gangster flicks from the thirties. In the end, he stuffed the cigar into his breast pocket. 'His name is Martin Maxwell.'

'Doesn't ring any bells.'

'It won't. He didn't use that name when he was on active duty. Called himself Dean Crow. Thought it sounded tougher than Marty Maxwell. More befitting a United States Secret Service agent.'

'Sounds like a complete dickhead,' I offered. 'But, I must admit, I do recall something about him. Some low-level scandal involving a presidential candidate's wife wasn't it?'

'He was relieved of duty after he was found supposedly looting the good lady's wardrobe for what he called in interview "a token of his skill".'

'He's a fucking knicker sniffer?' I asked.

Walter shook his head. 'Nothing so gross. He cut a patch from one of her blouses is all.'

My forehead furrowed, recalling the missing swathe of cloth from the old woman's blouse after she'd been held hostage next door. I was about to note this when Walter added, 'I say, supposedly; the truth is the good lady was wearing her blouse at the time. Marty said he took the token to show her how vulnerable she was, how much she relied on him at all times.'

'Crazy fucker.'

'Yeah. Supremely crazy.'

'So how'd he get through the net? Surely the psych tests should've singled him out before he achieved agent status?'

'Some psychos are good at covering their true identities. Up until that point Marty Maxwell was well-respected and had seniority. It came as a surprise that one of their most able men was crazy as a fox.'

I grunted. 'And all that happened was he was discharged from service. Why didn't anyone keep an eye on him? Surely the signs were there, that he was capable of spiralling out of control?'

'Secret Service kept an eye on him as best they could. Only thing was – crazy or not – he was no fool. He knew that he'd be under surveillance for the foreseeable future. He wasn't prepared to let that happen.'

'He went underground?'

'More than that, Hunter. He faked his death. Supposedly, in an act of shame, he killed himself. And the other members of his family. Wife and two kids.'

'Oh, God . . .'

'Shot them dead in their beds, turned the gun on himself, stuck it under his chin and blasted off his head. He'd set up an incendiary device to burn the lot of them. Left only charred corpses in the burnt-out ruin of their home.' Walter hung his head in shame, but I guessed it wasn't in memory of Maxwell's wife and children. 'Their identity wasn't in dispute. That was an end to it. They fucked up, Hunter.'

'You're telling me. Obviously the DNA wasn't matched or they'd have known before now that the bastard was still on the loose.'

'I don't fully understand the science. They were happy it was Marty Maxwell. Considering he'd blown away half his head they had no teeth for a dental comparison, his fingerprints had been burnt off down to the bone. With the odds-on favourite that it was him, where would you have put your money?'

'Considering the training he'd had, what he'd have known, I'd have looked at the possibility that there was more to his death than met the eye. Who was the fourth body? If not Marty Maxwell? His father? A brother?'

'According to Marty's file he was a single child. Both parents died years before. Mother died following complications during childbirth, father from congenital heart disease. Let's not forget that, until then, he hadn't committed any crimes. It was put down as a murder-suicide. They believed Maxwell was dead and that was that. Case closed.'

'But obviously he did have a brother?' I asked.

'Turns out he had a half-brother called Robert Swan. Daddy Maxwell had been a naughty boy on his stag night, got an old sweetheart of his pregnant. It was Daddy Maxwell's best-kept secret. We only found this out afterwards when the brother's mother noticed he was missing when her paychecks stopped coming. She's a lush, lives alone in a tenement up in the Bronx; seems like the son was sending her money whenever he could. A good boy. Looked after his ma, like any good boy should.'

'But Maxwell found out about his brother? I thought you said it was a secret.'

Walter grimaced. 'Daddy Maxwell must've come clean in the end. Maybe he confessed his transgression on his deathbed. His wife was already on the other side; I guess he could've been seeking absolution before he went over to face her. From what we've been able to put together Maxwell sought out his half-brother, but still kept his identity secret from everyone else. Makes you wonder if he had the brother in mind for this very purpose all along, doesn't it?'

I ruminated on Walter's story; wondered what level of insanity it took to not only murder your family but to plan it for God knows how long before carrying out the act.

'If Maxwell had had the foresight to kill his brother's mother, we would probably be sitting here right at this moment wondering how the fuck a dead man had risen from the grave,' Walter said.

I asked, 'So what has the Cain reference got to do with it? Other than the arsehole likes assumed names?'

'His half-brother was a musician,' Walter said as if that would explain everything to me. I looked at him blankly. 'Genesis. Like you said, everyone begetting one another.'

'I'm still not with you.'

Walter raised a stubby finger again. Sermon part two. 'Well, if you've read your Bible you'll know that there was an old blind guy named Lamech.'

'I must have missed that bit.'

'Lamech had two sons. Jubal and Tubal.'

'Yeah,' I agreed. 'I remember now. Jubal and Tubal Cain.'

'Jubal was the inventor of music,' Walter began.

'Tubal was the forger of knives and swords,' I completed. 'Shit, I see the connection now. If the brother, a musician, is synonymous with Jubal that makes the Harvestman Tubal Cain.'

'Took a shitload of FBI profilers to come up with that one.'

'Hence Maxwell's love of knives?'

'Yup.'

'And the bones?'

'Some of these profilers have it in mind that he's set himself some kind of mission, that he's taking the bones from his victims for some express purpose.'

'What?' I asked. 'Other than he's a demented fuck?'

'Believe it or not, they believe he's feeling remorse for the killing of his brother, that somehow he's attempting to make amends.'

'Why his brother? Why not his wife and kids?'

Walter gave a body shrug. 'It's just a theory.'

'It'd make sense, I suppose. If he has this notion that they're Jubal and Tubal Cain reborn, it'd only be right that he'd attempt to make amends. You think the killings are symbolic, y'know, Bible-related?'

'Nothing in the Good Book that extols the virtues of offering up body parts,' Walter said.

I was flummoxed. 'So what do you think he's doing?'

'No idea. Could be making soup stock for all I know.'

'John said that they had an arrangement, that he was willing to see it through to the end. That he'd sacrifice himself for the old woman. You don't think that he was *literally* talking about sacrifice?'

'Hmm,' Walter said. 'Sacrifice is something that appears in the Old Testament. Maybe it's something that would appeal to Maxwell.'

I was off the bed in an instant.

'We can't stand around here any longer,' I said. 'Where's Rink?'

'Cooling his heels next door,' Walter said. As I started for the door, he said. 'Hold it, Hunter.'

I rounded on him, my jaw set. 'You aren't in a position to stop me, Walter.'

'I don't intend stopping you. That's not why I was brought in; I want to give you my blessing. And to ask you a favour.'

I stirred restlessly. 'A favour?'

'A favour. When you kill the son of a bitch, you don't breathe his name to anyone. Ever.'

I scowled at him. Then nodded slowly.

'Help me, Walter. Give me the resources I need to find the bastard and I promise you Marty Maxwell – or Tubal-fucking-Cain or whatever his name is – will be buried without a trace.'

'I knew I could count on you, Hunter.'

36

Back on the road again.

I knew then, even as we sped away in a comman-
deered government SUV, that this journey was bound
to end in bloodshed. The only thing that gave me heart
was that I wouldn't be the only man doing the bleeding.
The Harvestman had an abundance of blood to spill,
too. By the grim set of Rink's features, the same notion
was burning in his heart. Cain had made two implac-
able enemies in us; I could almost pity the fool. Almost.

Rink drove. I held the Global Positioning Satellite
receiver supplied by Walter. On the display screen a
red cursor blipped on an overlaid map of the Los
Angeles Bay area. Periodically the cursor shifted on the
map, denoting not only that Cain was still on the move,
but that he hadn't yet realized John was in possession of
the mobile phone.

It could only be a matter of time before Cain discovered John's duplicity, or that the makeshift tracking
device became obsolete when John was buried in a
dumpster or sunk to the bottom of a river.

Going for us was the fact that Cain was taking
diversionary tactics to shake off pursuit. Guessing that
he might be followed by more conventional methods,

he was taking surface streets and alleyways to navigate the sprawling city. Though he had more than an hour's lead on us, we'd been able to pull back much of that time by following a direct route. Another thing that very quickly became obvious – even though he often backtracked or ran parallel to his intended target – Cain was making for Interstate 10, the main eastward route out of Los Angeles.

Initially picking up the 405, we hurtled north past Redondo Beach towards LAX, struck eastward on the 105, then again headed north on the 110, hoping to cut Cain off where the two major routes converged near to the downtown LA Convention Center. It was apparent that it wouldn't be as easy as that when Cain jinked north-eastward, skirting the centre of the city on its northern border while we continued east again towards Interstate 5 and became snarled in traffic hold-ups.

I watched the cursor skip across the map, pick up Interstate 10 and continue past the Rose Bowl as Rink cursed and pressed on the horn, attempting to force our way through the traffic.

After twenty minutes of very little progress, the traffic began to open out ahead of us and Rink pressed the throttle with disregard for the speed limit. Slaloming in and out of lanes, he gained open road and booted the SUV.

Picking up Interstate 5, we made the short trip northward before meeting Interstate 10 again, and swung in pursuit of our quarry that was now more than thirty minutes ahead of us.

'We can still make it,' I told Rink. 'The prick's certain that he's in the clear. He doesn't seem to be travelling much over sixty.' I glanced over at the odometer. Rink was pushing the SUV at 120 miles an hour. 'If you can keep this up, we'll catch him in no time.'

'Darn tootin' I can keep it up. If all these goddamn Sunday drivers would get the hell outa my way.' To add weight to his promise Rink laid his hand on the horn, causing vehicles ahead to swerve to let us through.

It was an exhilarating ride. If it wasn't for the fear of arriving too late to save John, I think I'd have whooped and howled like a kid on a rollercoaster. Instead I stayed grimly silent, my gaze on the GPS screen. I didn't have to be so observant. Cain was already out of the urban sprawl and was headed out towards the vastness of the American interior.

Even at breakneck pace, it was almost an hour before we caught sight of the Dodge hijacked from the house at Long Beach. We were tempted to continue at speed, attempt to catch and then force the Dodge off the road. Though I didn't want to believe that John was dead, now, at least, we could stop the Harvestman's reign. Of course, stopping him here would bring further complications.

Conclusion? It would be more prudent to follow at a safe distance and then act when there was no likelihood of an innocent passer-by being caught up in the gunfire.

Cain wasn't a fool. He was a crazy, murderous bastard, but he was also shrewd. Along with that, he'd also been trained as a government agent and it was a given that he was an expert driver, versed in all manner of countersurveillance measures and reactive driving. We fell into line, allowing more than quarter of a mile, and at least four vehicles, to separate us. Though that was a meaningless exercise.

'He knows we're here,' Rink said.

I looked across at him. There he was again, reading my thoughts.

'He knows we're here and he's taunting us,' Rink embellished.

I nodded. 'Probably.'

'Back at the house, it was almost like he was challenging you to find him. Makes me think that's why he spent so long in the city; to let you catch up.'

I realized Rink was right. 'Yeah, he was taking a big chance driving through the centre of LA when there could've been an APB out for him. He could've easily switched vehicles, too. Looks like he wants us to follow him.'

'You want me to get up a little closer? Put some pressure on the squirmy bastard?'

'No. Just hang back where we are. Let's see where he wants to take us.'

'My guess is it's going to be somewhere remote. He's looking for a showdown. Doesn't want anyone else getting in the way.'

'If it's a showdown he wants, it's what he's gonna get.'

Rink and I exchanged a glance.

'He's certainly made this personal, ain't he?' Rink asked.

'He made it personal when he took John prisoner,' I pointed out.

'Maybe so,' Rink said. 'But I'm referring to him and you. When he found out who you were, I could see it in his face; it was almost as if he was excited. As if he'd found a worthy adversary, y'know? You think he's looking to die, Hunter? I heard that some of these sickos like to go out in a blaze of glory. Apparently, it's the latest phenomenon: suicide by cop. Do you think he's looking for you to kill him?'

'Whether he is or he isn't, that's what's going to happen,' I promised.

'Yeah,' Rink grumbled in his throat. 'But be wary, man. Even if he has a death wish, he probably intends taking you with him. If he's looking to bolster his reputation, who better to have on his dead list than you?' Rink looked across at me again. 'Apart from me, of course.'

Even in that moment, Rink could find humour. It made me smile in response. 'Of course.'

'No, man, I'm serious. The asshole's looking to make himself famous.'

I shook my head. 'You really think that anyone will ever know the truth about him?'

Rink's eyes crinkled. 'Not if it's left to Walter.'

'The proviso he made – allowing us to bring the Harvestman down – was that his name never gets mentioned again. How likely is it that my name hits the news if the bastard manages to take me out?'

'Not very, I suppose. But then again, what about your folks back home? Don't you think they're going to want answers, that they won't raise hell if anything happens to you?'

'Diane knows what my line of work entails. She'll receive a call from Walter's office. She'll be told to keep quiet. She wants a quiet life, she'll comply.'

Rink grunted. 'An' here was me thinking you really understood your ex-wife.'

I squinted across at him and he looked at me as though I was a complete idiot. 'Hunter, man. You're not in that game any more. How many times do I have to remind you? There's your mom and dad. Jennifer. An' you really think for one goddamn minute that Diane ain't gonna scream to the rafters if anything happens to you? You think she'll give a shit what line Walter tries to feed her about the Harvestman's identity being an embarrassment to the United States government?'

I exhaled. He was right again. Of course Diane would want – no, demand – answers. Suggesting otherwise was doing her an injustice. I nodded in agreement.

'Not only that,' Rink went on. 'But don't you think I won't raise the subject? I don't owe Walter a goddamn thing. I never made any promises to hide the identity of his little black sheep.'

'No, Rink. I made the promise for both of us. Coming along on this ride, you bought into the agreement. You have to stand by my word.'

Rink's face twisted, but he conceded the point.

We drove for another hour and a quarter. Contemplative silence reigned over the many miles.

'Look familiar?' Rink suddenly asked.

I glanced towards a rest stop across the carriageway to our left. There was a diner and rest area, beyond them a cul-de-sac of single-storey cabins. I shook my head.

'That's where the couple was murdered. The man and woman who picked John up in their car.'

'You mean the couple who gave Martin Maxwell or Tubal Cain or whatever it is he calls himself a ride? It's obvious now isn't it; what really happened, I mean?'

'You're saying that, somehow, the Harvestman ended up with John's car – the one he stole from Petoskey – and it was him, not John, who the witnesses saw?'

'Yeah. Exactly.'

'So how do you explain John and the Harvestman tying up together again? I mean . . . it's a bit of a stretch, ain't it?'

'Not unless something happened between John and Cain. Something that ensured Cain would hunt him down.'

Rink gave an expansive shrug. 'Who knows? They coulda been acting together long before any of this happened.'

'No. I don't believe that. Chance threw them together. I think John became an unwilling puppet of this man. The evidence is all there. Remember that it was John who saved the old woman, that it was John who gave us the tools to hunt Cain down. It was his decision to take my mobile phone. Do you really believe he'd have done that if he was working with Cain?'

'No, I don't. An' I don't think he'd offer himself up as a sacrifice either. I'm only playing devil's advocate here, Hunter. I don't suppose we'll ever know the true story.'

'Only way we're gonna find that out is to save John,' I said. 'If I have my way Cain won't be around to do any explaining.'

Out here on the fringes of the Mojave Desert, there was a surreal cast to the early evening sky. Behind us, hovering above the Pacific Ocean, the sun's final attempt at holding on to day made the sky a mother-of-pearl banner. Alongside the road, Joshua trees cast elongated shadows like accusing fingers, pointing the way to the showdown ahead.

Four vehicles in front, Cain flicked on his lights, ensuring we could follow him as the night began to drop its hood over the desert.

While he drove, Rink drank mineral water courtesy of the government. He offered me some. Pity that the bottle didn't contain something a little stronger. Nonetheless, I accepted it from him and chugged down a grateful mouthful.

Really, I should've been thirstier than I was, I should've felt the need for food. Neither of us had eaten anything since early that morning. However, the continued release of adrenalin ensured that nothing would pass my lips that required my stomach to hold on to it. Anything more solid than the spring water, I suspected, would end up projected out the window a couple of miles hence.

As night fell, Rink pushed the SUV on. One of the cars between us turned up a side road and Rink filled the gap it left.

Two further hours Cain led us a merry dance, then – as if concerned that we might miss him turning off the main route – he flicked on his indicators, slowed down dramatically and crawled to the intersection.

Two of the cars ahead of us overtook him before he reached the turn-off. As Cain swept to the right, the remaining car continued on into the east, and I saw Cain flare the brakes a couple of times, ensuring we didn't lose him.

'Considerate son of a bitch,' Rink muttered.

Then Cain was on the flyover, crossing the interstate, heading north. On the bridge he slowed to a crawl, watched as we swung onto the off ramp, then he gave the Dodge throttle and peeled away.

'I guess we're getting close now, and he wants time to prepare,' I said.

The GPS tracker had been obsolete for some hours now. Throughout it had travelled cradled in my palms, for no other reason than it stopped me fiddling with my gun. Luck, or maybe foresight, caused me to check the screen. The cursor indicating the latest triangulated location of the mobile phone had finally stopped moving. I didn't even bother to frown. Cain had discovered our deception. Maybe he'd found John was carrying the device as soon as they'd left the house at Long Beach; maybe it was much later. Whatever. When he'd slowed down it wasn't to taunt us, it was to throw away the phone.

It was apparent he wanted us nearby. More apparent was his need to buy a little time before we arrived at his prearranged meeting ground.

'Put your foot down, Rink.'

'I can still see his lights,' Rink said. 'I won't lose him.'

'He won't let you lose him,' I said. 'He'll make sure we know exactly where he is. But he'll be prepared for our arrival, and I don't want to allow him that advantage.'

37

'You don't look so good.'

Cain studied his passenger.

His words, he decided, were an understatement.

John was spread across the back seat of the Dodge like yesterday's fast food wrappers: cold, soiled and greasy. Blood from the wound he'd picked up at the shoot-out on the yacht caked his clothing down his injured side. His hands were also reddish-brown and he had smears on his forehead. Thick beads of perspiration oozed from him like water from a perished boiler.

'I said that you don't look so good, John,' Cain said, watching John's eyelids flutter in the rear-view mirror.

'Turn off the light, willya?' John mumbled incoherently.

'I need to check that you're OK,' Cain said, but he reached up and flicked off the interior lights.

'Why? You're gonna kill me,' John said, his voice coming out like marbles over tin sheet. 'Or have you forgotten?'

'You keep saying that. I might have a change of mind.'

'Yeah, right.' John forced himself to sit upright.

'Lay back down.'

'I'm fine.'

'The road gets kinda rough up ahead. It would be better if you were lying down. Less chance you'll open up your wound again.'

'My wound's fine.'

Cain gave a humourless laugh. 'Suit yourself.'

'Better than suiting you,' John said with little conviction.

Cain drummed his fingers on the steering wheel. 'You know, I'm not sure this old heap will get us where we're going. Not in any shape, at least.'

'Won't matter,' John told him. 'You won't need it for the return trip. You'll be getting a lift in the coroner's car.'

'Ha!'

'I mean it. You fuck with my brother, you're booking your own body bag.'

'Keep thinking that way, John. Optimism's what you need to keep you alive.'

'I'm not gonna get outa this alive. I know that. I've known it all along. My only hope is that I see you die first.'

'If anyone ends up dead, it'll be your high and mighty brother. Chances are I'll have to do Jared Rington too.'

'You're so full of shite you actually believe that?'

'Are you saying that confidence in my abilities is a bad thing? Shame on you, John. What a horrible thing to do; trying to tarnish my self-esteem.'

'Nothing I say would make you think badly of yourself. You're a fuckin' psychopath.'

'Sticks and stones, John. Sticks and stones.'

'Stop being so fucking patronizing. Why don't you come clean and tell the fuckin' truth? You've intended killing me all along, haven't you? Fuck, I can't believe you saved me from drowning, so that you can murder me. That's so fucked up, nobody would believe it.'

'Doesn't matter, John,' Cain said. 'You're here now. Makes no difference whether you believed me or not. Fact is . . . it's immaterial.'

'Fact is,' John snapped. 'You're gonna get your head handed to you on a plate. My brother isn't like me; Joe *will* kill you.'

'Nah, I don't see things turning out that way.'

John gave a disgusted cough, squirmed down in the seat. Either his strength was failing him or he'd decided that it was pointless talking. Not that it made a difference; if Cain wanted to talk, then he would talk. 'Now then, where is the big bold Joe Hunter?'

Cain squinted into the mirror, adjusted it. Some distance back he could see the headlights of the pursuing SUV. In response, he turned off the Dodge's lights. 'Don't want to make things too easy, now, do we?'

'I thought you wanted him to follow you?'

'I do, just not too closely.'

'You may as well give up. Joe isn't gonna be reading you your rights and putting you in cuffs. As soon as he sees you he's gonna put a bullet right between your eyes.'

'Then I'll just have to make certain he doesn't see me, won't I?'

Cain grinned into the darkness.

The road had become a dirt trail, pitted with ruts and sprouting colonies of sagebrush along its centre where the desert sand gathered. The moon hanging low over the horizon offered a little light, so Cain could make out the road ahead. Not that he needed to concentrate; he knew this trail as intuitively as he knew his own dark heart's desires. Despite his misgivings about the worthiness of the Dodge, he pushed it to greater speed, smiling at each jounce and the wince of pain it elicited from his surly passenger.

'I bet you wish you hadn't pulled that stunt with the cell phone?' he asked. John didn't answer. 'Right now you're thinking that not only have you signed your own death warrant – but that of your brother as well. Deep down some errant grain of honour is festering like a malignant cancer, eating away at your insides. You're thinking: I should've taken my dues and spared the others. Now I've put my brother in terrible danger.'

'No,' John said, forcing a grunt of disdain. 'I'm thinking you're so full of shite I can't stand the stench any longer. I'm outa here, you arsehole!'

Then John was pressing down on the door handle. He thrust open the door, squirmed towards the opening with his shoulder. The rush of wind banged it back against him.

Cain would never admit to panic, but realizing John's insane plan he let slip a shout of denial. He immediately stamped on the brakes. John's body was thrown forwards, and his forehead slammed the back of Cain's neck. The shock of the collision forced Cain's hands off the steering wheel, and momentarily he had to fight both the movement of the vehicle and the wave of agony washing over him. In those few seconds, John threw his weight against the partly open door and he was snatched away into billowing dust.

'Son of a bitch!' Cain screamed, stamping on the brake pedal a second time. The Dodge fishtailed, sending up plumes of dirt, ending up crossways abreast the trail. He threw open the door and lurched out, eyes scanning the road for John's battered form. Not on the road. He began running. In the distance came the telltale lights of the cavalry charge headed by Joe Hunter.

Forty or so paces along the road he found John sprawled at the base of a gnarly cactus. Momentarily he feared that John was dead, but then he saw the fire in the man's eyes as he squirmed round to face him.

'You stupid, stupid idiot,' he snarled.

'Fuck you,' John grunted in response.

'No, fuck you.' As John attempted to rise up against him, Cain's foot thrust him down again, pressed savagely on the wound in his chest. John screamed. Cain pressed harder. The screaming stopped as consciousness fled John at last.

Cain grabbed him. He thrust his arms round John's chest in a bear hug, began back-pedalling. Dragging the groaning man, Cain looked up. Hunter's lights were some distance away, but looming nearer with vengeful resolution. 'I should just leave you here to die, you goddamn ass. Leave you in the road so your freakin' brother rides right on over the top of you.'

It was a hollow threat. He still had a plan for John Telfer.

38

The enigma that was Tubal Cain kept impinging on my thoughts. How does a psycho like Martin Maxwell bluff his way through the rigorous selection processes employed by the Secret Service? How does he manage to conceal his true self – a depraved stalker and murderer – and pass himself off as normal?

Not only that, but to his wife and kids he was the epitome of the family dad. What had gone through their minds when they'd finally seen his true face?

What had his long-lost brother imagined when first they'd met? That they'd pick up on their missing past, that they'd shoot pool together, share a couple of beers, become bosom buddies? I bet he never imagined that he'd end up a scorched corpse in a house he'd never known, the ghosts of Cain's wife and children keeping him company.

'You're doing it again,' Rink said.

I looked over at Rink, who was doing a good job of glancing at me without taking his full attention from the trail.

'Doing what?'

'Wearing that face.'

'What face?'

'The face that says you ain't worried about what's to come. The one you always wore on missions.'

'I'm worried, Rink.'

'Don't look like it.'

Then he changed the subject.

'Heads up, Hunter. The lights have just gone off.'

I peered into the darkness ahead. I couldn't see the Dodge's tail lights. They'd long taunted us and their sudden disappearance brought an uncomfortable feeling of foreboding. Like a hole had opened up and the Devil had escaped us by fleeing back to hell.

'You think he's stopped? Maybe fixin' to escape?' Rink glanced my way again, back to the road.

'No. He's running blind. He wants to get ahead of us so he can set up an ambush.'

'Time we played catch-up, then,' Rink said. The SUV surged ahead, bouncing over the higher ruts, blasting directly through others so that gravel and small rocks banged and clattered in the wheel arches.

Now the chase was truly on.

Again, I checked my SIG. Full clip. Two spares in my waistband. Then I reached down and tickled the hilt of my military issue Ka-bar where it was tucked in my boot. Somehow, I suspected that the knife would be my weapon of choice when I finally came eye to eye with the murderous bastard.

Stars twinkled in the vault above us. Out here, in the middle of this empty space, the sky appeared endless, the starlight sharply defined. Shadows were stark and the sand and gravel had a faintly luminous quality. Rocketing across the nocturnal landscape, the beauty of the desert was lost on me. I didn't give any of it a second's notice. How could I think of beauty when I was chasing something as loathsome as Tubal Cain?

I was inclined to check the night sky for another reason: as we'd used the technology given to us by Walter, I'd no doubt that we in turn were being tailed equally astutely. They wouldn't be coming in cars; they'd have command of helicopters, possibly even an AWACS high in the heavens to plot our course. In the end, I didn't bother looking; helicopters would be piloted without running lights and a high-altitude spy plane would be impossible to spot.

'When we find him we do him quickly,' I said to Rink.

'My intention all along.'

'Walter's goons will be coming,' I added.

'They won't try and stop us.'

'I know. They'll be coming to mop up, to make sure that everything's clean. I don't want John falling into their hands.' I looked pointedly at Rink, and he jerked his chin in response. 'They'll make John disappear. They might even make us disappear.'

'They'll goddamn try, frog-giggin' assholes.'

I returned my attention to the road ahead. The brush country was giving way to a higher elevation. On the skyline, I could detect a deepening of the shadows, as if a colossal wall had been raised across the desert.

'You any idea where we are?' I asked Rink.

'Nope.'

I looked for the GPS, switched it on and studied the faintly glowing map on the LED screen. Tightly knit bars showed that the terrain became more mountainous ahead. The road wasn't marked on the map, but that came as no surprise. I placed the GPS down in the foot-well. 'Keep on going. Looks like we're heading for those hills.'

Rink obliged. But we'd travelled no more than a quarter of a mile before I slapped my hands on the dashboard and commanded him to stop. I craned round so I didn't lose sight of what was at the side of the road. Rink brought the SUV to a halt even as I was opening the door to get out.

I jogged back the way we'd come, slowed down and came to a halt twenty metres from what I'd noticed protruding from a clump of parched brush.

I listened.

Nothing moved in the sandscape. All I could hear was the throaty hum of the SUV behind me, the rushing blood in my veins. Still, I remained motionless, using my peripheral vision to probe the shadows. What is often missed when viewed directly can be picked up peripherally, the slightest movement amplified tenfold. It's a prey animal thing, a throwback to the days when man was hunted by carnivorous beasts.

Finally satisfied that this wasn't part of Cain's ambush, I advanced. A quick inspection showed that the dirt and gravel at the side of the road was disturbed. More concerning, I saw a damp swathe of blood where a body had been dragged through the earth. I was no Sherlock Holmes, but I guessed that John had made some effort at escape, only to be captured again and forced back into the Dodge. Cain had John, yes, but he hadn't noticed the briefcase hung up in the bushes further along the trail.

I trotted over and snatched the Samsonite case from the brush. I was in no doubt that it was the case I'd seen John clinging on to when we were at the beach house. Chance could have dumped a briefcase way out here in the desert, but not one glistening with tacky blood. I didn't spare the time to check its contents, noting only that it was heavy before I stuffed it under my armpit and headed back to the SUV.

When I was back in the car and Rink had set off after Cain, he asked, 'You thinking what I'm thinking?'

'Money,' I said. I thumbed the catches and opened the case on my lap. Bundle upon bundle of bills filled it. Rink gave a low whistle.

'Counterfeit?'

I checked.

'No. The real thing.'

'So that's what this is all about,' Rink said.

I shook my head. 'I don't think so, Rink. It was never about the money. Cain wants blood.'

'Bones,' Rink corrected.

'But I do think this is what it's all been about for John.'

'Goddamn greedy fool.'

I shook my head. 'Believe it or not, but I don't think he did this out of greed. I think he sees it as a way to put things right.'

'Yeah,' Rink said with no conviction. I shrugged. I knew John better than that. I believed that he'd changed. The old John wouldn't have jeopardized his safety for the old woman; he wouldn't have risked lifting the mobile phone from my pocket for fear that Cain saw him. To me, John had turned a corner in his life where something meant more to him than his next fix.

Back there on the trail, he hadn't attempted to escape at all; he'd jumped from the Dodge with the intention of leaving the cash here for me to find. The money wasn't for him; it was for Louise, it was for Jenny, it was for his children. Stuffing the case beneath my seat, I put the discovery to the back of my mind. I could see to it later.

39

'How do you like the place?'

Oblivious to Cain, John slumped against the wooden support-beam, smearing it with blood as he attempted to force himself upright. John's head lolled on his shoulders. He mumbled something incoherent.

'You could act a little more enthusiastic than that. I've gone to a lot of bother to get the place ready for *my* brother. Put a lot of time and effort into the decor. Don't you think the ambience is just right?'

John staggered. Cain clutched him under an armpit, heedless of the way his fingers dug into flesh. 'Watch that first step; it can be a real bitch.'

Then, with a shove, he pressed John forwards. Watched as his captive tumbled down the short flight of steps into darkness. Only semi-conscious, John made little noise. He fell as if constructed from rags that made only soft contact with the steps. A grunt was all that marked his resting place.

'That'll teach you to pay attention,' Cain said. He wasn't happy that John had lost the case of money. Though neither was he unnecessarily concerned. Either Joe Hunter would fetch the money for him, or he could backtrack and collect it when all this was

over. Concern was unnecessary, but a little cruelty
would remind John Telfer what it meant to cross Tubal
Cain. Taking one last glance behind him, Cain followed John into the darkness.

A short way down, the steps levelled out on a floor
made of bedrock. Last time Cain had been here he had
swept the desert sand away, but already he could feel
windblown dust beneath his feet; it was the main
downside to his hideaway that he had to continually
maintain it by brushing and sweeping to keep the
desert at bay.

He prodded John with a foot, moving him aside as he
reached out in the dark and clutched for the padlock
that held the metal door shut. Holding the lock in one
hand, he ran the fingers of the other up the near wall,
found a narrow niche he'd dug into the sandstone and
pulled out the concealed key. The key opened the lock
with little resistance. Cain pushed and the door swung
inwards on well-maintained hinges.

The smell buffeted him.

He smiled.

Even in his semi-unconscious state, John gagged at
the stench.

'What the fu . . .?' John groaned.

Cain didn't comment; he bent down and grabbed
John's shirt, hauling him to his feet. He pushed John
into the room before him, urging him into the charnel
stink. John gave some resistance, refusing to breathe, a
steeling of his shoulders as he attempted to ward off the
sickening odour of rotted meat.

'Get inside,' Cain said, almost a whisper.

'No,' John gasped.

'Yes.' Cain pushed him into the cloying darkness.

Cain entered the room with a breezy exuberance. He fairly skipped over to the nearest lamp, scratched around until he found the butane lighter beside it, then he set flame to wick, casting writhing shadows round the room. That done, he emptied his pockets of the bones garnered during his latest trip. They made quite a mound. Then, hands on hips, he surveyed the space before him.

'Now what do you think, John? Do you think Jubal would be pleased?'

On the floor, John was curled into a foetal ball. One arm covered his face, but Cain could see the whites of his eyes reflected in lamplight. From under his ineffectual shield, he searched the room with a mix of fascination and revulsion. His pupils were like pinpricks in yellowed snow. Yes, Cain decided, John was very impressed.

40

'Remind me not to invest in a holiday home out here,' Rink said. 'Could be a bitch letting it out during the winter season.'

'It'd be a bitch in any season,' I told him.

The Mojave Desert occupies more than 25,000 square miles, bordering California and portions of Arizona, Utah and Nevada. Where we were at that given moment I couldn't even begin to hazard a guess. I was only pleased that we had a vehicle along with us. If we'd had to walk out of there in the daytime, I didn't wager much for our chances of survival.

Not that it was a desert in the true sense of the word. It wasn't made up of mile after mile of dunes like I'd experienced in the Sahara a number of years ago. But one look at the blasted landscape told me it was every bit as arid.

We were climbing higher into the foothills. All around us the night sky was torn along the horizon by weird shapes that I knew were Joshua trees. In my imagination, they appeared to be misshapen giants waving us on to our doom. The road was now little more than a memory and all Rink followed was the faint trail Cain's Dodge had left upon the earth.

During the day, this area was hot, and through the middle hours of the night the temperature could drop uncomfortably low, but we were driving through those hours when the heat stored during the daylight hours leached from the rocks and gravel, making the night tepid. Still, even with the heating cranked high in the SUV, I felt the first hint of the cold. I shivered, found myself tightening in reflex. Rink snapped a glance my way.

'You OK, Hunter?'

I mumbled assent.

'Everything's gonna go fine, you just mark my words,' Rink offered.

'I'm OK, Rink,' I reassured him. 'Just felt like someone walked over my grave.'

Rink fell silent. Maybe my words were too prophetic for his liking. He concentrated on guiding the SUV up an incline towards a pass into the foothills marked by two gargantuan crags. Nearing the summit, he turned to me. 'It's Cain who's gonna die.'

I exhaled. 'I hope you're right. That it's all over with tonight.'

I looked at him. He coughed deep in his throat, a low grumble. 'Cain's number's up, Hunter. That part'll be finished. But what about the rest?'

'What rest?' I asked, but already the question was rhetorical. He was referring to John, to Louise Blake, Petoskey and Hendrickson, Walter, the Secret Service. All the victims of the Harvestman and their families. Maybe Cain would die tonight, but how long would the hubbub last afterwards? There were other deaths –

Cain's victims aside – involved along the way. In particular, the hitman killed at Louise's house, the other I'd killed back at the beach house. How were those going to be resolved?

'We're gonna have us a three-ring circus out here,' Rink said. 'Big top, ringmaster, the whole shebang! Let's just hope that we don't end up looking like the goddamn clowns.'

I shook my head.

'Walter will see to it that that won't happen.' Just as he'd see to the disappearance of the hitmen I'd dispatched.

I stared straight ahead. The two gigantic pillars of rock dominated the skyline. Against the purple sky, they looked like monoliths, stones to mark the tombs of twin giants. And we had to pass between them.

Driving between the huge crags, I concluded that we'd just gone beyond the point of no return. Clichéd, yes, but true. Once more, I checked my weapons. They were still prepared, just as they'd been minutes earlier. Momentarily I wondered if they would be enough.

Beyond the rock gates was a flat expanse of sandstone. It sloped gently towards the horizon, shelf built upon shelf of petrified sand. Millions of years ago, this area had been the bed of a prehistoric ocean, teeming with weird and astonishing life forms. But now, far above present sea level, the vastness of rock was devoid of life. Only dust devils moved here, tiny zephyrs plucking and whirling particles of grit across the unresponsive land.

'Looks like we just touched down on Mars,' Rink breathed.

It was apparent by the way the table of rock disappeared into the night that we were on a massive shelf of land, and I cautioned Rink, urged him to slow down. Just something about the colour of the night beyond the scope of our vision gave me pause; as though we were standing at the edge of the world and an unwary step would pitch us over the edge.

Rink pulled the SUV to a halt. We both leant forward, craning our necks to look down on the mist-shrouded valley below us. We shared a glance. If Rink hadn't stopped when he did, we would've dropped sixty or more metres to our deaths.

'Which way now, Daniel Boone?' Rink asked.

'Anyway but forward,' I said and we both laughed.

Careful not to slip us over the rim of the cliff, Rink edged the SUV to the left, then drove with the caution of someone suddenly struck blind. Here the sheet-rock became rutted with deep crevasses and Rink drove back inland, did a complete U-turn, then swung back the way we'd come. Out of the night loomed queer shapes. Only as we drew alongside them did I realize that we were travelling amidst the husks of burnt-out vehicles. Predominantly they were camper vans and Winnebagos, the occasional minivan. Cain, it seemed, had a major gripe with their drivers. Then we found the Dodge. It was immediately apparent that the car had been abandoned. Both front doors stood open and the interior light was a yellow glow against the night sky.

Nothing stirred inside the car. Cain could've been stretched out across the back seat, waiting for us to blunder over and poke our heads inside so that he could shoot us. Or he could've hunkered down behind the car. I dismissed both ideas.

What fun would that be?

He hadn't brought us all the way out here just so he could hit us with potshots while we were out in the open. Cain had planned a more interesting game than that.

But we still had to check it out.

We disembarked the SUV fifteen metres shy of the Dodge. Rink went one way and I went the other, guns out in front of us. I circled to the front of the Dodge while Rink came up behind it. Then, in a position where we could each see both sides of the vehicle, we approached front and back.

As I trained my barrel on the interior of the car, Rink moved in and checked the rear seat.

'Clear?' I asked.

Rink nodded to me to come closer.

'Check it out, Hunter.'

I did. And I could do nothing but groan. The back seat was awash with blood; not pools of the stuff, but enough streaks and smears to indicate John didn't have much time left on this Earth.

While I continued to stare at the mess within the car, Rink quickly checked the trunk of the Dodge, finding it locked. Cain wasn't about to slip out from inside it when our backs were turned. Rink came to stand beside me. Gaining my attention, he nodded to our front.

Patches of scuffed rock marked someone's passing. So did the periodic droplets of blood that glistened darkly against the paler surface.

We were off again. Moving apart so that a dozen paces separated us, we edged forwards. Then no more than a hundred metres from the parked car, we gained the brink of the cliff. Out of the confines of the SUV, we could approach nearer to the cliff than before, so the void below us no longer appeared so empty. The cliff fell more than sixty metres to a sloping embankment of shale and sand, before levelling out into a natural amphitheatre that stretched further than I could see. It was a great bowl shape, alkaline white, with gathering mist hanging over it like a multitude of spectres. The sun-bleached basin reminded me of only one thing: the scooped out, hollowed interior of a human skull. I hissed. If Cain could call any place home this would be it.

Outlined on the escarpment's rim we made easy targets for anyone positioned below. We stepped back.

'Over there,' Rink motioned. 'Looks like a way down. Has to be the way they went.'

I saw the fissure in the earth and nodded. When I got near, I peered over the edge. At a casual glance, you probably wouldn't notice the fabricated steps leading down the cliff-side, but they were what I'd been looking for. Cain had been here many times in the past; the steps were testimony to that.

'I'll take point,' I told Rink. Then without waiting for acknowledgement, I set off. The steps weren't as sheer as they first appeared, and, surprisingly, it was not necessary to be mountain-goat nimble to climb down them. However, burdened with John, I did wonder how Cain managed to do it without tripping and carrying them both to their deaths. The thought gave me a healthy new respect for what the man was capable of.

I'd cautioned myself previously, reminding myself that he was a trained Secret Service agent, that he was probably whalebone-tough beneath the unassuming exterior. Now I had to credit him with above-average strength and determination. He wouldn't be easy to take out in a chest-to-chest fight, though that was my intention.

Rink didn't need guidance on how to handle our descent. He waited until I'd gained the bottom of the fissure before he set off.

While he came down, I covered him. When he reached the bottom, I stalked forwards. Rink followed, scanning left and right, periodically behind. We traversed the slope of the bone-white hollow in that fashion until we found level footing. The ground was no longer as treacherous as it had been on the descent, but the mist rose up before us, obscuring our view. That was bad enough, but it also played tricks on our ears. As I stepped out on the sand, I could've sworn I heard the tinkle of music. I paused, turned back to Rink.

'You hear that?'

Rink's eyebrows knitted. 'That a radio playing?' he whispered.

I shrugged, moved on. Between patches of mist, I thought I saw something move. In response, my hand swung towards it, fingertip caressing the trigger of my SIG. Again the tinkle of music. Then the mist writhed and the shape I'd glimpsed was gone.

'What the fuck was that?' Rink hissed at me. Which confirmed I wasn't hallucinating.

'Don't know,' I replied.

'Freaking ghost,' Rink muttered under his breath.

Music tinkled from in front of me like the dissonant chimes of a musically challenged orchestra. Once more, I snatched a glimpse of the conductor waving his baton. And, inured to horror as I'd become, even I cringed back from what stood before me.

'Shit,' I breathed.

Rink had been right: the monstrosity before me was indeed best described as a ghost.

41

Cain whistled while he worked. He kept harmony with every wince of agony from John, exhaled loudly in time with every grunt of pain, laughed when John ground his body against the rock wall in an effort to pull away from his slicing administrations.

'The pain will go away soon,' Cain reassured John. 'Once I'm through the dermis, as far down as the bone, I'll be beyond the nerve endings.'

John howled in fresh torment.

Cain moved closer, eyes like lasers, guiding the scaling knife with a surgeon's precision. In such deep concentration, the tip of his tongue poked from beneath the slash of his lips, writhing like a fat worm as he plied his tool. Beyond flesh was bone, and that would require effort. His whistling stopped, and now he moaned more often than John did.

John was travelling that road beyond agony now. Beyond the point of human endurance. Cain sighed. His work wasn't the same, didn't hold the same satisfaction, if his subject wasn't around to appreciate it. Shaking his head, he stepped away. Then, hands on hips, he surveyed his work of art.

'Not bad, I suppose,' he told himself. Though it still lacked a certain flamboyant statement to finish it off. If this was to be the magnum opus of both Jubal and Tubal Cain, he required a truly magnificent centre-piece to finalize it.

With that in mind, he slipped the scaling knife into his waistband, retrieved the empty gun from where he'd laid it on the floor and headed out into the night.

42

I've often wondered if there's anyone more super-stitious than a soldier. You'd think that with such a reliance on fact, science and technology, the basis of modern warfare, there'd be no room for anything supernatural. But, as I've already mentioned, in many a soldier's mind resides the firm belief that paranormal skills can add to the warrior's arsenal. I for one swear by the presence of a sixth sense, the heightened ability to detect the unseen watcher, the sniper on the rooftop or the tiger hidden in the long grass. It's so widely believed that it has even been granted a term: Rapid Intuitive Experience, the soldier's very own ESP.

I accept the proof of such a thing is subjective, but it has saved my life enough times that I give it full credence. Up until now, though, despite my fanciful notions during the assault on Petoskey's building, I didn't give the existence of ghosts much credence. How could I? The amount of men I've killed, I would go insance if I dwelt upon the number who must haunt me.

Still, for more than a heartbeat I genuinely accepted that the thing in front of me was a vengeful spirit risen from its grave to exact retribution. I stepped back, eyes wide, mouth hanging open. And, if the blade it held in its clawed fist had been animated, I doubt that I could've stopped it scything the head from my shoulders.

'Holy Christ!' I heard the words, but was unsure whether Rink or I uttered them. Maybe we both did.

Point shooting is based solely and entirely on the natural posture, the natural reaction to lifting the gun and firing wherever danger presents itself. When confronted by this diabolical creature, my reactions failed me. The SIG hung useless by my side.

Then Rink was beside me. He laid a hand on my shoulder. 'Hunter . . . we gotta keep moving, man. Can't let this damn thing throw us.'

'It's a little hard not to,' I croaked.

A paralysis gripped me, and it was an effort to shake free of it. When I did, it was through the exhalation of pent-up fear.

'What the fuck is it?' I heard Rink enquire.

I looked again at the spectre in the mist. A human skull grinned back at me. But I could see now that there was no life behind the recessed sockets, no drool dripping from its widely splayed teeth. It was a simulacrum, given the illusion of life by Cain's artistic insanity. The skull was mounted on a pole pushed into the sand. A tattered blanket was draped over a cross spar to give the semblance of an ethereal body. Hands and forearms – withered skin and tendons holding together the bones – were bound to other poles concealed within the blanket. I shuddered.

'It's a warning,' I finally managed. 'Or a gatekeeper. I think we've found him, Rink.'

'You're not kidding,' Rink whispered.

We both heard the music again: a sonorous piping this time. I stepped closer to the skeletal form. The music was coming from its bones. Tiny drill holes along the radius and ulna of the forearms made for a maniac's idea of a flute. When the wind picked up, it disturbed the blanket and a racket like a wind chime kicked up.

'Son of a bitch's crazy as a bag of weasels,' Rink offered.

As we walked on, I couldn't help peering back at the ghostly form. Who do those bones belong to? I wondered. Is there a family someplace who to this day hopes that their loved one will turn up one bright morning and announce that they are fine; that they only needed to get away for a while but now they are back? I promised myself that I would see to that return, that I would take this person home again. The day wouldn't be bright, and neither would he be fine, but he would be going home.

As would the further twelve skeletons we came across as we walked.

It was an unholy baker's dozen.

All were posed in similar styles to the first, strung up on poles, bodies formed of blankets. But some were in reclining postures, others placed to give the impression of flight, two of them strung together as though engaged in a slow waltz. Cain was indeed crazy and as dangerous as a pit of venomous reptiles. And every bit as sly.

Across the amphitheatre we went, and with every step my dread grew. I wondered if we were already too late; if John was already strung up in an insane tribute to Cain's madness.

The tiny bones strewn in the sand gave me an even greater loathing for Cain than before. Many were the remains of tiny animals and birds fallen out of the sky, but here and there, I saw the phalanges of human fingers protruding from their graves as though clawing their way to an afterlife denied them. Rink looked equally disturbed. I didn't know what 'face' I wore, but I was sure if my friend studied me now he'd see that I, too, could fear.

The wind was picking up. The mist – not true mist, but formed of particles of the alkaline desert borne on the wind – billowed around us. It invaded my mouth and nostrils, caused me to squint. From everywhere came the clamour of rattling bones, suffused with the ghastly pipe music. Judging by the orchestra making the music there were many more corpses strung up out here than those we'd already encountered. I had the horrifying notion that the desert was actually formed of particles of bone and I gagged and spat in reflex. It was an absurd notion, but it was there. I pulled my shirt up over my face as scant protection against inhaling dead men's dust.

'Hunter.'

I heard Rink's whisper. He was over to my left, crouching down, gun trained on something I couldn't see. I stopped, took up a crouch of my own. Rink indicated something beyond him that I couldn't pick out from the shifting veil of sand. Duck-walking, I made my way over.

'There,' was all Rink said. And as the breeze tattered the mist, I could make out a hulking formation of rocks jutting out of the desert like the ruins of a mythical castle. Like the sand, the rocks were chalk white and glowed with phosphorescent eerieness against the night sky. If this amphitheatre had once been the floor of an ocean, then the rocks were millions of years old, ancient testimony to volcanic activity that had shattered the sea floor in a cataclysmic upheaval. Directly ahead of us, two more spectral forms marked a fissure in the rocks. This time they truly were gatekeepers.

This had to be the final place: Cain's place.

43

Alone, either man was a formidable enemy. Together, Cain had no hope of defeating them. Not when he was armed only with his scaling knife while both of them came armed with semi-automatic handguns. The only chance he had was to separate them; use their loyalty for each other against them. It was a weakness Cain immediately read in the men. Though they were fearless warriors, neither wanted to die, nor to lose their friend. Cain on the other hand had no such qualms. He was prepared to die to achieve his aims.

Both Joe Hunter and Jared Rington transcended the level of even the most hardboiled soldier. Their training, no . . . their indoctrination, had seen to that. Maybe they were beyond the normal psychological and physiological responses to the death of a friend guaranteed to halt even the sturdiest warrior in his tracks. Perhaps, like Cain himself, they had reached that ultra-cognizant level where they could elevate themselves above the ken of mortal man, to float on the seas of chaos where the 'natural' order of being meant that nothing was as it seemed. This was the realm in which Cain existed; what if these two had achieved the same level of consciousness? What if, after all these years, he had found worthy opponents, contenders for his title of Prince of Chaos?

He chuckled to himself, careful that the sound didn't betray his hiding place.

Not a chance.

44

Standing at the threshold to Cain's domain, I balked at entering without a full reconnaissance of the area. Yet, at the same time, I knew that time was of the utmost importance. John was in terrible danger, possibly with only seconds to live, and I was dithering at the entrance to his torture chamber. Still, that unnatural talent for spotting the viper in the grass was screaming at me and I had to heed it.

I had to choose between my own and John's well-being, and at the end of the day I was left with very few choices. If I waited, he'd be dead. If I charged in, he could still end up dead. I had to act.

I stepped forwards.

Rink was behind me. I knew that Cain couldn't come at me from that direction. Rink on the other hand had me as a buffer if Cain chose to charge us from the rocks. I went slowly, gun out, eyes and ears scanning for any sign of life. Periodically I looked up.

The rocks towered over me. They were sheer enough that I didn't believe Cain could scale them, but more than one soldier had lost his life by ignoring what was lurking above his field of vision. In Vietnam, many a jarhead was taken by surprise by a noose dropped round their throats, or even by the constriction of an assassin's legs dropping from an overhanging bough. The martial art named Viet Vo Dao is based upon that very premise.

I know I was crediting Cain with more tools than he perhaps possessed, but at that moment, before meeting him in combat I had to credit him with everything possible. In my line of work to underestimate an individual is to invite death.

The twin sentinels watched my progress. They were larger than those skeletons we'd passed earlier. More formidable to the eye, with their bison skulls and hulking forms of tattered rags and strips of leather. They looked like something out of a Tolkien novel: chimera-like demons guarding the door to the lower realms.

Beyond them, I came upon a well-beaten path that led to the centre of the rock formation. The fissure in the rocks was natural, but here and there I detected evidence that Cain had helped widen the doorway by way of hammer and chisel. Also, he'd marked his progress with weird symbols and pictograms straight out of a Hieronymous Bosch painting. In retrospect, I believe the paintings on the rock surface depicted a history of his killings, but at the time, I couldn't give his demented story much more than passing notice.

Rink was disciplined enough that he didn't immediately follow me into the passage. I was aware of him somewhere behind me. I could hear his breathing as he crouched at the entrance to the passageway, the strange acoustics amplifying his trepidation. But no words passed between us now. Talking would identify our position. We had to rely on stealth, and not a little bull-headedness, to get us through this thing unscathed. I walked on, mindful of stepping on a loose pebble or stick of wind-blown brush that would alert Cain to my presence. Sweat moistened my brow, tickled between my shoulder blades. My vision was constricted to a narrow tunnel of focus and my blood rushed in my ears. Not the ideal conditions for hunting. But it was a response to the adrenalin racing through me and there was nothing I could do about it.

The passage widened out, opening into a cul-de-sac hemmed in on three sides by the towering rock formation. There was only one way in; the ideal location for a trap. Quickly I scanned the rocks above me, my gun at the point of my vision. Nothing stirred; there was nothing to indicate an ambush would come from above. I stepped into the cul-de-sac, circling on my heels to cover all directions as best I could. Soon I found the hole in the ground. Steps leading down into darkness. Breath caught in my throat.

I couldn't make out anything beyond the first few steps. The night had fully descended, and though my eyes had adjusted to the darkness the steps descended into a realm I can only describe as being devoid of *anything*. It was beyond night, beyond black.

I couldn't bring myself to step into the hole. I even looked back for moral support from Rink. If he could've seen me then he would've seen the face of terror. I couldn't allow that; quickly I traced the first step with the toe of my boot. Then, before my desperate boldness fled, I descended the stairs as rapidly as I could.

When I reached the bottom, I could make out the faint outlines of a door before me. The reflection of a guttering flame seeped out from beneath the door. Beyond the door a lamp burned. That knowledge gave me the courage to reach out and tug on the door handle. I did so sharply, then stepped into the space it revealed, my gun searching for targets.

The smell hit me first.

I gagged. That was bad enough.

Then my eyes began to make sense of what I was looking at and, for the first time in my career, I retreated with a cry of alarm.

45

Oh, what an idiot. You're baring your neck to the headsman's axe. You deserve to die with ignominy, you stumbling, sightless fool! To think I credited you with respect when you're as blind as all the rest. Die, cretin. Die, Jared Rington.

Rington was there, no more than an arm's length from him. The big lummox's nerves were strung taut, shredded, fraying under the pressure. His head swung from side to side. He didn't know which way to look. Because of that, he didn't look anywhere. He saw everything, but in doing so, he saw nothing. His mind was so full of stimuli that it was unable to process what was right before his eyes.

And that was all Cain required. He would use Rington's blindness to his advantage. He timed the rhythm of Rington's movements, watched and discerned the momentary gap where the eyes swung a fraction of an instant before the barrel of the gun followed. Into that fraction of space, Cain would insert himself. Before Rington could make any sense of his appearance, it would already be too late.

A one and a two and a . . . now.

From within the shroud of blankets comprising the body of the bison-skulled monstrosity to Rington's left, Cain erupted. He made as little sound as possible, and didn't so much leap out as jut forwards from his waist, arm streaking down at the juncture of Rington's neck and shoulder. It was a guaranteed instant kill. The point of his blade jabbing down to puncture the heart from above. Rington would die instantly, drop like a slaughtered steer. No shout of warning to Joe Hunter.

Except Jared Rington wasn't as blind as he looked.

He detected the shifting shadows and he jerked away. The blade still slid into flesh, but instead of finding that pinpoint where the blade could be forced down into the heart it found resistance in the form of his sturdy clavicle. The metal scoured bone, but it was deflected away from the vitals and into the pectoral muscle.

'Sumbitch!' Rink grunted, his gun coming round. He fired in an arc, not waiting for the target to present itself before jerking on the trigger. Three times he fired. Two bullets cut chips from the rocks, one snatched at the blanket swathing Cain's form. Then Cain's knee thumped against his forearm halting the gun, and the knife once more cut a swathe through the night. Rink staggered back, blood from his sliced forehead invading his vision.

Move, move, move. A mantra for both men.

Even as Cain extricated himself from his hiding place, Rink was firing again. Blind, but with determination. One bullet scoured Cain's left thigh, another plucked hair from his head. But then he was out of the line of fire and he cut again at Rington.

Sliced to the bone, Rink kicked back. His foot caught Cain in the gut, propelled him backwards. Cain was too canny a fighter to be caught out so easily. Instead of floundering for balance, Cain allowed his momentum to take him over in a roll that brought him immediately to his feet. And in that instant he was already coming back at Rink. The man was big, powerful beneath his clothing, trained to deal with dangerous foes, but unprepared for one as determined as Tubal Cain, Father of Cutting Instruments. The Harvestman.

Rink shot again. But the bullet passed through space that Cain had occupied a second before. He was already two paces to the left. As Rink swung towards him, he arced his blade under the barrel of the gun, felt the telltale thud of his fist against Rink's abdomen and knew he had scored. Cain gained the space below Rink's armpit, squirmed under and behind the big man and looped his free arm round his throat. He jerked backwards, tugged the blade free of the gut and sliced at the throat. Rink fell flat on his face, blood mingling with the chalk-white sand.

Finally, Cain gave voice.

But all he had to say was, 'Ha!'

He stepped forward. Rink didn't get up. Cain smiled. Leaned down and plucked the gun from his grasp.

Distantly, he caught the sound of someone calling his name.

He turned and headed into the narrow passage.

46

I should have expected something like this. Cain's history as narrated by Walter should have prepared me: the photographs of his victims viewed on Harvey's computer, the skeletons posed out there in the desert, the grotesque art daubed on the rocks. But nothing primed me for the chamber I now surveyed.

The chamber wasn't huge, less generous than a medium-sized living room. The far wall was no further than eight metres away; the side walls separated by little more than five. But Cain had used the space economically.

There wasn't a surface more than the width of my hand on walls or ceiling that wasn't decorated with human skulls, scapulae or pelvic bones. Femurs, humeri, radii and ulnae formed strange mosaics. Spinal columns had been arranged as borders to separate one insane montage from another. Interspersed between the human remains were countless bones gleaned from road-killed wildlife. Equally disturbing in their own way, myriad patches of cloth snagged from unsuspecting parties were woven between the bones. Human ribcages dominated the far end of the room like shields on a coat of arms. And there, as the living embodiment of Cain's insanity, was his centrepiece.

'Oh, my God. John?'

My voice came out as a wheeze. I reached out with plucking fingers. My feet wouldn't follow them.

'John?' I asked again.

He was displayed like all the other of Cain's exhibits, fixed to the walls of the cave by iron spikes hammered through his forearms, his chest against the bedrock. Cords were looped round his throat, woven round his skull and fixed to a hook in the ceiling. His head was forced back on his spine so that he peered upwards. His arms were outstretched, the skin peeled from his back stretched taut beneath them like demonic wings. I could see what Cain was attempting to portray. He intended that John be seen as a supplicant, beseeching a higher spirit in the heavens above him. A fallen angel begging for God's grace?

Walter said that FBI profilers concluded that Cain might be attempting to make amends for slaughtering his own family. Perhaps John represented the demon that was Martin Maxwell and in reality it was he who begged grace from God. Maybe we'd never know the true meaning, and everything was simply the product of his depraved mind.

It wasn't just the pose that shocked me to the core. In itself it was terrible; the way in which Cain had stripped the flesh from John's back, exposing the musculature, went way beyond awful. Yet, that wasn't the worst. What made me shrink inside was that John still shivered with life.

Caught in a snapshot moment again, eternity was measured by the thrum of one heartbeat.

Then I was moving with no sense of volition.

One moment I was standing at the threshold, the next I was cradling John's head between my palms. My SIG was lying in the dust at my feet, forgotten in my urgency to help my brother. All that was in my head, my heart, my soul, was to give John a modicum of comfort by my presence. He wasn't conscious; not in the correct sense of the word. He stirred. I didn't want to look at his wounds, but inexorably my eyes drifted down to the glistening ruin of his torso. My eyes screwed tight, blocking the awful image, but I knew I'd see for a long time to come.

'Oh, my God,' I moaned again. Beyond reason, the prayer was for my own mortal soul. I gently caressed John's head and this time he responded.

He shrieked.

He pulled away from me, shrieked again.

'John. It's all right. It's me. It's Joe. Your *brother*.'

Still John squirmed away from my touch.

'John. John.' I couldn't find words to comfort him. To let him know that he was going to be OK. I was there; I wouldn't allow the beast to harm him further. I would save him. Find him medical care. I would do all those things, but I was useless. I averted my face and allowed my frustration to escape me in a ragged howl of fury and loathing. All the while, I hung on to John so that – if nothing else – he would be aware of my presence.

I pressed my face to his shoulder, held him. I was talking to him, though I can't recall my words. They were nothing more than low, gentle platitudes that issued between wrenching sobs.

Finally I reached across and tested the iron nails that had been hammered in the wall. The nails were slick with blood and I couldn't get a grip on them. So, instead, I started pulling free the cords that bound his head. Only distantly was I aware that the cords weren't synthetic, but wholly organic; the dried tendons and ligaments stripped from previous victims. I managed to pull them free and John's head lolled on his shoulder.

The resilience of human nature is outstanding; the terrific injuries bodies can endure before life finally flees. That John was not only alive, but in charge of his faculties was truly remarkable.

'Joe?' he croaked.

'Yes, John.' I almost burst out crying again. 'It's Joe. I'm here to help you—'

And just as I said it, I heard the gunfire.

I spun from John, stooping for my SIG and lifting it towards the door. The gunfire was from somewhere outside. Rink, I thought. Killing Cain. Or being killed. I took three hurried steps before catching myself. I turned back to John.

'Everything'll be OK, John,' I promised. 'I'll be back.'

'No,' John moaned. 'Don't leave me. . . .'

I shook with indecision but my training took over. 'I'll be back. I promise.'

And I started for the steps leading out. I had to defend this place. If Cain had taken Rink out then he only had to keep me penned inside with no recourse but to watch my brother perish. If there was any way possible that he'd survive his horrific injuries, John required immediate medical help.

Even as I reached the steps, I heard gunfire again. A second of nothing, then one last shot followed by silence. I quickened my pace up the steps, taking them in three bounds, till I was out in the night air once more. Searching for targets, finding none. Immediately I set off in the direction of the narrow cleft between the rocks.

The cleft was a dark slash between the towering boulders, but I thought I could detect movement there. Instinctively I pulled the trigger. And as reactively, someone shot back. I felt the wind of its passing as the bullet punched through the air next to my head. In mid-run I dropped and rolled, came back to one knee firing again. A return shot tugged at loose cloth at my elbow. I didn't let it stop me, kept on firing. Six shots in rapid succession, directly into the narrow passageway where I just had to get at least one killing shot into Cain's body mass. I heard him curse, knew that I'd hit him.

I dropped to my belly, fired the remaining two rounds in my gun, snatched backwards at my waist-band for a fresh clip even as I ejected the spent one.

It was a practised movement I could achieve in less than two seconds, but it's surprising how much ground a determined man can cover in less than two seconds. Even as I pushed the clip into my SIG, Cain came charging at me out of the gloom.

Point.

Shoot.

The bullet caught Cain. It struck his left arm. Yet he didn't recoil; he fired back. Kept on coming.

Bullets punched the earth in front of me, spraying me with salty dust. I felt fire sear my left calf. I grunted. Fired again. And this time Cain doubled over, though it didn't stop him. He launched himself at me.

Prone, I was at his mercy.

I had to move.

I twisted sideways, barely avoiding the elbow that Cain thrust at my skull. Then I twisted back towards him, fired at point-blank range. Only Cain had also twisted away and my bullet missed him. He slashed at my gun hand and the stiffened edge of his hand struck the nerves on my forearm. The SIG fell from my lifeless fingers. Cain's gun swung towards me. I kicked at his chest and his aim went wide. Then we'd thrown our bodies together and even as I thrust at his throat with my left hand, Cain jabbed his knee into my groin. I headbutted him in the face, snatched at his gun hand and wrenched his gun from him. He chopped at my wrist and I allowed the gun to drop so that I could return the blow.

We rolled across the sand, and there was no reason behind the strikes we aimed at each other, only that they were vicious and aimed at vulnerable points. Delivered with evil intent. Neither had the advantage. We both carried wounds. Both of us were insane with hatred. Both of us wanted only to kill our enemy. At any second one us would achieve our aim. Then the earth gave way beneath us and we were falling into space.

Somewhere deep inside I knew our battle had taken us to the lip of the stairs leading to Cain's lair. We caromed against the steps, each taking the bone-ringing force as we somersaulted downwards. Only at the bottom did I experience momentary respite from the agony of blows as the force of our collision separated us on the floor.

I pulled myself to my knees, my teeth bared as I spat blood from my mouth. Cain was in a similar pose. There was a wound along his scalp that made his pale hair jut up like the crest of an infuriated lizard. Another wound above his right hip leaked blood. His eyes were pinched; pinpricks of fury.

'I'm gonna rip your fuckin' head off,' I promised him as I pushed up from my crouch.

'Come on then, tough guy,' Cain beckoned me. But even as I advanced, he spun round and charged into the chamber. I half-expected him to throw the door shut, and I primed myself to throw my shoulder against it. However, Cain did nothing of the sort. He took half-a-dozen running steps into the chamber then turned to face me. Almost languidly, he drew a knife from his waistband, held it up before his eyes, grinned at me. 'Come on. If you think you're up to the challenge.'

I stooped, drew my Ka-bar. Nodded. Entered the chamber.

'Ding, ding. Round two.' Cain looked like he was enjoying himself.

'Sick fucker,' I called him.

Cain's lips pinched. 'I can see where John gets his colourful language from.'

I swung my head.

'Let's leave John out of this. It's between you and me, Cain.'

He jerked forwards. I feinted at his gut, and we both skipped back out of range. Cain prowled to my right. I turned with him. He hopped to the left. Three metres separated us. Beyond him, John hung on the wall, an unwilling witness to our duel. I spared him only a second's glance. I couldn't take my eyes off Cain, not for one instant. Cain also glanced John's way.

'You see this, John? The great liberator has arrived. You really think he can help you? That it makes one iota of difference to your fate?'

'I said to leave him out of this,' I snapped. 'Me and you, Cain. If you've really got what it takes.'

Cain smiled as if he was hiding a great secret. 'Oh, I've got what it takes. Believe me. But what about you, Joe high-and-mighty? You know, up in Washington I often heard your name whispered. Like you're some sort of silent killing machine that even presidents are afraid of. Me, I think it was all hyperbole. I don't think you're anywhere near as good as they say you are. Me, on the other hand, well, just look around, Hunter. I reckon that the proof of the pudding's in the eating. Just take a look at what I did to our mutual buddy, John Telfer.'

John made a noise, a hiss of anguish. I lunged at Cain, cutting at his torso in a bottom-to-top oblique slash. Cain skipped away laughing. My knife-edge had missed by a mile. But that was OK. I'd only cut to get Cain to move, allowing me to leap through the space he'd left and position myself before John. Realizing his mistake, Cain shook his head. Made a tut-tut noise.

I wiggled the fingers of my left hand at him, beckoned him to me. 'Come on, arsehole.'

Cain did come on. He dropped low, thrusting at my abdomen. As I shifted to block his knife, he twisted to one side. He slashed in an 'S', bringing the blade perilously close to my throat, a centimetre shy of my carotid artery. Only I was also ducking and my return stab forced him back on his heels. I followed him, jabbing at his throat, at his groin, back to the throat. Cain shouted in forced humour. Slashed back at me. I struck at his knife blade with my Ka-bar and sparks danced.

I thrust my left foot into his gut. Cain absorbed most of the kick – but not all. He went into a wall, scattering bones and artefacts of his madness across the floor. Immediately he spun, struck at me. It was all I could do to save my throat, at the expense of a deep cut across the back of my left hand. I flinched, and Cain saw that as a weakness. He came at me again, emboldened by success. To show him I was no weakling I jabbed my blade into his thigh. I'd have preferred to rip out his femoral artery, but the meat was as good a reminder of my potency as anything was. Cain didn't like it. He jumped back, slapping his free hand over the wound.

He stood there, breathing deeply through his nose as he slowly lifted the blood-smeared hand before us.

I nodded at him. There you go, you son of a bitch. I repositioned myself so I guarded John from his blade and inclined my head, inviting him in.

Cain postured. He did an adjustment with his feet reminiscent of a young Muhammad Ali – a show of bravado to indicate that the wound wouldn't slow him any. I smiled knowingly. Bravado was the tool of a frightened man.

'What's wrong, Cain? Not so sure of yourself any more? It's one thing cutting up helpless people. What's it like to have your victim turn on you?'

'Fun.'

'I bet.' I took a slow step towards him. 'Bet it isn't as much fun as when you murdered your wife and kids?'

Cain stiffened slightly.

'Or when you killed your brother, huh?'

'Leave *my* brother out of this,' Cain said.

I gained another half-step on him. 'What was it like, Cain? Murdering those that loved you? Was it a thrill? Some sort of sick fantasy come to life?'

Cain growled. My taunting was having the desired effect. For one thing, my words were angering him. An angry man doesn't reason. And when reason goes, so does training. Secondly, my speaking was forcing him to consider the actual words. Even if his response was only to swear, his brain was engaged as he deliberated his answer. While he was measuring those words, he wasn't capable of planning his next attack. It was a lesson I learnt many years ago. Ask a question of your enemy. As they answer, hit them.

'Did you watch them burn, Cain?'

'Yes,' he replied. 'Watched them burn like torches.'

'Bit of a waste, though. Bet you wish you'd brought them here, eh? What a waste of good bones.'

Cain paused. I could see that there was regret behind the scowl. He opened his mouth. I didn't wait for his response. I leapt at him.

It should have ended then. My knife should have found his throat. He should have fallen to his knees gripping at his wound, attempting to halt the flow. But, as I'd always been cautioned, 'should haves' and 'could haves' mean nothing in the reality of blood and snot combat.

Even as I speared at Cain's throat, he was already lifting a hand. Instead of the soft tissue of his throat, I found a sinewy forearm. All right, I wounded him sorely. If he didn't staunch the blood loss, then he would ultimately weaken and die. But he was still in the fight. Unfortunately, my Ka-bar was wedged in muscle and bone. And Cain's blade was still free.

47

You've undoubtedly heard that old story about how at the moment of death your entire life flashes before your eyes. It's not true. Well, not for me it wasn't. I guess that my life had been way too eventful for that.

Not many people get the luxury of playing out a billion reminders before sinking into oblivion, not when death comes in an instant. Instead of the whole panoply of incidents from an event-filled thirty-nine years, only two things flashed through my mind. First, the face of my ex-wife, Diane. It wasn't a genuine image, but one a future event I imagined. She was standing at my grave, but she wasn't grieving. She wore a face of disgust, reproof, anger, as if she'd always known that this was how it was going to end.

Second – and equally poignant – an image from only minutes before. John beseeching me. 'Don't leave me.'

On reflection, those two images whirled through my mind in less than a heartbeat, so I suppose the important episodes of my life could've been played out within seconds. But I didn't even have the luxury of seconds. If I was to live at all, I had to act now.

I loosed the hilt of my Ka-bar. It was pointless attempting to wrench it free. While I tried, Cain could have cut enough of my hide to fashion himself a new pair of boots. Instead, I stabbed my fingers into his eyes. It didn't stop his knife parting flesh and grating on bone, but it was enough to deflect it from my heart. It also forced us apart. It was a slow release and I swear that I could feel every cold centimetre of steel as it sucked free of my chest. Cain went backwards, eyes screwed tight as he tried to fight the response of tears invading his senses. I went to one knee, clutching at my chest.

Cain backed to the wall again, his shoulders brushing fresh detritus on the floor. He scrubbed at his eyes, cursing me in short guttural snatches of sound. I remained kneeling, almost overwhelmed by the agony. His knife hadn't killed me, but at that moment, I wasn't sure that the pain wouldn't finish the task for him.

Ignoring the agony, I craned up to see where he was, and already Cain was coming for me. He was half blinded, but he didn't need eyes to know I was at his mercy. He was armed. I wasn't. I was severely wounded. It would be a matter of seconds to finalize the job.

But in combat 'would be' is a phrase that sits alongside 'should haves' and 'could haves'. And only I understood that at that moment. Cain hadn't seen Rink step into the doorway behind him. Rink was bleeding from his belly. He had a deep gash across his chin, another across his arm, his face was plastered with gore from another wound across his forehead, but life seethed in his furnace-hot gaze.

Cain faltered as something in my face alerted him. He stumbled to a halt, swinging round to face Rink.

'Drop the fucking knife,' Rink roared as he lifted a gun and aimed it at Cain's face.

Cain laughed. 'You found my gun? I wondered where I dropped it.'

'Drop the knife, Cain,' Rink said again. He stepped closer, the gun trained between Cain's eyes.

'Sorry. Can't do it.'

'Drop it now or I blow your goddamn head off.'

'I'm surprised you're still alive,' Cain said, as if he genuinely cared. 'I really thought that I'd opened you up back there.' Cain sucked air through his teeth, noting that Rink's throat was wholly intact. 'Didn't realize that you got your arm in the way. I suppose that'll teach me for rushing the job, eh?'

'Don't fuck with me,' Rink warned. He looked unsteady. Loss of blood was making him weak. 'I know what you're trying to do. Do you think you can get me with that pig-sticker before I blow a hole in you?'

Cain glanced my way. I could see a gloating smile begin across his face. 'You know something, Rington, I believe I could.'

I knew it. Cain knew. Even Rink knew it. The gun was empty.

'Shoot him, Rink,' I shouted.

Rink pulled the trigger.

A click as the hammer fell on an empty chamber.

But it was enough. Cain almost swaggered as he advanced on Rink. As he did so, I was already moving. I snatched at the clutter on the floor, came up with the first thing my grasping fingers found, and with all my might I forced the broken end of a human rib into the soft flesh in the hollow of his throat.

The result was instantaneous. Cain shuddered, his knees gave way. He stumbled towards Rink, who was already coming at him. I snatched at his left arm even as Rink grappled his right, pulling the knife from Cain's listless grasp. Cain twisted towards me. His eyes were wide, as though he was caught in an epiphany. His mouth was wide too, but nothing issued forth other than a gurgle. My own face was flat, emotionless, as I plucked my Ka-bar from his flesh.

We could have done it then. A frenzy of stabbing and slashing. Doling out an equal amount of the torment Cain had subjected his victims to. But neither of us succumbed to our base instincts. We did something immeasurably crueller: we allowed Cain to suffer the ignominy of a slow and painful death. And the realization that it had been his own egocentricity that had brought him down. If he hadn't revelled in displaying the trophies taken from his victims it would have left me weaponless. No doubt about it . . . he'd have won the day. Instead, he had to suffer his last few minutes of life in the knowledge that he'd fucked up.

He collapsed to his knees. He searched our faces. We both grinned at him. Miraculously he found a laugh. But it was lost on us. We weren't afraid of his insanity. He was simply pathetic. And he knew it.

He sobbed. Lifted a beseeching hand to me. I shook my head. He lifted faltering fingers to the stub of bone protruding from his throat. Blood oozed from the hollowed-out core.

His eyes said it all.

'Yes, *Harvestman*,' I told him. 'You reap what you sow.'

Cain laughed a final time at the irony of my words.

48

Just as I suspected, Walter arrived like a celebrity at a Hollywood bash. There's no show without Punch. He entered the chamber only after the storm troopers had given him the all-clear. Medics were in the throes of strapping John to a gurney – belly down, of course – hooking up IV bags and inserting all manner of hypo-dermic contraptions into his failing system.

Sitting in the dust, I watched it all with a strange sense of distraction.

Medics fussed over Rink and me too, but I gave them as little notice as I did those working to save John. I was only concerned with Walter. I wasn't troubled that any of us would end up buried under the dirt as I once contemplated. Walter was seeing this through the right way. Showing his gratitude. Otherwise, the armed strike force wouldn't have given ground to the medical team; they'd have simply shot us where we sat.

'What kept you?' I asked.

Walter came to stand beside me. He even gave me a fatherly pat on the shoulder. But his eyes were on Cain. We had left him where he'd come to rest, slouched on his knees, hands folded in his lap, head tilted forwards on his chest. Apart from the blood dripping on his breast, he looked like a supplicant at prayer.

'I didn't want to step on your toes,' Walter said. 'This was your gig, Hunter.'

I spat phlegm and dust and God knows what else on the floor.

'You could've come sooner. You were monitoring us all along. Why didn't you send in your team before now?'

'And would you have thanked me if I had?'

'No,' I answered truthfully. 'I suppose not.'

'Then all's well that ends well.'

I gripped the dressing a paramedic had placed on my chest wound. All's well that ends well? 'Yeah.'

Walter walked away from me then. It wasn't that he didn't care for my well-being, only that Cain held a more immediate fascination for him. He went and stood over Cain, stared down at him for a long time.

'He's dead.'

'As disco,' I said.

'You know,' Walter said. 'There's many a profiler up at Quantico would've given their eye teeth to speak to him before he died.'

'My heart bleeds for them,' I muttered. In hindsight, considering how close Cain's knife had come to finishing me, they weren't the most appropriate words. Even Walter glanced at me to see if I was serious. I shrugged.

Returning his attention to Cain, Walter went on, 'Don't know how he managed to elude us all this time.'

'Maybe you didn't look hard enough.'

Walter nodded. Then, totally out of character for a man who'd ordered plenty of wet work but never got his own hands dirty, he gripped Cain's hair and pulled back his head. A shadow crossed Walter's face. He looked to the medics.

'See to this man,' he ordered.

I jerked. Walter stepped in front of me, pressing me down as Cain was loaded on to a gurney. 'Don't worry, Hunter. I'm going to bury him.'

'He is dead?' My words were more question than fact.

'We don't bury the living,' he pointed out.

That wasn't necessarily true, but I wasn't of a mind to argue. Walter never talked straight.

As Cain was rushed away, Walter and I watched him go. Walter sighed, and I should have guessed what was coming. 'We were looking in the wrong place.'

I squinted at him.

'It's not him.'

'What?'

'It's not him,' Walter repeated.

I experienced a moment's panic.

'What do you mean *it's not him*? It's definitely Cain.' To emphasize the point I threw out a hand, inviting Walter to take in the sheer horror of his surroundings. Walter lifted a palm, a calming gesture, but I struggled up from the floor to stand beside him. My nose was centimetres from his. 'Can't you see what the son of a bitch did here?'

'Easy now, son,' Walter said. 'It's Cain all right. No doubt about it.'

'So what the hell are you talking about?'

'It's not Martin Maxwell.'

'What?' I stared into Walter's face. Searching for the lie. Not that it helped. I didn't know Martin Maxwell from Mickey Mouse. Only thing I was sure of was that I'd stopped the Harvestman.

'It's the brother,' Walter explained.

'The brother? You mean . . .?'

'Uh-huh. Robert Swan. The musician.'

I got it then. 'You need a name to give to the press? And you want Swan to take the blame? To protect the good name of the Secret Service?'

'Yes.'

At the end of the day, it didn't much matter to me. Whoever Tubal Cain ended up being, it was unimportant in the great scheme of things. He was a demented killer regardless, one that I'd put down like a rabid dog, and for that I was thankful. If Walter needed to spin the world a line of bullshit, then so be it.

I grunted, looked Walter dead in the eye. He stood there expressionless. Then I nodded. 'The musician? If you say so, Walter.'

Walter winked. 'I say so.'

I turned my back on him and limped towards the exit door. It was still night outside, but the sky was ablaze with searchlights from the helicopters coming and going. As I reached the stairs, Rink joined me. He placed a hand on my shoulder. I couldn't determine whether it was to support his own weight or mine. It didn't matter. As always, we'd support each other.

'You going to be all right, Rink?'

'Fine and dandy,' he said, yet, involuntarily his hand went to the dressings on his face and chin. 'He got me good, Hunter. Slashed my gut, but luckily only got the muscle. He came close to getting my throat, too. If I hadn't been knocked cold by that bang on the head the son of a bitch might really have finished me off.'

'It was a close one,' I said.

'Too close,' Rink said.

With no sense of volition, I'd made it up the stairs and found myself standing ankle-deep in the white sand. The cul-de-sac wasn't large enough to accommodate all of the choppers and personnel brought in by Walter but there were a fair number of men and women in jumpsuits and body armour. They stood around with their weapons cocked, as though Cain continued to pose a threat.

Leaning on each other, Rink and I made our way to the cleft in the rocks. It was awkward walking through the gap shoulder to shoulder, but we made it.

Outside was as Rink had earlier described it. A three-ring circus. Helicopters dominated the sky. Hummers and SUVs prowled along the lip of the escarpment in the distance. Undoubtedly FBI and Secret Service, but this was now Walter's gig, and he was calling all the shots. Everyone else had to make do with prowling on the periphery. The only thing that concerned me was the presence of the air ambulance Walter had had the foresight to call in. And even as I confirmed its presence, paramedics rushed past us with John strapped to the gurney.

'Think he'll make it?'

I remembered the awful wounds on his back and couldn't see how.

'It's amazing what the doctors can do these days,' Rink said, his words sounding hollow. Even he doubted them.

'He'll pull through,' I said softly. 'He has to. Otherwise all of this will have been for nothing.'

'Not for nothing, my friend.' Rink slipped an arm round my shoulder and pulled me into an embrace. 'We've just stopped a monster. Me an' you, Hunter. Just like the old days.'

49

In the days that followed, Walter attempted to explain the thinking behind it all. Martin Maxwell hadn't gone off the rails as he'd first suspected. All right, he'd messed up his life when he'd gone playing with the governor's wife's lingerie, but that it turned out was his only transgression. Other than a sleazy penchant for women's underwear, he wasn't the fiend he was suspected of being.

Some would even argue that Maxwell was a decent enough fellow. After all, he'd sought out his less privileged brother, taken him into the fold of his home, given him the kind of lifestyle he'd been missing. But it appears that the man who would become Cain wasn't one for gratitude. His was a soul festering with jealousy, with dark fantasies and desires he couldn't achieve as a no-name musician in a nation of musicians whose talents far outshone his. So Cain instead coveted something that could never rightfully be his. He stole the skills of his brother. Maybe Martin gave the knowledge willingly. He had to have taken the brother under his wing, for Cain's adeptness with weapons, particularly the knife, didn't come without many hours of practice. Nor did his understanding of tracking and surveillance.

The most troubling aspect with regard to Walter's take on Cain was how he could have known my name. But that was easy enough for Walter to explain: he simply omitted me from the equation. As far as anyone would ever know, it was federal agents who'd taken Cain out.

In the end, I gave up thinking about it. Let Walter play his games. It was what he did, after all. What better way to cover up the depraved actions of a government employee than deny that he was the same man? Plausible denial. That was what Walter thrived upon. If he wanted the world to believe that Martin Maxwell wasn't their man, then so be it. I knew otherwise.

I had other more important things on my mind.

John for one.

He was currently recuperating in a military hospital beyond the prying eyes of the media. As far as anyone else was concerned, Cain had left no living victims. I was happy enough with the arrangement. It got Hendrickson's men off his back. Walter promised me that on his recovery John would be entered into the witness protection programme. In effect, he would disappear. New name, new identity, the works. The only time he'd be drawn back into the limelight was if charges were brought against Hendrickson and Sigmund Petoskey for their part in a counterfeiting ring. Then John would be returned to obscurity.

For him it meant never going home. But given that he'd been gone so long, that his time with Louise Blake was now behind him as well, maybe it was for the best that John started over.

My next concern was for Rink. My best friend, who'd given so much for me. Who had suffered as much as I had.

We went off to the hospital together. My chest wound turned out to be superficial, as did the wounds to Rink's chin and arm, but the slash to the gut meant he had to undergo observation for a few days.

After Rink was cleared from any signs of complications, Walter extended his hospitality to the use of his Lear. A few hours later we were back in Florida. We spent two days at Rink's condominium in Tampa. The rain had passed and we spent those forty-eight hours reclining on sun beds and drinking. Of course, it wasn't all partying.

We still had work to do. A certain briefcase liberated from a boat at Marina Del Rey required our attention. Not to mention the seven hundred grand that was inside it. I'd no qualms about putting the money to good use; John had paid in blood and agony for this reward. As far as anyone was concerned, the cash had burned along with Rhet Carson's yacht. The problem being, blood money never brings happiness. It was handed over to Walter as evidence that would help bring down John's enemies.

As a sweetener for my time in the US, Walter transferred a sizeable sum of money into a fund set up for Jennifer and the kids. This was cash from his department's budget, so did not reek of agony and blood. It was clean. So was my conscience.

I spoke to Harvey Lucas, who told me he was looking after Louise Blake. Something in his tone made me smile. He was looking after her? I bet he was.

Job done, Rink was as affable as ever. The scars would forever be a reminder of how close to death he'd come. But he wasn't too upset. The ones on his face gave his rugged good looks even more appeal to the ladies, or so Rink maintained. There were tears in our eyes when we said goodbye at the airport.

My final concern. And the most pressing. Going home. Wherever that turned out to be.

EPILOGUE

Jubal's Hollow.

A sun-blasted landscape in the middle of nowhere. The G-men had come and gone. An army of anthropologists, medical examiners and crime scene investigators had picked the barrens clean. The remnants of Cain's depravity had been listed, labelled, sealed and shipped off in packing crates to a secret location. And with them, the media hubbub had died down. The Harvestman story was old news now, other atrocities in the world taking centre stage. The camera vans and anchors in starched suits and starched hair departed for more immediate bad news stories.

Now there was nothing but scrub, sand and more sand.

As it should be.

But there were visitors. Hundreds of them. People came to stare and shake their heads, twisted souvenir hunters who came away with nothing but fragile bones from birds or lizards, although to the casual observer true remnants of the Harvestman's ossuary. A number of entrepreneurial tour operators made a killing from the fascination wrought in the minds of the ghoulish tourists who sought out more than the glitz of LA. The

Harvestman was big business. Big money. He was, after all, the most despicable of all murderers this side of the new millennium. He had achieved the notoriety and fame he'd desired.

However, under constant armed supervision, the patient known only as John Doe must have found it difficult to curse through his ruined throat. For though the Harvestman was the name on the lips of every person with a penchant for dark history, Maxwell meant nothing. To the world, Robert Swan, a mediocre guitar player with hopeless dreams of the big time, had at last achieved his fifteen minutes.

ACKNOWLEDGEMENTS

A very big thank you from the bottom of my heart to all those people who have helped me along the way. To Denise, who is everything to me. To all my family, particularly my father, Jacky, and brother, Jim, who have helped me immensely in writing this book. To Luigi and to Alison, I owe you a massive debt of gratitude for having faith in me and championing me all the way. To Sue Fletcher and David Highfill, editors extraordinaire, for all your brilliant work and guidance. To Lee Child for your kind support. To Jeanette Slinger for making everyone take notice. And to everyone else in the background on both sides of the Atlantic for all your hard work.

Matt Hilton

Meet Joe Hunter's next deadly opponent in this exclusive extract from JUDGEMENT AND WRATH

Caitlin Moore opened the door to her living room and stepped into Hell.

Or that's how it seemed for the remaining three minutes and twenty-seven seconds of her life.

The clock began ticking when she pushed the door to with a nudge of her hip and reached for the light switch with an expertly aimed elbow. It was the usual Friday evening routine. Coming home from Collinwood High School with her arms filled with books and test papers for marking, she could hit the switch every time.

Except this time blackness prevailed.

'Goddamnit,' she muttered under her breath, swinging round to place the papers down on the sideboard next to the door.

It was the creaking of the easy chair by the TV that made her pause.

'Are you awake, Nate? How about giving me a hand here? The power's down.'

Nathaniel Moore was also a teacher at Miami's Collinwood High. But Caitlin's, husband was a track coach and didn't have to attend the Friday evening tedium of the faculty meeting. He always got away three hours earlier, picked up Cassie from the sitter and went home. Once Cassie was tucked up in bed, and a couple of Jack Daniels were residing in his belly, Nate would doze in front of the wide screen with the Discovery Channel doing its best to cover his snores.

Routine.

'Nate?'

But tonight's routine was blasted into smithereens.

There'd be no supper. No cuddling on the couch while watching a late movie. No fondling their way to bed where a rejuvenated Nate would prove he was still a jock when it came to stamina-based sports.

'Hello, Caitlin.'

The voice was soft, but still enough to shock her to the core. She jerked, her spine knocking on the sideboard, papers spilling from the pile. That wasn't the voice of her husband.

It wasn't the voice of anyone she knew.

The easy chair creaked again, and there was a shifting of the darkness around her. The owner of the mystery voice was on the move.

She almost turned for the door.

Then she remembered Cassie.

Eight-year-old Cassie would be asleep in her room. If she ran, what would happen to Cassie? What *had* happened to Nate?

A flashlight was thumbed on, the beam stark in Caitlin's eyes. She croaked, throwing an arm across her face.

That rush of movement again and a hand clamped on her throat. The fingers were long and slim, but they felt like steel where they dug into her flesh. Caitlin's lungs bucked in her chest.

She had no way of resisting. Air gone, she didn't have the strength or the will to fight. She was turned in a lazy circle then ushered to the centre of the room. Sparks popped and fizzed behind her eyelids. Without air she'd be unconscious within seconds. Then the fingers were gone from her throat and she was retching: gag reflex on overdrive.

'Hello, Caitlin,' the voice said again.

'Who are you?' Caitlin gasped. 'What do you want?'

The light was still in her eyes. She couldn't make out the figure behind its beam. Did she know the voice after all?

'I want to give you a choice.'

The flashlight went off and darkness slapped its hood over Caitlin's head. Around her a breeze eddied. The stranger was on the move again. Caitlin swung with the breeze, trying to determine where the stranger was now.

'Do you love your family, Caitlin?' The voice was barely more than a whisper.

'More than anything. Please! Don't hurt them. I'll do anything you say.'

'Anything?' the voice sounded strangely disturbed. 'You'd debase yourself for them? You'd lie down and give yourself to a stranger?'

'Anything,' Caitlin sobbed. 'Money! You want money? I'll get you money.'

'I don't want money, nor do I want your body.'

'Then, what?'

'I told you. I want to give you a choice.'

There was a metallic click above her. A bulb being turned in its socket. Pearlescent light bathed the room.

And Caitlin saw the figure and knew that her life could be counted in seconds.

He was tall. Slim almost to the point of emaciation. His face was too pale, a wax mask that made Caitlin think of a reflection in a steamed over mirror. His hair was silk-fine, as pale as his skin, and hung to his shoulders beneath the wide, circular brim of a hat. His coat was shabby: a long, ankle-brushing raincoat that was missing all but the topmost button. A thin silver chain looped from one side to the other, where something bulged in the pocket. On his feet were grimy deck shoes that were threadbare where his toenails pushed against the fabric.

The stranger had a look about him that spoke of sleeping under cardboard, drinking from bottles concealed within brown paper bags, and ranting at alcohol-induced phantoms.

But Caitlin knew: this was no street person who'd found access to her home. This man was the type that even the hardiest of the street-wise shunned.

Two things told her.

The silenced pistol he held loosely in his hand.

And the stone killer intensity of his eyes.

'I'm going to give you a choice,' the man offered again. 'Who will you save, Caitlin? Nate or Cassandra?'

Caitlin followed his gaze. On the opposite side of the room, two wooden chairs had been dragged from the kitchen. In them sat the people she loved most in the entire world.

Nate was bound and gagged. He strained at his bonds, his eyes huge. In contrast Cassandra was very still, her features lax.

A wail swelled in Caitlin's throat.

'Make your choice, Caitlin,' whispered the man.

How could she? How could she? How . . .

'Cassandra has been anaesthetised,' the stranger said. 'If you choose Nathaniel she will never know. Do I kill her, Caitlin?'

Nate's veins were standing out on his temples like blue ropes. He was shaking his head in denial. Caitlin met his eyes and he sank back in the chair.

'Please,' Caitlin said, 'don't harm our daughter.'

The stranger nodded. Then shot Nate in the forehead.

'You made the best choice. Your child will be safe now, Caitlin. You can rest easy.'

Then he lifted the gun to Caitlin's face.

Sometimes you make rash decisions that you instantly regret. Other times you just have to go with the flow. Like when I walked into Shuggie's Shack – a roadhouse north of Tampa, Florida – and parked myself on a stool at the corner of the warped and stained bar.

Shuggie's is the kind of place that self-respecting souls avoid unless they're dragged inside by the hair. The tables are planks nailed to barrels, seats 1970s retro-vinyl from the first time around. The atmosphere is redolent with beer fumes and cigarette smoke, and the stench of unwashed bodies. Tattooes seem to be the order of the day. Muscles and hair, too. And that's just the women.

You finish your meal of grease over-easy, and the kind of gratuity you offer the staff is thanks that you get out with your face still intact.

I was made as a cop by every man, woman and beast in the place within the time it took me to catch the bartender's eye. Every last one of them was wrong, but I wasn't averse to letting them wonder.

'Beer,' I said. There didn't seem to be any choice. It was that, or chance the brown liquid masquerading as liquor in the dusty bottles arranged on the shelf behind the cash register.

The bartender moved towards me reluctantly. He glanced around his clientele, as if by serving me he was betraying their creed. Not that he looked the type to worry about people's feelings. He was a massive man in one of those cut-off leather vests designed to show the size of his biceps. He had a black star inked into the rough skin beneath his right eye, and a scar that parted his bottom lip and ended somewhere in the braided beard on his chin.

'Don't want any trouble in here, mister,' he said as he set down a beer in front of me. 'I suggest you drink up and get on your way.'

Holding his gaze, I asked, 'Is that what you call Southern hospitality round here?'

'No,' he sneered, 'in these parts we'd call that good advice.'

Besides the long hours I'd already put in at the wheel since leaving Tampa, I could foresee a long night. A relaxing drink would have helped my mood. Maybe a little pleasant conversation would have helped, too. Didn't look like I was going to find either in here.

'Thanks for the heads up,' I said.

Flicking dollars on the bar top, I stood up and walked away, carrying my drink. It felt warm in the glass. By contrast, the barkeep's gaze on the back of my head was like ice.

Passing a group of men sitting at a table, I inclined my chin at them. They looked back with the dead eyes of men wary of the law. One of them shivered his over-developed pectoral muscles at me and they all sniggered.

In the back corner of the bar sat a man as incongruous to this setting as I was. A small bird-like man with nervous eyes and a way of oozing sweat through his hair without it moisturising the dry skin on his forehead. His right hand was in continuous motion, as though fiddling with something small in his palm. I may have caught a flash of metal, but his hand dipped to his coat pocket and it was gone.

Without asking his permission, I placed my beer on the table and took the chair alongside him. The barrel made it awkward to sprawl, so I leaned forward and placed my elbows on the planks. I turned and studied the man but he continued to watch the barroom as though fearful of who might walk in next.

'When you said I'd know you when I got here, I see what you meant,' I said. 'You don't strike me as the type who hangs out in biker clubhouses.'

'We agreed on this place for that very reason,' the man said. 'It isn't as if anyone I know is going to be here.'

'It wasn't a good idea,' I told him. 'If you wanted anonymity, you should have chosen somewhere where you'd blend in. Where *we'd* blend in. Check it out; we're on everyone's radar.'

Maybe the bartender's advice wasn't so bad after all.

'We should go,' I told him.

The men gathered at the table further along had turned their attention to the spectacle we presented sitting in their midst. They didn't seem pleased, as if we spoiled the ambient testosterone.

The man wasn't listening. He dropped a hand from the table and dug beneath a folded newspaper. I saw the corner of an envelope.

'Everything you need is in there.' He quickly grabbed at his own drink, taking a nervous gulp. 'The balance will be paid as soon as I get the proof that Bradley Jorgenson is no longer a threat to me or any of my family.'

Sighing at his amateurish attempts at subterfuge, I left my arms resting on the table. It gave me cover for when I dipped my right hand under my coat and caressed the butt of my SIG Sauer P228.

'I'm not sure I want the job,' I said to him.

The man stiffened.

'I'm not who you were expecting,' I said.

He finally glanced at me and I knew what he was thinking. Is this a set-up? Was I a cop like everyone in the damn bar thought?

'You can relax, Mr Dean. I am Joe Hunter.' I folded my fingers round the butt of my gun, placing my index finger alongside the trigger guard. 'What I mean is I'm not a hit man.'

'Jared Rington told me that you would help,' Richard Dean whispered harshly.

'I will help,' I reassured him. 'I'll get your daughter away from Jorgenson. But I'm not going to kill the man without any proof that he's a danger to her.'

Dean nodded his head down at the envelope. 'Take it. You'll see what I mean. All the proof is there.'

There was movement among the men at the next table. One man with jailhouse tats stood up. He picked up his beer, held it loosely in his hand. He gave me a look that said we'd outstayed our welcome. He sniffed, then jerked his head at the two men nearest him.

Matt Hilton

Oblivious, Dean said, 'Please, Mr Hunter, I need you to get my daughter away from that monster. If it means killing him to do that . . . well . . . I'll pay you any price you want.'

'Pass me the envelope,' I told him. 'Under the table. I've got your phone number. I'll be in touch with you, let you know my decision.'

Dean had panic in his eyes. Whether it was about relinquishing the cash already in the envelope without a firm agreement, or because there was a *real possibility* I was going to do as he asked, the nerves got a grip of him. He wavered, his fingers plucking at moisture on his glass.

'Two seconds and the deal is off,' I warned him.

He quickly slipped the envelope into my out-stretched left hand.

'OK. Now go.'

He opened his mouth and I gave a slight shake of my head. Suddenly he was aware of the Aryan Brother-hood approaching us. Coughing his excuses, he started from his seat, dodging round the tattooed man and his two compadres. They heckled him but allowed the little man to go.

Pushing the envelope into my waistband, I stood up.

'I'm going, guys. You can relax.'

The man with the jailhouse tats barred my way. He lifted a grimy nicotine-stained finger to my chest.

'You're not welcome here.'

'Didn't you just hear what I said?'

'Can't say I did. What is that funny accent?'

I get remarks like that occasionally. Comes with being English. And northern to boot.

'Look, guys, you've caught me in an awkward predicament,' I said to Tats. 'You don't want me here; I
don't want to be here. Truth is, normally I wouldn't
sully myself by entering a shit hole like this. But here I
am.'

My words had the desired effect.

I got a laugh.

Stepping forward, I found they parted for me.

That should have been it. Playing on the paradox of
self-deprecating humour, I should have got myself out
of Shuggie's Shack and there'd have been no injuries.
The problem was two things got in the way.

First, Tats' question; 'What did that little freak hand
you under the table?'

Second was the surly mood I'd been in when I
arrived. Which wasn't helped by the bullshit Richard
Dean had subsequently laid on me.

'None of your fucking business,' I told him, plea-
santly.

The jukebox was spitting out heavy rock music. Ear-
jarring stuff, but expected in a place like this. It played
on. If there'd been a pianist in the bar he'd have
stopped at that moment.

'You're in *my* place,' Tats pointed out. 'That makes
it *my* business.'

'Oh, so you must be Shuggie, then?' I swept my gaze
around the barroom. Shook my head at what I saw.
'You know, place like this dump, you should be
ashamed of yourself.'

'I ain't Shuggie, asshole. And that's not what I
meant.'

'Yeah, I know what you meant.'

'I own this place. I own what goes on under this roof.' He stuck out his grimy hand a second time. 'Hand it over.'

I shrugged.

'OK.'

The SIG was between his eyes before the smirk had fully formed on his lips.

Chairs scraped and there was a chorus of shouts as just about everyone leapt to their feet, pulling out guns of their own. A couple of the more delicate customers headed for shelter.

It was like DefCon Five had just been announced and anarchy was the new world order.

It kind of matched my mood.

'This is how it's going to be,' I said. My words were for everyone in the room. 'Everyone relaxes, puts away their weapons and gets the hell out of my way. The alternative is that Biker Boy will be throwing his very own wake in the near future.'

'He's only one fucking pussy,' an anonymous voice shouted from out of the crowd. 'We can take him out.'

'One pussy with a gun at your stinking boss's head,' I reminded the shouter. Turning my attention to Tats, I asked him, 'How would you like things to go? Bit of a party animal, I guess. Should be a good turn-out for your wake.'

'Put down your goddamn guns,' Tats yelled. 'Any of you muthas with itchy fingers, you're gonna answer to me!'

Smiling at him, I grabbed a handful of his denim cut-off.

'Me and you are going to walk out of here together,' I told him.

He was shorter than I was, but bulkier round the chest. Slightly awkward for getting a hold round his neck. Making do with bunching his cute little ponytail in my left hand, I stuck the SIG under his ear. That way we moved towards the door.

A man to my right maybe still had it in his mind that I was a cop. Cops will always warn before they shoot. He lurched at me, trying to grab the gun away from Tats' throat.

But I'm not a cop.

My sidekick found his knee. There was a tendon-popping twang and his leg now had a two-way joint. His face screwed around the agony, a good target for my elbow. He went down, but at least in his unconscious state he wasn't in pain any longer.

In the fraction of a second that it took to take the idiot out, the SIG had never wavered from its target.

'Any more of you assholes want to test me?' I growled.

They hung back like a pack of hyenas, wary of the lion in their midst, starving but too afraid to try to snatch away its kill.

Taking that as my cue, I dragged Tats backwards and out of the door. Arrayed along the road outside was a row of chopped and converted Harley Davidsons and other bikes I didn't recognise. I shot at a few of them, putting 9mm ammo through their gas tanks.

One of them went up in the air like the space shuttle, trailing fire and burning fuel that splashed most of the others. Rapidly I dragged Tats away from the conflagration, even as others began to spill out of Shuggie's. Suspended between their desire to get Tats free and saving their beloved bikes, there could only be one winner. I was able to bundle Tats into my Ford Explorer without anyone else trying to play the hero.

Screeching out of the parking lot, I pushed the SUV into the eastern lane approaching eighty miles an hour and gaining.

'Fuck, man!' Tats said from the passenger seat. 'You didn't have to go as far as blowing the bikes to hell.'

I smiled. The action had done my bad mood the world of good.

'Had to make it look real, Ron, otherwise they might've guessed you were a willing hostage.'